THE AMAZING STORY OF THE MAN WHO CYCLED FROM INDIA TO EUROPE FOR LOVE

PER J ANDERSSON

Translated by
ANNA HOLMWOOD

ONEWORLD

A Oneworld book

First published in North America, Great Britain and Australia
by Oneworld Publications, 2017
This mass market paperback edition published 2017
Reprinted twice in 2017, three times in 2018 and twice in 2019

Originally published in Swedish as New Delhi – Borås
by Forum, 2014

A CIP record for this title is available from the British Library

ISBN 978-1-78607-208-5
ISBN 978-1-78607-034-0 (eBook)

Printed and bound in Great Britain by Clays Ltd, Elcograf S.p.A.

Two images on p.296 © PA Images

Oneworld Publications
10 Bloomsbury Street, London WC1B 3SR, England
3754 Pleasant Ave, Suite 100, Minneapolis, MN 55409, USA

Praise for

THE AMAZING STORY OF THE MAN WHO CYCLED FROM INDIA TO EUROPE FOR LOVE

'Charming...epic...a journey repeatedly facilitated by the kindness of strangers, but also fraught with danger and pitfalls...[a] 7,000-mile journey across continents, lasting almost five months – all in the name of love.' *Daily Mail*

'This wonderful book does so much to explain why Indian society is the way it is. The story of PK, growing up an 'untouchable' at a time when such labels should have been abolished, is touching, harrowing and ultimately enlightening. The writing is humorous and tender, the cast of characters joyous, and best of all – it's all true.'

Vaseem Khan, author of
The Baby Ganesh Detective Agency Series

'This is a story of human connection that spans continents, class and race.' *Library Journal*

'This fab book tells the beautiful true story of PK, who was born into a poor family in a small Indian village. One day, while studying at art school in New Delhi, PK paints a portrait of a young Swedish woman named Lotta. This chance meeting changes his life forever... we follow his journey as he heads 7,000 miles, across continents and cultures, armed with just paintbrushes and a secondhand Raleigh bike, as he searches for the woman he loves.' *Closer*

'Filled with sumptuous prose.' *Publishers Weekly*

'A beautiful, epic tale of love and perseverance.' *Booklist*

'A must-read...you won't find any other love story that is so beautiful, touching, and – above all – true.' *Grazia*

Contents

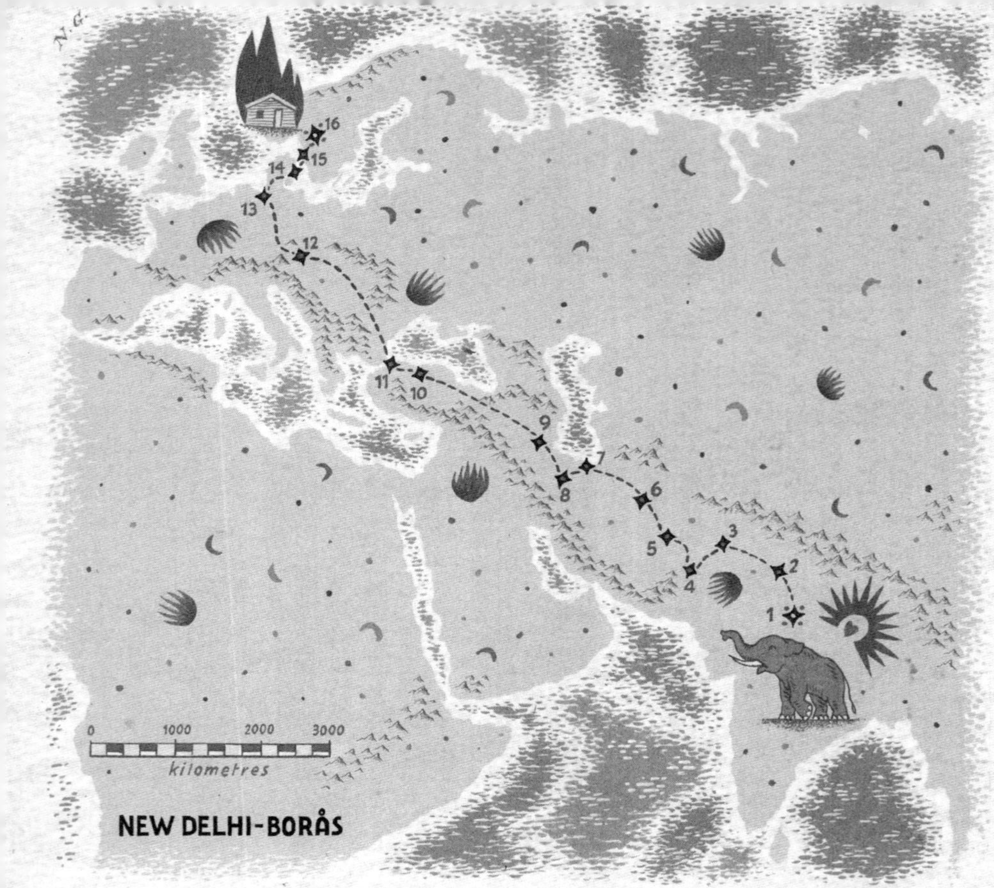

1 New Delhi, India
2 Amritsar, India
3 Kabul, Afghanistan
4 Kandahar, Afghanistan
5 Herat, Afghanistan
6 Mashhad, Iran
7 Sari, Iran
8 Tehran, Iran
9 Tabriz, Iran
10 Ankara, Turkey
11 Istanbul, Turkey
12 Vienna, Austria
13 Hamburg, Germany
14 Copenhagen, Denmark
15 Gothenburg, Sweden
16 Borås, Sweden

The Prophecy

Ever since the day I was born, in a village in the Indian jungle, my life course has been steered by a prophecy.

It was winter and almost time for the New Year celebrations, which remained a tradition, even though the British who had introduced them to our country had left two years earlier. It rarely rained in December, but that year the north-eastern monsoon lingered on the Orissa coast. Eventually the rain subsided, but the forested slopes on either side of the river remained hidden in the dark clouds that doused the landscape in twilight, even though it was morning.

Suddenly, the sun cut through the darkness.

And there I was, laid in a basket inside one of the village huts, destined to be the protagonist of our story although I did not yet have a name. My family gathered around, marvelling at me, fresh to the world. The village astrologer was also present, proclaiming that I had been born under the sign of Capricorn, on the very same day as the Christian prophet.

'Look!' cried one of my brothers.

'What?'

'There, above the baby!'

Everyone looked up and saw a rainbow that had formed in the beam of light that fell through the little window.

The astrologer knew what it meant.
'He will work with colour when he grows up.'

It did not take long for the rumours to spread around the village. A rainbow child, said one. A great soul, a Mahatma, is born, said another.

When I was only one week old a cobra strayed into the hut where I was sleeping, oblivious to the impending danger. It rose above my cot and flared its muscly hood. My mother saw it and assumed it had already bitten me. She ran to me just as the snake slithered away outside. But I was fine. Indeed, I was lying there quietly, my dark eyes gazing out into the void. A miracle!

The village snake charmer told my parents that the cobra had extended its hood to protect me from raindrops dripping through the ceiling directly above my cot. The rain had been hammering at our roof for the past few days and it was now leaking. Cobras are considered holy and this was a sign from the divine. The astrologer nodded as the snake charmer spoke.

Yes, indeed. I was no ordinary baby.

The astrologer returned to tell my fortune. He took a sharpened stick and scratched my future on a palm leaf. 'He will marry a girl from far, far away, from outside the village, the district, the province, the state and even the country,' it began.

'You needn't go looking for her, she will come to you,' he whispered to me alone, looking straight into my eyes.

At first, my father could not make out the rest of the words. The astrologer held an oil lamp underneath a candlestick smeared with butter and let the soot that formed fall into the grooves scratched in the porous leaf. The text appeared before my parents' eyes. He did not need to read it out loud, my father could see the curly Oriya script for himself and read it to my mother: 'His future wife will be musical, own a jungle and be born under the sign of Taurus.'

I have lived with the prophecy on the palm leaf and the stories of the rainbow and the cobra ever since I learned to understand what the adults were saying. Everyone was sure my future had been set.

I was not the only one to have my future told. The fates of all children are written in the stars the moment they are born. That is what my parents believed, and so did I, growing up.

And in some ways, I still do.

His full name is Jagat Ananda Pradyumna Kumar Mahanandia.

A joyful name. Jagat Ananda means universal happiness, and Mahanandia means optimism. But this is not his full name; this is just the short version. Including all the titles passed down from grandparents, tribe and caste, it runs to 373 letters.

But who can keep track of 373 letters? His friends settled instead on two. P (for Pradyumna) and K (for Kumar). PK.

PK's family never used any of his given names when they called out after the little boy as he ran through the village or climbed up high in the mango trees. His father used *Poa*, meaning little boy, his paternal grandparents always said *Nati*, grandson, and his mother chose *Suna Poa*, golden boy, because his skin was just a shade lighter than that of his siblings.

His first memories of the village by the river on the edge of the jungle were from after he had turned three. Or maybe he was four. Or still only two. Age was not so important. No one cared about birthdays. If you asked the villagers how old they were, their answers would vary and were never precise. Around ten, forty-something, nearly seventy, or merely young, middle-aged, very old.

However old he was, PK remembers standing inside a house with thick walls made of mud and a roof of yellowed grass. The picture comes into focus. Fields of corn with their dusty tips rustling in the evening breeze and clumps of trees with their plump leaves set alight by flowers in the winter and heavy with syrupy fruit in the spring. A stream flowed through the village and into a large river, behind which a solid wall of foliage and branches rose up from the ground. It was the beginning of the jungle, from which came the occasional trumpeting of an elephant or the growl of a leopard or tiger. Wild animal tracks could often be spotted in the mud, along with piles of elephant dung or the imprint of a tiger's paw, accompanied by the buzz of swirling insects and the singing of birds.

PK's horizon was the edge of the jungle, but his universe extended beyond it and into the woods. The village and the jungle. There was nothing else. The forest was endless, mysterious, secret, but also familiar and safe. It was an adventure and yet also a certainty, a comfort. The city was somewhere he had heard about but had never seen for himself.

He lived in the hut with his mother, father and two older brothers. And his father's parents, of course. That was how most families lived; tradition dictated that the oldest son stayed with his parents, even after he had married and started his own family. Shridhar, PK's father, held fast to those traditions.

PK did not often see his father. He worked as the postmaster in Athmallik, the nearest town, which had markets, teashops, a police station and a jail. As the twenty-kilometre journey was too far to cycle every day, his father had a room with a bed at the post office where he slept during the week. Every Saturday night he would make the journey home with PK's two older brothers, who lived in the town's boarding school.

PK felt like an only child. During the week his mother devoted all her attention to him. Most days it was just the two of them and his grandparents in the house in the village on the edge of the forest.

Sunlight flooded the village, breaking through the thick canopy that often kept the forest floor in relative darkness. Most of the houses were built in the same style: round or rectangular huts of brown, dried mud, greying palm leaf roofs and bamboo enclosures for the cows and goats.

Beside them, vegetable patches had been cut into the soil and stacks of hay were piled up to be used for feed. There were some brick houses scattered around the village, built for the untouchables by the British in an act of mercy. But monsoon rains had destroyed these houses before anyone had been able to move in and now they stood empty, their ceilings collapsed. Aside from this, PK's world contained only a primary school and another building where the village council meetings were held.

PK's mother used to say that they lived in India's largest forest and that Kondpoda was its most ancient village. It was home, she said, to both the living and the dead. The sandy banks of the river were used as a cremation site, where the souls of the departed gathered at night to sing and dance. A whirlpool in the river had taken two women in recent years, both newlywed and pregnant. She had seen their bodies laid out on the beach, their foreheads embellished with dazzling red dots, shining symbols of their pure, unblemished lives. Their eyes were open wide as if searching for something, their mouths gaping as though they had screamed for help in their final moments. In reality, she told him, it was because that was how their souls had left their bodies; they had merely forgotten to close the door behind them.

At night his mother lay beside him on the straw mat, whispering stories of souls, gods, goddesses and black magic. She jangled her jewellery to create ghoulish sound effects. PK shuddered and held his breath, his heart pounding. He listened as the ghosts edged closer in the darkness, gasping, panting. But then came the warmth of his mother's body. She sensed that she scared him and pulled him close. He had gone from the laughter of the afternoon spent playing in the forest, to the bedtime horror of the valley of death and into the safety of his mother's embrace. Comforted by that feeling, he fell asleep.

His mother was not scared of the dead. She believed the best way to keep malicious spirits at bay was to show confidence, which she considered herself to possess. Only self-doubt would put you within reach of death's grip.

'As long as you are brave, no one can hurt you, not even the dead,' she would say.

Before PK started school he had no idea what a 'caste' was. No one had told him that people were divided into four main *varna*, and then into thousands of subcastes within them. He had never heard of the ancient *Rigveda* verses, thousands of years old, in which the four castes were described. He knew nothing of the mythical, primeval cosmic being Purusha, who was himself divided into four. He did not know that the Brahmins, the priests, came from Purusha's mouth. That the Kshatriya, the warriors, came from his arms, the Vaishya, the merchants, craftsmen and farmers, from his thighs, and the Shudra, the workers and servants, from his feet.

Nor had he heard of the Indo-Aryans who had come riding south from the plains of Central Asia three and a half thousand years ago and had taught the people of the Indian subcontinent's forests how to grow crops before themselves becoming priests, soldiers and administrators, assuming their position in the upper castes. He had not been told that the darker-skinned indigenous forest people ended up being consigned to the lowest groups to work as farmers, craftsmen and servants, like PK's father's family, or else lived as hunters among the trees and were known as tribal people, like his relatives on his mother's side.

By the time he reached adulthood PK had come to the conclusion that the caste system was no stranger than the feudal and subsequent class systems of Europe.

'It's not that hard,' he would say, when Westerners said they could not understand the Indian divisions.

'Okay, maybe it's a little more complicated,' he sometimes admitted.

And so he would explain that Indians were born into one of the *jati* – meaning birth – a group whose categorization functioned much like the European guild system. Jati were the subgroups of the four varna, the Sanskrit word for colour. These were the four main castes as laid out in the ancient texts of Hinduism.

'So there are only four varna but millions of jati,' PK would add.

'Millions of jati! How on earth do you keep track of them all?' the Westerners would ask. And when PK replied that they could not, no Indian could, his friends would give up and the conversation would turn to another topic.

Unless pressed, PK preferred not to tell his friends that his own family did not belong to any of the four varna and instead had no caste, that they were untouchables. Historically the designation 'untouchable' came about because they were engaged in occupations that were considered to be unclean and polluting. It was not exactly something he was proud of. And yet had he not been an untouchable, his life would have turned out very differently indeed.

The Father of the Nation, Mahatma Gandhi, had wanted to raise the status of the untouchables and so called them *Harijan*, or 'God's children'. It sounded beautiful, PK thought, but in fact this word described someone who had no proper father. Gandhi wanted to give them a pleasing name, PK supposed, a name to improve their situation in life. But somehow the label was still offensive, a rejection of the legitimacy of his flesh and blood, and one PK would disdain as an adult. After the British had left, the Indian authorities classed untouchables officially as 'Scheduled Castes', giving them cheaper train tickets and quotas to make it easier for them to attend university and be elected for public office. These well-meaning gestures of benevolence were supposedly designed to improve their lowly lot in life.

Anti-discrimination laws were drafted to combat the injustices, but laws are useless if left unenforced. Ancient prejudices are embedded in people's minds like layers of bedrock.

PK has since come to realise that change must come from within – from the heart.

In a country many thousands of miles away, Lotta had longed to visit India ever since she was twelve. She still remembers that first taste of the East, even now, when her class was shown a film about the Ganges. She watched as the sun rose over the river, accompanied by the whirr of the projector. She can recall perfectly the clang of the sitar emerging from the loudspeakers, the ringing of the temple bells and the splashing of the pilgrims as they descended the steps into the water until submerged to their waists.

This black and white film was her first introduction to India. It affected her more than anything else she was taught at school. They were asked to write essays about it; hers was a long and emotional text.

I will go there one day, Lotta said to herself.

She wanted to become an archaeologist. She loved to dig in the soil, looking for things. She dreamed of sensational discoveries, untangling the twisted yarn of history into neat threads. She chose to draw a large picture of the pyramids in class and read about the British Egyptologist Howard Carter and his discovery of Tutankhamun's tomb. The curse of the pharaohs fascinated her, excitement building in her stomach as she read about the mysterious deaths of twenty of his excavation team. Lotta wanted to spend her life solving puzzles just like these.

During her teenage years a fascination with outer space began to take over. She borrowed books about UFOs from the library and travelled to Gothenburg to listen to lectures about life on other planets. She subscribed to a specialist magazine and read every issue with feverish delight, convinced as she was that humans could not possibly be alone in the universe.

Most of all, she was interested in a life different from the one she was living. She used to fantasize about being born in the sixteenth century and living with her family in a hut in the woods. No modern luxuries or fancy gadgets. Everything stripped bare, simple, close to nature.

The only person who really understood little PK was his mother. Her name was Kalabati. She had dark blue tattoos on her face, a golden heart in her nose and moons in her ears. All that remains of her now is a brass ceremonial candlestick in the shape of an elephant. It was her favourite candlestick. PK thinks of her every time he looks at it, sitting on the mantelpiece in the yellow house in the woods.

It was Kalabati who painted the traditional magic figures on the walls of the village houses before every major festival. She had an artistic eye and was good with a brush. Her skills were in demand across all castes, including the high-caste Brahmins. As the holy days approached she rose early, washed the mud walls of the family house with cow dung and began to decorate them. Once she had completed their own home she moved on to the neighbours' houses. The day before the festivities were due to begin she worked from dawn until dusk, painting figures with spindly limbs alongside vines and flowers with slender leaves. She made the white pigment herself with rice flour and water. When she was finished, the village houses sparkled in the first pale yellow rays of morning light. These were Kalabati's great masterpieces.

PK watched his mother paint and wondered why she never worked on paper.

Kalabati was born into the Khutia Kondh tribe.

'Ordinary tribespeople like us are the descendants of the dark-skinned forest people who have lived on this land for as long as we have known, or who came here, at the very least, thousands of years before the plains people moved in and cut down the trees and began growing wheat and rice,' she told PK. 'War and disease followed them. It was the people of the plains who divided us into the worthy and the worthless. Before the Hindus came, we didn't make distinctions between people. Nobody in the forest was superior to anyone else.'

Ma was the only person who felt real to PK; the rest of his family were like strangers. An odd feeling bubbled in his stomach when his father and two older brothers rode into the village at the weekend. They only ever spent Sundays at home. Every Saturday evening his father propped his bicycle against the wall and reached to pick him up, but PK was afraid of him and cried every time.

'Don't cry – look, your father has brought sweets for you,' Kalabati would say.

He would fall silent, sniffle and then take one of the crispy sugared *burfi*, moist *gulab jamun* or chewy English toffees from his father's hand, before crawling up into his mother's lap.

Every morning Kalabati bathed PK in the Kondpoda stream. They went to the water's edge, where the fragrance of the surrounding wild flowers mingled with that of the round patties of cow dung that had been laid out to dry. His mother warned him not to swim out too far. She scrubbed his back with a fold of her sari and rubbed him with coconut oil so that he gleamed in the sunshine. He would climb up onto a stone polished smooth by the rushing water and dive into the river, before climbing back up again. He could go on like this forever. He was never cold and he never got sick, because he was protected by a layer of grease so thick that the water slid off him in pearls, keeping him warm until the sun rose high in the sky.

At the start of every summer the rivers were all but dry, awaiting the monsoon rains. The new Hirakud Dam, built a few days' canoe journey further upstream, had stripped the Mahanadi River of its wilder rapids. By June, only the smallest trickle remained in the centre of the channel. This lack of water had become a scourge on the village. It would have been one thing if they had received electricity as compensation, but the power produced in the plant was directed elsewhere. When dusk fell they turned to the crackling fires and the flames of oil lamps. Kalabati and the other women of the village took to digging makeshift wells in the large sandbanks; holes stretching down for metres, from which the water that seeped in from the sides was collected and carried home in dented tin buckets. One bucket balanced on the head and one in each hand.

According to the priests, untouchables made dirty everything that was pure and holy: they threw stones at PK whenever he approached the village temple. The year before he started school, PK decided to have his revenge. As the rituals began and the priests emerged carrying clay pots filled with water, he took his slingshot, scrabbled for stones around him, loaded and fired. Clonk, clonk, clonk! Water began to seep out of the cracks in the pots. The priests saw him and chased him through the village.

'We'll kill you!' they shouted.

He hid in a bank of cacti, the thorns digging into his flesh. Bleeding, he limped home to his mother. Even the plants want to hurt me, he thought.

Ma stroked his back and whispered softly of everything that was good, even though she knew that for untouchables and tribespeople like them, the world was mostly vindictive and unfair. He did not know why the Brahmins disliked him so much, nor why they kept him out of the temple. He had no explanation for the stones that were hurled at him. All he knew was, they stung.

His mother held back from telling him the truth and instead drew him the most beautiful pictures with her words.

When the high-caste children touched PK by mistake,

they ran away and washed themselves in the river.

'Why do they do that?' he asked.

'Because they're dirty,' his mother replied. 'They need a wash! Eugh, so stinky and dirty!' she repeated until he no longer took their actions as a reflection of his own self-worth.

Kalabati had never been to school and so could neither read nor write. But she knew a lot about the world, nevertheless. Like how to make pigments, paint intricate designs and mix leaves, seeds and roots into natural remedies.

Her life was shaped by routine. Chores were always performed at the same time every day. She got up before the sun, her alarm the crowing roosters and the morning sun's position in the sky her clock face. PK lay on his straw mat and listened as she scrubbed the floor, veranda and yard with a mixture of water and cow pat. He thought it strange that she used dung for cleaning, until she explained that it was far more effective than any white chemical powder you could buy in the village shop.

After cleaning the house, Kalabati went to fertilize the family's field of corn and then bathe in the river. She returned and stood in her dark blue sari on the newly swept veranda. Her wet, curly hair glistened in the morning sun as she slowly squeezed the water out with a cotton cloth.

She sang softly as she watered the fragrant green-purple leaves of the holy basil bush. Then she went to the kitchen and dipped her index finger in a clay pot of red cinnabar powder and pressed it to the middle of her forehead. She looked at herself in the cracked mirror that hung on a hook by the stove. Leaning towards it, she painted thick black lines around her eyes with homemade kohl, a mixture of soot and ghee.

Then it was PK's turn to get up. He rolled up his straw mat and he received a dot of kohl in the middle of his forehead to protect him against evil. This was then followed by a dab of ghee, which soon melted in the sun and dribbled down his face. The butter was Kalabati's way of telling the rest of the village they were not as poor as they seemed.

'Not everyone can afford butter and milk,' she told him, 'but we can.'

Look! The Mahanandia family lets the butter run down their children's faces! At least, that was what Kalabati hoped they would think.

His body clean, hair combed, kohl and butter smeared on his forehead, PK was ready for the new day.

His mother's ancestors, the tribal people, had hunted among the trees and farmed in the glades for thousands of years. Nowadays, most of Kalabati's relatives worked making bricks by the riverside. They collected mud from the bottom of the river, shaped and fired it. PK's uncle, however, held fast to the old ways and made his living with a sling, hunting in the forest. PK received a peacock feather from him, which he tied to a string and fastened around his head while he played at creeping about the forest, pretending that he too was on the hunt.

Kalabati secretly wished for a daughter, so had let PK's hair grow and helped him tie it up in braids. PK was proud of them, and liked to tie stones to their ends. 'Look how strong my hair is!' he roared at the other children, swinging the rocks from his braids.

The other boys, who wore their hair short, were impressed. They had never seen anything like it.

He usually played naked save for some wristbands and a belt strung with white shells. All Khutia Kondh children ran around like this. The caste Hindus thought the tribal people strange; their children were covered up.

Kalabati worshipped the sun and sky, monkeys and cows, peacocks, cobras and elephants. She worshipped the liquorish scent of the tulsi bush, as well as the peepal sacred fig and the neem tree, whose antibacterial sap was used for cleaning teeth. To her, the divine had no name, but it was present in everything around them. Several times a week she went to a grove where the trees grew so close that they formed walls on all sides. Inside this secret temple hewn from nature, she gathered stones and fresh grass, laid out a small amount of butter and sprinkled red cinnabar powder over it. There she prayed to all the living things in the forest, but especially to the trees, which, along with the sun, were the most holy of all.

Just like the other tribes of India's eastern forests, the Khutia Kondh had never divided themselves into castes, nor made any distinction between chiefs and subjects. Everyone had the same right to worship the gods and communicate with the divine. But then something happened. Kalabati told PK how the people from the north-western plains came, and how they began to cultivate the valleys and riversides. They regarded the forest people as primitive and uncivilized.

'In the end, we were forced into their caste system,' his mother said sadly.

The forest people tried on occasion to revolt. The British had to send troops to restore order. But it was an uneven battle in which PK's people were uniformly defeated. When PK was in his twenties, he read that Maoist guerrilla warriors called the Naxalites had once again taken on the fight for the rights of the tribal people. Gradually, the conflict escalated and the Indian army went in with force. Blood was shed, hatred took hold, and the newspapers called the conflict a civil war. PK did not like this violent turn. He realized that many of his mother's kinsmen felt all hope had been lost when the mining companies started exploiting their sacred mountains, trees and shrubs for minerals. At first, he too thought the only solution was to fight back. But then PK's hate subsided. No man was worth so little that he deserved to die, not even an oppressor or a murderer. PK agreed with Mahatma Gandhi when he said, 'An eye for an eye makes the whole world blind.'

Athmallik had been one of India's 565 princely states during the years of the British Empire, a Lilliputian country of some forty thousand inhabitants. Not that it was ever a 'real' country: the King had been subordinate to the British and was forced, like all the others, to abdicate when the Empire retreated in 1947 to make way for a modern state apparatus and democratically elected politicians.

The founding of the kingdom of Athmallik was shrouded in mystery. The royal family claimed to be heirs to a traditional ruling clan from Jaipur in Rajasthan. One of the King's sons, named Protap Deo, left their crumbling palace in Jaipur with his brothers and travelled eastward to conquer Puri, the grand temple city by the shores of Bengal Bay. But their plan failed, and they were forced to flee up the Mahanadi River, inland towards the forests. After a few days' march upstream, Protap Deo founded his kingdom, taking over a collection of villages nestled in a clearing. He killed the local indigenous chief and installed himself on the throne.

People said that before the kings arrived, when the tribal chiefs still ruled, the god Jagannath lived in a cave hidden in the forested mountains of Athmallik. The god was represented by a wide-eyed, limbless wooden statue worshipped by the indigenous Sabar people. But one day, Hindu priests arrived along the river by boat and kidnapped Jagannath, installing him in the main temple of Puri, where he has remained ever since. The god was thus brought into the Hindu pantheon to be worshipped by millions of pilgrims from all over India. In Athmallik, Jagannath is believed to have once been adorned by what was then the largest diamond in the world, before became known as the Koh-i-Noor and joined the British royal family's collection of crown jewels via the Mughals, Persians and Sikhs.

In 1827, a British colonel named Gilbert arrived and was made director of the South-west Frontier Agency in Athmallik. The King, he discovered, was in conflict with the neighbouring Boud on the other side of the river. The King of Boud regarded the King of Athmallik as his subordinate and demanded he pay tribute, but because the rulers of Athmallik did not consider theirs a vassal kingdom, they refused to pay. The British colonel noted that, every now and then, the King of Boud made incursions into Athmallik and stole livestock and other valuables. Gilbert must have rubbed his hands in glee. A local dispute! The area could not be better placed for a takeover, perfect for the British and their policy of divide and rule.

When PK was a child, the people of Athmallik still talked about the days of princely rule. That time was doused in a shimmer of nostalgia. PK's relatives did well during that time, and his paternal grandfather had the great honour of being assigned the task of capturing wild elephants for the King and taming them for service in court. According to custom, the elephant catcher's children and grandchildren were held in high regard by the royal family.

The kings of Athmallik did not fight the British. They acceded to the demands of the imperialists for political supremacy and control of trade, and accepted gratefully the offer of protection. The British rewarded their acquiescence in 1890 by upgrading their raja, Mahendra Deo Samant, a king, to the title of Maharaja, Great King.

And yet despite their relative privilege during the time of the princes, it was under the British that PK's family was really to prosper.

When King Bibhudendra died in 1918, the heir to the throne was only fourteen years old and too young to accede, so Colonel Cobden-Ramsay took over temporarily. Ramsay was known to his subjects as the White Raja, and he governed the princely state of Athmallik for seven years. According to PK's grandfather, those were the seven best years in living memory.

'Cobden-Ramsay wasn't a racist like the other Englishmen,' his grandfather would say. 'He didn't pay attention to caste.' The British, in contrast to many Indians, cared about the common good and not just how to enrich themselves.

'Can you name one single Brahmin who treated anyone outside their own caste with even a shred of respect or dignity?' his grandfather would ask. 'Have any of them ever done anything to benefit the lower castes? No, exactly! But the British did, all the time. They acted on behalf of everyone and never discriminated against us untouchables.'

PK's family liked and respected the British. It was the first time they had known rich and powerful men who did not see them as ritually unclean. They knew India's elite hated the British. But PK's grandfather used to say that he had never met an untouchable who resented the British colonial masters.

Mahatma Gandhi said the British were racists. That might have been true, but PK's grandfather believed Gandhi never understood that the worst racism to plague Indian society was the treatment of untouchables by high-caste Hindus.

PK's grandfather, grandmother and father had all attended Victoria Vernacular School in Kaintragarh, the tiny kingdom's capital, where they learned to read and write and even speak a little English.

'Before the British came, there was of course no school for us,' Grandpa said. 'But then everyone got to go to school!' he shouted, almost triumphantly. The British did not make distinctions between the local population – high caste and low were of equal worth. 'It didn't matter which caste we belonged to. Oh, it was such a joy to get to learn. For the first time, we saw that someone outside our group wished us well.'

During Queen Victoria's birthday celebrations every year, Grandpa was allowed to raise the British flag at school while the other children sang the British national anthem. Many years later, PK's European friends found it hard to understand that his relatives could feel joy at performing such a ceremony when his country had been colonized, occupied and subordinated to a foreign power. But Athmallik had almost always been ruled by outsider kings, he explained. Hundreds of years ago, King Ashoka was conquered by Emperor Kharavela, who was succeeded by the Sultan of Bengal and then the Maratha Empire.

'The British were only one in a long line of foreign rulers,' PK said. 'But as long as the foreign kings didn't interfere in the lives of the ordinary people, the locals didn't care too much who was in charge.'

Yet British rule changed the power dynamics within the villages for the first time. They did not understand the caste system, at least not in the way the Brahmins wanted them to. The British hired untouchables to work in the post office, the civil service and on the railways. And anyone who wanted to could attend Victoria Vernacular School.

'No, the British have nothing to be ashamed of,' was Grandpa's opinion.

The kings of Athmallik had not been extravagantly rich. Not like the maharajas of Rajasthan in western India who lived in enormous palaces and kept hundreds of elephants, hung hunting trophies on their walls and filled their drawers with diamonds. And certainly not like the maharaja who owned twenty-seven Rolls-Royces or the maharaja who married his daughter off to a prince in a wedding *The Guinness Book of Records* described as the most lavish in the world. Or like the maharaja who arranged a wedding for two of his dogs, dressing 250 canine guests in gemstone-encrusted brocade outfits to receive the 'bridegroom' astride a train of decorated elephants. Such profligacy was unknown in the miniature kingdom in which PK grew up.

By the time PK was born, most of the maharajan palaces and office buildings were already abandoned and dilapidated. Liana vines had begun to wrap their strong stems around the increasingly monsoon-mouldy walls and collapsed roofs. The son of the last ruling maharaja of Athmallik left the palace when India became independent, but as the owner of a successful business, he moved instead into a stately mansion. PK and his family were always welcome there for a chat, a cup of tea and to gaze at the framed sepia photographs of the British dressed in pith helmets and Indian princes in turbans. Indeed, PK is as welcome there today as he was as a child.

Despite their status as untouchable, PK's father, grandmother and grandfather still belonged to the Hindu faithful. His father performed Hindu rituals at home, but not all untouchables did so. PK suspected that his father's beliefs were inspired by his high-caste colleagues at the post office. Shridhar put together a small altar with pictures of Lakshmi, the goddess of prosperity, Ganesh, the elephant protector, and a statuette of Vishnu, the Sustainer of the Universe, surrounded by incense and oil lamps. Every day, wrapped in sweet smells and smoke from the fire, his father prayed to the gods for a happy life for himself and his family.

As long as there were no Brahmins nearby, untouchables were able to approach the Shiva temple. But no untouchable ever dared enter the innermost rooms where the statues of the gods were enthroned. Such impudence would have thrown the Brahmins into an ungodly rage.

Local custom claimed that hurting or killing snakes brought bad luck, so they had made the village temple their home. The priests fed the snakes every day because they believed it to be Shiva's wish. PK liked that the villagers looked after the snakes. He had peered into the temple and spotted a metal cobra glinting in the darkness, its neck extended as it protected the gods just as the real cobra had done when he was a baby. The snakes were mankind's friends, PK was sure of that.

The temple was also the place you went if you were bitten by a snake. There, you would be laid on your stomach in front of the entrance and told to pray to Shiva. Sooner or later, the Auspicious One would answer and heal your wounds. PK saw it with his own eyes when his aunt had suffered a particularly fierce attack. As custom dictated, she went to the temple, lay down on the steps and prayed. Then she went home and slept. The next morning she got up and announced that she was fully recovered. It was a miracle by Shiva's own hand, everyone could see that.

Shiva's powers were not limited to snake bites. One of PK's aunts had been married for twelve years without bearing a child. She went to the temple, lay down on the steps to pray, and there she stayed for four days and four nights. She neither ate nor spoke; her devotion took all her energy. She returned home weak and tired, and had to be brought to the table to be fed rice. Nine months later, she gave birth to her first baby.

The gods did not confine themselves to the temples. A nearby clump of cacti was home to Sat Devi, the Seven Goddesses who had their origins in the beliefs of the forest people but had since come to be feared by the Hindus. The goddesses possessed great powers, people said. Bad things happened if they were not respected.

The priests performed ceremonies to appease the goddesses before the villagers went out to collect seeds for the next year's crops. But one man did not wait for the ritual to be completed, and before long, he was struck down with aches and a raging fever. The muscles in his legs atrophied, until they became as thin as twigs. He never recovered. For the rest of his life he was forced to drag himself around on crutches. That was what happened if you defied the goddesses.

An old tree grew at the eastern end of the village, where bats and nocturnal birds lived. And witches, said PK's grandmother. Every night, a conference of birds could be heard chatting in the tree, only to be drowned out by the shrill squawks of the crows, the most fervent talkers of all. But PK thought that these noises were actually the desperate cries of people who had been cursed by the witches and damned to spend this life in bird form.

A large wooden cart was usually parked on the outskirts of the village. During the summer festivities it was used to parade the black, white and yellow gods: Jagannath, Lord of the Universe, his brother Balarama and sister Subhadra. They were gods of the forest people, ones his mother's family had worshipped since ancient times even though the Hindus had made them their own. Jagannath became a revelation of Vishnu, while the Buddhists saw him as an incarnation of the Buddha.

In autumn, festival season came again. This was when Durga, Shiva's wife, was honoured. The priests sacrificed goats on a hill outside the village, staining the soil dark with their blood. The Brahmins said that blood gave Durga power to fight the demons that threatened the divine order.

The Hindus have so many gods, PK used to think. He never understood how they all fitted together. But he felt their presence and ignored the contradictions. As an adult, he realized that his mother and father were not allowed to participate fully in the festivals. They could join the processions, but were forbidden to touch the statues or the wooden cart in which the gods travelled. They could pray, but not next to the upper castes or in the temple. They were permitted to perform the rituals, but preferably in the background so that the Brahmins did not see them. If the priests had been free to decide, they would have made the untouchables stay at home, away from everything that was pure and holy.

A great deal of Indian entertainment focused on relationships between mothers and daughters-in-law, the core conflict at the heart of the Indian family and thus the subject of many soap operas and Bollywood films. This was perhaps only natural when multiple generations lived together under one roof. Men may be the masters of the mountainside, but women reign over the hearth. To this day, mothers-in-law maintain a firm grip over the domestic realm, while daughters-in-law bring habits inherited from their own mothers. How should the chapatis be rolled, the dal boiled, the corn harvested and the children raised?

PK was three years old and too young to notice what was going on in his own family, but his older brothers later told him about the time their mother fell out with Grandma.

Kalabati had given birth to her fourth child three months earlier, a girl named Pramodini. But her mother-in-law was on the attack.

'That beloved wife of yours is a witch,' she told Shridhar.

And then she turned to Kalabati. 'You can't stay here. You bring trouble on us all.'

Kalabati's eyes darkened, but she did not reply. What good would it do to protest? It was understood by all that Grandma made the decisions. The house belonged to her and her husband. PK's mother was the outsider who had moved in. The only person in a position to defend her was Shridhar, but he said nothing. He swallowed the anger, vexation and shame. He showed no emotion, no displeasure at his mother's behaviour.

Silence descended on the home. That Monday, Shridhar left for the city without comment and Kalabati went about her chores. But after a week had passed and Shridhar was about to return for the weekend, Kalabati turned to her mother-in-law. Without letting even one tear run down her cheeks, she announced that she would be moving back to her parents.

'With the two youngest.'

Grandma put her foot down. 'Take the girl, she's just a baby, but the boy stays with me.'

Kalabati accepted without a word.

PK stood on the veranda with his arms crossed and his cheeks wet with crying as his mother took her possessions in one arm, his little sister in the other, and, weighed down by a heavy frown, walked out of the house and down the path. She turned several times to look at him; he waved and she waved back. To this day, he can still see her disappearing behind the sugar cane and feel how his world suddenly became quiet and empty.

His mother and little sister were gone. As his Bapa Shridhar lived six days a week in the city, PK was alone with his grandmother and grandfather.

He cried for days, weeks, maybe even months. Tears showered his cheeks as the monsoon clouds expelled sheets of rain that turned the dirt roads scarlet and made the straw ceilings smell of damp and mould. Everything was a wet haze of loss. Once he had cried out all his tears, he fell silent. He stopped talking, laughing, even smiling. He spent days with the same pinched face. He refused to let a word pass his lips. Most of his waking time was spent sitting by himself in a corner, staring into space. He refused food, but soon he did not have the strength to fight when Grandma forced him to eat. The rice and lentils had no flavour any more. Food was just texture in his mouth.

Then, one Sunday, a man came riding up on a bicycle. He had a message from Kalabati's family; she had been taken ill. She no longer did her chores, the messenger said. She just sat and cried. Shridhar received the news and, without letting anyone know what he was thinking, walked quietly out into the back garden, fetched his mother, who was digging in the soil, and led her off to the cornfield.

'We can't go on like this!' he cried, finally releasing months of imprisoned anger.

His mother made no reply.

'You are driving my wife insane!' he continued.

Still she said nothing.

What could she say? She was too proud to admit that she had made a mistake. And deep down, she probably thought she was in the right. She was a stubborn woman. Unyielding. She represented reason and logic in the face of a world gone mad.

When PK's Bapa returned the following Saturday, he sat PK down and told him that he had purchased a piece of land near the post office in the town of Athmallik.

'We are going to move there, to our new house,' he said.

'Who's we?'

'Us. Just us.'

'We're going to live there by ourselves?' PK asked. He had never heard of anyone who did not live with their grandparents.

'Yes, it will be our house. Just ours,' Shridhar confirmed.

The rain polished the sugar cane and churned the red soil into mud, so that cows and people squelched and bicycle wheels scored deep combat-zone furrows in the muck. Black clouds gathered above and the landscape was enveloped in semi-darkness, cheating the villagers of precious daylight hours.

Bapa lifted PK up onto the cart, which was tied behind two glossy oxen. It had a roof of plaited bamboo, and a couple of burnt clay pots filled with milk from Grandma and Grandpa's cow had been loaded onto the back. The driver belted the animals with his whip and the wheels started to roll, settling into a leisurely rhythmic creak as they made their way through the village.

Bapa walked behind with Grandma and Grandpa, talking, while PK sat close to his mother, who had placed his little sister in her lap. He could not hear what his father was saying, but he hoped that he was explaining why they could not stay, that they were moving to make his mother happy again.

After a few short minutes, the cart stopped by the spirit tree outside the temple on the outskirts of the village. PK looked back and saw his father kneeling down before Grandma, his forehead lowered to the ground. He was touching her feet with his fingertips.

It started to rain again, the plump drops saturating Grandma's grey hair and yellow sari. But no tears ran down her cheeks. The ox cart continued to roll along the narrow earthen road between the fields. PK looked around again as the temple and the cornfields receded and then disappeared completely in the lingering fog.

Grandma dissolved away with the rest of the village, a quivering yellow dot in the grey, before becoming one with the monsoon and the nightfall.

He laid his head on his mother's lap. She covered his naked body with a piece of thin, soft cotton.

The cart rocked along the road, winding through woods, past flooded rice fields and across narrow wooden bridges that hovered above hurried streams and rivers. The rain clouds blocked out any residual light from the stars or the moon. PK looked out into the darkness and saw nothing. But his ears were attuned to the creaking of the wheels and to the familiar sounds of the forest: croaking frogs, singing grasshoppers and screaming foxes. He felt the warmth of his mother's soft thighs and was calmed by the rhythm of her breathing.

He awoke as his mother stroked his forehead to announce their arrival. Paralysed by fatigue, PK was helped down from the cart. He stared into the darkness, but there was nothing to see. Where was their new house?

Father lit an oil lamp and their new home emerged from the shadows. Long grass tickled his legs.

'Where are we?' he asked.

'Liptinga Sahi,' replied his mother. 'Close to Athmallik, near where your father works and your brothers go to school.'

Father disappeared to get some food from the kitchens of the private school. He soon returned with metal lunchboxes filled to the brim. They sat on the floor of their new home and ate their first meal in their new village, far, far away from Grandma and Grandpa. Life had suddenly taken on a new colour, thought PK, as he watched the insects fly into the white glow of the gas lamp. Even the dal had been made with different spices, he noted in amazement. Taste had returned. The cloud of grief that had hung over the family began to fade into the past.

Nobody would ever be able to separate him from his mother again.

The new house sat alone, separate from the others. But PK frequently heard the sound of children shouting and laughing.

'They are our people,' his mother said, patting him on the head.

'Our people?'

'They belong to the same caste as us.'

It was the first time he had heard the word, even if he had experienced its vicious sting back in the old village. He understood, however, that it meant the children would not mind playing with him. That they belonged together.

'Caste?' he repeated.

'Yes, they are Pan, just like your father.'

'What about you, Ma?' asked PK.

'I'm Kondh. Khutia Kondh.'

He was learning so much in this new place.

A path cut through the cornfields, passed their house and the others further beyond, and on towards a crumbling, yellow concrete building with a small hatch window secured by thick metal bars. It was along this trail that the long stream of village men stumbled to get their hooch. They shouted to the man inside and out came large bottles of beer and smaller bottles of spirits wrapped in brown paper bags. They turned up in the early morning until the sun disappeared for the night, singing and wailing, the whites of their eyes shot through with blood. This was PK's first encounter with alcohol. He had never seen a drunk before.

Another narrow road went from the house down to a large reservoir. He liked following the paths and exploring where they led. Every day he ventured just a little bit further than the last. But he was always careful to avoid the hooch shop because the men, stinking of spirits, shouted after him, grabbed him and slurred so badly he could not understand what they were saying.

At his grandparents' house they had bathed in the river. In Liptinga Sahi they washed in the reservoir, which was covered in lotus flowers and teaming with fish. Many of the villagers took their morning bath here, along with birds and bears looking for breakfast. His mother would dig damp clay from the wooded embankment close to the water's edge and take it home in a basket. She used the mud to wash her hair and clean the plates, pots and pans.

'Gravel and clay mixed together work better than soap and water,' Kalabati said. She made a virtue out of buying as little as possible from the shop, so that she could save their money for more important things.

By the time the first monsoon clouds had passed overhead and the autumn sun was high in the sky, PK had begun to feel at home. It almost felt as if they had never lived anywhere else. He adapted quickly; indeed, he always had.

If you don't adapt, you drown, he came to realize many years later.

One day, his mother took him on a walk to the two largest trees on the outskirts of the village. They were home to eagles and vultures. Under the trees men worked skinning dead cows, preparing the hides to sell to the shoemaker to make into shoes and bags.

'They,' she said, pointing to the men, 'are our people.'

'Do we know them?' he asked.

'No, they belong to the same caste as us.'

But that was not entirely true. The men who took care of the animal carcasses came from a group of families that belonged to the Ghasiara caste. They lived in the forest, beyond the cornfields. But they were also untouchables, which was what his mother meant. The Ghasis lived in terrible conditions. The Brahmins considered them even dirtier than the Pan because not only did they work with dead animals, but they handled the carcasses of cows. God forbid. Even their shadows were dirty. The merest sight of them was considered a bad omen.

But as darkness fell, the Ghasi women were no longer untouchable, that much Kalabati knew. At night-time the men from the surrounding villages came, men who were ritually clean and distinguished, to buy sex from the women. Even Brahmins, who spat on them during the hours of daylight, were drawn to their tents at night.

Kalabati did not tell her son about this. She wanted to protect him from the cruel reality of life for the untouchables for as long as possible.

PK stood in the cornfield and watched the Ghasi men drag a dead cow towards the village spirit tree. Their second monsoon in the new house was upon them. He watched as they laid the heavy body out on the ground and began separating the skin from the flesh and the flesh from the bones. Flies swarmed around the mounds of meat and vultures circled ever lower. Finally, the birds shot down from the sky like arrows. But rather than tear into their dinner, they waited, like stone statues, patience winning out over greed. It looked to PK as if the vultures had been possessed by the gods, or at least, they did not act like predators. He could not understand why they were not eating. He looked up. Two more birds were flying above. Then, suddenly, they too swept down with such force that their wings whipped the air into cyclones.

PK dreamed of being able to do the same. He took off down the sloping path that meandered towards their house, howling like a vulture, his arms stretched out like wings.

'Ma, if I sat on the back of one of those vultures, would I be able to fly too?' he asked when they were home.

But instantly, his dreams of flying were dispelled.

'Be careful of vultures!' his mother replied quickly. 'They will peck your eyes out and turn you blind!'

'Why did they wait before eating?'

'Vultures,' she said, 'are just like people. They have kings and queens, sons and daughters and live in families too. When a cow dies the vultures tell their king and queen where the body is located. They daren't eat before the king and queen. That's why they wait so patiently like that.'

Then she continued: 'The king and queen are the most beautiful of all the vultures. Look closely next time: their feathers shimmer like gold in the sun.'

She put her hand on his forehead.

'Their world is not so different from ours.'

PK's maternal grandmother lived alone in a small village a few kilometres further into the jungle. Her house was even humbler, with walls made of bamboo and mud and a thatched roof that often collapsed during the monsoon rains. The garden had been overtaken by tall maize plants, which attracted wild animals when the corn was ripe. Regulars included the bear, with his long, black coat, and the fox. When Grandma tired of seeing her precious maize crop being taken, she built a scarecrow out of straw and placed it high up in a clump of bamboo. She hung a brass bell that tinkled in the breeze from one of its arms. This kept most of the animals away. But not all of them.

PK and his little sister Pramodini were visiting their grandma one evening when a family of *hathi* came to visit. The children were already asleep when the walls around them began to shake. Two adult elephants and their baby were trampling the vegetation and chewing on the bright yellow corncobs. But Grandma was not scared. She went out on the veranda with a bundle of dry grass, set it alight and started waving the flames at them. Unfortunately, the elephants were not scared either. The papa elephant snorted, scuffed the ground with his hind foot and charged straight at Grandma. She threw the torch and ran back to the hut, slamming the wooden door behind her and locking it.

The elephant threw his weight against the fragile building, cracking the mud and bamboo walls. Grandma woke the grandchildren, told PK to get out of the way and, with little Pramodini on her hip, began banging at the opposite wall with her one free fist, managing to beat a hole in it large enough to escape through. She nudged PK outside and they ran through the thorny undergrowth and cacti. PK remembers feeling nothing as the thorns ripped through his skin. Blood gushed down his legs, but he was numb. Was he awake, or still asleep and dreaming?

Finally they stopped, exhausted. PK had no idea how far they had run. Their escape was quick but it felt infinitely long. Soaked in blood and sweat, they collapsed against a tree trunk and waited for the sun to rise. The night air was filled with the buzz and chirp of mosquitoes, grasshoppers and crickets.

'What if the elephants are angry with us? What if they come after us and trample us to death?'

But luckily they never did, and Grandma, PK and Pramodini were sore but safe.

In this northern country no wild elephants roamed. Instead, mosquitoes buzzed in the reeds that edged the wooded lakes of Borås. Willow warblers serenaded each other, while moose and deer grazed among the fir trees in the hundred-year-old forests. Rainwater glistened in the tracks left by large forest machinery. Grey smoke rose from the chimneys of the red summer cottages that dotted the glades.

Lotta's family were regular church-goers. Lotta's mother grew up fearing purgatory, haunted by the priest's descriptions of the eternal punishment that awaited sinners in the next life. Her father joined them at the weekly service even though he was not himself a believer. Lotta was never sure what he thought about religion and the Church; he rarely expressed his opinions about anything. He was a hard man to get to know. There were moments when she thought she might understand him, especially when they sat side-by-side in silence. Somehow, she felt a deep connection to him despite the lack of conversation.

When Lotta was eight, one of her aunts fell ill while pregnant. The family prayed to God, but her aunt's condition worsened. Both aunt and baby died, and the faith Lotta had once felt was subsumed by anger and disappointment.

She was confirmed into the Swedish Church, but not because she had faith. No, she did it mostly because that was what everyone did. She was easily influenced by parents and friends. It was hard to be different, to do her own thing. People turned against those who broke the norm, stuck out too much. Lotta had no strong beliefs in any case; she found it difficult to attach too much weight to any one idea. There was a hint of truth in most things people said and she took little interest in politics. How could one put one's faith in a party, or an ideology, one hundred per cent? To do so meant that everyone else had to be completely wrong. No, party politics was not for her.

Sometimes she found herself humming a song that she had first learned at the age of three. Its message: a light shone over all of humanity, despite its vanity, its ambition and its pettiness.

That light exists inside me too, thought Lotta. But it was not God, it was something else:

> Clouds come, clouds go
> Sometimes the heart goes cold
> But up above us, in the sky
> A wishing star behold.

Instead, in her teens, her imagination turned eastwards. She read the *Upanishads* and continued with the *Vedas* and the Buddha's sermons. There were similarities between the ancient Hindu texts and the Bible's Sermon on the Mount, she observed. But there was something wrong in the way Christianity expressed its teaching. It excluded more than it embraced. Christians seemed more interested in drawing boundaries between people. Everyone, whether they were believers or not, was driven by the same vital energy. The heart beats for the same reason in all of us, no matter your beliefs, she thought. All atoms in the universe belong together. Everything is connected.

The Asian philosophies made a strong impression on her, especially the idea that all humans and animals dissolve after their death and come alive again in other living things. Yes, that's it, she thought. If you want to know the past, look at the present. If you want to know the future, look again at the present, as the Buddha said.

Life is recycled and recreated again and again. We have all been soil and water and it is to soil and water we will return, thought the teenaged Lotta.

When the Pan men shot a sambar deer, PK's grandfather would be invited to sample the meat. Around festival time, villagers came with auspicious gifts of tiger skins and bird feathers. Grandpa's elevated social standing rubbed off on PK, and among the untouchable children he was king. He was proud of his grandfather and liked to imitate him. With a bow and arrow Grandpa had given him as a present, he led groups of friends on expeditions into the jungle, naked as usual save for a peacock feather and a belt and bracelet shaped like snakes. They crept along paths and pretended to hunt tiger and deer. They howled with excitement at every squirrel that scampered up a nearby tree or eagle that circled above the forest canopy.

They pretended that PK was their chief while the other children took turns acting as his spiritual adviser. This boy would pick fruit for PK and present it to him with a bow. Then they ran down to the river to fish or ventured into the woods to strike at beehives hanging high up in the branches.

The beehives were PK's domain. He climbed up with a bundle of dry grass, set fire to it and held it underneath to smoke out the bees. He clasped a stick in his mouth, which he used to jab at the hive to scare away any bees still brave enough to remain inside. Sometimes the bees launched their own counterattack. But no matter how badly he was stung, PK refused to retreat without having first tasted the sweet nectar inside. With one hand wrapped around the tree trunk, he greedily sucked on his stick as the honey ran down his cheeks and dribbled onto his chest. Then he let some drip down to the others, waiting below, their mouths gaping as the sweet, sticky drops fell from the sky.

* * *

PK was also becoming the village artist. He collected big, smooth stones along the road out of the village, and drew on them in charcoal. Sunrises, sunsets and wooded mountains.

PK's skills advanced quickly. He took the neighbouring children to a large, flat rock near the river, told them to close their eyes, and then declared that with his magical powers he could lure a tiger and make it stand before them. They were sceptical, but obeyed. He started working. There, on the stone, he drew a tiger with its mouth wide open in a roar. 'Look!' he cried. The other children stared in astonishment. Were they frightened? Had he convinced them? Maybe it was just wishful thinking. Then they laughed in delight.

At least I can make people happy with my drawing, he thought.

He expanded his repertoire and honed his technique. He painted in every spare moment he had, before and after class, and all of Sunday. He found stones in a variety of colours, not just beige and grey. He discovered how to use leaves and flowers to produce pigments other than black. He learned to make plates out of clay from the river and then paint designs on them, which he brushed with a layer of egg yolk to make them fast. He also worked on paper and favoured jungle motifs such as leaves, flowers and trees.

Every stone within a hundred metres of their house was transformed into a work of art. Here was his gallery. And inside, a row of decorated plates stood proud on a shelf.

These games in the woods are among PK's most treasured childhood memories. The forest spoke to him and his desire for adventure. It was full of secrets and surprises that he knew would only reveal themselves gradually. The rest was destined to remain mysterious and unknowable. He has held onto this feeling to the present day. It is enough to comprehend only a small part of life. He is content knowing that there is much he will never understand.

PK's father pedalled energetically, a whistle dancing from his lips. He was in a good mood. The road wove between cornfields, mango groves and clusters of mud houses. His white shirt beat in the wind as he swerved potholes, stones and twigs. PK was just as happy. He sat on the carrier, his father's shirt a sail spread out before him. They were on the way to town, away from the safety of their people, but he felt brave and adventurous, and relished the feeling of uncertainty.

Finally, he was starting school.

The teacher of his new primary school in Athmallik had promised Shridhar that his son would be allowed to join the class even though the semester had begun a month before. Perhaps his mother and father had delayed the decision, fearful about how PK would be treated. In light of their own bitter experiences, no doubt.

The school was made up of a row of ochre classrooms built in mud, sharing a long veranda that faced a sandy schoolyard. The outer boundary was marked by a dense wall of greenery made from bamboo sticks and vines.

PK peered into the classroom. There sat his new teacher, his belly large and round. The teacher turned to look at him.

'Just like Ganesh,' the old man chuckled as he patted himself on the stomach.

Then he turned back to the other students, and pointed to the letters written on the blackboard. The children sang back the words in unison.

So many children, so many new friends.

The teacher stopped and gestured to his place. But his finger was not pointing in the direction of the other children, but to the veranda outside.

'There,' he said. 'You sit there, Pradyumna Kumar Mahanandia!'

PK sat cross-legged on the sandy floor outside. He felt confused and disappointed. Why am I sitting on my own out here? But his father took no notice. What was it that he knew that PK did not? He pressed PK's hand, said goodbye, and walked over to his bike leaning against the bamboo fence.

PK was alone with all these unfamiliar people. Did they want to be his friend? He was no longer so sure. The excitement of the ride had now dissipated. Why was the teacher angry with him? Why was he not allowed to sit on the floor inside the classroom, with all the others?

The teacher soon came out to the veranda to help him with the writing exercise. He spread a thin layer of sand over PK's wooden board and showed him how to draw the letters with his forefinger in the grains. PK noticed that the teacher avoided touching him. He sat close, but was careful not to make contact. Why was he acting like this?

From the veranda, PK could see into the classroom as the teacher turned and began to write the letter 'ma' on the blackboard in Oriya. 'Repeat,' he instructed.

'Ma, ma, ma, ma, ma,' chanted PK and the rest of the class.

The teacher rang a brass bell to announce time for play. The students rushed out into the yard, so PK stood up to follow them.

'Where are you going?' cried the teacher.

The question rendered PK mute. Was it not obvious?

'You're not to play with them!' continued the teacher.

PK adapted surprisingly quickly. On the first day of school, he spent break time by himself in a corner of the playground, fighting back the tears. On the second day, he discovered a pond behind the school where he could play on his own. Within a week, he found himself longing for those solitary moments. He did not understand why it had to be like this. He gazed at his reflection in the water. He searched the rippled image for the features, the colour perhaps, that made him different from the others. Maybe his nose was too flat, his complexion too dark, his hair too curly? Sometimes he thought he looked more like the forest creatures that played on the dark surface of the water. Other times he concluded that, in fact, he looked just like all the other children.

After a week, he finally asked his mother what he should have asked the first evening, but was too confused to formulate into words.

'Why do I have to sit outside the classroom?'

His mother was squatting by the fire in the kitchen, grilling corn on the cob and baking chapatis. She looked at him.

'Why am I not allowed to play with the others?' he continued.

'We are jungle people,' she said at last.

He looked at her and felt even more confused. What did she mean?

'Once upon a time, our people lived deep in the woods. We probably should have stayed there and led our lives among the trees and not moved to the village to live with people from the plains.'

She picked him up and sat him on her lap.

'We are not allowed in the temple, because it makes the priests angry. You already noticed that. We are not allowed to draw water from the same well as the others. That's why I go to the river or the reservoir and not the common well. But there's nothing we can do about it. We just have to accept it.'

'Why?' he asked.

'Because we are untouchable, because we have been born to a lower caste... or... to no caste at all.'

She caught his eye.

'It will all work out, you'll see, only if you focus on the truth...' She wiped her tears. '... And as long as you are honest with yourself and other people.'

That evening, he lay on his straw mat and pondered what his mother had told him. The whooshing of bats and howling of dogs were the accompaniment to his thoughts. Ma gathered sticks for the fire and rattled stainless steel bowls. These were his safe sounds, the ones he fell asleep to every night. But somehow he could not quiet his mind. What did caste mean? And untouchable? He sensed that it explained his teacher's strange behaviour, but where did it come from? Why was everyone so obsessed with it?

PK's class had been assigned a piece of land in the kitchen garden at one end of the playground. In it the students planted cucumbers, okra, aubergine and tomatoes. When the vegetables were ripe, they were allowed to pick them and take them home to their families. PK was given the task of watering the plants. No one minded him touching the seeds and the water.

At harvest time, he was given his own basket, while the other students shared another. This, he realized, was because they did not want their vegetables contaminated by his impurity. But he did not care any more. Instead he focused on all the lovely tomatoes he would be able to take home to his mother. The thought of joining in the harvest excited him, and he ran towards the patch. And tripped. He stumbled over a water hose and into the class basket, spilling the topmost fruit. PK bent down, picked them up and put them back.

'What have you done?' the teacher exploded. 'Now they are all ruined!'

PK froze, petrified, and watched as the teacher snatched the basket from him. He sensed that something unpleasant was about to happen. Teacher raised it above PK's head and poured the tomatoes over him. A rain of round, red fruit thudded against his skull and tumbled all around, while the rest of the class stood in a ring and watched in silence. Teacher then declared that PK might as well take them all home, seeing as no one else would be able to eat them.

Crying, PK bent down, picked up the tomatoes and placed them in his basket.

Ma's face lit up when he came home with the bounty, but when he told her what had happened, she looked depressed. Maybe he would be expelled and the other villagers would harass them?

'You never know with caste Hindus,' she said. 'Sometimes they like to humiliate us in public.'

But the next day Teacher pretended as if nothing had happened. And neither PK nor the rest of the family observed any other repercussions.

PK thought about it. Teacher had explained to him that whatever he touched turned dirty. So what would happen if he touched the other students? Would they be angry? Or would they pretend that nothing had happened?

I have to try, the young PK decided.

The students were lined up in rows in the schoolyard as they did every morning. This was his moment. He made a dash for it, reached out and ran his hand over every stomach down the line. Then he ran up to his teacher and the headmaster, and patted them on their bellies.

Teacher was dumbstruck. He glared first at PK, then at the headmaster, and finally at the other children.

'Come!' Teacher cried, turning to his students. 'We are going to the well to wash. PK, you stay here. I'll deal with you later.'

Teacher used to beat the students with his cane when they broke the school rules, but PK was never whipped because Teacher did not want to soil his cane and thus spread the infection to the others. For PK, Teacher came up with a special form of punishment; he was made to stand still on the veranda with his eyes closed. Teacher then edged back and began to throw stones, small, sharp rocks that stung as they assailed his skin, and left ugly bruises.

PK cursed the teacher, but recalled his mother's words with resignation; this was their destiny, what life was like outside their home. This was how he would always be treated. There was nothing he could do about it.

Now and then it made him angry, and he fantasized about getting his revenge or having divine justice intervene on his behalf. Bittersweet thoughts came as he rode home in the afternoons, as he lay awake in the moments before dawn, as morning's first light filled the sky and his mind still clung to the events of the previous day.

And one day, divine justice seemed to play its part. Teacher had fallen asleep at his desk while the students were reading morning prayers out loud. PK could smell the moonshine on his breath and the snoring filled the classroom as Teacher's mouth gaped ever wider. Then something amazing happened, something that he would never forget. One of the pigeons that liked to sit in the beams above suddenly relieved itself. The poo fell towards Teacher's lectern, down towards Teacher's chair and, to the delight of all the children, plopped straight into his mouth. Teacher jumped up, screamed and began cursing his students, believing that one of the boys must have played a prank on him.

Had the pigeon read PK's thoughts? Whatever the case, PK took great pleasure in his teacher's shock and disgust.

The mood at school changed dramatically when the schools' inspector came to visit. His main task was to check whether the school was obeying India's anti-discrimination laws that made prejudicial treatment on the grounds of caste illegal. Dressed in a blue blazer, white shirt and white trousers with creases pressed into them, he possessed a natural authority. His smiles were polite, but they masked an iron will.

That morning, PK was instructed to join the class inside, as if his untouchability had been nothing but a bad dream. Suddenly he was one of them and allowed to play with the other students during break time. Nobody told him to go away. He felt ecstatic, liberated. But tragically, he had no idea that this was all a sham, that as soon as the inspector left, he would be cast right back into the hell of exclusion again.

Had he been a little less naïve, he would not have let himself feel such happiness.

In the evening, he told his mother how he impressed the other children by correctly answering the inspector's questions. She was visibly proud of him, and felt so moved that she cried. This made him feel better, that in her eyes he was important and valued. Years later, in his teens, he thought that perhaps his mother's tears had been shed because of the hypocrisy, that she had known all along that such treatment was only temporary, make-believe for the benefit of someone who would leave again.

He used to dream of the inspector's return. The inspector would sit diagonally behind the teacher, watching eagle-eyed over the class. Nothing escaped his gaze and he saw to it that everyone treated PK fairly. PK sat in the middle of the classroom, surrounded by the other students. He raised his hand, answered all the questions correctly and was praised repeatedly.

But such sweet sensations evaporated when he opened his eyes. He lay still, the warmth lingering in his body for just a moment longer than the dream. The pressure in his chest returned as soon as he was up and sitting out on the veranda greeting the sun, and he would replay the post-inspection ritual in his mind. It went like this: immediately after the inspector had mounted his bike and pedalled away, PK's Brahmin teacher and caste classmates would form a procession and proceed down to the reservoir to cleanse themselves with soap and water. They washed carefully and slowly, scrubbing every last trace of the stench of his presence from their skin.

The first time it happened, he went home and cried desperately.

'They were dirty,' his mother soothed. 'They needed a wash. You did them a favour, making them go for a swim. They stank!'

She would keep repeating these words until he stopped crying. Although he knew she was lying, the words were soft and warm and wrapped themselves around him like a blanket. At least someone in the world accepted him.

This charade was not performed for the inspector alone. In his third year of school, they received a visit from a British colonial official who had remained in Orissa after Independence. He and his wife stepped stiffly into the classroom, he in a dark suit, she in a floral dress. Their faces were as white and smooth as yogurt. The Brahmin girls in the class placed flower garlands around their necks. To mark the occasion, PK was once again allowed to sit with the others inside the classroom, as if the daily humiliation was nothing but a figment of his young imagination. The children stood up together and sang for their visitors, a loving family reunited.

As the British couple were leaving the classroom, the woman approached PK and patted him on the cheek. She looked him straight in the eyes and smiled.

'I can touch you, because I am also untouchable,' she said as she removed the garland of flowers around her neck and placed it on PK.

The sense of acceptance was intoxicating. This time he knew it was temporary, but he did not allow its transience to settle; no, he swatted it away like a mosquito, desperate to let the moment last a little longer.

When the British were in earshot, caste did not exist. Maybe life was better for us when they were in charge? His grandfather thought so.

He glanced at the white woman and remembered the astrologer's prediction: she will come from far, far away, from another country even. Was he destined to marry a woman in a floral dress and a face as white as yogurt?

Lotta's longing for the East only grew. *The Beatles are off to India to meditate*, the Swedish newspapers announced. She read about how George Harrison had travelled to India, met with spiritual masters, learned to play the sitar and performed an Indian song in a Hindu temple in London. She also read an interview with Maharishi Mahesh Yogi, guru to the Beatles, who said that the Fab Four had cosmic potential. India was everywhere, impossible to escape.

Lotta often thought about her grandfather, who died when she was only two. It had been his dream to travel, his greatest wish to take off for countries far, far away. He had been a weaver by trade and made friends with a travelling textile dealer from Bombay. He read books by Rudyard Kipling, Jack London and the Swedish explorer Sven Hedin, and talked constantly about having his own adventures in the Orient.

Lotta often took out the yellowed copy of the magazine *Idun* where he had circled an advert for cruises to India. Grandfather had never realized his dream. Instead, he brought the world home to him. One day he found an old incense burner at the local junkyard, which turned out to be from Persia. No one knew how it had ended up on a rubbish heap in Borås, but what did that matter? Lotta's grandfather treasured it. It was his adventure.

When he died, responsibility for looking after the censer fell to Lotta. Many years later she ended up hanging it in a niche in her home in the clearing in the woods. I'm not going to settle for a censer, Lotta said to herself, I'm going to do what Grandfather never managed.

The family home was a small, three-room apartment. They were often short of money and lived frugally. Her parents ran a fabric shop they had inherited but never really wanted, and when business dwindled, eventually they were forced to shut down. Lotta's father began working on managing the family forest, while her mother took a job as a nurse at her brother's dental practice.

It wasn't obvious from their modest lifestyle, but Lotta's family was descended from a knight. They were nobles, the von Schedvins. But what to others was a name to be proud of, to the teenaged Lotta felt like a weight around her neck. It was no fun to bear such a fancy name. Lotta wanted to be like everyone else. And yet she also felt guilty for begrudging her privileged background.

The family drove an old, rusty car that often broke down. But Lotta and her sisters wanted a horse. So the family sat down to discuss it: which was the more important investment, a horse or a car? It could not be both, it was either or. Lotta's mother held the deciding vote.

'It's more important the girls have a hobby,' she said, 'than we have a new car.'

She turned to Lotta and her sisters.

'You must learn to take responsibility for something other than yourselves.'

Lotta once saw a film at the cinema about a boy who rode around India's dense jungles on an elephant. I will have a friend like that, she thought. And before long she was writing to pen pals in Nairobi, Japan, Austria and San Francisco.

One day, a bracelet made from elephant hair arrived from Nairobi. She wore it to school the next day with pride.

India's first Prime Minister was Jawaharlal Nehru who was sworn in on 15 August 1947, the day India gained independence from the British Empire. He believed in modernity, industry, urbanization and the railways. In a speech laying out his vision for India, he talked about how the new must replace the deadwood of the past. It inspired many of PK's fellow countrymen. Indeed, his father was one of Nehru's greatest admirers, as was his school's new headmaster.

On the first day at his new job, the headmaster gathered the students in the playground to tell them about all the machines and other modern things he had seen in the city. First he described the telephone, then something so strange and magical, PK remembers it to this day.

'The locomotive,' the headmaster said with a sense of drama, 'is very long. It looks a bit like a giant snake that reaches from where I am standing here all the way over there.' He pointed to a grassy slope a few hundred metres away. 'It also moves like a snake, zigzagging through the countryside. I travelled on one for three days and two nights to get here. There was over a hundred of us sitting on it.'

PK listened carefully and imagined the train as a long, man-made snake slithering through the sand, with the people sitting astride it, as if they were riding a horse or an elephant.

'Any questions?' the headmaster said finally.

PK raised his hand.

'Can it jump up like a cobra?'

He recalled not only the cobra that had protected him as a baby, but also the one that had bitten him when he was a mere five years old. He had been so furious that he grabbed the snake, bit through its scaly skin and let it bleed until it hung lifeless in his hands. He pictured an animal many times larger than that one, shiny and powerful.

The headmaster snorted and sniffed theatrically.

'It's too heavy to jump; it's made entirely from metal,' he said.

Yes, it must be terribly heavy, PK realized. It couldn't possibly jump off the ground. But he had one more question.

'Will it come to the village?'

Now the headmaster lost his patience.

'No, it most certainly will not. It travels only on metal. Roads made of metal. And we don't have those here.'

Amazing! Roads of solid metal! Imagine how much you'd need to build a whole road! More than in all of Grandpa's arrowheads, and he had more than anyone else in the village. Perhaps if I took all of them and melted them down, it might be enough... to make a metre? Not more. And Headmaster said he travelled for three days and two nights!

He tried to imagine such a thing, but the scale of it only made him dizzy and he had to shake his head to rid himself of the feeling.

After five years, he moved on to boarding school and, just like his father and brothers, returned to his mother only one day a week.

He walked along the corridors of his new school and looked up at the ceiling. They were decorated with strange objects he had never seen before: round glass globes that hung from thin strings. A puzzling sight. Oil lamps? They were so bright! They must guzzle oil, he thought. He examined them from all angles, looking for the reservoir.

'How do the townspeople refill their lamps?' he asked his father on his first Sunday home.

Shridhar replied that he need not trouble himself with such questions, and that he would learn how everything worked in time.

'But get used to it! The Prime Minister has promised us that we will have those kind of lamps in our village soon,' he added.

From the very first day at his new school, his untouchability was apparent to everyone and his new teachers and classmates treated him accordingly. Indeed, now he carried in his pocket a folded caste certificate issued by the local authorities. This gave him access to the quotas reserved for '*Scheduled Castes*', '*Scheduled Tribes*' and '*Other Backward Castes*', which included untouchables and tribal people like him:

> Caste Certificate. Case Record No 44 of 1975. Certified that Sri Pradyumna Kumar Mahanandia, son of Sri Sreedhar Mahanandia of village Kandhapada P S Athmallik in the district of Dehnkanal belongs to schedule caste. His subcaste is Pan.

There it was, black and white proof that he was untouchable, a pariah, a second-class citizen. The certificate afforded him cheaper train tickets and would one day give him easier entry to university, that much was true. But mostly he regarded it as a stamp of his humiliation. He was nothing but a poor wretch who needed special treatment just to survive.

One of his new teachers also happened to be director of a shelter for *Dalits* (untouchables), which made him qualified to tell the young PK exactly what was expected of him and how he should behave. He was not to enter the kitchen or the dining room if anyone else was present, and, instead, should sit on the floor in the hallway and wait there for his food. The cook would come out to serve him last, and separately.

The cook came out with his pans and poured a portion

of rice, dal and vegetable curry from such a height that his ladle did not touch PK's bowl. Some days, PK was given only rice as the other food had run out. When he complained the cook only sighed, as if he was as powerless as PK in the situation.

'It's karma from your past life. You must understand and respect that,' was his only answer.

This was not the first time he had been given this explanation, invariably from Brahmins or people who had been brainwashed by them. It's not their fault, he would say to himself, they have been indoctrinated, taught to treat untouchables like lepers. But still he felt the rage swell inside him.

The school employed a Dhobi wallah, a man who washed clothes for the boarders. Except PK's. When he realized this, PK's fury turned into a deafening scream, but he was too scared to let it out. Instead, he slipped down to the riverbank, and just as he had done as a little boy with the priests at the temple, shot at the Dhobi wallah's water pots with his slingshot. Yet again, he was caught.

That week, a letter arrived for PK's father from the Dhobi wallah: 'Your son must understand and respect our rules and traditions. How would it look if he did as he pleased all of a sudden?'

Shridhar replied that he knew all about these traditions and so, no doubt, did his son. 'But,' he wrote back, 'these rules are unjust and shameful for a country that wants to be modern and compete with the successful nations of the West.'

Had the laundry man heard Prime Minister Nehru's speeches? Did he not know that the politicians in New Delhi dreamed of an India free from caste hierarchies? Had he not read Nehru's most wise pronouncement that people are creatures of free will, and are not controlled by ancient customs? Life is like a game of cards, Nehru once said, the cards you are dealt are predetermined, but life is all about your skill in the game. That is your free will.

The following week, the Dhobi wallah approached PK as he sat alone eating his meal in the corridor. 'Get your clothes for me tonight,' he whispered, 'but be sure no one sees you. I'll wash them and you'll get them back tomorrow night when the others are asleep.'

A half-victory, at least.

Indian society was full of contradictions, PK was more than aware of that. A good example was how the caste system had affected his paternal grandfather. Grandpa was a respected man when it came to secular activities. Yet it was unthinkable to the Brahmins to receive food or a glass of water that he might have touched. He was refused entry to the temple until the day he died.

The Pan had worked as weavers for hundreds of years, but his grandfather broke with tradition and took an office job in Athmallik. While the Brahmins treated him like elephant dung, the British respected him. They would do anything to annoy the Brahmins. They appointed him *chatia*, chief of the village, and tasked him with arbitrating local conflicts, as well as reporting all births and deaths and crimes committed to the colonial authorities. There was no police station or national registration office in the village, it all fell to Grandpa. The role was also punitive. If anyone violated the law it was Grandpa who beat the offender with his wooden stick, as per British orders. But most of all, this position made him an official representative of the British Empire, because the imperialists did not trust the Brahmins.

'Brahmins have so many taboos when it comes to food, as well as strange social rules, so you never know if you are insulting them. Only they seem to understand the rules,' one of the British in Athmallik was reported to have said.

The British knew that the scepticism was mutual.

Orthodox Brahmins despised the colonialists and called them Beefeaters. It was meant as an insult.

Grandpa used to tell PK how much he liked the British.

'They keep their promises; they are good people. Unlike the Brahmins, they shake hands with us. They don't mind touching us,' he said. 'Stay away from Brahmins,' he continued in his gravest tone. 'If you don't keep your distance, it will be your undoing.'

During his teenage years, PK found sanctuary and companionship in a most unexpected place: the travelling circus. They arrived one day without warning, pitched their tents, parked their elephants and built their itinerant amusement park nearby. The first evening, a queue formed for the Ferris wheel and the carousel, powered by men on reconstructed bikes. The rusty attractions squeaked, blinked and whined. It was a ramshackle affair perhaps, but PK was nevertheless impressed by the spinning, rattling machines. Yet it was the circus tent that fascinated him the most, without really knowing why. He wandered among the caravans, patting the horses and elephants and introducing himself to the jugglers and lion tamers.

PK was careful to let them know he was untouchable. Out of consideration. Then they could choose to keep their distance or shoo him away. That way he would not contaminate them.

'We don't care about stuff like that!' said one of the lion tamers.

'We're Muslims, we understand you. They treat us as if we're untouchable too,' said a juggler.

No one had ever told him that India's Muslims were treated as badly as the untouchables. Technically, Muslims did not belong to the caste system. But in fact, they too had once been low-caste Hindus who had escaped their untouchability by converting to Islam. Not that it had helped. They were excluded and humiliated just the same.

The caste system is an incurable epidemic, PK concluded.

He went to the circus after school every day. Finally, he had found a place where he was treated with common respect. The circus people were friendly, open and curious. They answered his questions and listened to his stories. It was an unfamiliar feeling. After a few days, they offered him a job. Why not? He did not care if his school work suffered. That was his way. He did not think before he acted, and good offers were so rare that he never said no.

He was flattered. For the first time in his life, he felt accepted.

For two weeks, he carried hay to the animals and ladders to the tents. He also painted their posters.

'Become our clown and join us on tour!' the circus director said to him one day.

Sure, why not? It was the beginning of the summer holidays anyway. He was given a long striped coat and a red plastic nose. He learned some tricks and sketches, and realized that it was not so hard. Best of all, the audiences laughed. The attention was easily earned and at first it was intoxicating.

The circus performers liked him. But after a few weeks, when the director asked if he wanted to join them on a longer tour of several states in eastern India, he hesitated. Something was not quite right. He had started to feel that playing the clown was the ultimate confirmation of his exclusion. What was a clown if not a failure who tried to cover up the fact by making himself a fool? He was among like-minded people, he had a job, he was even earning money, but somehow the laughter of the caste Hindus in the audience sounded scornful to him. No, he did not want to be the clown.

Exams at school were an unrelenting torture. PK would sit, staring at the questions, dumbstruck. He could barely answer a thing. Maths and physics were the worst. Had he understood nothing the teachers had been saying?

I'm untouchable, and stupid, he said to himself, full of self-pity.

If he did not pass his exams, he had no future. Then he would have to be content to clean toilets for the wealthy, or become a weaver or a brick burner, professions destined for untouchables who, like himself, were unable to make anything of their lives.

He went down to the river with the intention of surrendering himself to the rapids, to find his final relief, to obtain his own, better, revelation. He plunged forward, to end all suffering. Something else awaited him, surely.

But just as the water rushed against his skin, he had time for one thought: what would his mother say? Emotions inside him started to fight against the current that pulled him towards darkness.

He still wanted to live.

He came to the surface, swam to the shore and climbed out onto the narrow, shingle beach. Yet, an impulse told him he should try again. He jumped in, but his body struggled against the water. He surfaced. One more time, he said to himself. As his body reached the bottom of the river, he grabbed hold of a rock to keep himself underwater. He wanted this ultimate escape.

There was no turning back now.

Suddenly the stone dislodged from the riverbed and he rushed to the surface. Soaking wet and defeated, he went back to school, lay on the floor of his dormitory and stared at the ceiling.

He began processing recent events. He hated his teachers, the Dhobi wallah, the cook and the other students. He hated the way they accepted everyone's predetermined place in society. And yet, he could not shake the feeling that all these things happened for a reason. Nothing in life was meaningless. Even failure had its purpose. This sense of exclusion had its purpose, the suicide attempt had its purpose, and the stone loosening at just the right moment had its purpose too. In the search for consolation, he brought his thoughts back to the palm leaf and the horoscope. The prophecy. The woman he would marry. He imagined her, drew her in his mind. The image of a light-skinned woman took shape in the darkness before him. She was beautiful and her smile was gentle. He felt the warmth of a body as he closed his eyes, and he was convinced there was a light surrounding him. His mother. He did not know how he knew, but there was no doubting it. She was sitting on the floor beside him, stroking him.

'There now,' her voice came to him, 'they are the stupid ones; you're doing everything right. One day, you will meet the woman from the prophecy, your future wife.'

The darkness could not get any darker, but it was his mother, her light, that sustained him and stopped him from taking that plunge into the void.

It feels so nice when you sit beside me. That was the last thing he remembered saying to her that wretched evening, as he drifted off to sleep.

Military training camps were mandatory for all boys about to start their final year of secondary school. India had fought two wars with Pakistan and one with China. There were battles in humid jungles, hot salty deserts and icy glaciers. Even schoolboys had to be prepared to serve in the next conflict, because everyone knew it was only a matter of time before war broke out again.

It was time for PK to attend the National Cadet Corps youth camp in Baulpur. Over a thousand young people from all over Orissa gathered in the summer heat to practise drills and learn to shoot. They lived in tents on the banks of the Brahmani River, under mango trees weighed down with ripe fruit that fell around them in the sand. The exercises were monotonous and boring, but PK was fascinated by the uniforms, the caps and medals, and the heavy leather boots. The outfit gave him a feeling of authority.

One day, he and two other cadets were charged with guarding the tents while the others marched a kilometre along the river to cook dinner. Navy, rain-filled clouds had been hanging low above the trees all afternoon. Wind had now caught up with them. Not long after the others had left, wet hail the size of kernels of corn started swirling in the air.

The cyclone hit faster and with more force than anyone had anticipated. In less than ten minutes it had levelled the entire campsite. The dense blackness was illuminated by an occasional flash of white-blue light, and PK stumbled into a ditch he and a few others had dug that very day. A sudden gust dropped another cadet beside him. A large branch was torn from one of the mango trees like a tooth pick. A smaller branch came flying and hit PK. The pain ripped into him. He looked up and saw blood gathering in pools where he lay, the scarlet liquid soaking into his clothes. Within seconds, he was drenched in it.

He looked down at his body, but he was not bleeding. That was when he realized: the blood was his friend's.

PK woke up several hours later, an irritatingly bright light hanging above him. He was lying on a hard stretcher in the hospital in Dhenkanal. He had broken his leg. His friend had been crushed by the larger branch, and was dead.

***

Before he knew it, the time for exam resits arrived. Just when all had felt so utterly hopeless, hope returned. His bad luck had finally run out. His memory began to function again. The blockage was released.

He passed. Just.

Some of what he had been taught had gone in. He was not completely useless after all.

His father saw again his chance to push PK towards the career he had chosen for him. Become an engineer, son. A job with prospects, a bright future for PK and for India, built on rationality and science, not the superstition and prejudice of the priests.

Bapa told him to apply to a science college. PK did as he was told and was accepted for the following autumn. But he soon tired of the course and instead took to drawing caricatures of the faculty staff during lectures.

'Untouchables have no brains!' his maths lecturer yelled upon discovering them.

But being thrown out of class did not cast PK into despair this time. He knew what he wanted and it was a different life to the one his Bapa had envisioned for him. He hated the natural sciences: physics, chemistry and mathematics were his worst subjects. Leave the nation building to someone else.

The same lecturer approached him the next day and gave him some sound advice.

'Pradyumna Kumar, this isn't working,' he said.

'Then what should I do?'

'Apply for art school!'

He took his teacher's advice and fled with the grand sum of fifty-five rupees in his pocket. At first he did not know where he was going, but then he remembered the Bhima Bhoi spiritual centre in Khaliapali, a couple of hours' bus ride from home. PK knew the monks welcomed lost souls like him. He was received warmly, given a straw mat to sleep on and food to eat. These people shared his values, so he took his place on the floor beside the monks, who were naked save for scraps of bark that covered their genitals.

PK was fascinated by the movement's founder, Bhima Bhoi. The monks told him that he had been an orphan boy from the neighbourhood and had formed the sect out of frustration with India's caste hierarchy, class divisions and hypocritical Brahmins. He had quickly gained followers.

The monks sang their guru's songs and recited beautiful poems that told of a just society in which people lived together and were not divided into competing factions. PK found solace in hearing his own thoughts sung out loud. Here, he was among equals. The monks felt the same way about the Brahmins as he did.

And yet, something told him he could not spend the rest of his life in meditation. The life of a monk was not for him; he needed to taste cravings and desires before he could renounce them. He would marry, the prophecy had told him so, and he wanted to see the world out there, beyond Athmallik.

He continued his journey, and stole onto a train travelling north to West Bengal. The creaking train was carrying him to a new life, and as he sat watching the world pass by the window, he recalled the headmaster who had once described trains as metal snakes. To think that he had pictured passengers astride a giant serpent as it wound its way along roads paved with metal. He laughed at his own stupidity. There was so much he had not understood.

His next destination was Kala Bhavana, an art school in the village of Shantiniketan founded by the Bengali poet Rabindranath Tagore. He checked in at the school's hostel.

Only one rupee a night for a bed? That much he could afford. But the classes were much less reasonably priced and he was forced to abandon the idea. He could not possibly write to his father for help. Instead, they told him about an art school in Khallikote, back in his home state of Orissa, designed for students from less affluent backgrounds like him.

With renewed hope, he sneaked back onto a train going south and arrived at the art school, located in an old colonial house with marble floors and a cast iron fence, nestled between towering mountains and the vast Chilika Lake.

The school was exceedingly popular because it was free. Competition for the thirty-three available places was fierce, and PK was one of hundreds of applicants. The selection process consisted of a series of tests in how well candidates could work with paints, ink and charcoal. The school set up a still life in the yard – one pot, one bunch of grapes and three mangoes – and the hopefuls formed a ring around it.

PK glanced at the other drawings and felt confident. The next day, the teachers came to announce the results. First came those who had been unsuccessful. Then, the lucky ones, graded and ranked by order of skill.

PK was placed number one.

He told no one at the art school in Khallikote that he was untouchable. And no one asked him. The teachers and students came from all over the country and they socialized together, as if neither caste nor class existed. It was a new and powerful sensation. This was a different India, and it reminded him of the itinerant Muslim circus he had briefly joined as a young boy.

Another life was possible.

That year in Khallikote was crowned by his greatest achievement so far. The teachers singled him out for his talent and in the spring invited him to apply for a scholarship to continue his studies in New Delhi. He put in an application and waited for the answer, which arrived finally to the accompaniment of the clap and roar of the summer's monsoon rains. His father, the postmaster, brought the brown, official-looking envelope home and presented it to his wife, who ripped it open, only to hand it back to her husband to read out loud.

'You got the scholarship!' Kalabati said when PK called home.

The ground beneath his feet swayed.

'You're moving to the capital,' she continued, and began to cry.

His father congratulated him, having finally given up on the idea of his son becoming an engineer.

His mother cried and refused to eat for three days before his departure. The move, for her, was a tragedy. And yet her emotions were more complex. She was also proud. Indeed, in front of the neighbourhood women, she was triumphant:

'My son is travelling by bus and train, and then he is going to fly in a silver bird over the jungle and the mountains and further away than any of you could ever imagine.'

The Transformation

It was late summer, and a perfume of fermenting fallen fruit and monsoon rain assailed his nostrils. PK was about to leave for New Delhi. He knelt before his mother and lightly brushed her feet. She cried. Holding back his own tears, he stood up, hugged her and jumped onto the cart. He signalled to the driver, and the ox responded by shaking the flies from its eyes. It then began its leisurely walk along the bumpy dirt road, the wagon PK was sitting on creaking behind it. As he made his way to the train station, PK was reminded of his horoscope: he would marry 'a girl from far, far away, from outside the village, the district, the province, the state and even the country'.

The next morning the train arrived at Bhubaneswar, the capital of the state of Orissa, an exuberant city that hit PK with a riot of new sensations. Wide, straight boulevards with traffic police clad in white positioned at the intersections. Rows of Hindustan Ambassador taxis with men dressed in starched cotton clothes sitting in the back seats. Ancient, stately sandstone temples surrounded by manicured gardens. Bazaars where the goods seemed to pour out into the streets. The delicious aroma of cooking food wafting from rows of small eateries. Cows sauntering among tinkling bicycles and roaring motorized rickshaws. And in the evenings, glistening temples, tall glass houses and lights spilling from shopfronts. It was a gleaming spectacle, an unearthly creation. How, then, would New Delhi shimmer?

He was twenty-two, or twenty-one, or possibly twenty… he did not know exactly. His illiterate mother could not be sure. Birthdays were not celebrated in his family, and there was no such thing as an identity number in the India of those days. The year was 1971: the calendar that hung on the wall at school told him so, as did the front pages of newspapers for sale by the side of the road.

His childhood had been characterized by the gradual realization of what it meant to be untouchable; the loneliness, the humiliation, which had overwhelmed the pure joy of the early years in his mother's care. Village life had been cruel. But now he stood on the threshold of a new kind of freedom, an anonymity unavailable to him back home. Everything – the houses, the streets, the city bustle, parks, temples, the vendors shouting in the markets – they were like picture-perfect visions of a dream-world.

When running to schedule, the Utkal Express between Bhubaneswar and New Delhi took two and a half days, but by the time they rolled into their final stop, they were more than eight hours delayed. What happened? The man on the bunk beneath him shrugged.

'What *hasn't* happened?' he replied. 'But we should rejoice that we have made it and not worry about the things in the past we cannot change. I mean, what can you do about it anyway?'

This sounded like good advice. Look forward, to the future. Celebrate the fact that he had made it out of the village, away from the constant bullying, to the capital, where fantasies were realized and ambitions took flight.

PK slept deeply that night, in his brave new world on the fifth floor of the Orissa Bhavan state guesthouse, the club and guesthouse for Orissans living in the city. The next morning, he got up and went to the window in the hallway. But as he stood, rubbing his eyes in the early morning light, he started to feel scared. He had fallen asleep so full of courage and wild ideas, but was awakened by fears leaping around inside his chest; a feeling that, most of all, he wanted to go back to safety, to his bed, to his village in Orissa, and to his family.

He looked out on New Delhi below: wide roads of dark smooth asphalt, white and beige hunchbacked cars, buses dented from the constant battering of dense traffic, trucks painted rainbow colours, black and yellow motorized rickshaws, swarms of motorcycles and towering buildings of concrete, steel and glass that glittered in the scorching September sun.

Will I ever feel at home here?

He started to wonder if he would even dare to go out. Maybe they would not understand him here? He spoke Oriya, his native tongue, and English, which he had learned in school. But the capital spoke mostly Hindi, of which he had gained only a working reading knowledge in secondary school; it most certainly was not a language he was comfortable speaking. *Mai Orissa se ho*. I am from Orissa. *Mai tik ho*. I am well. In Hindi, his conversation would be stiff, formal and childish.

He let his finger trail across the map from the guesthouse to the art school. It was a long way. He had no idea how to navigate the city's buses. What if he made a mistake? What if he could not find his way back? What if he was robbed or cheated? What if the city people noticed how awkward he was – unsure of himself and badly dressed – and laughed at him?

For the first week, he walked to and from the school in order to avoid having to figure out which bus to take. But he soon found it exhausting; he would have to catch a bus after all. As he approached the bus stop, fear grasped him.

The Delhi Transport Corporation's dilapidated vehicles trundled by in a steady stream, tilting heavily as cones of black smoke spewed from their exhaust pipes and passengers hung like bunches of grapes in the doorways. The bus drivers did not halt their vehicles but slowed as they approached the stop, so that people could jump on and off.

Somehow he managed to press himself onto one of the buses. After what felt like hours stuck in the depths of the sweaty human mass, he noticed the tall buildings and roundabouts were being replaced by small mud huts, then fields and thickets.

The bus, he realized, was not going in the direction of the school. He had gone the wrong way.

He jumped off at the next stop, crossed to the other side of the road and stuck out his thumb for a ride back into town.

The next day he decided to walk. The more he got to know the wide boulevards, passed the towering high rises and navigated the giant roundabouts, the less scary New Delhi became. What once seemed dangerous and hostile began to feel familiar. He felt relief. This was freedom. Here he was not the untouchable Pan boy, son of Shridhar Mahanandia, Athmallik's untouchable postmaster, and Kalabati Mahanandia, the dark-skinned tribal woman. No one had even heard of Athmallik, let alone knew where it was. He had no choice over where he had been born or his place in the caste hierarchy. But here, so far, no one had asked about any of that.

The teachers at the College of Art were modern, if not radical. They were vehemently opposed to the caste system, and just like at the art school in Khallikote, he sat inside the classroom along with the other students. High caste and low were treated the same. PK heard teachers say things like, 'The caste system is an evil that must be destroyed.'

They said it loud and proud, almost triumphantly, as if they wanted to free their young students from this obsolete and outdated culture. PK even ate with the others: in the same room, at the same table, from the same deep bowls. No one flinched as he approached and no one shunned his presence or touch. It was like living through a revolution. He walked home at night with a bounce in his step. New Delhi, the city, was his future.

The scholarship from the state of Orissa was supposed to be paid once a month and be enough to cover school fees, art materials, books, rent at the guesthouse and food. But after a few months the money stopped coming. The fifty rupees his father sent every month was only enough to cover his living costs for a few days. Someone at the government grants office was probably siphoning off the money into his own pocket. PK kept returning to the window where he was supposed to receive it and the same answer came back at him again and again:

'Sorry! No money. Come back in a month and see.'

His first year at the art college started so positively, but it quickly came to be characterized by poverty, hunger and anxiety about where he would spend the night. For the first three months he stayed with various school friends. But he did not want to trespass on their hospitality for too long. After a while, he began to sleep on the floor of New Delhi railway station along with the day labourers, the disabled, the beggars and families from the country waiting for the dawn trains. The station was full of people wrapped in blankets, big bags made from sheet metal, jute sacks filled with grain and straw, milk pots, farm implements and sometimes the occasional goat.

It was warmer and more comfortable inside the station than out on the streets. Delhi nights were not as hot as at home in the village; they were rather damp and at times bitterly cold. Moreover, he could wash in the station toilets, and therefore did not have to attend classes stinking of sweat.

Some evenings, however, he was too tired to walk all the way to the station. Those nights he crawled inside a nearby telephone booth and fell asleep.

Aged eighteen, Lotta moved by herself to London to study nursing and undertake her practical training in a local hospital. She needed no moral support, no friend to hold her hand. On the contrary. It felt liberating to go alone.

She got a job at a renowned hospital in Hampstead, where the long-term patients and staff were like family. Lotta had chief responsibility for an old and very sick man who wanted to be addressed as Sir.

'Promise me, Lotta, never, ever let yourself turn hard inside,' he said, holding her hand, on her last day.

She has carried this advice with her all her life.

In London she ate Indian food in small neighbourhood restaurants where the aroma of cumin and chilli scratched at her nose. She went to the Royal Festival Hall to see the Indian Odissi dancers with bells around their ankles and to the Royal Albert Hall to see George Harrison and Ravi Shankar's concert for world peace. For a short while, she even dated an Indian immigrant from Delhi.

And then there was the photo diary she found at the hospital. One of the pictures was of a large, stone wheel. It looked to be very old and was fringed with small sculptures of humans and elephants. She tore out the picture and stuck it to the wall above the bed in her lodgings. In the evenings she lay, staring at it.

'It's as if the wheel is pulling me,' she wrote in her diary, 'as if the image is speaking to me, deep inside, about something big that I have known, but have forgotten.'

PK started skipping class. The days he could not afford to eat, he was too tired to listen to the teachers or complete the exercises they set. Instead, he took to walking aimlessly around town. He often ended up in the area around Connaught Place, a large roundabout in the centre of the city surrounded by white colonial houses with columns and arcades. This was where the best restaurants and fanciest shops were located. In the middle of the roundabout was a park with a lawn, bushes, a fountain and a pond. In its own peculiar way, it smelled of the metropolis: the stench of stagnant water, diesel fumes and human waste mixed with the sweet incense of flowers and fruit stalls, as well as the cigarette smoke from the porters who lay on the grass inhaling *bidis*.

Next to the park, in one of the squat, white buildings, was the Indian Coffee House. This was where the capital's students, journalists and intellectuals gathered. A new kind of guest had recently started making an appearance, the European hippy. They parked their painted VW vans and converted postal trucks outside, bearing slogans, such as INDIA EXPEDITION 1973–74, NEXT STOP HIMALAYAS and OVERLAND MUNICH–KATHMANDU TOUR.

PK went to the Indian Coffee House almost every evening. He liked the atmosphere and the mix of people. Signs on the walls explained that the café was a member of the Indian Coffee Workers Cooperative. He looked up at the sepia advertisements from the 1950s: 'A fine man…' (a proud coffee farmer with a white beard and cotton cap), '… a fine coffee' (coffee beans) and finally the punchline, 'and both are Indian!' The waiters wore white pajamas with broad green and yellow belts and headdresses adorned with fans of starched, snow-white cotton. They ran barefoot on the rough coconut fibre mat and served hot, black coffee and tea with thick buffalo milk in white porcelain cups and saucers. Here, he used to sit for hours nursing a cup of tea, a pencil and a sketchpad.

He drew both waiters and guests, but especially the foreigners. Bearded, long-haired guys with cotton scarves and shirts in Indian patterns. Girls with henna-dyed hair dressed in jeans and tight T-shirts or colourful, baggy cotton shirts. Sometimes he would offer them his drawings, but he was too shy to ask for money. A cup of tea was enough. Some guests gave him a few coins nevertheless, which he used to buy paper, paints and brushes. Others asked if he was hungry, and took him to eat deep-fried samosas, pakoras, chickpeas and potatoes fried in spices and served in small bowls made of dried leaves.

When PK could no longer afford canvas and oil paint, he settled instead for thin copy paper, brown wrapping paper and black ink, which he bought for a few paisa in the narrow streets behind Connaught Place. He began to draw people on the verge of starvation, expressionistic depictions of poverty that frightened those he showed them to. For PK, famine was an important subject. The scratchy ink lines perfectly conveyed how it felt to be hungry. He was giving voice to the world's starved masses. Drawing the suffering of others alleviated his own and afforded him some moments of temporary relief.

He stopped paying his school fees, and after six months was deleted from the student register. His teachers did not mind if he continued to sit in on classes, but it felt pointless and so he stopped going. He even stopped making art altogether. He had more important things to do, such as obtain food.

After four days without eating, his stomach began cramping. It was as if a rope had been tied around it. The pain grew in intensity, surging before releasing again and turning back into a general, background ache of hunger. The physical effects were schizophrenic: he was listless and depressed one minute, lively the next. When his energy was up, his mind fixated on food. He pictured freshly made chapatis, steaming paneer and large bowls of cauliflower doused in thick, hearty sauces.

He wandered aimlessly in search of anything to eat. On one of his worst days, as he was drifting along Ferozeshah Road in Delhi's upmarket government district, he encountered a powerful aroma of spices. He could not stop himself. A wall surrounded the stately bungalow, but the gate was open. He looked inside. In the courtyard, marquees had been erected and furnished with long tables covered in red tablecloths. He saw waiters in white turbans and blue jackets running to and fro, carrying trays laden with gold-edged glasses, and musicians wearing dark blue jackets with glittering decorations as they played on scratched brass instruments.

PK was naturally cautious, he did not do things that were illegal or could get him into trouble. But hunger had crushed all such integrity. He stepped into the courtyard where the wedding party was in full swing. Hundreds of guests were chatting and eating from the buffet. Spinach lamb, cheese in red chilli sauce, tandoori chicken drumsticks with mint sauce, golden samosas, chickpea masala in yogurt, potato and cauliflower dip with cumin and coriander, chapatis, nan, pakoras...

His stomach was cramping. It was now or never. He took a plate, piled it high with food, and retreated to a corner.

He ate like a starving dog. He tried to restrain himself but could not. Worried he would be seen, he kept turning and looking around him. But no one was looking. Everyone was busy enjoying their meal.

Once his plate was empty and his stomach full, he

sneaked towards the exit. Three more steps and he would have made it, undetected. Then, a tap on the shoulder. Forceful, authoritative.

He froze, felt panic wash over him.

That's it, he thought, I'm headed for a police cell. Then I'll be sent back to Orissa, and all the shame and humiliation that awaits me there.

'Coffee or tea, sir?'

He turned. It was one of the waiters, with his gold embroidered waistcoat and white turban. At first PK did not understand what the man had said. He had not mentioned the police, he realized. Tea or coffee? Was that really what he said? A pulse of pure joy surged through him.

'No, thank you,' PK stammered. Satisfied no one else was watching, he ran out into the street and scampered between the Ambassador cars and scooters parked along the tree-lined street.

He ran up to Mandi House roundabout and then sailed along the wide avenue up towards Connaught Place. He stopped only when he was at the Indian Coffee House. Panting, he took a moment's rest. He smiled. The dull ache in his stomach was gone.

Some days he ate only jamu berries that grew on the trees along Parliament Street. In the autumn, after the monsoon rains, they dripped with purple-blue pearls. When no one picked the berries, they fell onto the pavement, staining it with pools of wine red. They were sweet and gave him energy. He washed them down with water from street taps. But eventually he became so sick that he burned with fever and his body sank from fatigue. He was unable to hold down the little food he managed to find.

He rapidly lost weight and his vision began to suffer. His whole being was now focused solely on the pursuit of stilling his hunger.

Autumn turned to winter and night temperatures sunk to just a few degrees. He slept under Minto Bridge by Connaught Place, and warmed himself beside fires of burning leaves. He had no friends left. Indifference was like an infestation crawling inside him. He could not even muster the energy to draw people in the café. Instead, he took to writing pleading letters to his father asking for money. When he heard nothing back, he wondered if his letters had arrived. Surely salvation was on its way?

When spring came, the warmth returned. Summer followed with its blistering heat. Temperatures in Delhi were approaching forty-five degrees, bubbles formed in the asphalt, pavements were deserted between dawn and dusk, and he felt sick day and night. His stomach hurt constantly and once again his thoughts turned to suicide.

Delhi, India, the world! He was more and more convinced that in actual fact, he belonged nowhere. He was poor wherever he went, equally useless and unwanted.

My birth, my whole existence, has been nothing but a mistake.

It was time to end the pain. He walked as if in a trance, his legs shaking, towards the Yamuna River. As the water once more rushed against his skin, he hoped desperately that he would never have to get out again.

But halfway to the bottom of the brown, filthy river, PK's subconscious took over. He fought his way to the surface for air, just the same as last time. His body refused to obey. It was as if his limbs were controlled by another force, which would not give up on him.

He crawled up onto the riverbank and started walking along the searingly hot streets. He did not know where he was going, but somehow he ended up at a set of railroad tracks. This was where he would put an end to it all. He would rest his head against the rails and wait.

But the metal was red-hot in the afternoon sun. He leapt up. The burn mark on his neck throbbed and he understood the folly of his plan.

Instead, he sat down.

I'll jump out in front of the next train, he said to himself. Only two steps, and it will all be over. So simple, so easy. Was that all it took to go from one world to the next?

Hours passed, but no train arrived. What was going on? Eventually a man approached along the track, cloaked in twilight. PK stopped him to ask if he worked for Indian Railways.

'Yes, I'm a train driver,' he said.

'So why aren't you driving trains?'

'Don't you read the papers?'

'No.'

'We're on strike.'

'Strike?'

'You can't sit here. Go home to your wife!'

'But I don't have a home to go to, and no wife. I'm so hungry my stomach hurts. Why do you think I'm sitting here?'

The driver shrugged and disappeared.

Moments later, a policeman came the same way.

'Go away, before I lock you up!' he shouted, shaking his wooden baton.

The next day he came across a copy of *The Times of India* and started reading. A railway strike, he read, led by George Fernandes, the president of the railway workers' union. Fernandes had persuaded several other industries to down tools in solidarity. Seventeen million Indians in total. Their anger was directed against rabid inflation, corruption, food shortages – and ultimately the Indira Gandhi government. It was potentially the largest strike in history, one columnist wrote.

I'm not the only one on the verge of collapse, he thought. The whole of India is breaking down.

Imagine, the largest strike in history had saved his life. He was not meant to die, at least not yet. A higher power had plans for him, and he had to respect that.

It could not be a coincidence that these suicide attempts repeatedly failed. He must instead focus on the prophecy. What did it say? A woman from a foreign country. He recalled the English woman who had visited his school, with her yogurt skin and floral dress. There was someone out there, looking for him. She was his destiny.

Her image grew in his mind. She became giant, occupying more and more of his waking time. And yet, it was to be an Indian friend who would pull PK out of his hunger and delirium. As for the woman from the prophecy, he would have to wait.

PK started returning to class. His attendance was sporadic at first, but then he met Narendra. They started going to the Indian Coffee House together, where Narendra would buy him tea.

'And maybe something to eat?' PK suggested.

Narendra was a medical student and, like PK, untouchable and alone in Delhi. He had gained a place to study medicine as part of the low-caste quotas, and he was doing well. Better certainly than most of the Brahmin students who refused to associate with him. The first day they met, PK told him about the hardships, the hunger and the despair of recent months. Narendra comforted him and gave him money so he could start eating more regularly, something other than the berries and leftovers that had been his only sustenance of late. After two weeks, the fever disappeared.

'You've probably been suffering from a shigella infection,' Narenda said, 'a malignant salmonella bacteria.

Otherwise known as Delhi belly.'

'What should I do?'

'It will get better by itself. As long as you eat and look after yourself.'

Just a few more weeks of hunger, one more step into the abyss, and he would have faded away forever. He was sure of this. One more week of berries and dirty water, and the illness would have broken him.

After his meeting with Narendra, even the scholarship money, which had so mysteriously vanished, reappeared. Good fortune begot more good fortune. PK's father began to answer his letters with excuses about how he had not understood how bad things had been for his son. His first letter in months contained an extra one hundred rupee note, which would be enough to cover food for a week if PK was careful.

He began to pay his school fees and attend lessons again. His desire to learn had returned and colour flooded back into PK's life. He was eager to make new friends. One of the other students had also been forced to sleep rough, and PK used to meet him under Minto Bridge. However, PK was to become close to someone who could never imagine what it meant to starve.

The majority of his classmates came from rich families. Not merely the middle class, but from the capital's political and economic elite. One had a father who was the head of the Indian Postal Service, another was the daughter of the Indian ambassador to Bulgaria, a third came from a rich Parsi family from Bombay. Her style was metropolitan, with an attitude to match.

'I grew up in the heart of Bombay,' she would say, flicking her long hair behind her as she spat chewing gum out onto the floor.

PK was shy around her. He felt inferior in her company. How could he assert himself when faced with such self-confidence and entitlement?

As long as the students spoke English with each other, he felt a bit better. On the occasions he received more money than was required to fill his stomach, he bought the *Reader's Digest*, perfect for expanding his vocabulary. In Hindi, things were more difficult, and conversation became more uncertain. He had a decent understanding of the language, but struggled with the Devanagari alphabet, which was different from the one used to write his native Oriya. He lived in constant fear that someone would point to something written down and ask him to read it out loud.

But PK wanted to overcome these feelings of inferiority and so he began chatting to a young man in the school café who looked like he might be Muslim, and therefore would not be so concerned with his caste. PK's guess turned out to be correct.

'My name is Tarique, Tarique Beg,' he said in refined English, before boasting that he had come first in the school entrance exam. 'Although, that was not my own doing,' he added.

'What do you mean?'

'Ask my father,' Tarique said, without a hint of pretension.

'Your father?'

'My father, Mirza Hameedullah Beg. Haven't you heard of him?'

'The name sounds familiar... Is he famous?'

'He's a judge of the Supreme Court.'

'Oh, Tarique, you are the son of a powerful man.'

'Yes. Unfortunately.'

'Unfortunately?'

In each other they found a common interest in philosophy. But neither was attracted to the Hindu scriptures that so enraptured the Brahmins. They spurred each other on to read the texts of Buddhism and Jainism, as well as those written by Sufi mystics. They would sit for hours in the school café, talking about human nature and how to expand consciousness, only to look up suddenly and find the janitor had come to close the school for the day.

PK was still homeless and Tarique took him in.

'You can sleep on my floor. I'm sure Father won't mind.'

The Beg family lived in a Baroque palace of twenty bedrooms and nine bathrooms among the leafy bungalows of south Delhi. Shortly after PK moved into Tarique's room, the family hosted a lavish wedding party for his sister. The buffet table in the garden groaned under the weight of the delicacies that had been specially prepared. Large sections of India's political elite were in attendance, and even Prime Minister Indira Gandhi made an appearance. Needless to say, PK was not welcome. As the guests arrived through the main entrance, he lay on the floor in Tarique's room, which had been locked from the outside. Tarique had promised to return with a smuggled plate of food. PK felt like a mutt, waiting to be fed.

He listened to the murmur of conversation and the jangling of music coming from outside. He heard laughter and smelled the delicious aroma of spices. Finally, late in the evening, Tarique came.

He lived in Tarique's room for months. Despite the breathtaking discrepancy between their family backgrounds, they had so much in common. But philosophical discussions could only take place after PK had dealt with a more pressing question: 'Do you have anything to eat?' When, many years later, PK and Tarique resumed contact again via email, this was Tarique's prevailing memory of his poor young friend: 'You were constantly hungry, it was the first thing on your mind.' Only once the roar in PK's stomach had been quelled could they deal with the Buddha.

Tarique's father became increasingly sceptical of his son's impoverished friend. The judge was polite to PK, greeted him respectfully as befitted a well-mannered former student of Trinity College, Cambridge. He never said directly that PK was not welcome, not to his face anyway. But Tarique was often forced to endure long interviews with his father, in which he begged for mercy on PK's behalf.

Tarique told PK that his father was trying to convince him to make friends with the children of better-known and wealthy families. The situation became more pressing as each day passed. Eventually, Tarique lied to his father and said PK had moved out. Tarique sneaked plates of food to him from the family dining room. When Tarique's father came from his side of the palace to talk, PK hid in the wardrobe. He felt so ashamed, standing in the dark and listening to the rumble of the judge's voice outside.

He kept himself hidden from Tarique's father and the rest of the family throughout the spring of 1973. Quite how long he stayed, none of them can remember. Perhaps he moved out one day in May, when the mercury was about to rupture the glass thermometers and the asphalt on the Connaught Place roundabout had turned sticky like English toffee. Maybe it took until the summer monsoon pulled in the lead-coloured clouds, swept the streets of the capital clean and cooled the hot air. No one can say for sure. But Tarique never threw him out. He was the best friend a person could hope for.

During those hot spring nights on Tarique's floor, PK was assailed by terrible nightmares. He usually forgot what they were about as soon as he awoke, but the horror and fear lingered. One night, soaked with sweat, he opened his eyes and saw his mother approaching in the pitch black of Tarique's room. A faint grey dawn glow clung to her and her sari was wet and pulled tight around her body, as if she had just come back from her morning wash in the river. As usual, her black hair was damp and she carried a clay pot filled with water on her head.

How can Ma be here? In New Delhi?

'Everything will work out,' she said sombrely and placed the pot on Tarique's floor.

'My journey is over now,' she continued. '*Sona Poa*, you must take care of your sister. Promise me that. You have only one sister!'

He opened his eyes and was wide awake. There was no one else in the room, apart from Tarique who lay asleep, his chest rising and falling with heavy breaths. It was half past three in the morning. But he could still feel his mother's presence, soothing him, just as she had done all those years ago when he slept in her arms. But then he knew: she was telling him that something was wrong. The more he thought about those final words, the harder his heart thumped in his chest. He could not remain on the floor as if nothing was happening, much less go back to sleep.

He packed his bag, crept out of the house without waking Tarique, and made his way to the railway station. He jumped into the carriage where passengers with unreserved tickets crowded onto wooden benches. Less than an hour after he had awoken from his dream on Tarique's floor, he was on his way back home.

After three days, four changes and a long bus ride along potholed roads through the forest, he was standing outside his childhood home in Athmallik.

Shridhar came out, surprised to see his son standing before him with crumpled clothes and messy hair, sticky with sweat and dust.

'How did you know that your mother is sick?' he asked.

'I didn't,' PK replied. 'Or... well, I did. I dreamed it.'

'Kalabati knew you were coming,' Shridhar said. 'We didn't believe her. I tried to persuade her otherwise. But she is stubborn. She kept saying, "I know my son is on his way." Come, your mother is waiting for you. Our bird is about to fly her cage forever.'

The family gathered around Kalabati's bed. She was only about fifty, her hair was not yet grey, but a recent stroke had robbed her of her previous sparkle, or at least that was the explanation given by the medical centre in Athmallik.

Kalabati stared at PK. Then she spoke without any unnecessary greetings: 'You must never drink alcohol, and never make your future wife unhappy.'

Then, just like in his dream, she added: 'And you must take care of your sister. Promise me. You only have one sister.'

The conversation with her son was to be her last great effort. Her condition worsened rapidly. By that afternoon, as PK gently poured water into her half-open mouth, she could no longer swallow. A gurgling emanated from her throat, followed by exhausted splutters. Laboriously, she turned onto her side. Her eyes could no longer focus and her breathing was slower and lighter.

And then, Kalabati died.

That same afternoon, Shridhar sent a message to the village carpenters that he needed a load of wood for the cremation. PK and his father carried her body down to the river, helped by his younger brother Pravat. They placed the stretcher on the sand and squatted by the edge of the bank where the ground fell steeply to meet the water below.

There they waited patiently. The sun went down, the wind stirred and clouds clogged the sky. Rain began to fall and the ground shook as thunder and lightning cut through the darkness, just as it had all the other monsoons that had come before. PK sat with his mother's body in his lap, afraid that the storm would take her from him. He held tightly to her feet, as if it would stop her from leaving him.

The night was as black as soot, but in the flashes of lightning he caught glimpses of his mother's pale face and stiff, grey feet. Several of the untouchables gathered to witness the upcoming cremation, only to leave in the belief that evil spirits had taken possession of the riverbed.

But PK was not afraid. He felt sad, but also secure. Peaceful.

At last, the carpenter arrived. But he approached on foot. They had broken down a good distance from the river, and he was unable to deliver the wood. There could be no cremation that night.

'You can't sit all night in this storm with your mother's body in your lap. She'll begin to rot soon,' his father said.

PK and his brother had to do something. They climbed

down the sandy slope to the edge of the water and there the three of them dug a half-metre hole with their bare hands. They gently placed Kalabati inside it. In the absence of a cremation, they would have to settle for a sand burial, in the hope that the river would take her body into its swirling embrace.

His father and little brother showed no emotion, but PK sobbed. Then, suddenly, he jumped into the grave on top of his mother. 'Bury me with her!' All was quiet for a few seconds. The rain whipped against them, but no one said a word. Silently, Shridhar pulled his son up and onto the sandy bank. Then he began to shovel the sand over his wife's body.

PK set off for Delhi the next morning. He did not stay to attend the funeral, which was to be held a few days later, as, according to tradition, he would have had to shave his hair. PK did not want to get rid of the long, flowing locks that had taken an age to grow, inspired by the hippies he had met in the Indian Coffee House. Moreover, he had already said his goodbye to his mother on the riverbank.

The invulnerability he had felt as his mother lay in his lap quickly dissipated, replaced by a feeling of emptiness as the train rattled across the Ganges plain on its way back to his life in the city.

Invisible bands had been broken, he would later write in his diary. 'Sometimes we fly, but we always land back in our mothers' laps. Now she's gone I have no ground to stand on. Life is unstable. The ground is collapsing under my feet. I'm falling.'

Term ended, and PK and Tarique decided to take a trip together. They had talked about visiting PK's father and brothers, and also wanted to make a pilgrimage to the holy sites of Buddhism.

They began with PK's village. They hitchhiked around Orissa and called in on a dejected Shridhar, who had not yet recovered from his wife's death, before taking a winding bus up to the slopes of the Himalayas and the Kathmandu Valley in Nepal. It was the first time either of them had left Indian soil, the first time they had seen snow-capped peaks or trampled through puddles covered in a thin film of ice.

Everything sparkled; colours were bright and distinct. The sky was so clear and blue, there was none of the dirt-brown haze that hung over New Delhi. One afternoon, as PK sat drawing trees in Kathmandu's Ratna Park, a man approached. 'Namaste,' he said politely, bringing his hands together and bowing his head. 'Do you draw people?'

PK hesitated. 'Yes. Sometimes.'

The man's face was marked by a straight nose and framed by a Nepalese style of hat that looked like a forage cap. His profile was distinctive, and thus not too difficult to capture. The man seemed satisfied with the picture and asked if he might buy it for a few rupees. This aroused the curiosity of a passing man who asked if PK might do a drawing of him too. As the sun disappeared behind the peaks of the Himalayas, a crowd had formed an orderly queue as paying customers waited to have their portraits done.

After four hours of drawing, his right arm ached, but his pockets were bulging with coins and crumpled bills.

The money paid for four days of breakfast and dinner at the cafés of Freak Street. Just being able to pay his own way and not have to rely on Tarique's generosity was liberating. PK could feel the weight of his poverty being lifted. Things might work out, after all.

Tarique and PK were like two exotic birds among the Western hippies who frequented two of Kathmandu's most popular cafés, Patan and the Snowman. An untouchable jungle boy and the son of a rich Muslim judge. Neither of them belonged with the adventurous children of Europe's middle classes. The young hippies shunned the West while PK and Tarique longed for it. For PK's part, it was not the wealth or their advanced technology he so admired, but the fact that they did not seem to have Brahmins, or a caste system. They probably have poor people in Europe too, he thought, but they can't be as oppressed as India's untouchables, surely?

Nevertheless, they did their best to fit in with the Europeans, who spent their evenings disparaging materialism, smoking hashish and eating apple pie. The Westerners must have found them fascinating, natives dressed in jeans, well read and well spoken.

Things were about to change radically for PK. For the first time, he was making money. Their last evening in Kathmandu was going to be his new beginning, the start of a life in which he would never again have to starve.

Back in New Delhi, Tarique told PK he was too scared to have him back in his house, for fear of his father's wrath. PK did not blame him. He would have done the same. But this meant that once again, he was homeless. Some nights he slept with friends from the art school, other nights he was back on the stone floor of the train station. Despite his optimistic mood only weeks before in the cafés of Nepal, the depression returned with force. He felt doomed to these endless setbacks.

But this time, he had a way out. He was going to become a commercial artist. And he knew the perfect place to set up shop: the fountain in Connaught Place Park in the centre of Delhi.

Guests from the Indian Coffee House often came to watch as PK made his portraits by the fountain. Every afternoon a crowd formed around his newly purchased easel.

But the spectators also began to attract the police.

'Sir, honourable Police Commander, please, I need to earn my living somehow, right, sir? Do you not agree, sir?'

Most of the police officers turned out to be decent, however, or at least open to bribes. The Chief of Police used to be satisfied with a portrait.

'Then you don't have to pay the fine,' he would say.

The walls of the police station began to fill up with PK's pencil and charcoal drawings.

When this did not work, he would be taken to the police station. But PK did not complain. He quickly understood the advantage of not demanding instant release. This way, he got a warm cell, was offered food and even got to shower. He would then be free to go the next morning, clean and rested.

He began cooperating with one of the police officers in particular, who came to arrest him only after his peak hours were over for the day. Their agreement: PK got a bunk in a cell, and the officer took fifty per cent of his income. This lasted for some time, until the officer's colleagues began to be suspicious and PK's policeman felt obliged to ask him to lie low for a while.

But PK had to make money, so he moved his business out to the area around the airport. Which was where he happened to be working on Republic Day, 26 January 1975.

People had lined the main boulevard from the city centre out to the airport. Vehicles were banned and police formed human chains to prevent the crowds from surging into the road. People moved as one, shoulder to shoulder, facing the direction of the terminal. Some carried placards, others flowers. PK saw men with cameras and notepads. Suddenly a wave went through the crowd, someone was pushed and fell, and shouts rose up, only to be drowned out almost instantaneously by an excited murmur. Who was everyone waiting for?

Two police jeeps appeared, and then two more. The cortége crept towards them, making a show for the audience. The murmur grew louder. PK penetrated the crowd and found a spot with a good view. That was when he caught sight of the woman in the jeep. Her skin shone milky white in the strong, summer sun.

She has come from somewhere far away, he realized.

'Valentina, you're our hero!' someone shouted.

PK was pressed in between a group of tall Sikhs and a class of schoolchildren. The children cheered. PK joined them. As he had no flowers, he began instead to sketch the woman. She had dropped from the sky, landed at the airport, and was now being transported like a queen towards the centre of the city. He pushed past people to get closer. The jeep had stopped. PK reached over and tried to hand the sketch to the woman in the open top car, but a security guard blocked him with his wooden truncheon. The man took the drawing instead, looked at it, and smiled. He passed the picture to the woman. PK saw her examine the portrait, then look up at the guard, who pointed to PK. He met the woman's gaze. She leaned forward and murmured something to the guard, who turned to PK.

'Madame wants to speak with you,' he said.

'Now?'

'No, you idiot! How would that work?'

He was given a piece of paper with an address. *The Embassy of the Union of Soviet Socialist Republics, Shantipath, Chanakyapuri,* it said.

'Tomorrow at noon. Bring your picture and don't be late,' the guard added brusquely.

He approached the Soviet Embassy in the tidy diplomatic quarter of Chanakyapuri. Indian government officials and Russian diplomats were standing at the entrance, surrounded by journalists and photographers. There she was, a little further inside the building, deep in the pit of people and framed photographs of Soviet leaders. A guard shoved him towards her, she took his hand and thanked him in broken English.

'A beautiful portrait,' she said, introducing herself, 'Valentina Tereshkova.'

'A beautiful face,' replied PK.

Who was she? They smiled together at the cameras. Tereshkova? He had never heard the name before. There was only time to exchange a few pleasantries. With so many diplomats and journalists in the room, he could not add anything personal, like a question: are you married?

Instead, he was hit with questions from curious journalists as soon as he came out.

'Who are you? Where are you from?' they wanted to know.

PK asked the journalists to tell him instead who Valentina Tereshkova was.

'Oh my God, how ignorant can you be? The world's first female cosmonaut!' cried one of the journalists.

PK was delighted. He did not need to know more. Outer space! That was enough for him. He answered their questions, telling them about the village in the jungle and his tribal mother and untouchable father. The reporters scribbled intensively. Indians love a feel-good story and the journalists knew this dark-skinned young man was gold. PK, the poor, low-caste boy from the jungle, had been given the chance to meet the world's most famous female cosmonaut.

***

That evening, he sat at the coffee shop on Connaught Place and thought of Valentina Tereshkova. By now he had read the day's newspapers. Once a textile factory worker, on the morning of 16 June 1963, Valentina had donned her spacesuit and stepped up onto the bus that was to take her out to the launch site, the newspaper said. The rocket had roared and the controls had buzzed. After a two-hour countdown, the engines were fired and they had lift off. Valentina, codenamed Gull, began her journey up into Earth's orbit. She spun forty-eight times around the planet over two days, twenty-two hours and fifty minutes, before coming down again in a small cone of steel equipped with parachutes, and landing on the barren steppes of Kazakhstan. Back on Earth, she continued as a researcher in aeronautics, and became a member of the Supreme Soviet of the Soviet Union and the Central Committee of the Communist Party.

And now she was in India.

There was something otherworldly about a woman travelling in a vehicle out in space. What could it mean? He thought of the elusive goddess Durga, usually described as a saviour figure, the mother of the world who fights the demons that threaten the divine order. Durga is mostly depicted standing on a severed buffalo's head while carrying the sort of large weapons usually sported by male gods, or else she is portrayed riding a lion or a tiger.

Valentina Tereshkova had escaped Earth, but had come back again. A woman from a place beyond everything. A woman riding a roaring lion, a fire-breathing rocket. A cosmonaut.

Maybe she was the woman the astrologer had prophesied?

He fantasized about a life spent with her. But it was hard to imagine. He pictured himself following her back in a motorcade as it drove into the sunset, then arriving, after a long journey, in her hometown in the Soviet Union. She stood beside him in a floral dress, he wore a dark Western-style suit. When he tried to envisage their surroundings, things became more diffuse, the emotions weaker, the colours paler. He had never seen a Soviet city, let alone a cosmonaut's house. He did not know how they lived in the Soviet Union, what their food tasted like, the shapes of their cars or the height of the trees.

He read about the poor Kazakh villagers who had gathered around her capsule upon landing. The woman in the spacesuit stood face to face with the hungry, hollow-eyed shepherds and farmers.

'Wait!' she said, and turned back to the capsule where she rooted around for some small packages, boxes of biscuits and other food left over from her trip into space.

'Here, take this!' she said, and offered what she had.

She was later chastized by the Space Agency welcoming committee; she should not have given away her space food.

PK imagined Valentina landing her spaceship in Athmallik and handing out the packages of dry food to the needy. The thought made him warm inside, because he knew there were good people in the world and Valentina was one of them. She did what she could to reduce human suffering.

But the dream was fading. He knew deep down that she was not the woman from his prophecy, she was not his wishing star. Such ridiculous thoughts! He walked through the dark, deserted streets of the city in search of a cardboard box or telephone cubicle to sleep in.

The next day he scoured the newspaper stands that lined the pavement outside the railway station. *The Navratnam Times. The Times of India. The Hindustan Times. The Hindu. The Indian Express.* What they had written about him?

'Is that you, in the papers?' a chai man nearby asked.

'Yes, that's me,' he said as he paid the man thirty paisa and received a rough terracotta cup of steaming tea. The man looked up at him from where he was squatting by his dented aluminium kettle, which bubbled over a crackling fire. He was impressed.

PK bought *The Times of India* and flicked through its pages.

There they were, on page twelve. Valentina and PK, standing in the embassy. *Boy from jungle meets woman from outer space*, the headline read.

His head was filled with noise. His life story, not someone else's, right there in the paper.

That day PK was the talk of Delhi's bus queues and teashops. Several newspapers carried the story. People greeted him as he made his way from the station, taking his usual detour through the bumpy main street of Paharganj market. People stopped and asked if he was well as he walked past peeling façades and loosely hanging billboards and out onto the wide Panchkuian Road towards Connaught Place.

After a summer working in Stockholm, Lotta was back in England, on the south coast, learning English. As part of her studies she had to prepare a special project, and hers was going to focus on India, obviously. She took the train up to London from Portslade-by-Sea and made her way to the Commonwealth Library. Over the course of a few weeks she worked intensely, putting together an exhibition about the tribal people of Orissa and their ceremonial murals in particular.

As she sat looking at the pictures of Indian ikat fabrics, she thought the patterns felt familiar. Then it hit her. They looked just like some of the material used in the traditional festive clothing of Sweden. In fact, they were almost identical to the ones made in Toarp, a small community on the outskirts of Malmö. How could Indian and Swedish fabric be so similar?

Everything happens for a reason.

India had problems. Inflation was out of control and unemployment was on the rise. PK read in the newspapers that Prime Minister Indira Gandhi had described the situation as 'increasingly difficult to contain'. The Hindu right wing threatened to incite religious strife.

PK, however, walked his usual route between the station where he slept and the fountain where he made his living.

A neatly dressed man stood to the side as PK was drawing another customer.

'A portrait, sir? Ten minutes, ten rupees!' PK said without looking at him.

'Not for me,' the man answered. 'Come, so we can talk undisturbed.'

'Why?'

'Our great President, the honourable Fakhruddin Ali Ahmed, wants to invite you to dinner. He also wants you to do his portrait,' said the man, who introduced himself as the President's secretary.

A few days later, PK was driven to the Presidential Palace in a white Ambassador with red lights on the roof and sirens blaring.

Originally built by the British for the last viceroy, the Presidential Palace was an imposing sandstone building that radiated power and strength.

He was received by the Presidential Guard, which consisted of a few sturdy Sikhs in turbans. They could crush me with one hand, PK thought, as he was ushered inside. Everywhere he looked, there were gold, mirrors and chandeliers, the shine of the old Empire. PK was impressed. He'd never seen anything like it, except in pictures. It was almost unthinkable that he, of all people, should be here, in the centre of power in the middle of the nation's capital, about to meet the President.

He put his palms together and bowed deeply as a gesture of respect. The President sat next to a small round table on which stood a vase of flowers. PK began work immediately. The secretary glanced at his stopwatch. 'Tell me when you are done,' he said.

Thirteen minutes later, PK called 'stop' and the secretary pressed the button. The President looked at the drawing. He sat studying it for a long time without saying anything. Then he turned to PK.

'Lovely,' he said.

The President then started to make jokes. He had a laugh like a scooter start engine. Just like any other ordinary Indian uncle.

As PK was leaving, he heard the President say to his secretary: 'Don't forget to send money to my daughter.'

PK liked him; the President of India seemed to be a loving parent, worrying about how his children were getting on now they had left home. It made him seem more human. As he left the palace, PK was met by a wall of shouting journalists and flashing cameras. The press wanted to know what the President had said.

'He said he had to send money to his daughter,' PK replied, believing the journalists would interpret it the same way he had, that the President was a caring, likeable man.

But the reporters did not find it nearly so charming.

'He should be worrying about the country, not his family,' one said.

'India's future is more important than his daughter,' complained another.

'You get the leaders you deserve,' said a third.

The next day, all the major newspapers published articles about his visit to the palace, illustrated with photos of the President, PK and his portrait. The fact that the drawing had taken only thirteen minutes to complete was a major focus of the reports, as if he had been an athlete, not an artist.

In the spring of 1975, the police were becoming ever more aggressive in their treatment of crowds. The government was afraid that the political unrest might escalate into violence, riots and rebellion.

PK had installed a sign at the fountain: *Ten rupees, ten minutes*. The queues grew. He started to become so popular that the police saw him as a security risk. The chief of the Connaught Place station came to see him personally, declaring: 'This cannot continue!'

So they took him in again.

After he was released early the next morning, he went to the art school, his stomach full and body rested, and then straight back to the fountain to take up where he had left off the night before.

In addition to the commissioned portraits, PK hung landscapes and expressionistic oil paintings from his starvation period on display. These paintings grew in number. Every evening, between six and nine, the fountain and the sunset mirrored each other in the most beautiful spectacle PK had ever seen. The last rays of the day created rainbows out of the atomized water droplets. This was the most inspiring gallery possible for his art.

Gradually, the police grew politer in their dealings with him. They still arrested him on occasion, mostly for show, so that people knew they were taking action. Increasingly, however, they left him in peace. The newspaper articles earned him the moniker 'the Fountain Artist'. The teachers at the art school admired his industriousness and gave him encouragement. Students who had not previously noticed him wanted to be friends. Within the space of a few weeks he had gone from a nobody, to a celebrity. Everybody loves success.

After the meetings with the cosmonaut and the President, he began appearing in the media on a weekly basis it seemed, as he was interviewed for television, radio and magazines. He became the subject of conversation from the country's slums to the parties of the elite, and the queues around his easel grew ever longer. His reputation spread, reaching the centre of power, and two MPs, who had seen his picture in the paper, invited him to the Constitution Club of India on South Avenue, close to the Prime Minister's residence.

That was where they were sitting and talking when Parmeshwar Narayan Haksar happened to see him.

Haksar was Indira Gandhi's principal secretary. The government was in trouble and Haksar knew they needed good publicity. PK could be just the right person, went his thinking. He came from the very bottom of society, but he also personified the drive that Haksar thought many privileged Indians lacked. PK was a victim of society's evils, everything that Indira Gandhi and the Congress Party wanted to change about India. The untouchables represented a large potential voter base, a fifth of the country's population. If Indira Gandhi could win their support, she would be able to implement the drastic measures she was hoping for and still win the next election.

PK quickly realized that Haksar was an important person whom Indira trusted. He was her media adviser, personal think-tank and political strategist all in one, and a persistent advocate of more socialist government policies. He belonged to the inner circle of radical Brahmins from Kashmir. Some political commentators claimed that Haksar was behind the government's nationalization of the banks and the excommunication of certain emblems of capitalism such as Coca-Cola.

Haksar introduced himself and asked: 'Would you agree to do a portrait of the Prime Minister?'

'Yes, sir,' PK replied, jumping up from his chair.

'Where can I reach you? Phone number?'

'Sir, I have no phone.'

'Address then?'

'I sleep one night at the railway station, the next at the police station, sir.'

'Shhh!' Haksar whispered. He leaned closer. 'I'll arrange somewhere for you to stay.'

Indira Gandhi was an impressive woman. Motherly and authoritative, and yet jolly at the same time. She made jokes about the recent news and the objects that decorated the Prime Minister's residence. PK did not fully understand them, but her entourage laughed and PK decided it was better to laugh along too.

He had imagined she would be tall, that he would have to crane his neck to speak to her. But she was barely five feet seven, around the same height as him, but with a fine womanly figure and beautiful eyes. Just like a movie star.

Indira asked PK politely where he came from and about his future plans.

His voice trembled as he answered.

'Orissa, I come from Orissa, but now I go to art college here in Delhi,' he said, trying to sound dignified.

'I see,' Indira said, somewhat distracted. She paused and looked at the flowers in the pots by the window.

'Hello,' she said, turning to the man standing by the door. 'You must remember to water the plants. Don't forget to water the plants.'

She then sank back into her ruminations.

Indira and PK looked through his portfolio of oil paintings, charcoal drawings and pencil sketches. The Prime Minister had attended Tagore's art school in Shantiniketan, this much PK knew, so she had a genuine appreciation of art. She flipped through his work, registering a partial interest with a few nods and ah-has.

'This one is nice,' she said, holding up a drawing, 'but the others... Hmm, well, you will have to practise more. That's the only way to get better.'

She praised him nevertheless and said she earnestly hoped that he would become famous. 'You deserve it.'

They then went into another room to eat lunch, served by uniformed waiters. They sat at the table, Indira Gandhi, the world famous Prime Minister, and PK, the homeless jungle boy. But Indira did not know that PK slept in the railway station; Haksar had not told her.

If only Ma could see me now.

He glanced at Indira as they ate. She peeled her own cooked potatoes. Strange. Couldn't the servants do that for her?

After this first meeting with Indira Gandhi, PK went straight to Orissa Bhavan. He was going to meet a friend from school who was working as a cook in the clubhouse. PK was looking forward to being given another meal, but was greeted by a crowd of strangers as soon as he stepped through the door. People looked at him differently now, he could sense it. They were curious, expectant. What was he going to say? Now they assumed it would be interesting.

'I've prepared a special meal for you, PK,' his friend said and bowed deeply as if he was talking to a state official.

'Who are *they*?' PK asked and pointed at a group of men nearby.

'Journalists,' his friend replied and smiled. 'They want to know what she said.'

A journalist from *The Navbharat Times* approached and asked for an interview. PK responded willingly to his questions. He liked the attention, and the fact that they were asking him, of all people, about the Prime Minister. It made him feel important. But the journalists also seemed to want to make the meeting more remarkable than it really was.

In reality, it had been nothing more than a conversation about art with an influential woman. Not just any woman, to be sure. But it was not that amazing, was it?

He had been nervous and unsure of himself during that first meeting with Indira Gandhi. Indians worshipped the Prime Minister as if she was a goddess and he had not known how to behave.

But there were to be more meetings with Indira. Three in all. And it was all down to Haksar. The second time they met, his fear eased and she seemed like a genuinely good person. He did not need to be afraid of her.

On the third occasion, he allowed himself to be photographed in the gardens of her residence together with the Prime Minister and a group of untouchables from Orissa. Indira's photographer took the pictures and they appeared on the front pages of several newspapers the next day. She stood in the middle in her lion-yellow sari, her undulating hair shimmering from a distinguished light grey to black, while the untouchables squatted in the grass, as if they were her disciples.

After all these meetings, rumour spread back home in Orissa that the Prime Minister, the 'Mother of the Country' as she was known, had adopted PK. He was no longer the son of Kalabati, the tribal woman who had been dead and buried for several years. He was born of Indira Gandhi now, even though he was not in need of a new mother. Perhaps in these troubled times, Indira Gandhi's government needed him more.

Lotta was not the type to obsess over setbacks. They were nothing more than passing rain clouds that she let float by as she went in search of sunshine. What was important was the here and now. There was real misery in the world to be sure, but still, it was best not to over-identify with the darker aspects of life. Many people got stuck reliving their past again and again, as if only comfortable when in pain.

She started practising yoga, and in it found a philosophy perfectly suited to her personality. The movements and breathing techniques were grounded in an idea she had already embraced: it takes guts to change yourself, but you cannot be a slave to your mind forever.

Everyone wants to find happiness, but it is difficult to live by such principles. We need reminding of them every day, so as not to stagnate, she told herself.

But how was it possible to be happy in the knowledge of the way people treated each other and the horrible injustice of the world? Yes, it was important to be politically engaged, and yet she could not bring herself to be so. There are many different and equally valid opinions. No ideology should claim to be absolutist. She belonged to no religion, wore no badge to declare her political allegiance. She could no more call herself Christian, Hindu or Buddhist, than conservative, liberal or socialist.

Take a little bit from all of it.

Despite her Christian upbringing and a natural affinity for yoga and the Eastern philosophies, Lotta was critical of organized religion. She was a humanist. That was enough. Everyone had within them the same energy, regardless of ancestry or skin colour. It was simply impossible to be racist, thought Lotta.

The money PK earned from his portraits went towards paints and canvases, which enabled him to make ever larger artworks with a greater variety of techniques and subject matter. Most were sold to foreign tourists by the fountain or inside the Indian Coffee House.

Haksar had promised to arrange an apartment for PK, but was taking his time. In the meantime, PK rented a small room in Lodi Colony, one of the city's more affluent suburbs just south of a large, leafy park, home to a grand mausoleum to the medieval sultans of Delhi. But his new accommodation was anything but grand. The bare room contained only a bed and a bedside table, three hooks screwed into the unpainted cement wall for hanging his clothes on, and a couple of square metres of floor space for hosting his homeless friends.

He was starting his third and final year at art school and was often the talk of the canteen. The other students increasingly regarded him as some sort of guru. Even the teachers and experienced visiting artists more than twice his age came to ask him for advice. They wanted to know about technique, what materials he used, whether his parents were famous artists, about his thoughts on art in general and what Indira Gandhi was really like in person.

One of the students from the year below was especially keen to make contact. She did not say much at first, but PK thought he could sense she wanted something. Finally, she gathered her courage and introduced herself.

'My name is Puni,' she said softly, as if ashamed to be so forthright.

But her question was surprisingly direct:

'Will you have lunch with me?' she asked.

'Yes,' PK responded without thinking. He rarely said no

to an invitation. But Puni seemed to doubt his sincerity.

'I'm not disturbing you, am I?' she asked anxiously.

'Yes,' he replied. 'You are a bit! I'm in the middle of work. But it's a nice distraction to be invited to lunch by you.'

After a pleasant meal in the school cafeteria, she invited him home.

'My mother wants to meet you,' she said. 'Can you come by on Sunday?'

'Your mother? Why does she want to meet me?'

'She wants you to do her portrait.'

The traffic, which consisted mainly of Ambassador cars, imaginatively painted trucks and worn-out buses, crept like cold syrup. It mixed lugubriously with a stream of bicycle rickshaws pouring out of the narrow streets around the Jama Masjid market. PK sat on the passenger bench in the back of a pedal rickshaw, gazing out at the chaos and the crowds. It was a wonderful feeling. He had never before allowed himself the extravagance of being driven by a bicycle taxi, to sit and watch as a man carried him forward on pure strength alone. He thought of the landowners, merchants and Brahmins accustomed to having servants wait on them, as if they somehow deserved it. In that moment, he felt he deserved it too, to have a man do the heavy work for him.

They snaked through the increasingly dense throng at Chandni Chowk, past jewellers, fabric shops, signs advertising chilled tap water and photographers with their wooden box cameras taking pavement portraits. The rickshaw driver swerved into alleys, dodging cyclists, wandering goats, other bicycle taxis, wobbly cows, yapping dogs, women in grey scarves and men with crocheted skullcaps. They passed holes in the walls and jute sacks filled with flour and chillies. It was an exhilarating sight.

Delhi's markets still felt like exotic fairytales for the boy from the jungle. The city smelled of history and power, but also overcrowding and poverty. The air stank of the black, sticky mud that festered in the open sewers, but it was also mixed with the seductively sweet scent of patchouli smoke from courtyards flaunting their syrupy mangoes and figs.

Finally, he had arrived. He got out, paid a handsome tip to quell his bad conscience, and knocked on the old wooden door.

'Welcome!' came a voice from behind the door. It was Puni.

She looked tense. 'Can I get you something to drink?'

'Water is fine,' PK replied.

She giggled. She was nervous, PK realized.

'Tea or coffee then.'

'Maybe later.'

All was quiet. He looked around. The walls were decorated with pictures of India's superstar actors and actresses, and fashion magazines covered the coffee table. Puni returned with a glass of water on a tray. A smell filled the room. She must have made a detour via the bathroom and sprayed on more perfume. The sweet scent of jasmine and roses tickled his nostrils. He looked at her. She looked different. She was wearing a shiny salwar kameez, her cheeks were daubed with rouge and her lips painted red. She wanted to look older, gone was the sincere and undecorated art student.

He gulped down the water.

'Where is your mother? I can start right away.'

'Oh, my mother had to leave just before you arrived. Something came up... something urgent at work.'

He suspected at once something was not right.

'Wait, she'll be back,' Puni said in a gentle voice.

But he was uneasy and decided he had to leave at once.

'Sundays are my best day at the fountain. The customers

will be waiting. I have to go make my living. Goodbye!' he said and left.

'Good morning!'

He recognized the voice behind him. He turned in the corridor. It was Puni again.

'My mother bought two tickets for the movies tonight, the late show at the Plaza. But she changed her mind and doesn't want to come with me. Do you want to come instead?'

'What film?'

'I don't know, but my mother is very selective.'

'Let me think about it. See you at lunch.'

He went to his studio to tidy up the previous day's mess. Screwed the caps on some tubes of paint that had leaked onto the table. Threw away a brush that was caked in dried paint. Cleaned another two with turpentine. Stared at a half-finished painting and examined the sketches strewn all over the floor. Then he picked up a brush and started to paint.

He tried to picture Puni, but could not. A veil seemed to descend over his eyes. He heard sounds, muffled then high pitched. It was as if the colours in the painting were speaking to him, as if they were people. They did not articulate words as such, rather chords and tones that represented different feelings. He worked fast, with zeal and energy.

The school bell rang for lunchtime, but he continued as if nothing had happened. Suddenly, someone appeared at the door. He saw a faint shadow moving in the glare of the wet paint on his canvas. He carried on, pretending he had not seen it. He knew who it was and he was not happy, which surprised him. She was interrupting him and he wanted to be alone.

'That's a really fantastic painting,' Puni said, stepping into the light streaming through the large studio windows.

He turned to look at her.

'So, do you want to come tonight?' she asked.

He giggled, uncertain.

'Wait one moment!' he said, and ran out into the corridor, down the stairs and into Tarique's studio on the floor below.

Tarique was sitting at his table, working on an illustration.

'Puni, from the first year, she wants to go out with me tonight...' PK started.

Tarique looked up.

'... So, should I go?' he continued breathlessly. 'She suggested going to the cinema.'

PK looked expectantly at his friend.

Tarique sighed.

'Jesus, Pradyumna, she's not going to kidnap you! Go have some fun!'

They waved down a motorcycle rickshaw and rode together to the cinema. They were going to see *Ajanabee*, a story about a middle-class boy who falls for a rich and beautiful upper-class girl. They sat down in the back on a cracked vinyl two-seater sofa. The dramatic opening music came blasting through the loudspeakers. It turned out to be a shocking tale. The girl fell pregnant but did not want to keep the child – how un-Indian, PK thought – because she wanted to become a model. The couple split and the girl moved back home to her father. The shame.

He liked the outdoor scenes, the singing and dancing. It was the most romantic movie on release at the time, that much he understood. He was lost in the spectacle until Puni wrenched him back to reality by reaching out and searching for his hand. Their fingers interlocked.

'My mother asked me where you keep all the money you earn from your art,' she whispered in his ear. 'If you want, she can take care of it for you.'

'No need, I opened a bank account,' he whispered back.

They sat in silence for a few minutes. The screen was alight with a passionate love scene. The hero kissed his girl, one of those typical Indian film kisses where everything is left to the imagination. Still, he squirmed with embarrassment, shook a little even. She squeezed his hand even harder.

'What's the matter?' she asked.

'Nothing,' he hissed back.

'But you're shaking.'

'It's cold. I'm cold.'

She leaned her head against his shoulder. 'No it's not.'

'Really?'

'I love you,' she said, and sighed heavily.

He felt confused, uneasy, weak even.

'I haven't... ever thought about love,' he faltered.

'Now you can,' she said.

'Well,' he tried again, 'according to the customs of my village, you can't fall in love unless you're married.'

The moustached leading man shot at a pickpocket who had just stolen his jewel-laden bag. The thief fell to the ground, dead.

'Oh, don't worry,' she said. 'Write a letter to your father and I will ask my parents. My mother likes you, she will convince my father. And then we can get married.'

She continued: 'You make a living from your art and I... well, I will also be an artist. We can be very happy together.'

He did not know what to say. All these dreams and plans. Maybe she was right? Maybe she was his future? Maybe he should write to his father and ask permission to get married? He was unsure how he really felt, but perhaps this was his fate. Everything happens for a reason.

Luckily, the ending of the film was a happy one, or he might have cried; with the couple reunited, the credits finally rolled.

They left the cinema hand in hand, hailed a rickshaw and rattled along the Vivekananda Road, glittering in the rain, towards Old Delhi. She jumped off near the Great Mosque and the rickshaw turned south towards his rented room in the suburbs.

Once home, he began to write a letter to his father. Puni's proposal sounded good, he thought, despite his somewhat conflicting emotions. She was right! She must have been the woman the astrologer meant. She certainly was not from his village or state. Not exactly from another country, but close enough.

A girl had fallen in love with him, he wrote, and they wanted to marry. Would his father give them permission?

He rubbed his eyes and looked at the clock. Half past midnight. He lay down on his bed, his thoughts spinning. A pack of wild dogs barked as they passed outside. The sound of a creaking bicycle came and disappeared. The rain had stopped and the window cast a milky white square of light on his dirty cement floor.

It had all been decided... And he drifted off to sleep.

The entrance hall to Puni's home was thick with the smell of spices; paratha, chicken curry, palak paneer, aloo ghobi. He was amazed to think that all this food had been prepared for him, that they had made such an effort for his sake. The dining room table was invisible under the sheer number of plates and bowls. There was no space left even for the napkins, which their servant girl had instead placed on a side table draped in a floral cloth.

He was starving.

'Namaste,' he said, placing his palms together as he bent down and touched her father's feet, a greeting he thought would satisfy any would-be father-in-law.

'Welcome, brother. Stand up,' Puni's father replied. 'We are modern people, let's shake hands instead.'

They were joined around the table by Puni's two brothers and their wives, while Puni sat in the next room behind a door covered by a curtain, where she could still hear their conversation.

This was how it was done, he knew that, but at the same time, it seemed absurd. He was here to be interviewed by her parents, not to see her.

But I'm supposed to be marrying Puni, not her father, he remembers thinking.

And her father's first question? 'What is your caste?'

PK felt his cheeks grow hot. This was not a good start. He knew the family belonged to a high caste. If they were traditional, there was no way he would be accepted as their son-in-law. Yet her father had just said they were modern people.

PK answered with a question. 'Do you believe in the caste system?' Full on counterattack was his only chance. Before Puni's father could answer, he continued: 'What does caste matter? I may have been born in a tribal region and my father may be untouchable, but the blood in my veins is still the same colour as your daughter's, is it not? We share the same interests. I hope we can be happy together.'

Puni's father looked him in the eye. No doors had yet been closed. A positive outcome was still within the realms of possibility.

'You were born in a tribal area to an untouchable family?'

PK did not answer this question.

'And my daughter is already in love with you?'

Everyone in the room fell silent. No one moved or made a sound, not even to clear their throat.

PK thought he heard her father's slow breathing and the sound of his own pulse. He looked around. All smiles were gone, faces flickered with uncertainty.

Finally, Puni's mother broke the silence. Or rather, the

sound of her hand slapping against her forehead did: 'Oh my God!'

Her father stood up, pointed at the door. 'Please leave my house!' he bellowed. 'Now! And never, *ever* contact my daughter again!'

PK stood up and walked out with barely a whispered goodbye.

Sobbing, he threw himself down on his bed. After the first violent convulsions of emotion had eased, he continued to lie there for some time, staring up at the ceiling. He was destroyed, empty and small. Memories of his school days in Athmallik came rushing back, the exclusion and rejection. That familiar feeling of inferiority had been secretly lying in wait, under the surface, demanding to be set free. His heart pounded, his skin burned, sweat drenched his body. He shook as if engulfed by fever.

He lay there for the rest of the night, his thoughts churning: Why, why, why was I born untouchable?

He saw her again a few days later, while he was drinking tea in the school café. She was talking to a male student. He approached but she turned away and left with the other man.

At lunch they ran into each other again. This time she made eye contact.

'Forget me!' she said quickly. She neither believed in, nor cared about, the caste system, but her father did, she explained. 'I cannot defy my father.'

He was dumbstruck.

'Did you see the guy I was talking to?' Puni said. 'He's reading engineering. My father had already arranged for us to marry, but he was prepared to change his mind because I told him that I was in love with you. But that was before he knew anything about your background.'

PK stared at her in amazement. She had pursued him so relentlessly, and yet within a few days, had agreed to marry someone else.

'It's over,' she said.

'Do you love him?' he asked.

'Yes,' she replied without moving a muscle in her face.

What kind of love was this? She's lying, PK thought. She's scared to defy her father.

'Puni, listen! I'll fight for us. Legally, no one can stop us. Not your father, not your family. We can get married without any of your relatives or a priest if need be, and then we can move to a place where no one can find us, where no one knows about us, or even cares.'

But she did not seem to be listening. She turned her head and her eyes flickered as she glanced down the corridor and into the canteen.

'Don't ever talk to me again,' she interrupted. 'Forget about me!'

'Don't you like me any more?'

'I like you, but I can't marry you.'

'Why not, Puni?'

'I can't make my father unhappy.'

PK had read in the newspapers about the Dalit Panthers from Bombay. Inspired by the Black Panthers in America, they had written a manifesto in which they claimed that Brahmin control of India was worse than British colonialism, just as his grandfather and father used to say. Hindu leaders held tight onto both the entire state apparatus and an inherited feudal power in the form of spiritual oppression, they wrote. 'We will not be easily satisfied now. We do not want a little place in the Brahmin alley,' their manifesto declared.

The untouchables had their own newspaper, *Dalit Voice*, in which the Dalit Panthers likened their discrimination to racism against blacks in the United States. African-Americans would never be free, they claimed, as long as their blood brothers and sisters in Asia were still suffering. Indeed, the Dalits were in an even more desperate situation, which could be compared to the height of slavery two hundred years earlier. PK was at home in his room in Lodi Colony, screaming at the walls:

'You Brahmins and the rest of you high-caste snobs! You prejudiced, stuck-up, narrow-minded creeps! What have we ever done to you?'

He could not sleep for all the hateful thoughts coursing through his head. He woke at four and lay in bed, wrestling with these voices, until the sun rose three hours later. Anger was followed by bitterness and self-pity.

A thin green book with yellowed paper, cloudy ink and slightly sloping text lay on his bedside table. He picked it up and began reading, to forget Puni.

> One day, in Kerala, southern India, Shiva decided to teach the Brahmins a lesson.

Ah, this is perfect, PK thought, and continued reading.

Shiva, the book said, wanted to put a stop to the overblown pride of the Kerala Brahmins and decided to humiliate the highest and brightest of them all, the exalted spiritual teacher Adi Shankaracharya.

The guru was close to enlightenment. The only thing preventing Adi from being freed from the cycle of rebirth was his own arrogance and pride, his refusal to accept that he was of the same flesh and blood as all other humans on Earth, no matter what caste or social position.

Shiva and his wife Parvati wanted to play a trick on him. They transformed into a poor, lowly couple of the untouchable Pulayar caste. Their son Nandikesan joined them, turning himself into their wretched child. They were dressed as day labourers, their clothes smeared with dirt from the fields. In addition, Shiva conjured up the smells of meat and alcohol, taboos for virtuous Brahmins. Shiva reeked as if he had been drinking all night. Just to reinforce his point, he carried a jug of palm wine under one arm and had a half coconut shell of the pungent liquor in the other.

And so, on one of the raised paths through the paddies, Shiva, Parvati and their son encountered Adi Shankaracharya. Custom dictated that an untouchable should jump down from the embankment and into the mud when faced with a Brahmin. But Shiva and his family kept walking straight towards Adi and asked *him* to step aside so that they might pass.

The arrogant Adi was enraged.

'How dare a family like you, dirty, smelly, drunk, meat-eating untouchables, walk on the same path as a pure and unblemished Brahmin? You smell like you haven't washed once in your lives. I've never seen anything like it,' Adi thundered, and threatened to behead them, on the grounds that this was a crime that even the gods would never forgive.

Shiva replied: 'I admit, I have partaken of a glass or two, and it was a while since I last bathed. But before I climb down into this muddy field, I want you to explain to me what makes you, a clean and high-caste Brahmin, different to us dirty untouchables. Let me ask you a few questions.'

If Adi was able to answer them, Shiva promised he and his family would let him pass as propriety dictated.

'My first question,' Shiva began. 'If we both cut our hands, is not our blood the same colour? My second question: Do we not eat rice from the same field? My third question: Do you not give bananas, grown by the untouchables, as offerings to the gods? My fourth question: Do you not adorn the gods with flowers picked by our women?

My fifth question: Do we not dig the wells that provide the water you use in your temple rituals?'

Adi could not answer Shiva's questions, so continued:

'Just because you eat on metal plates and we on banana leaves does not mean that we belong to different species. You Brahmins ride elephants and we buffaloes, but that does not make you elephants and us buffaloes.'

Adi was not only dumbfounded by the wretched man's words, they confused him. How could this poor, illiterate untouchable, who had hardly any schooling, come up with such sophisticated and profound philosophical questions? So Adi began to meditate right there on the path and opened his sixth sense. At once he understood: the dirty Pulayar family faded and in their place appeared the gods, Shiva, Parvati and their son Nandikesan, in all their splendour.

Horrified by what he had done, Adi fell to his knees and recited a poem in honour of Shiva.

Shiva forgave him.

Adi asked him why he had turned himself into an untouchable when he appeared to him, his most devoted follower.

'Yes, you are a wise man on your way to salvation and enlightenment,' replied Shiva. 'But you will never get there unless you understand that all people deserve respect and empathy. I took this form to teach you this. You must fight against prejudice and ignorance and help people from all castes, not just your fellow Brahmins. Only then will you achieve true enlightenment.'

Thousands of years ago, Shiva had taught the Brahmin a lesson. And yet here was PK, all these years later, the poor untouchable still drawing comfort from Shiva's story.

There was hope, he realized. In Kerala, where Shiva is particularly celebrated to this day, many people saw an heir to this story in the doctrines of Karl Marx. PK understood in that moment that God was not merely a tool for oppressing the poor, but also a shield against the arrogance of the privileged, a potential catalyst to effect change in the world.

PK went to see a psychologist, who told him in no uncertain terms that he was not to mope around at home alone in Lodi Colony, but rather he should get out and socialize.

'Try to enjoy life,' he said encouragingly.

PK consulted a friend at school, who told him to try alcohol. It had given his friend solace after the particularly painful end to a love affair.

'It helped,' he said.

PK had never let a drop pass his lips before, indeed the idea had never occurred to him. Alcohol was for the weak-willed. But feeling desperate, he went to one of the shops in the backstreets behind Connaught Place and bought a small bottle of Indian-made foreign liquor. He found a spot in the shade, hidden behind a load of mattresses. He poured half the bottle down his throat, hissed, coughed and spat out what remained in his mouth. Then he sat down on some steps and waited. And waited. But he felt nothing.

After some time, his surroundings began to feel soft, like cotton wool. It was a nice feeling, as if the pain and grief of recent weeks were floating away. His friend was right: alcohol helped.

He went to the fountain to work but could barely hold a pencil. He apologized – he was sick, he said – packed up his stuff and hobbled home. He slept the rest of the evening and through the night, only to wake up late the next morning and reach immediately for what remained of the bottle of whisky.

He drank more and more. For the next few weeks, alcohol was the first thing he tasted in the morning and the last thing at night. It made him feel like someone, or rather something, cared for him. The hard edges of the world were wrapped in a gossamer mist. Corners became round and worries faded.

Wobbling up Parliament Street with a sketchbook under his arm, he ran into one of the policemen he had drawn in the past. The officer could smell the booze on his breath and was blunt in his greeting: 'Why have you started drinking?'

PK started to tell his story. He told him all about Puni, the trip to the cinema, how he had been shaken by love, the invitation to meet her parents, all the food they had made for his visit, her father, his banishment, the humiliation and his fear that no one would ever love an untouchable like him. He stank of whisky and his monologue was loud and energetic. He had difficulty keeping his balance, swaying back and forth like a mast in the wind. Then he cried.

The officer stood and listened patiently without interrupting him, except to ask him to repeat the parts he could not catch through PK's mumbling and slurring.

The further he got into the story, the better PK started to feel.

'Oh, don't be stupid,' the policeman said finally. 'May I see your hand?'

PK held it out. The officer studied the lines on his palm.

'Look here, it will all be fine! According to these lines, you will marry suddenly and unexpectedly, and the marriage will be a wonderful and happy one.'

'But,' PK continued in his garbled speech, 'I'm untouchable. I'll never be able to marry a Hindu woman, at least not one who can read and write and comes from a decent family.'

'Maybe she won't be Indian,' came the policeman's simple reply.

That night, as he lay in bed navigating the borderland between wakefulness and sleep, bitter memories ambushed him. He was eternally doomed and yet also fated to something better.

She came to him in his dream, an angel in white. She had travelled across the wheatfields of the Punjab and over New Delhi's rooftops, and landed here, in his room. They were so close now they could touch each other.

He drank in her presence, her breath, her scent and her soft hair as it fluttered against his bare shoulders. He felt her warmth and affection and somehow knew things his conscious mind did not. She was somehow bigger than him, not physically, but spiritually.

He awoke, but she felt more like vapour, faceless and cold. And yet, her presence lingered with him into his waking hours.

She returned the following night. This time she came with melodies he had never heard before. It's beautiful over there, he thought. Just like the fortune teller said.

It was the spring of 1975, and violent demonstrations had broken out against rising food prices and the internal bickering of Hindu nationalists. Discontent was reaching boiling point.

Even Indira Gandhi was unhappy. She was angry with antagonistic judges, critical journalists and quarrelling opposition politicians who she believed did not have the necessary skills to take responsibility for the country. What infuriated her most, however, was that she stood accused of electoral fraud. A court ruled that she had bribed voters in the last election and, contrary to the law, spent government money on her own personal election campaign. She was stripped of her seat in Parliament and forbidden to stand again for six years.

But Indira was not going to stand idly by and watch as her opponents moved against her. She took matters into her own hands and, on 25 June, she asked the President to issue a state of emergency, citing 'internal disturbance' as the justification. In this one move, she had annulled the court's decision to limit her powers and instead grabbed hold of the reins of government herself. Early the next morning, while the first monsoon rains of the season fell across New Delhi, she gathered together her ministers to tell them what was happening, and then took to the airwaves to inform the people.

'There's no reason to panic,' her voice sounded in millions of crackling radios as clouds clogged the sky above.

From then on, she was the sole person in charge. Indira was India, and India was Indira, as the Congress Party spokesman told the press.

But before her speech was broadcast to the people, politicians and government officials had already whispered the news to the sleepy chai boys on Parliament Road, to the Sikh taxi drivers parked under the trees of Patel Chowk, and to the itinerant sugar-cane vendors in Tolstoy Marg. Like fire through the forest, word engulfed the city's colonial arcades, spread among the bus drivers who goaded their crowded vehicles along Radial Road No. 1, and to the waiters at the Indian Coffee House, who served it to their guests alongside their hot drinks. Within five minutes, everyone in the city already knew what Indira was about to say.

In the aftermath, the press was censored, opposition politicians were imprisoned, and trade unions subjugated. Journalists and intellectuals criticized the Prime Minister. But Indira was convinced that the landless and the oppressed supported her, that PK and his brothers and sisters, India's millions and millions of poor, stood by her side.

It was their backing she had to win if she was to remain in power. And PK believed she would bring order to the country. Leaders who looked after the poor had justice on their side.

Delhi was papered with Maoist-sounding slogans. As he walked his usual route to the fountain at Connaught Place, posters screamed out at him:

> Courage And Clear Vision – Your Name Is Indira Gandhi
>
> A Small Family Is A Happy Family
>
> Work More, Talk Less
>
> Efficiency Is Our Cry

And the one that sounded like an advertisement for the Indian Coffee House:

Be Indian, Buy Indian

Otherwise, it was mostly business as usual.

The country's most prominent businessman, Mr JRD Tata, claimed that the strikes, boycotts and demonstrations had gone too far. The parliamentary system had not adapted to the country's needs.

The middle classes, shopkeepers, businessmen and government officials said they were tired of the chaos, and that they preferred the police to receive new powers that would allow them to disperse threatening crowds by force if necessary, to lock up the petty thieves and ensure that the slums that had grown up along Delhi's avenues were demolished. In the Indian Coffee House, PK heard comments like:

'Opposition politicians, intellectuals and journalists just complain about the state of emergency. But we ordinary people, we like it.'

And:

'Delhi needs a strong hand. The slums are everywhere these days.'

Even:

'Now, crime has fallen, the trains run on time, the streets are cleaned and people are sterilized so that we don't have ten children in every slum shack. But the newspapers only complain about human rights violations and rubbish like that. Things are finally improving.'

But Delhi's teachers, journalists and academics were shocked and angry.

'How could she? It's her son Sanjay who's behind it, the punk. And the President? He's nothing but a joke, Indira's stooge.'

Raids took place around the capital and prominent politicians, lawyers and newspaper editors, who Indira now saw as enemies of the state, were arrested. People resigned in response. The protests began to tail off. But a minority persevered and continued to demonstrate in the streets against 'Indira's madness', as their placards called it.

Once a month, the Sikh People's Front for Civil Rights organized protest marches on the streets of Delhi. PK heard how they roared their slogans as they passed the café. He went outside to watch. The procession of men dressed in traditional ankle-length robes and blue and orange turbans floated down the avenue towards Parliament.

'Indira is mad and so is India!' the leader chanted.

The city was boiling over, that much was obvious, but the newspapers gave the impression that all was calm and peaceful. Not a word was printed about the protests.

Opposition to Indira became increasingly inventive, coming up with methods to fool the censors. A post in the obituary section of *The Times of India* reported the anonymous contributor's regret at the tragic death of *D. E. M. O'Cracy*, survived by his mourning wife, *T. Ruth*, his son *L. I. Bertie* and his daughters *Faith*, *Hope* and *Justice*.

How gullible can the censors be? PK laughed to himself.

PK liked Indira, but the state of emergency was too much, even for him. He was forced to report to Haksar that some police officers were becoming more aggressive in their methods. They chased people away from his queue, ripped up his paintings and shouted at him to leave. It was as if one half of the force did not know what the other was doing. One day he was met with friendly concern, the next with a stinging slap. Their treatment of him was inconsistent to say the least.

Haksar listened silently and then told PK he would make some calls. He assured him that he would ensure the police left him alone.

The next day, Delhi's governor arrived at the fountain in his official car, his advisers and servants in tow. Police harassment would cease immediately, he reported. Henceforth, no officer of the law would be allowed to arrest him because he used a public place as his private gallery.

A few days after the governor's visit, men from the State Electricity Board arrived to install lighting so that he would be able to work late into the evenings. He was also assigned a personal assistant, a man who would run his errands, buy food, drinks, pens and paper, as well as pack up and lock away his paintings in a specially arranged store when he finished for the night.

'Anything else I can help with, sir?' his assistant said with a salute as he closed the store.

Haksar explained that the area around the fountain was going to become New Delhi's Montmartre. Just like the Place du Tertre in Paris, artists would be allowed to work freely. PK would become a tourist attraction.

The Statesman published an article a few days before Christmas 1975 about PK and the other artists around the fountain. *Your face is his fortune*, it declared. Just as in Paris, portraits were the mainstay of their business, rather than the more thoroughly considered works, the newspaper noted.

> It takes ten minutes and ditto rupees to get a pencil likeness of yourself from Pradyumna Kumar Mahanandia... One among the seven artists holding their exhibitions in the basement of Delhi's Connaught Place Fountain, PK has been the most successful. He earns anything between Rs 40 and Rs 150 every evening sketching passers-by and visitors to the exhibition.
>
> 'Few people want to invest money in a landscape or on a modern art painting, but no

> one minds spending just Rs 10 for a portrait of theirs – especially if it's done in ten minutes,' observes Jagdish Chandra Sharma, one of the other exhibiting artists.
>
> After an unprofitable month exhibiting paintings that never got sold, Jagdish took a leaf out of PK's art book and started making portraits. And soon his pockets too were jingling.

PK lay on his bed, reading about Robert Clive, a strange Englishman who after his death became known as Clive of India. PK was fascinated by the story, and recognized himself in the foreign man's unwillingness to give in to his father's expectations, in his yearning for adventure and even his unsuccessful suicide attempts. He could have been reading about himself.

Robert Clive was a disappointment to his father. He was born in 1725, the most rebellious of thirteen children, hyperactive, stubborn and insubordinate. He was deemed so unruly by the age of three that he was sent away from the family estate to be taken care of by childless relatives in town. But they were unable to cope, and he was sent back to the village after a few years.

At the age of ten, he used to climb up the clock tower in a devil mask and scare passers-by below. By his teens, he was a petty criminal. Exhausted, his father eventually found him a job – on the other side of the world. He was to work as a bookkeeper at the East India Company's offices in Madras. The family were relieved to be rid of him. It was well known that the odds of returning from India were only about fifty-fifty: he was just as likely to die from some tropical illness as make it back to the shores of Great

Britain. But the eighteen-year-old Robert Clive was happy to be finally embarking on his own adventure.

The job in Madras turned out to be deathly boring, however, and suffering insomnia, anxiety and depression, he put a gun to his temple and pulled the trigger. *Click!* He tried again. *Click! Click!*

PK could not put the book down.

Everything happened for a reason, Clive concluded. God must have had a greater plan for him.

Just like me, PK thought. It was all decided at birth.

Robert Clive established the East India Company as a powerful military and political entity, helping to lay the foundations of the British Raj that allowed the British Empire to flourish.

After returning to England, Clive was honoured with the title of Baron. Yet he spent his last years fighting to clear his name after being accused of misconduct. Despite eventual success, he committed suicide in 1773. His fellow countrymen were reminded of his story every time they visited the Tower of London museum, where his elephant had been stuffed and put on display in its armour. Who knows, perhaps it was one of PK's ancestors who had captured that very animal, and tamed it for the local king, who had then sold it on to the Englishman?

PK closed the book. Robert Clive had played a part in securing India for the British, and had even been posted to Orissa. Had it not been for him, perhaps India would have become French. Or remained under the rule of the Muslim kings or Hindu autocrats. PK's family said that British victory had been the best of all possible outcomes, for untouchables like them at least.

He read in *The Times of India* about another book, this time about two famous Englishmen who visited the jungle he grew up in.

According to the article, the book was almost one hundred years old. He saw in the picture the gilt lettering embossed on a brown leather cover, with two long stalks of grass, a coat of arms and two crossed spears: *Jungle Life in India*. The author, an Irishman by the name of Valentine Ball, called himself a geologist and ornithologist and had spent almost twenty years travelling around India, documenting everything from the stones he found at the bottom of rivers, to rocks scattered in the dirt and birds nesting in the treetops. But the thing that caught PK's eye was that he had lived many years in Orissa, wandering through the same jungle that PK had played in as a child and along the very river he washed in with his mother.

He put the newspaper down. A strong smell of burning leaves came wafting in through the open window, probably from the evening fire the neighbourhood street sweeper made to keep himself warm in the chilly winter night. Beeping scooters and barking dogs provided the bedtime lullaby.

But it was still too early to sleep. His head was full of all the Europeans who had visited his homeland. Wide awake, he picked up his copy of Rudyard Kipling's *The Jungle Book*. It was odd that a white-skinned English gentleman would write a story about an Indian boy raised by wolves. The same story that Grandma, who had never heard of Kipling's book, used to tell him as he rolled around on his straw mat before bed. He knew by heart the story of the boy who lived with wolves. His grandma had even begun varying the storyline, expanding it with new details and plot twists in an effort not to bore her grandson, or herself. It was a widely known myth of the jungle in India, long before Kipling was even born.

PK only learned that the Englishman had written a book based on the story when he got to school. He read the protagonist's name again and again to himself:

'Mowgli, Mowgli, Mowgli...'

Why did Kipling name him that? Monguli, as it was pronounced in Oriya, was a common boy's name where he came from, but barely heard elsewhere in India. Kipling claimed the book was inspired by the Pench National Park in the neighbouring state of Madhya Pradesh, but his choice of name for his protagonist suggested that Kipling had also visited PK's forest.

His grandfather and Bapa used to talk about an English author who lived for some time in the State Forest Agency guesthouse in Kansab Kurab, a few hours' walk north of the shores of the Mahanadi River. Which meant Kipling must have read Valentine Balls's *Jungle Life in India* and come to Athmallik himself, heard the name and given it to his main character, albeit with a new spelling.

Kipling wrote that Mowgli meant frog in the language of the forest. Mother and Father Wolf chose the name because Mowgli had smooth skin with no fur and never sat still. But there was no forest language in real life. And why would parents give their child a name that means frog? In Oriya, Monguli described the dawn and meant light, hope and optimism.

But the story was fading, along with his childhood and the forest, and his thoughts turned back to 1975. The imprisonments, the censorship and the sinking morale, they would all be temporary, that was what PK had thought at the time. The darkness wouldn't be permanent either, not for India and not for him. Indira Gandhi would release her iron grip. One day, the untouchables would be free and he would meet the woman from his prophecy.

'I'm going to India. I've decided. It's my mission in life,' Lotta told her parents.

They did not object. Lotta had expected opposition, but they remained calm and told her she knew best, as if she had announced that she was taking the bus to Gothenburg. Neither said much in general, anyway. They were used to it, she thought. She was only twenty but had already spent a year living abroad on her own in the UK. Moreover, she knew they too had dreamed of travelling the world but circumstances had prevented it.

They would have done the same in my situation, she thought.

There was no heroism in her plans. Lotta was not doing it for the spectacle, to break records. She was not writing an adventure story. There were no boats between Europe and India and flying cost a fortune, so that was out of the question. The train went as far as Mashhad in eastern Iran, but after that the plains gave way to mountains through which no train could travel, all through Afghanistan up to the border with Pakistan. No, the train was too complicated. There were regular bus services all the way from London to New Delhi and Kathmandu. One company, calling itself the Magic Bus, had already become an icon of the hippy era, with its colourfully painted coaches and dirt cheap prices.

Lotta considered her options, but really, she had already decided. Driving was the only sensible option. She had a licence, and companions: Leif, an ex-boyfriend of her sister, and her best friend, with her Indian husband and their baby. They would drive to Gothenburg, take the ferry to Kiel, proceed along the autobahn to the Alps, continue over the Balkans and then roll into Istanbul, the gateway to the East.

As for the specifics, they'd work them out along the way. They had maps but no guidebooks, for the simple reason that no guidebooks yet existed for the route. And why plan a trip that would keep changing? The journey was to be like life itself, unpredictable and exciting.

They bought a green 1971 VW van with help from Lotta's father. The vehicle had already done one round trip to Iran and back after which the engine gave up in exhaustion, but it had since been replaced. Newly serviced, the van was as good as ready, if not new.

Her mother offered only one piece of advice: 'Behave in such a way that you can always feel proud of yourself. And never do any harm to anyone else.'

It was October 1975. Lotta sat behind the wheel of their hippy dream and drove out into the world. There was no waving, no big goodbye, no fanfares sounding in the streets of Borås. But the adventure had begun.

It was a cold December evening. The coloured lights had been switched on and shone in patterns on the water's surface. For once, there was no queue of waiting customers and no crowd of curious onlookers watching as he drew. PK was done for the night anyway, so he began taking down his paintings from the cardboard sheets on which they were displayed.

Out of the darkness, a young European woman appeared and asked if he would be at the fountain the next day. She wore a yellow T-shirt and tight, flared jeans. He noticed that she did not wear make-up. She seemed different from the other European women he usually talked to at the Indian Coffee House, more serious and thoughtful. But she was in a hurry. He answered her, and she gave only a quick 'thank you' before disappearing into the night.

Was she afraid of me? Would she come back?

The next afternoon, he took his place by the fountain earlier than usual. He was hoping to meet the serious white woman again and had therefore put on his new jeans with their snaking yellow stitching on the back pockets, and the short-sleeved green checked shirt that his neighbour Didi had so kindly ironed for him. He had trimmed his moustache that morning to reveal his upper lip and combed his hair with coconut oil to tame the unruly curls. The tourists were already waiting for him. As he and his helper unpacked the canvases and began rigging up the easel, a queue formed. He looked around for the unadorned woman with the sober face. But she was nowhere to be seen.

At nine o'clock he gave up his wait, packed away his equipment and walked home to Lodi Colony. The disappointment wore heavily on him.

She had specifically asked him if he would be there, why

then had she not come? He had already woven together a full fantasy out of their minute-long meeting. At home, sitting on his bed, he began to pray, listing all the names of the gods he could think of, not only from the Hindu pantheon, but Allah, Buddha, Mahavira, the Dalai Lama, the Christian God and Maharishi Mahesh Yogi. There, in his dingy room, he prayed to them all, every god, guru and prophet his memory could conjure into existence.

The next day, a thick winter fog enveloped the city, as was usual for this time of year. He decided to go to the Shiva temple to pray that the woman with the soft voice would come back. He appealed to the Auspicious One for a full hour. He had never done that before. Normally, he did not go in for religious entreaties. But this time, he was desperate.

At home in Athmallik, he was forbidden from even entering the temple. But here in New Delhi, people from different castes, classes and ethnic groups gathered as if it were the most normal thing in the world. No one kept watch nor cared about caste. The anonymity and diversity of the big city gave him at least a partial sense of his longed for freedom.

After the temple, he made his way to Connaught Place. The columns and pilasters of the Romanesque buildings stood like mysterious figures in a dream. Just before dusk, the pale winter sun broke through the mist. There were even more people today. Some sat on the grass as they had their ears cleaned by men with dirty cotton buds. Others lay on their stomachs as men kneaded their muscles with their feet. But most sat or reclined in groups, content to chat, shell peanuts, smoke, and chew on paan, spitting out the blood red juices where they sat. Today, perhaps, she would come.

Her mother had always wanted pencil drawings of her daughters, Lotta recalled as she stood by the fountain on Connaught Place. *Ten rupees, ten minutes*, the sign said.

The queue was usually long, but that evening, she caught sight of the street artist in a rare moment of solitude, gazing at the cascading water. She stepped out of the shadows and asked him a question. What it was, she can no longer recall, but the conversation was brief. She then said goodbye and quickly left. There was something about him that both attracted and frightened her, and she decided she could always return the next day to have her portrait done.

Two nights later, she was back in the queue by the fountain. When it was her turn, she told him she wanted a portrait in pencil. He stared at her, as if it was a remarkable request. She examined his moustache and the frizz on the top of his head that he was obviously trying to tame with a slick of grease. He flipped to a fresh piece of paper and prepared himself. His hair glistened under the streetlamps. A darker version of Jimi Hendrix, she thought. He was clearly copying the hippy style. And yet he also looked like the curly-haired forest boy from Elsa Beskow's picture book, *Bubble Muck*, who lived among the lily pads and presented a fairy with a shiny ring.

It was just after seven on the evening of 17 December 1975, and the smog-filled sky over Delhi shimmered a peach colour in the glow of the streetlights. This was to be the first time they really saw each other.

A throng of people had gathered around the fountain as usual, but he saw her, there in the crowd. Her long, blonde hair. Finally! She was waiting in the queue. When her turn came, he told her to sit down on the stool. His hand was shaking as he traced his pencil over the paper. An audience stood around him as always, but he was used to them; they were not the ones making him nervous.

His marks were so unsteady that he had to give up.

'I'm sorry, I can't draw,' he said. 'Would you be willing to come to the art school tomorrow instead?'

'Sure, we'll come,' she said.

He looked up. A white man was waiting behind her.

Her husband? Please no.

'Yes, both of you,' he said cheerily.

'My name is Lotta, this is Leif. He's a photographer.'

She didn't say boyfriend, or husband, he thought hopefully.

He showered, put on some clean clothes, examined himself in the mirror and said her name to himself again. At first he thought she had said Lata, which was the name of the singer whose songs he heard all the time in the movies.

No. She said Lotta.

His neighbour Didi came out onto her veranda.

'Are you going for a job interview?' she asked.

'In a way,' he replied.

When he arrived at the school he fetched three wooden chairs, placed them in the sun on the lawn outside the café, and sat down to wait. They arrived at ten on the dot, as agreed. Yes please, to coffee.

It was a nice feeling, to sit in the clear December air with a cup of steaming coffee in his hands, opposite these two new friends. He had not yet asked where they were from.

'Sweden,' she said suddenly, as if she had read his thoughts. 'We come from Sweden.'

'Far away,' he said.

They nodded.

'In Europe,' he added. A guess.

She smiled.

'Come, let me show you the school,' he said, when they had finished their coffee.

Leif stopped to talk to some students in the ground floor corridor, while PK and Lotta went around on their own. He introduced her to his teachers and showed her the lecture halls and studios that occupied the seven-storey building. It was as if she was an old friend, he thought, even though they had only known each other for half an hour.

After they had examined every nook and cranny of the building, he asked her what she liked most in life.

'Music,' she replied. 'I play the flute.'

He asked her star sign.

'Taurus,' she said.

She will be born in the sign of Taurus and be musical…

He gathered his courage, and asked politely: 'Is Leif your husband?'

'What?'

He had mumbled, spoken too quickly, fearing it would sound ridiculous. Had she not heard him? Was she offended? Maybe one should not ask such questions of a woman? He repeated his question.

'No,' she laughed. 'Leif? We're not married. And he's not my boyfriend either.'

They continued their tour. The other students whispered to each other and pointed as he walked beside the foreign woman. Even Puni, who had not so much as looked in his direction in recent months, came up and said hello. He enjoyed the feeling, letting her see him with Lotta.

He asked if Lotta and Leif wanted to come to his room in

Lodi Colony. 'Not that there's much to see really,' he added, but he was keen to show her his prints and oil paintings. She accepted the invitation without much enthusiasm.

Maybe she was just shy?

His room was as desolate and dirty as it had ever been. Lotta and Leif stood behind him on the veranda as he gazed inside. It was a sad sight. A broken cup had been thrown into a corner. The room was almost empty of furniture. He had not wiped the table. The floor was covered in gravel. Dust bunnies had collected by the back door and the walls were plastered with charcoal drawings and scrawls that he had made while drunk. One read: *I was born untouchable. I have no right to anything, not even love*. But most embarrassing of all: *I will marry a European girl as the astrologers have predicted*. He blocked their entrance, but it was no use. They had come to see how he lived, and he had to let them in.

He selected some prints and gave them to Lotta. She said nothing.

Had she read what he had written on the walls?

Then she smiled at him and thanked him for the gift.

She agreed to see him again, and the next day they met at Connaught Place to do a tour of the city on a motor rickshaw. They visited the great Jama Masjid mosque and listened to the call to prayer.

'It was built by a powerful man called Shah Jahan, Ruler of the World,' he told her and slowly repeated the call: '*La Allah illah Allah, Mohammad Resul-allah*,' he said, stressing every syllable, before translating, 'There is no god but God, and Mohammed is his prophet.'

They climbed to the top of one of the mosque's minarets and looked out over the people below and the Red Fort. From there, he told her, the Mughals, Persians and Britons had all ruled. They looked the other way to the

Gate of India, the main boulevard of the Republic and the Presidential Palace.

'It's amazing,' he said quietly.

'What's amazing?' asked Lotta.

'You see over there, the red bridge? That's called Minto Bridge. I used to sleep under it. I have spent nights cold and hungry there. And over there...' – he raised his hand slightly and pointed at the Presidential Palace a few kilometres further in the distance – 'the President of India invited me to tea.'

She searched across the cluttered landscape of Delhi until eventually she found the large dome.

'It's like a fairytale,' she said, but looked somewhat sceptical. Maybe she thought he was making it up?

They jumped into a rickshaw and headed south to Humayan's Tomb, one of the city's top tourist attractions. They chatted the whole way. It was so easy to talk to her. He thought again about the prophecy: she would be musical and born under the sign of Taurus.

And would own a jungle, the astrologer had added.

She could not possibly own a jungle, surely?

Lotta carried on with her travels. The next day, she and her friends took the VW bus for a trip out of the city. They headed for the temples of Khajuraho by the Ganges, where they could drink in the sight of pilgrims bathing in the holy water at Varanasi. PK missed her, but he had doubts. She was a tourist, she would soon be leaving India again. Life had so much to offer her, there was no way she would stay with him. Why would she? One moment. An eternity. His misgivings mixed with the memory of her gentle voice.

On Christmas Day, his birthday, he received a hand-pressed envelope with his name and address written on it in neat block capitals. He opened it with a pounding heart. He removed the colourful card with a drawing of a happy fish jumping out of clumsily drawn waves. Vulgar, his teachers would have said. Commercial. Infantile. But he had never received a birthday card before. He held it up to the sun so that the fish glowed.

> Imagine, we had to travel so far to find a nice friend like you. Happy birthday,
>
> Lotta.

The days before her return were sweet torment.

He caught sight of Leif and his large backpack in the rust-red dusk of New Year's Eve. PK ran through the crowds gathered around the fountain. Leif was alone and proceeded to tell PK about their trip to Khajuraho and the thousand-year-old temples with their erotic sculptures. Did PK know of a good, cheap hotel?

'Don't stay in a hotel, stay with me.'

He gave him the key to his room in Lodi Colony.

'What about Lotta?' PK ventured.

'She's renting a room in a palace. We met the family on the train.'

'She'd also be welcome at mine,' he said listlessly.

He had no hope that she would exchange a bed in a private room in the plush villa of a wealthy family for his cramped and filthy quarters.

The next day, as he sat gazing out along the street, a yellow-red dot appeared in the shade of the trees. It began to grow, slowly transforming into the contours of a woman. She was wearing jeans, a yellow T-shirt and a red backpack.

It felt like a personal triumph. He wanted to shout out in glee: she chose my poverty above their luxury!

But his greeting was more neutral, more controlled: 'Welcome, Lotta!'

Leif slept in PK's broken *charpoy*, a wooden bed with a braided rope base. For Lotta, he rolled out a thin bamboo mattress. He slept directly on the cement floor.

'Don't worry, I'm used to sleeping on hard ground,' he reassured them.

What bothered him most was that he had no linen to offer. But she looked happy enough as she rolled out her sleeping bag on the bamboo mat under the window.

He prepared masala omelette, toast and tea on a gas stove on the veranda. Then they took a motor rickshaw to Connaught Place, where they switched to a pat-pattie, a three-wheeled motorcycle overloaded with passengers, and headed for Old Delhi.

The city, of which he had been so afraid three years earlier, was now a part of him. She has to experience the markets, he said to himself. They are the reason I am the man I am today.

They wandered around the old town and through a narrow opening, wedged between two small restaurants, into an alley that swelled to form a small courtyard lit by fluorescent lights.

It smelled of charcoal and fried meat; plumes of steam rose from the outdoor kitchen, and diners sat at tables in the four different rooms around the courtyard. They peered inside one of them: there were floor-to-ceiling tiles and guests eating kebabs and thin, floury bread.

They walked around the groves and man-made lakes of Delhi Zoo housed in a dilapidated fort, talking and laughing. He felt giddy. And yet, anxiety began to ripple inside him as soon as they sat down on the lawn. He was waiting for tragedy to strike; his luck always ran out at some point. That was his experience of life so far, and it was how it would be now. Happiness was merely the premonition of impending misfortune. He was not created for true happiness. Lotta would travel back to Europe, and he would remain in India. She had come like a flash of lightning and would disappear again just as suddenly.

He had one semester left at the College of Art, and no money for travel.

It's impossible, he thought, our romance has no future, our meeting is doomed to be a short but pleasant memory and nothing more.

But he did not share these feelings with Lotta.

They continued on to Paharganj, Delhi's main market. They pressed tight against each other as they wove between fruit stalls and teashops. He felt at once consumed by her and by the pleasure of that moment. They talked with baker boys who flattened lumps of dough in red-hot tandoori ovens using only their hands. They met the bloodshot eyes of old men and women who lay outside on their charpoys, wrapped in grey sheets. They nearly tripped over a man who had dismantled a gearbox and had laid out the pieces, down to the washers, in a neat pattern on a piece of cardboard in the middle of the road. They picked their way through a herd of goats. They patted the shiny skins of cows, smelled the warm wet fabric of a woman ironing shirts with a steam iron. They laughed at the man who whipped milk with a converted electric drill. And they stood for several minutes watching an old man building a pyramid out of hundreds of chicken eggs under a naked light bulb. 'If one falls, they all go,' the egg man said. They laughed.

They saw dogs sashaying through the crowds, women sewing, silver necklaces being repaired, a girl who swept the street before her door. They breathed in smoke heavy with the smell of burnt leaves and listened as a woman snored. People sang, talked, rolled dough, played cards, and reclined in the shade.

He felt as if they were part of it all, the people and the streets, the smells and the sky.

***

They arrived at the fountain at around six o'clock, and PK started hanging out his paintings. Lotta helped him. He watched as she hooked them onto the cardboard screens. God, let this woman be my future wife, he thought, as he sat down on his stool. He then began working on the queue of people waiting. She sat close to him. He finished four drawings before they decided to pack up and go to the cinema instead.

Hundreds of people stood outside the Plaza. The queue for the box office snaked out into the street. *Sholay* had had its premiere six months previously, but it still drew full houses. They stood and looked at the hand-painted posters of Amitabh Bachchan pumping the bad guys full of lead from his machine gun. Once inside, they looked down on the stalls from their seats in the balcony and saw that most of the audience was made up of single men, gazing longingly back at them.

The movie started and he translated for her. But he paused when Lata Mangeshkar began to sing 'Jab Tak Hai Jaan', leaned back and just listened. Lotta moved closer to him during the film's more colourful dances, rested her head against his shoulder and put her hand in his. The fear, which he had been keeping at bay since leaving the zoo, returned with force. What did it all mean? Was there a higher power trying to tell him something? Was this how love began? He knew nothing and realized just how inexperienced he really was. He felt twelve years old again.

What will be will be. He had to overcome his misgivings. We have already started a new togetherness, he said to himself. Our souls are on the same wavelength.

He leaned forward and kissed her forehead.

'*Maheswari Ma, Ma Maheswari*', he whispered. A prayer to the same jungle goddess his mother used to call on in times of need.

It was winter in Delhi. The night sky was filled with stars but the fog held off until just before dawn. The air was ice-cold as they trudged through the deserted city past the fountain, which looked empty and desolate in the darkness. They walked along the main avenue south, past Raj Path and the triumphal India Gate, towards Lodi Colony. At first he held her hand, but as they were alone, he gathered his courage and put his arm around her. He felt the warmth of her body, but was also assailed by the feeling that he was doing something forbidden, that the streetlights were watching them. For a moment, he thought he had left his own body and was looking down, watching himself walking, side by side, with Lotta.

It was a long way home. But what of it? They arrived back at two in the morning. Leif was asleep in the rope bed, snoring loudly. They took a blanket and went out onto the veranda. They sat on the cement stairs and wrapped themselves up against the cold. Wild dogs yapped as they ran past. He held her, looked up at the stars, then at her and then up at the stars again. It was so romantic. And yet he was too shy to look straight into her eyes. The sky above was his escape.

They had been drawn together by a divine power, a power that had been working on him ever since he was born. He knew Westerners did not think like this. But that was how he had been brought up, that was how life worked. This was their night, their magic, their love, and it had been written in the stars. He kissed her again on the forehead, then on the cheeks. First the eyes, then the mind, and then the heart, love made its way through him. They had always belonged together, and together they would stay, for time in all its infinity.

He whispered her name. She did not answer. So they remained in silence.

'I love you,' he ventured. But instantly, he regretted it.

Why? Why did those words, of all the ones he could have chosen, have to leap out of his mouth? What if she got up and left? What if she laughed? What if she said, 'I like you, but not like that'?

Eventually, her answer came. 'So do I.' She leaned forward and kissed him lightly on the forehead.

Then, after another pause:

'I would be the happiest man in the world if you would marry me.'

She tensed.

'I haven't given any thought to marriage. Not yet! There's so much I want to do before then.'

'I don't mean now,' he said. 'I can wait. However long it takes.'

The conversation petered out. He did not want to push it.

They sat in silence and listened to Leif's snoring. Then they went inside. He lay down on the floor and she on his bamboo mattress by the window. He tried to sleep, but ended up staring into the darkness. He tossed and turned, then his body became rigid. He listened. She too was moving, unsettled. He wondered if he should say something. Just then, he felt a light gust of air and heard a faint rustling. A soft hand on his shoulder. Almost silently, she crept in under his blanket and lay down beside him on the cold, cement floor.

'You can't sleep either?' she whispered.

'No.'

'I feel scared over there, by the window. Can I lie here with you?'

'Of course,' he stammered.

She moved closer. His desire was reawakened and he grew braver. But she tensed.

'I'll go back to my bed if you can't control yourself,' she whispered gently. 'I didn't come for that. I want you to hold me, that's all,' she added.

So he held her. Who did he think he was? He was ashamed of himself. This was more than enough.

PK and Lotta were lying on the bamboo mat on the cement floor. He looked at her. She seemed so at ease when she slept. He remembered her reaction in the night. She had recoiled at the mention of marriage, but he knew no other way to express his feelings. They could not possibly live together if they were not married, and then the romance would wither. Love could not survive without a solemn vow and an official blessing. At least, that was how he felt. But Lotta wanted to wait, she had told him that much on the veranda. It was difficult for him to understand. If she liked him and her father agreed, why wait? In this, it was obvious they came from different cultures.

But he would keep trying.

'Come with me to Orissa,' he said as they ate breakfast. She gave him a curious look.

'And meet my father. And my sister and brothers.'

'Sure, why not,' she replied.

No counterargument, no questions. But did she really want to come? Had she misunderstood him?

They moved fast, as if they had to act at once, before she could be conquered by doubt. They pushed his things into her backpack and dressed quickly. He pulled on the same dirty trousers and shirt he had worn the day before. It did not feel right when there was a woman in the room, but what else could he do? He did not have any clean clothes.

How bad do I really smell? he wondered.

He turned and looked at Lotta. She was dressed in a newly purchased red sari in a style common to the Varanasi region. That blonde hair and red sari! She was so beautiful.

They took a rickshaw to Connaught Place to buy a gift for his father and some token presents for his siblings. They ate at a Chinese restaurant, threaded in and out of the shops, gazed at each other, laughed. Life was just like the romances he had watched on the big screen, and now they were building towards their climax. But how long before it all came crashing down? As usual, he kept his doubts to himself.

They climbed aboard the Janata Express, and before dusk the long train slithered out of the station and eastwards. A cool breeze wafted through the open window as the sun painted the plains a mango yellow. He watched Lotta's hair flutter in the draught and sometimes whip across her face. He was fascinated by its golden glow in the last light of the day.

Scenes from PK's childhood flickered through his mind. Riding his grandfather's elephant in the jungle at the age of five. His teacher throwing stones at him, shouting that this was his fate. His high-caste friend who was forbidden from playing with him once his parents realized he was untouchable. His thoughts turned to the here and now, as he sat in a train compartment with this beautiful, foreign woman. Characters in the movies were given flashback montages in their dying moments. It was an apt comparison; he was being reincarnated into a better life.

They ordered dinner, which was served at their seats in cardboard boxes. Vegetables, rice and chapati. They sat cross-legged on the green vinyl bunk and ate in silence. It was dark outside, the faint glow of the carriage lighting cast a gloomy blue over them. The train bounced on the rails, the horn bellowed and they rocked back and forth as if on a boat navigating stormy waters.

They climbed up into one of the narrow bunks above and lay close to each other. Lotta tried to read her book about Orissan religious festivals, but soon fell asleep. He lay, gazing at her, breathing in the stillness of her sleep, her closed eyelids, her luminous complexion.

He thought about the conversations they had had over the last few days.

'You've made me believe in God,' she had said to him.

'But I'm poor, I can't take care of you and give you a secure life,' he replied.

'You're not poor to me,' she countered.

'I'm an artist, that means I will never have money.'

'But I want to share my life with you.' It seemed that Lotta had decided to follow her heart after all.

A few hours before dawn, they stepped off the train in Bokaro, the city of steel. This was where PK's oldest brother worked. They huddled close to each other on the dark platform, wrapped in a soiled woollen blanket, and waited in silence for sunrise. Bundles of material scattered around them seemed to accommodate sleeping people. Maybe they were waiting for the train, or, like PK and Lotta, for relatives who would come to pick them up after dawn. They heard barking dogs roving the streets in packs on the other side of the station, and now and then the solitary trumpet of a bus horn.

As the sun rose above the horizon, Lotta went into the station, changed into a new, clean sari and covered her hair with a headscarf. From a distance it was impossible to tell that she was a foreigner. PK was sure that his brother would like her traditional style.

Suddenly, Pramod appeared. PK had not seen him in years. He was now a few kilos heavier, dressed in a Western suit, white shirt and tie. He looked important. He approached with a cautious smile. PK and Lotta knelt before him and greeted him with lowered heads and fingertips to the feet.

Pramod was a division manager on the Indian Railways and was very proud of his position. He was not unique, but it was still uncommon for an untouchable village boy to do so well. Most managers were still Brahmins or from other high castes, despite Indira Gandhi's insistence that state companies had to start obeying the anti-discrimination laws. Pramod's promotion was indirectly Indira's doing.

He showed them his office with its attached kitchen and servants, housed in a railway carriage. On the walls hung portraits of Indira Gandhi and the guru Sai Baba, his benefactor, guardian angel and prophet.

No one believed that PK's brother was the son of a dark-skinned tribal woman and an untouchable man. He was light-skinned and had, rather mysteriously, grown paler with the passing years. The young Pramod had often spoken of his desire to be as white-skinned as a wealthy and powerful European. And now it seemed that his wish had come true. PK knew that black hair turned grey then white with age, but he had never heard of skin getting paler too. But so it was. Pramod looked more and more like the Westerners he so admired, and many in the Soviet-sponsored city of steel treated him courteously, having mistaken him for a Russian guest worker.

PK was worried what his brother would think of Lotta. He did not want to break with local tradition, which decreed that the eldest brother must first approve a marriage, and then the father. He was not sure if it was entirely necessary to follow the custom, but neither did he want to provoke his family unnecessarily. He could not risk being ostracized by them too.

'My oldest and wisest brother,' PK began that first evening, 'may I marry Charlotta?'

Pramod did not answer.

'Charlotta is really the same as Charulata,' PK clarified in Oriya, then turned to Lotta and whispered in English: 'He will probably be more sympathetic when he hears that you have such a nice name. Charulata means vine in Oriya.'

His brother was silent, and then announced that he

needed to think. He would meditate for an hour, during which he would consult with Sai Baba and God.

PK's brother sat down in the lotus position on the cement floor of the living room, surrounded by photographs of snowy mountain peaks and fair-skinned babies. He closed his eyes and his expression turned grave. PK studied his brother nervously, but he could do nothing but wait.

After an hour, a smile broke out across his brother's face. PK knew that it would all be fine.

They took the Madras Express to Tata, switching to the Utkal Express bound for Cuttack and then a long distance coach up the river and into the forest. The vegetation thickened, the sky cleared and the air became easier to breathe. He was back in the village of his childhood. So much had happened since he had last visited.

At once it was clear that his father had no objections to the match.

'You should marry whoever makes you happy,' he said. 'And she fits with your horoscope,' he added.

His father began singing hymns in Sanskrit as if he were a Brahmin. The village priests would surely have been most disturbed by such a display, but Shridhar did not care.

'Why should the Brahmins have the sole right to perform sacred ceremonies?' he used to counter when his colleagues thought he was in danger of provoking the high castes.

PK and Lotta watched. Behind him on the wall hung a portrait of PK's mother. PK felt his Ma's gaze, as though she had returned from the dead, curious to see what he had made of his life.

Then his father brought together their hands, nodded and spoke.

'Pradyumna Kumar,' he said, looking at his son, 'make sure you never give her reason to cry.'

'I promise, as long as she's with me,' he replied.

'If tears run down her cheeks, never let them reach the ground,' his father continued. 'You should always be on hand to comfort your wife.'

Then he presented Lotta with a new sari. It was done. They were husband and wife. They would have to register the marriage formally at the local court, but they could do that later. For now, it did not matter.

With backpacks on their heads, they weaved through the mass of villagers who had come out to see PK and his white-skinned wife dressed in Indian clothes. They had never seen anything like it. They stared unabashedly, but no one dared approach her and say hello. PK's success in Delhi commanded their respect and admiration. He was no longer a pariah.

Rumour spread quickly that the boy from the village who had drawn a cosmonaut, a prime minister and a president had returned. In Bhubaneswar, the secretary-general of the art school invited them to lunch. He praised PK and pulled out their chairs so they might sit down. It was a display completely alien to PK. After lunch, the secretary general instructed his chauffeur to drive them wherever they wanted to go in town and sent a messenger boy to buy their train tickets. Lotta was presented with a silver hair clasp as if she were a queen. King Pradyumna Kumar and Queen Lotta. It was as if the whole world had transformed into their servants.

They took the bus to Puri and strolled along the wide sandy beach past other lovers, and then on to the Sun Temple in Konark with its carvings of erotic scenes from the Kama Sutra.

Before they reached the Black Pagoda, as the old-time sailors called the temple, PK told Lotta to stop. He cupped his hands and placed them over her eyes.

'Now, for something beautiful.'

He took his hands away.

'Look, up there!'

The temple with the stone wheel. The very same stone wheel in the picture she used to have pinned to her wall in London. She had stared at that picture and longed for India. And now, here she was, standing before the real thing. She started to cry.

They had only met a few weeks before, but here, in front of the temple designed as a chariot for the sun god Surya, their lips touched for the first time.

PK's ecstasy was once again blunted by doubt. It was all so surreal, so detached from reality.

How is it possible for an untouchable jungle boy like me to walk beside the woman I love?

The doubt swelled, occupying everything. He stumbled over the simplest phrases. He fumbled while performing the most basic manoeuvres, such as a caress of Lotta's cheek or avoiding piles of rubbish in the street.

On the bus back to Bhubaneswar he imagined throwing his old life away, the career in New Delhi, for a possible future with Lotta in Europe. He toyed with the idea and it scared him, precisely because it felt so perfectly feasible. Why had he left behind the beauty of his home in Orissa and gone to the capital? This was where his family was, and everything that felt familiar. The jungle was so bounteous, so rich, dense, mysterious and exciting. Mango trees and coconut palms shrouded in morning mist belonged to a landscape that made him question the ingrained notion that it was worth sacrificing everything for the new and the capricious.

As soon as they arrived back at his rented room in New Delhi a week later, his neighbour Didi came to tell him that a well-dressed woman and her daughter had been to visit several times in his absence. Puni and her mother, it transpired. Where was PK? they kept asking. In the end, Didi turned the question on them; why were they looking for him?

Puni's mother told Didi the story:

There was nothing wrong with Puni's fiancé, the engineering student. He was a nice boy. But the boy's father had asked for fifty thousand rupees in dowry. It was an unthinkably large sum, a dowry fit for a film star. Puni's father had been desperate for his daughter to wed the boy from the high-caste family, but eventually he too had to accept that they could not afford it. So Puni's mother had come to see if PK might take her daughter after all.

What an idiotic family! Why would he want anything to do with them, after her father had so humiliated him?

I'm a forgiving person, but there are limits, he thought.

To Didi and his friends, he said that he was already married to the woman from Sweden. This was not strictly true of course. His father had performed the ceremony so that they were united in the eyes of the gods, but they were not technically wed according to the law. But then again, who was going to check something like that?

They spent their nights lying beside each other on the concrete floor of PK's rented room, looking up at the cracked cement ceiling, while Lotta related stories about Swedish history and her ancestors.

'The King of Sweden at that time was called Adolf Frederick and the Queen Louisa Ulrika, and just like India, Sweden had four castes. The King's power had been limited and the country was ruled instead by four parliaments, one for each caste group,' Lotta explained. 'We called them the nobles, the clergy, the burghers and the peasants. Two parties contended for power, and they had the strangest names, the Hats and the Caps!'

'How strange. Imagine that happening in India!' whispered PK. 'People would laugh themselves to death.'

'Let me finish,' Lotta said.

'The King and Queen were furious that the nobles who controlled the Hat Party were attempting to seize power and limit that of the royal family. They even insisted upon raising the heir to the throne, Prince Gustav. This way, the Prince would grow up to be a fair and just king.

'The Queen refused. How could humans alter the will of God? It was madness. She called her advisers and told them about her plan to stop the Hats. They would enact a military coup and reinstate the King, as God ordained.

'One summer evening,' Lotta continued, 'in 1756...'

Just as Robert Clive was struggling to gain dominance over India – what a coincidence, thought PK.

'Have I told you about Robert Clive?' he interrupted. 'I must tell you his story.'

'Later!

'One summer evening, in 1756, chaos broke out in Stockholm. But the details of the Queen's plan had not yet been fully worked out. The agents of the coup did not have the necessary money, and the timing was wrong. But one of the Queen's closest men decided he would start the coup anyway. He collected together his friends and told them to set the plan in motion. Then he ran up the palace staircase to inform the Queen.

'Word of the plan reached the King and Queen's bodyguard and a junior officer of only twenty-two by the name of Daniel Schedvin.

'Had he obeyed the order, my family's history would have turned out very differently. Then we wouldn't have owned any forest,' said Lotta.

'You own forest?'

'Not me personally, but my family does.'

She continued. 'The King and Queen's men gathered their troops and marched on the Hat Party headquarters to arrest them. Daniel, however, went to his lord and told him what was going on, and then warned the leader of the noblemen.

'Sweden's warrior caste.'

'We call them Kshatriya in India.'

'The nobility mobilized their opposition and quickly stopped the Queen's attempted coup. The King and Queen were criticized in a sermon given by the high priest. Several others involved were executed. And my ancestor, Daniel, was rewarded with a large sum of money, which he used to buy forest and land. The nobility also forced the King to knight him. To be knighted, that means to change caste and advance upwards,' Lotta explained to an increasingly puzzled PK.

'Daniel became the owner of a large section of the Swedish forest and his family bore a coat of arms decorated in blue and gold, with two crossed swords, a green wreath with ribbons, and a motto in silver: *Ob cives servatus*.'

'What does that mean?'

'It's Latin, but I've forgotten what it means, unfortunately,' she replied.

The family shield was hung in the Stockholm headquarters of his new caste, and in a church in the area where he bought the land.

'That's why my family still owns forest,' said Lotta.

'So you're from a high and noble caste?'

'Yes, that's why my last name is von Schedvin. But I'm not proud of it. It doesn't make me better than anyone else.'

'Lotta, you belong to a high caste while I get less respect than the dirt on the soles of your feet.'

He remembered how Puni's father had shouted at him to leave their house and thought of all the doomed Indian love affairs that ended in honour killings because of similar mismatches.

How was their love affair going to end? he thought as he kissed her on the forehead.

'Yes, but those are just outdated prejudices,' Lotta said. 'That stuff doesn't mean anything to me.'

'You own forest. It's my destiny. If all that stuff hadn't happened all those years ago, the prophecy wouldn't have come true.'

'Yes, you're right.'

'Lotta, you know, everything happens for a reason.'

Lotta took the train to Amritsar, where her friends were waiting with the VW bus. They would go back the way they had come, over the Hindu Kush mountain range, through Iran's deserts and the peaks high above the Black Sea. She recalled the trip they had made only a few months earlier. She remembered how, in the Alps, a guardian angel had prevented the bus from becoming a burning pile of metal at the bottom of a ravine. In Turkey, they wormed their way along endless mountain roads, and the world had never been more beautiful. They almost turned the van to scrap once more in the traffic chaos of Tehran. Hours passed on the roads of Afghanistan without seeing a single person, only empty diners with dusty Coca-Cola signs and no drinks to sell.

Three weeks after their departure from Sweden, they had passed over the border between Pakistan and India. After a detour to the Taj Mahal, they arrived in Delhi late at night, where they collided with a wall and demolished the bumper. It was pitch black and the streets were emptier than usual because of the state of emergency, but they did not know this. They had not phoned home once, but now they contacted the Swedish Embassy and asked the receptionist to call their parents and tell them that they had arrived, having crashed only once, one hundred metres from their final destination. The embassy in New Delhi called through to Borås, but neglected to mention that they had not been injured in the accident.

The trip home to Europe did not worry her, she was now experienced and cleansed. She could have found her way back without a map. The trip went quickly and with no major mishaps, apart from an incident when the van skidded on a patch of ice on a mountain road beyond Trabzon.

They spun full circle and slid to a halt right at the edge of the precipice. But their guardian angel had not abandoned them, and they stepped out of the vehicle, unharmed but in shock.

Everything happens for a reason. And Lotta's destiny was to arrive safely back in Sweden.

It was spring 1976, and at home in Borås, she told her parents that she was in love. PK was the man she wanted to marry, and she would return to India that autumn.

But this time, her mother stopped her.

'PK hasn't finished art school and you haven't got yourself a proper education yet,' came her sober reply. 'Stay here and study. Keep in touch, write letters, get to know each other from a distance.'

It was not what Lotta wanted to hear, but as the memories of India began to fade, as the smells left her clothes, she began to think that her mother might be right. A conflict raged inside her. If she returned now she would surely remain in India, and never come back. But wherever she ended up, she needed a foundation on which to build her life and career.

PK promised he would come to Sweden as soon as he could. But weeks, then months, passed. Their agreed date for a reunion, August, came and went, and PK never appeared. A letter arrived in September from New Delhi. He would come, but he still did not know when exactly, as he was not sure how to get there.

Lotta was reconsidering if she would go back to India after all. She had started work in a kindergarten. The pay was low and she could not save for a ticket. She certainly did not want to borrow money from her parents.

Later, Lotta realized how scared her mother had been that she would not make a career. Women should no longer be only mothers and housewives, her mother said. She had missed out on the opportunity to educate herself, but she would not see her daughters make the same mistake.

New dreams began to take shape. Lotta had learned to play the piano as a child. She applied for a job as a substitute teacher at the municipal music school, as well as for a place at the University College of Music Education in Stockholm.

She got both.

India would have to wait.

PK returned to his previous routine, attending lessons at the art school, painting in the school's studio and drawing portraits by the fountain. But Indian society had changed. New Delhi was paralysed by the new and harsh laws of the emergency: press censorship, slum sanitation, sterilization campaigns, as well as bans on demonstrations and political gatherings.

Bulldozers tore through slums along the city's boulevards and police dispersed crowds. The usually obedient and politically tolerant capital was now boiling over in open rebellion and police repression.

And yet, PK never felt that Indira Gandhi was going too far. If we want to get rid of the corruption and the injustice, then India needed to take a hard line, he concluded. You cannot ask the Brahmins nicely to stop discriminating against untouchables and for employers to start giving them jobs. You cannot expect people to give up their privilege voluntarily, inherited or otherwise, in some false hope that they will act without a stick to encourage them. Politics was the antidote to self-interest, he had learned that from bitter experience.

It had now been over a year since Mr Haksar, Indira's principal secretary, had promised to organize a place for PK to live. Then, in the spring of 1976, Haksar got in touch again.

'It's all done,' he said. 'You're free to move in.'

'Where?'

'South Avenue.'

South Avenue! The road where India's Members of Parliament lived. The exclusive preserve of the country's elite.

'I'm going to live there?'

'Yes,' said Haksar. 'One of the apartments at No. 78 is yours.'

PK packed his belongings, barely filling one bag. He kept his easel and canvases at the fountain and walked all the way to his new home in South Avenue.

The apartment consisted of a large lavishly furnished living room, a separate bedroom, a balcony overlooking the garden, a kitchen, a dining room and two bathrooms. When hunger struck, all he had to do was pick up the phone and food would be delivered straight to his door. When his clothes were dirty, he left them for the Dhobi wallah who came every day to collect them.

One year ago, he had been sleeping under bridges and warming himself by bonfires of rubbish. Now he lived in a bungalow on the same street as the Prime Minister and was never short of money. He must have exhausted his reserve of bad karma; all the fighting and the struggle had filled his well full of better luck to draw on.

For PK, life during the emergency was one of success and increased self-worth. Indira Gandhi was a mother figure for the untouchables, for all of India's oppressed. And sometimes, a mother could be harsh and reprimanding.

She was their benefactor. What would India's untouchables have been without her? Where would he have been without her benevolence? Most certainly, in the gutter.

But PK was still hurting from missing Lotta, and he told anyone who would listen about his loss. The intensity of his feelings so moved people that Lotta received a steady stream of letters from PK, as well as messages from backpackers he met at the Indian Coffee House.

It was as if everyone making the round trip to Asia knew about their story.

Kate from Edinburgh wrote:

> I just got back from India. I met your friend PK while I was out there. He's a nice, honest guy and he misses you a lot. He was always talking about you, saying he hopes you haven't forgotten him. Not that I want to get involved, of course, but maybe you should write to him and let him know how you are.

And then a letter from Maria from Bohus-Björkö:

> I just got back from Pakistan on Sunday the 6th... I was also in Delhi in January. A friend from Lahore and I took a short trip to India. Another friend told us to look PK up and we did. We met several times and had a great time. PK gave us a book to give to you... PK is well, but he misses you a lot.

Beatrice from Pontoise, who thought he was called Pieket, said:

> I arrived home three days ago from Delhi. My husband and I met Pieket there and he helped us a lot. Pieket told me about you and we saw the beautiful photo of you two together. Pieket asked me to write a letter to you as soon as I got home to Paris, and it makes me happy even if my English is poor. I hope you will understand anyway what I write. Pieket have not heard from you in two months, and he is worried about it. He hopes that nothing happened to you and we hope it too.

PK had everything he had ever dreamed of living somewhere as lavish as the bungalow at 78 South Avenue, and yet he was miserable. The reason, of course, was obvious. He lay on the bed, looking out at the garden, and thought of how they had walked in the Mughal Garden behind the Presidential Palace and remembered the moment when, among the roses, tulips and temple flowers, he had placed a ring on her finger.

Despite his relative comfort, PK began to become more politically active. He wanted to change the lives of the untouchables with his art. His paintings would force the complacent middle classes to really see and understand their suffering. Outside the Congress Party Head Office, Haksar introduced him to a tall man who shook PK's hand so vigorously he nearly yelped.

The man shared PK's vision, and asked if he wanted to start a magazine for 'the oppressed'.

'Yes,' PK said.

'My name is Bhim Singh. You're the famous fountain painter?' he said.

'Yes,' PK replied again, more gruffly this time. He did not enjoy being treated like a celebrity. 'And what about you, Mr Singh?'

'I have travelled through 120 countries by motorcycle. I have been to Europe, America and Russia and also crossed the Sahara Desert.'

'Most impressive, Mr Singh! But why?'

'For world peace. I'm going to write a book about my experiences.'

'And now?'

'Now I'm going to start a newspaper.'

Singh seemed to be a strong-willed, dedicated man not content to stay in his comfort zone. Nor was he motivated by the pursuit of wealth. PK liked him instantly, and he liked PK.

'Would you be willing to design the newspaper's logo?' Bhim asked.

'Of course.'

'And to illustrate some articles?'

'Gladly.'

Bhim explained that he had already come up with a name: *Voice of Millions*. PK was appointed deputy editor there and then, and Bhim would be editor-in-chief. The two of them made up the entire editorial staff. Bhim would write, PK would illustrate.

They were given a corner of the Congress Party's veranda. Their office comprised a worn typewriter, a broken table and two rickety chairs.

The *Voice of Millions*'s two-man editorial team started work that very week. Every day, they sat on the veranda and composed articles describing the dark side of Indian society, the hunger and the oppression.

'We are the voice of the masses,' Bhim used to declare as fatigue set in and their pace slowed.

PK designed a logo in which the letters of *Voice of Millions* were filled with lots of small, emaciated faces screaming for food. The newspaper of the hungry. A cry against poverty and the caste system. But Bhim did not stop there; he was fighting for another cause as well: the independence of Kashmir. On this topic PK felt less informed, so he left that particular struggle to his friend.

Their first edition was ready. PK took a bundle and went to the streets around Connaught Place. Pride swelled his chest as he carried their newspaper, a newspaper he had helped to create.

He walked a few times around the roundabout, into the side streets, through the park and between the tables of the Indian Coffee House. He walked up to the station, into Paharganj market and then back to the roundabout.

'Get your *Voice of Millions*, the newspaper of the oppressed!' He must have cried this hundreds of times.

'The publication that will change India!' he began to add when no one took any notice.

After two days, he had only managed to sell a handful of copies. He dumped the rest on the pavement, saying: 'Take a copy, it's free! Take it! *Voice of Millions!*'

He returned to Bhim, who was sitting on the veranda, and handed him his resignation.

'India isn't ready for change,' PK said bluntly.

Bhim was not happy with PK's decision, but he decided to continue, at least until the day Kashmir had its freedom.

'Good luck with Kashmir, and the eradication of hunger,' PK said and returned to his easel by the fountain.

There, at least, people took notice and appreciated him.

When anyone Swedish came to the fountain, PK stopped what he was doing and talked to them. If he heard a Swedish voice at the Indian Coffee House, he introduced himself, offering them tea just to have an excuse to sit down and talk about Sweden. He changed his sign at the fountain. Now it said, *Ten Minutes, Ten Rupees. Free for Swedes.*

He wanted as much contact as possible with Lotta's fellow countrymen. Their voices and stories reminded him of her. It was his way of keeping the memories, the feelings, alive, of refusing to let her fade away.

That was how he got to know Lars.

Lars showed PK his Swedish passport and PK drew his portrait for free. He was a journalist and, just like all the others, had travelled overland from Europe to India. He had not driven, but hitchhiked. He thought PK could do the same.

Lars unfurled a map of Asia and together they sat for hours in the café, examining it. He traced his pen along the roads, which were coloured red, and read out the names of the cities. Kabul, Kandahar, Herat, Mashhad, Tehran, Tabriz, Ankara, Istanbul.

'You can make the trip in two weeks, easily. Then you only have Europe left, which you can hitchhike in a week, tops.'

Yes, perhaps I could hitchhike to Sweden, PK thought.

If Lars could, then he could. Three weeks sounded manageable. Sweden had felt like another planet, unreachable for a poor Indian like him. A plane ticket cost a fortune, and he did not dare write to Lotta to ask for money. He did not own a car. But three weeks! It had never occurred to him.

Lars, in turn, was entranced by PK's story of the prophecy and Lotta. He wanted more.

'That's as much as I remember,' said PK.

'There must be more. Try!' Lars said.

'There isn't.'

'It's like a fairytale,' Lars breathed.

One day, Lars told him that a Swedish director was in town, screening a film at the local film festival.

'He could make a movie about your story,' Lars said. 'Sjöman. His name is Vilgot Sjöman.'

'And he's famous?'

'Yes, in Sweden. And in America.'

'As famous as Raj Kapoor?'

'No, more like Satyajit Ray. A serious director. No singing and dancing.'

'What movies has he made?'

'Movies with a political message. And naked people. It was quite controversial.'

Lars wrote down the name of the hotel where the director was staying and told PK to go and introduce himself. But PK was sceptical. Movies with naked people! If the director's reputation was considered questionable in Sweden, imagine what Indians would think! Even kissing was considered too risqué for India. He thought mainly about his family back in Orissa. They would face the consequences if it got out that he had worked with a director who made films about naked people. No, Lars' proposal was not in the slightest bit tempting.

Nevertheless, Lars managed to get him into the film festival, which was being held in the Congress Centre. There, in the crowded vestibule, Lars caught sight of Sjöman. He rushed forward and tapped the director on the shoulder. Then he introduced PK.

The Swede had a nice manner, PK thought. He asked PK what he thought of the state of emergency and Indira

Gandhi and listened carefully to his answers. But PK did not tell him anything personal. He was adamant; no sex tape director was going to make a film about his life. He was not that liberal.

He said goodbye as politely as he could and slipped back into the crowd with a disappointed Lars in tow.

PK was convinced that Lotta would come back. They had agreed upon it. They would be reunited after six months, in August, she said. Either she would come to India, or he would go to Sweden.

He graduated from the College of Art, Delhi, in June 1976 and began to plan for Lotta's return. She can stay with me on South Avenue, he thought. No wife could be dissatisfied with an address like that. No tears would fall on his polished floor.

But he had to find work. He could not sit at the fountain and draw people for the rest of his life.

India Post was looking for illustrators and the art school helped him get an interview. They liked his samples and offered him a six-month in-house training contract in Pune, a city that described itself as cosmopolitan and 'every career-hungry Indian's dream'.

He had a place to live, and a steady job. Or almost. Lotta would be proud of him. India Post also had an agreement with the British Post Office, and the man who interviewed him suggested that there would be a possibility that, if he turned out to be talented and hardworking, eventually, maybe, possibly, he might have the chance to move to London. The very idea of it made him jittery. Imagine living in the colonial capital, together with Lotta!

But August came and went, and Lotta did not arrive. He had neither the time nor the money to make the trip to Europe. His savings were meagre and he was still waiting to start his training.

He waited the whole of autumn to hear from India Post, but nothing came. The disappointment was crushing. But it only made him more determined to be reunited with Lotta.

Their love would have its chance to bloom in person, and not only in finely worded letters. Otherwise, he risked losing her forever.

He organized a new passport and an International Youth Hostel card. Every day, as he made his way to the fountain, he gazed up at the giant billboard for British Airways that had been set up on Connaught Place. It promised another life, on the other side of the planet.

Weeks went by and he grew increasingly unstable from the intensity of his emotions and his longing for Lotta. He found it hard to concentrate, his drawings suffered and he withdrew socially.

One day, he decided to enter one of the main Delhi travel agencies he passed regularly. The girl behind the counter did not look pleased to see him standing before her, dressed in his washed-out T-shirt and jeans. How much for a ticket to Sweden? he asked. Why did he want to know? She had already decided he would never be able to afford it.

'Just tell me what the ticket costs!'

'Almost forty thousand rupees. Do you have that kind of money?'

No, he did not. He had been saving all summer, and yet his bank book showed the grand total of four thousand rupees. What good would all his hard work do? It would take him years.

Perhaps the prophecy had been wrong all along.

PK knew he could either sit around sinking further into despair, or he could make a move. Flying was out of the question: he couldn't afford it. Four wheels? He didn't own a car. Then he remembered Bhim Singh and his journey across 120 countries by motorcycle. Two wheels and a motor? That might be the answer, but it was too expensive. There was another way, though, on two wheels, powered by grit, tenacity and... love.

The Long Journey

New Delhi – Panipat – Kurukshetra – Ludhiana – Amritsar

PK arrives in Kurukshetra in the late afternoon of the first day of his journey. He has been riding since dawn, and decides he has chewed through enough gravel for one day. He dismounts his lady's Raleigh, bought for sixty rupees. Half the price of the men's model. Sixty rupees was a reasonable price for someone like him, who normally struggled to pay for train tickets.

He is on his way to fulfill his astrological destiny. All he has with him is a sleeping bag, a blue windbreaker, an extra pair of trousers given to him by a Belgian postman whom he met in New Delhi, and a blue shirt Lotta had sewn and sent to him. She embroidered his initials on it in the shape of an easel.

He draws his fingers through his dusty hair, rough like bristles on a broom, and squats in the long afternoon shadows of the acacia trees on the outskirts of a small village. He looks out over the fields. The sun sets in the west, so he knows to make his way towards it. Or rather, north-west. But just how many miles he has ahead of him, he has no idea. He has no grasp of the distance, no knowledge of geography. He would struggle to point on a map to all the countries and cities he had heard named in the Indian

Coffee House these past few years.

Stories of the world's creation, the sky and the gods, these he knows better. Tales of the origins of life and its future destiny, even events from the dawn of human history. He recalls the tales of the *Mahabharata*, the book all Indian children are made to read at school, and the great battle between two families that took place here thousands of years ago, right where his bicycle is now resting against a tree, on the outskirts of Kurukshetra. It was a fierce and bitter feud over who would control the kingdom. His teacher at primary school used to read it aloud to them. He enjoys these stories, they are a part of him. In that sense, he is as Indian as it is possible to be.

He looks out over the fields where spears were thrown, swords wielded, blood spilled, and the gods summoned for counsel when doubts crept in. The *Mahabharata* is a book about just war. He recalls a scene in which Prince Arjuna, one of the fighters, pauses and asks the god Krishna for advice. Krishna's response is so long and thorough, it is considered an independent poem. Go back to the field, Arjuna, because you are a warrior, and warriors fight.

It is advice that has been the cause of so much misery. If only they had asked the Buddha or the Jain prophet Mahavira, the world might be a different place.

In Hindi, the road he is travelling is called the Uttarapatha, meaning the northern route. In Urdu, it is known as Shah Rah-e-Azam. The Grand Trunk Road. The backbone of successive empires, a thoroughfare for kings as well as peasants and beggars, Greeks, Persians, Turks and Central Asians. For thousands of years people have taken this route between Afghanistan in the west and the Ganges and Brahmaputra rivers in the east.

Yes, its reputation is both impressive and ominous, but the road itself is not so very grand. Just as narrow and bumpy as every other thoroughfare in India. For two trucks to meet, the same courage and daredevil attitude are required, the same skirting of the asphalt. And along it, the same bellowing monsters of buckled metal slip out beyond the confines of the paved road, throwing up great tempests of sand and gravel that settle in a crackling film over all the other vehicles, pedestrians, grain threshers and ox carts. And bicycles.

Kurukshetra is one of many dreary villages along the way, home to roadside diners hidden behind rows of parked trucks so overfilled with cargo that they look like they might be toppled by the merest prod of a finger. Rickety wooden beds line up beside the trucks, mattresses consisting of nothing but braided rope. Here drivers sit and eat their dinner from metal lunch boxes.

He searches for something that could have borne witness to these ancient stories, but there is nothing old or remarkable about these fields. It's the same monotony of paddies and rows of wheat that have lined the road all the way from New Delhi.

India has been independent for thirty years, and the Prime Minister is trying to remake the country according to her version of Indian socialism. No longer should the people be fooled by superstition and myth. But as far as PK can tell, the legends have not left their mark, at least, not to the naked eye.

He has eighty US dollars sewn into his waistband and a few hundred rupees in his pocket. He must economize. This money has to last him all the way to Kabul, preferably longer. Who knows, maybe with a little luck he can make it all the way to Europe on just this measly sum.

Surely there are people along the way who can help him?

His address book is full of the names of travellers, vagabonds and hippies. Friends. They have described the special community of people bound together and strung out along the hippy trail. We help each other, they said. We share whatever we have. The thought of this big family keeps his nerves in check, even if there is a constant hum in his stomach. The road ahead will be difficult. But he wants it to be difficult, a struggle before a triumph. He wants the tension to drum a beat inside him. It will all work out.

He understands that he must be patient. Save your strength, he tells himself. Sure, he would like to be in Sweden tomorrow. But in the larger scheme of things, he will reach his destination soon. Assuming he makes it that far.

Looking out over the fields, he thinks of his father. Become an engineer, he said. Help build India in Nehru's vision... A memory bubbles up: Nehru and his daughter Indira arriving by helicopter and landing on a beach on the outskirts of Athmallik, there to inaugurate the construction of a new hydroelectric dam on the Mahanadi River. A dot in the sky that grew and grew until it landed next to the buffaloes and cows with their crooked, bony backs. He remembers the bafflement, that something moments before so small could suddenly become so large. 1964, it must have been.

Thousands of people gathered by the banks of the river to catch a glimpse of the Prime Minister. PK remembers Nehru placed his hand on his heart and looked to be in pain. A few weeks later, the Prime Minister died. Perhaps it was no great surprise, the villagers said; the local goddess Binkej Devi must have cursed him. Damming the river was a serious violation of the sacred will of nature, and Nehru had received his punishment.

But PK did not subscribe to such nonsense. He was fourteen at the time and no longer believed everything his elders told him. People died because they got ill. They had been taught that in school.

But just because the world is not governed by gods and demons does not mean there is no cosmic plan. The power of the stars to rule our lives should not be underestimated.

Nehru also had a plan, but a national, not a cosmic one. India was to pursue material wealth and technological progress. Poverty could be eradicated and superstitions and gods were to be replaced by rational thought and science. The nation would put its faith in socialism rather than religion, in Marx and Einstein rather than Vishnu and Shiva. Modernity must take precedence over tradition. If you had to choose, Nehru said, it was better to throw away the old in favour of the new.

And PK's father agreed. This was the best way to be rid of India's injustices. His father did not believe in the old superstitions; he too held firm to reason.

But PK had not become the son his father hoped for. Old injustices have to be replaced by something new and more egalitarian, PK agreed. If anyone hated the traditions espoused by the priests it was him, and yet he never really understood mathematics and science. He preferred to draw people rather than calculate equations. He had learnt it at school, and now, finally, he is escaping all that.

That first night, PK lies in his sleeping bag on the edge of a rice paddy. It is January, and northern Indian winters are cold and damp. He listens as dogs bark and trucks thunder past along the narrow, bumpy road with the grand name. He recognises the smell of stagnant water and watches the breath of the drivers caught in the streetlights. He shivers, zips the sleeping bag around his chin and closes his eyes.

He shuts out the sound of the crickets in the grassy ditch and thinks of Lotta. She knows he is coming. He wrote to tell her about his plan. She replied that if anyone knew the route between India and Europe, it was her.

It was an adventure to drive the VW van all the way to

India and back, and it will be a tough journey for you, she wrote.

Setbacks are often accompanied by crying. As are stories of the humiliation and oppression of others by those in power, or with money and status. PK is known for being governed by his strong emotions. Moments of joy and laughter are often followed by tears. His friends are more balanced and controlled. He envies them. He is unable to regulate his emotions so well.

Anger seizes him sometimes too. He fights them in his daydreams, all the people who have ever humiliated him. But the desire for revenge has softened. More often it is grief that agitates him these days.

He has arrived in Amritsar. But in his diary he writes:

> A week has passed since I was stopped in Kurukshetra. Now my Raleigh and the Grand Trunk Road have taken me to the holy city of the Sikhs with the golden temple. But unfortunately it seems that my adventure is over. I'm going to go see the golden domes and the nectar pond now, then eat dinner in the dining room of the temple given out for free to the poor before starting my ride back to New Delhi. So much for that dream.

Once again, joy has given way to despair. Tears flood his cheeks as a feeling of hopelessness overwhelms him. How can he continue his journey? He is going to have to stop, already. Yesterday, he reached the border with Pakistan. At first, the border guards had refused to let him in. No Indians allowed, they said. Not under any circumstances. They tossed his passport back at him and told him to turn around. But he took out some of the drawings he had made and showed them to the police. He could draw portraits of them, he suggested. Reluctantly, they agreed, and he took out paper and a piece of charcoal. He talked as he drew, telling them about the woman he loved and the country he was going to make his home. Their expressions grew ever more curious, and they began to relax.

It was a great story, and as soon as they saw their grim faces appear on the paper, they smiled. All severity was blown away. Just as he had hoped. It usually worked. To be drawn is to be seen at your best, to be flattered, and it softened even the thickest of skins most of the time.

'Okay, we'll let you ride through our country,' one of the Pakistani officers said.

'Are you sure we can do that?' another countered in Urdu, a language of which PK had passing knowledge.

'Yes, yes, what does it matter? He looks like a kind soul.'

They turned to PK and the man who seemed to be second in command said politely: 'On you go, sir!'

They opened the bar and he rode into Pakistan.

Half an hour later, he swung his bicycle into a leaky wooden shed with charpoys and glossy painted tables. He got down, and feeling pleased with himself, approached a man with a bare head and sullen countenance who sat in the shade of the jute awning, next to a cabinet of bulbous sweets clouded in a swarm of flies.

He ordered a huge plate of chicken biryani, and gulped down his first meal across the border, sitting on the edge of a charpoy.

He burped, washed his hands, and filled his canteen. Then, just as he mounted his bicycle to continue on, a police jeep swung into the yard in front of him.

'Passport, passport!' shouted one of the officers as he jumped out of the rolling vehicle.

PK pulled out his green passport with the King Ashoka lion on the cover, *Bharat Ganarajya* written in golden

Devanagari script and *Republic of India* in English. They flipped through its pages, from back to front and vice versa, before closing it and turning it upside down. They shook their heads.

The police then pointed to the bike and then to the jeep. PK understood what was being said. They threw the bike on the roof, told him to take a seat in the back, and proceeded to drive him to the border crossing.

All he had to do was ride the fifty kilometres back to Amritsar in India.

If the road to the future had already been determined, it was turning out to be peppered with pitfalls, thought PK, as if some higher power had decided that paradise could only be reached after first conquering seven earthly trials.

He sits on the hostel bed and watches the sun go down behind the rooftops, listening to the cries from the minarets drowning out the crows in the banyan trees. Hope has stirred in him again. His luck has returned.

That morning, he caught sight of a familiar face in the crowd at Guru Bazaar. It was Mr Jain! He worked in the Ministry of Information in Delhi. They had first met a few years before, and it turned out he was also a friend of PK's older brother. And here they were, bumping into each other in Amritsar.

As the melancholy sound of the minarets chases the darkness into his hostel dormitory, he feels fortunate to know such an educated, high-ranking man.

But he should have met him the day before yesterday. Then he would have dispelled some of PK's misconceptions. For example, that PK would be able to enter Pakistan, when Indian citizens were blanket forbidden, even when long-haired, pot-smoking hippies from America and England were welcomed with open arms into the Islamic Republic.

He knew he would need a visa for the Shah's Iran. But to Pakistan? India and Pakistan, two countries that were once one, that shared virtually the same culture, food and language, the same customs. Why was there even a border at all? But he should have known. He is ashamed by his ignorance. The conflict between India and Pakistan filled the papers daily: how could he have missed it?

But in Guru Bazaar that morning, Mr Jain had felt sorry for PK and announced that he wanted to buy him a plane ticket so that he could fly to Kabul without having to cycle through Pakistan. Fly high above the border police and all the earthly problems below.

'On me,' he said. It was the least he could do. 'You're not just anyone, after all. I've read about you in the newspaper.'

PK bowed deeply, shook his hand, knelt down and touched the man's feet. His lucky cobra, the snake that had been protecting him since he was born, had come to his aid again.

He meets a German hippy at the hostel and shows him the flight ticket. The German is on his way back to Europe with his wife. They are driving a minibus furnished with beds and a small kitchen.

'Okay, Picasso, we'll take your bike to Kabul on the roof of our van.'

They give him a cloth pouch to hang around his neck. 'To keep your passport safe,' he explains.

Now PK looks almost like all the Germans and other Europeans he has been meeting these last few years. A backpacker, one of the gang out on the hippy trail.

The engines roar. He is pressed into the back of his seat, feels a tickle in his stomach. Later, he would reflect on the moment in his diary:

> I look down at Earth from the aircraft and am filled with what I see, the snow-capped mountains, the arid steppes, the green fields; they are all larger and more true than my own life. Everyday problems seem petty from this height, the possibilities are endless and life is as wide as the sky. Worries are nothing but dots on a map.

Through the aeroplane window he looks down on empty cities, pavements with no people, roads with no cars.

'Up in the sky, it is difficult to make out the details down on Earth,' he writes. 'This is the first time I travel with a flying machine. I travel far away never to return. I can still not really believe it, but it looks like the prophecy came true.'

Amritsar – Kabul (almost) – Amritsar (again) – Kabul (finally)

Something is wrong. Just as they were about to land in Kabul, the plane started climbing and now they are circling the airport. Nervous, PK gazes out at the brown carpet scored with a grid of roads below. They go even higher and then start flying straight. The shaking ceases and is replaced by an otherworldly murmur. No one says anything over the speakers. After an hour, they are ready for landing and start their descent again.

As he looks out, he sees that they are back in Amritsar. There has been no explanation, and he is too scared to ask. Maybe the weather was too bad in Kabul? Maybe there was a hole in the runway?

He is back in India. Again.

But this time, he does not feel hopeless. They are put up in a luxury hotel at the airline's expense and given tickets to eat at the gourmet buffet several times a day. The Air India staff make an appearance and promise that flights to Kabul will resume the next day. And he is not disappointed. The next morning his journey restarts, and finally, he lands in Kabul.

The shuttle bus drives along empty boulevards towards the city centre. The roads are edged by trees that have lost their leaves. There is so little traffic in contrast to back home in India. Not that same urban crush. Light grey mountains rest on the horizon, standing against a crisp blue sky.

His mind returns again to Lotta as he watches Kabul slip past the window. This time last year, they were standing together at the railway station in Delhi, about to say goodbye. She was taking the train to Amritsar to meet up with her friends, where they were waiting with the VW van. She was bound for Europe, he was stuck in India. A thick voice came over the tannoy: *Two Nine Zero Four Golden Temple Mail bound for Amritsar is at platform number one.* The stationmaster rang the bell and blew his whistle, the signal at the end of the platform went from red to green and steam from the engine blasted up high above them.

'It sounds like a bomb going off,' Lotta said, and kissed him one last time before climbing onto the train.

'Yes,' PK laughed, not yet shattered by his grief.

She hung in the doorway as the train started to roll. He intertwined his left hand in her right, pressed his cheek against hers, and walked quickly as the creaking carriages gradually accelerated. He was so distracted by the softness of her hand and cheek that he did not see the rapidly approaching fence at the end of the platform. Their grand farewell ended as the metal poles struck against his chest, and he fell over. He screamed in pain, scrambled onto all fours, and watched the train disappear as his tears spotted the cracked cement beneath his hands and knees.

The train was gone. Lotta was gone. His future had been ripped from him and was disappearing into the distance.

He cried all the way from the station to the usually crowded street bazaar at Chandni Chowk, now desolate at this hour, just before midnight. He walked under Tilak Bridge and passed Delhi's old dilapidated fort and zoo, where they had walked only a few days earlier, holding hands. Lotta had been sitting beside him as he painted watercolours of the ruins and caged animals.

A pack of dogs, growing bolder now the sun had set, started rounding on him. They bared their teeth, barked, and drew close. But PK was not scared. Instead, he stopped, planted his feet, took a deep breath and yelled back at them.

'Eat me then, you mangy mutts! Eat me! I don't care!'

The dogs closed in, slowly. But something in their growling made PK imagine they were pondering what he had just said. They fell silent and wagged their tails. He opened the remains of his lunch, wrapped in a crumpled newspaper, and fed some of it to them. He sat among the dogs as they ate. All energy had gone from his body and he was numb, exhausted by the crying and the long walk. He lay down on the ground and the dogs rested their heads against his body.

That night, PK and five of Delhi's fiercest stray dogs huddled together on the pavement outside the city zoo. In his dreams, wild storm winds tore houses from their foundations and violent waves came crashing over him.

Before dawn he was awakened by the shrill screech of shock absorbers and the rattling of chassis as the first morning buses sped past. He sat up and looked around him, dazed. A cold wind had swept away the last of the previous day's heat. He felt chilled. The dogs, his blanket in the night, had disappeared.

He stumbled the last kilometres home to his rented room in Lodi Colony, where he was still living at the time. He stood in the doorway and looked in on the miserable scene inside: a worn bed, a dresser and a calendar depicting Lakshmi, the goddess of happiness and wellbeing, clinging to the mould-flecked wall.

As Lotta journeyed westward, PK waited for the merest sign of life from her. But his letters went unanswered.

Desperate, he sent telegrams to her home address: 'I'm worried by your long silence, please write to me when you get back home. PK.'

But Lotta was still on the road. Finally, a letter arrived from Maku in western Iran. 'My dear friend and companion,' it began. He read it quickly, starved of her words. The letter described the magic journey, the beauty of the snow-capped mountains on the border between Iran and

Turkey, the pale sun, the serenity of Maku, the transparent cold mist and 'the buzz of insects, nature's lullaby'.

She wished he could be with her, the letter concluded.

But then why did she leave?

Lotta's beautiful, poetic letters were unsettling; their mood somehow made him even sadder. Her long, engaged descriptions of places so completely alien carried almost a sinister tone.

He climbs down from the airport bus and starts walking through the throngs of men in ankle-length shirts and women with scarves wrapped around their heads, through the bazaars, and out onto the street with the funny name – Chicken Street, or Khosheh Murgha as the Kabul locals call it. There he finds a cheap-looking hostel.

All the wanderers gather here, with their long hair and their backpacks. They are dirty and bedraggled, as if they have been dragged through all the filthy streets of the world. His hostel is followed by another and another, countless English signs promising cheap accommodation and great service. Then comes a row of cafés and restaurants, menus also in English. He looks out along the street; for every Afghan in traditional dress he can see a white person in tight jeans and a T-shirt.

PK has been recording the trip so far in his diary with the intention of sending extracts to the newspapers in Orissa. He is confident they will be interested.

'Tens of thousands of Western hippies are heading East and West at any given time, whether they have been in India and are on their way home to Europe or vice versa,' PK writes. The cafés of Chicken Street are abuzz with stories of the road to Kandahar, where to stay in Herat, the best coffee shops in Mashhad, the top bargains in the markets of Istanbul and how to cope with the traffic chaos in Tehran. A Frenchman explains the itinerary to PK as they drink tea.

'The hippy trail,' he clarifies, 'isn't one single road, but in fact many that interlock.'

PK shares a room with four Europeans. It feels like they belong together. Everyone helps each other. He has met several of the other guests before in New Delhi.

'Hey, PK!' he hears people call out on the street, from cafés, in bazaars.

He hugs them, drinks cup after cup of tea, tells them what he's been up to and where he's going and listens to their stories in return. He asks about their upset stomachs, while they tell him how brave he is and how they wish him well on his long journey.

Some of the European girls wear shorts. The Afghan men stare so they do not see where they are going, colliding with each other on street corners. A Swedish girl he met several times in India walks towards him in thin balloon pants with bells around her feet. She is a thrilling sight for the local men, as she tinkles past like a tambourine. The men laugh and cast their eyes up to the heavens.

He is reluctant to rip open the seam in his trousers and start on the eighty dollars he has stashed. He is saving them. So he goes to give blood, as it is well paid. And he sits in the teahouses drawing people. It always works. People are curious, approach him, start asking questions, and are delighted when they see the results. It looks just like him! They laugh, point and shake his hand. They want to be drawn too, when he is done. And they pay handsomely.

The editor from *The Kabul Times* is impressed. He wants to see the other drawings leaning against the cement wall under the coffee table. PK shows him Afghan tribal women with their heavy silver jewellery and nose rings, as well as bearded Bedouin riding camels. The editor says he wants to interview him.

'Of course,' PK replies. He is used to journalists and knows the importance of publicity for a struggling artist.

The interview appears a few days later. The picture shows PK holding up one of his paintings of an emaciated black woman breastfeeding her equally starved child next to a white statue of the Virgin Mary and plump baby Jesus. *Faces fascinate me, says Indian portraitist*. The text is both courteous and admiring in tone:

> Pradyumna Kumar Mahanandia was the unusual caller at *The Kabul Times* offices last week. On his way to a round the world tour, the young portraitist from India came to Kabul recently on a fortnight visit.
>
> 'Faces fascinate me more than anything else. They attract me, vex me, provoke me,' says the soft-spoken, unassuming Mahanandia. His strongest desire is to paint human tragedy bringing out the inequality of one being and another. 'No matter rich or poor, all are starving for something or other,' he says.
>
> He earns a living from making sketches. 'I want to specialize in portraits and miniatures. Sketching is just a side business to keep myself going,' he added.
>
> 'To make his living is as important for the artist as to pursue his art,' says Mahanandia and is very emphatic about it...

PK laughs. Did he really say that? Yes, probably. He continues reading:

> It is the first time that the young Indian artist has visited Kabul and he is overwhelmed with the natural beauty of the place. He has met a number of artists in Kabul and seems quite impressed by their talents and works.
>
> Mahanandia began school as a science student but soon proved a flop and instead took up studies in art, which he had been practising since the age of three...
>
> Mahanandia observes: 'Few people are willing to invest money in a landscape or in a modern painting, but no one minds spending a few pennies on a self-portrait. Everyone has an egotistic streak in him that makes him want to see himself on paper. It is a perfect combination for a needy man.'

The article attracts attention. People on the street turn around and point; some come up and say hello. The journalist returns to PK's hostel and tells him that the editorial board has decided to exhibit some of his drawings in the newspaper canteen.

PK finishes hanging his paintings and steps back, looking pleased with the results. The journalists gather and examine his work. They seem interested, he thinks. The editor buys several of his drawings. The money is good. Very good.

Now, he has enough to last him all the way to Europe.

He has already received his bicycle from the German couple who drove it on their van from Amritsar. It is parked outside the hostel, but the chain is sluggish and squeaky, so he decides to spend some of his freshly earned cash on a new bike from one of the workshops on Chicken

Street. He trades in his Raleigh and pays the difference.

The new bike is red.

PK stays two weeks in Kabul, meeting old friends and gaining new ones. He may be an unusual figure among the backpacker community, with his dark brown complexion, but somehow, he feels included in their gang. Why have they accepted him? Because despite initial differences, he wears the same clothes as them, has grown his hair and speaks good English. But above all, he is an artist: the sketchbook and pencils are his entry ticket into the white world of the hippies. He is a mascot, a bohemian splash of colour in a world of rebellious middle-class Westerners.

He sits on a small stool, a sketchbook on the table and pens in his shirt pocket, and is bought tea, chicken, rice and yogurt. Evening after evening is spent like this, in his favourite restaurant, talking to other travellers and occasionally drawing them, or Afghans passing on the street outside.

They are so free, the backpackers. Anything is possible while in their company, everything is open for discussion and everyone is entitled to their opinion. It is so unlike back home in India, where people are constantly trying to work out where you are from and who your parents are. These vagabonds of Chicken Street are becoming his new family. They are his brothers and sisters, friends through thick and thin, not bound by tradition or prejudice. He learns that they have left home in search of something deeper than the materialism of where they come from.

'Factories operate at capacity, everyone has jobs, we all have enough to eat and we are surrounded by stuff we don't really need,' an American backpacker tells PK as they sit opposite each other, drinking tea.

His name is Chris and he comes from California. The

restlessness he embodies started in the detached houses of the suburbs and grew into a fury over an unjust war in Vietnam. Young people, just like PK's new friends in Kabul, gathered in parks to protest the injustices of the existing world order.

'Love won out there,' explains Chris. 'And then it conquered the city, took over the country, ended the war, and began to spread right across the rest of the world. That's why we're here now,' Chris continues, as they sit surrounded by other Westerners in Indian cotton trousers and brightly coloured T-shirts. 'Look around you. What you see is the embodiment of love. People like you and I can end all the hatred of the world. We are an army of deserters. We put flowers in the barrels of our guns. Yesterday America, Kabul today, tomorrow India and the rest of the world,' he announces confidently.

PK recalls how hatred and mistrust still linger in India, despite Mahatma Gandhi's speeches preaching non-violence. His home country may need more love pilgrims. Indians who talk about love, such as the Brahmins, are false prophets. They do not know what love is. If the Brahmins really understood the meaning of the word, PK thinks to himself, then they would never treat untouchables like me the way they do. But hippies? They seem to practise what they preach.

He sits on the bed in his hostel and writes letters to Lotta. The minarets call out for evening prayer.

'From my window I can see mountains covered with snow,' he writes. 'But the cold weather doesn't affect me. My heart feels warm because of the love from you, forever. Your love makes me joyful, always.'

Despite his longing to see Lotta, he is reluctant to continue his bicycle trip. He wants to rest first, meet other travellers and get more tips about the best route to take. And he needs a visa for Iran and that takes time, they say. But he has not even made the journey across the city to the Iranian Embassy to fill out the application. He was refused once in New Delhi, and he dreads another no in Kabul. What will he do then? Ride his bike through the Soviet Union? Was that even possible?

A young Australian woman by the name of Sara is also staying at the same hostel. They spend several afternoons together, sitting on the wooden chairs in the lobby, chatting about their travels, India and life in general. The sounds of Kabul's minarets bounce along the narrow alleys between the houses. Twilight descends and the shops on Chicken Street pull down their steel shutters for the night. And they talk for hours, forgetting to go out and eat while restaurants are still open. By the time they realize they are hungry, it is too late. The people of Kabul go to bed early, and now everything is closed. But what does it matter when there is so much to talk about?

'The West is doomed; the future belongs to Asia,' Sara says.

'For me it's the opposite. My future lies in the West,' PK replies.

And yet they have so much in common.

Sara takes him to a nightclub. It is his first time. She wears a yellow dress with a red spiral batik pattern, he wears the blue flared trousers the Belgian gave him in New Delhi and the shirt Lotta embroidered with his initials. Everyone looks at them. A dark guy with wild, tousled hair and a light-skinned girl. To the Afghans, they are an exotic couple. Maybe even sinful. They have never seen anything like it. He recognizes their envious, covetous glances. They dance to 'Yes Sir, I Can Boogie', 'Rivers of Babylon' and 'Dark Lady'. Just as the rich tones of Marvin Gaye come through the speakers, a man in a suit and neatly done-up tie approaches. He looks PK in the eye.

'May I dance with your girl?' he asks.

My girl?

'She's not my girlfriend. We're just friends,' PK replies. The man is polite. Sara looks at PK and nods. So he goes and sits down by himself at a table next to the dancefloor while Sara follows the man into the depths of the pulsating throng.

They dance and PK watches. As the evening draws to an end and the nightclub is about to close, Sara comes to his table. Her dance partner is Iranian and he wants her to go home with him. He works at the Iranian Embassy and owns a nice apartment in Kabul.

Who is PK to object? She is allowed to do what she wants. They are not married, they are not even together. But he is concerned for her, tells her to be careful, to be on her guard.

PK walks alone under the stars, back to Chicken Street.

Sara will be back at the hotel the next morning and they will continue their conversation then.

Sara comes running into the lobby, where PK is reading *The Kabul Times*.

'Come on, hurry up!' she cries. 'The Iranian works in the embassy's visa section. They're going to get you a visa, but you have to come now.'

Sara and PK are sitting in the back of a car with diplomatic plates and tinted windows, feeling important. They are usually nomads, living and travelling by simple, modest means. But now they feel like VIPs on a state visit.

In the car, Sara tells PK that she spent the night putting pressure on the Iranian to get him the visa. Sara is too kind, PK thinks.

They go to the embassy officer's apartment in the outskirts of Kabul. The driver parks the car, asks them to wait and goes in with PK's passport. He returns quickly, smiling, and hands the passport back to PK, who flips through to find the long-awaited visa.

But the stamp in his passport grants him only fifteen days' transit.

I'll have to ride fast, he thinks.

Kabul – Sheykhabad – Ghazni – Daman – Kandahar

He is travelling ever further away, but at the same time, he is on his way home. Fate has spoken. The prophecy was correct.

In his mother's youth, while PK was tucked up inside her womb, she had dreamed of a baby sitting on a cloud, drifting away. He is not sitting on a cloud now exactly, rather the new red bike he bought in Kabul, on his way south towards Kandahar. Grey mountains daubed with patches of snow stand out against the red of the horizon. He is surrounded by a lunar vista, the desert reaching out towards the sunset. The sky is blue, the air crisp and clear, the Russian-built concrete road ashen, straight and smooth. It beats a rhythm every time he cycles over the joints. Thump, thump, thump. Monotonous and unnerving, it makes him dizzy.

He watches his shadow. The further the sun rises in the sky, the shorter it becomes, but it never leaves him. It is his constant companion, day after day.

I am not alone, the shadow is my friend. It never lets me down.

He is spurred on faster as his shadow grows longer. He is not standing still, even though the landscape feels uninterrupted and unchanging. The length of his shadow tells him he is making progress.

He stops to rest. All is strangely silent: he can hear no birds, no insects, no trucks, no rustling of trees. There are no trees here. Afghanistan is desolate, just gravel and stone. A world on mute, where only the wind occasionally speaks to break the silence. The heat wobbles above the tectonic plates of cement. This place is so different, it makes him wonder: have I landed on another planet? He feels lonely but it does not bother him. Rather, it gives him peace. Is this how it feels to leave my homeland?

Suddenly, he spots a small group of Afghans standing by the side of the road. They are talking loudly, sound indignant, outraged even. There, halfway down the ditch, two cars lie crumpled in a heap, with broken windshields and dented hoods. He approaches and the smell of petrol fills his nostrils. Then he sees her. A girl, lying on a woollen blanket in the gravel. She is still conscious, but looks battered. Blood is pouring from her mouth and her forehead is covered in wounds. He bends down and looks at her. He asks her name and where she comes from. But she cannot speak. Her teeth have been knocked out and her lips are cut. He looks at her clothes and realises she too is a backpacker. She is white. A European heading home after an Indian adventure, perhaps. A strong feeling comes over him; he must help her. He must repay the kindness. She is one of his new family, the community of vagabonds, and you cannot leave a sister in need.

They hitch a ride on a truck back to Kabul. The bike, his bag and the white girl's rucksack and cotton bag with the Devanagari print have been thrown into the open cargo. The driver hums an Afghan song PK does not understand.

He is travelling back the way he came, the last two days of cycling will have been in vain, and yet he feels strangely elated. The twilight sun has turned the usually tough, brownish-grey desert peachy warm and silky soft. The truck's rumbling engine is also singing, 'Onward, onward,' even though he is actually travelling backward, backward, and the driver's song seems, in some mysterious way, to be whispering promises to him. He closes his eyes and imagines his own translation to the Pashtun lyrics: 'Be whatever you want, anyone you want. Be your own fate, make your own future.'

Lulled by the monotony of the landscape, he suddenly sees his mother sitting beside him in the truck. She is warm and soft. He feels her presence and hears her steady breathing. Her phantom hand brushes against his right side and he feels tears of happiness, sadness and longing pool in his eyes. If she had still been alive he might never have started this journey. Now there is nothing keeping him in India, only forces pulling him away.

He turns his head towards the feeling. Of course, there is no dark, round, safe mother, but instead a much leaner young girl. Yet her bruises remind him of the lines and dots tattooed on his mother's cheeks, forearms and hands.

The hospital in Kabul confirms that not only has the young woman lost nearly all her teeth, but she is suffering from a serious concussion. She still has trouble talking and the sores make it painful for her to move her mouth. She writes him a note instead. *My name is Linnea*, it says. *Please stay with me!* she adds.

'I will, I promise,' PK responds. 'Where were you going?'

Home, she writes.

'Where's that?'

Vienna.

'You'll probably have to wait, you can't go home all bruised like this.'

But Linnea wants to leave as soon as possible. She is back on her feet after two days and is discharged from the hospital. He goes with her to the Austrian Embassy and they organize a plane ticket back to Vienna. She had been driving her own car when the accident occurred, but it was totalled and she is in no condition to drive.

He goes with Linnea to the airport and takes in the details of her face before it is time to part. She smiles her toothless smile and writes one final note: *See you soon!* And then she locks him in a long, warm embrace.

He does not feel particularly noble or good as he rides the bus back to Chicken Street and to the same budget hostel he left only days before. He expects no chorus to sing his praises. The choice to help Linnea was an obvious one. How could he expect help if he refused to give it to others? Emotions can be rational sometimes. Cause and effect. Everything is connected. It was as simple as that.

And he will need help, he knows that. He does not even know if he is supposed to turn left or right or keep going straight ahead once he gets to Kandahar.

Three days later, PK is heading south on the wide cement road between Kabul and Kandahar for the second time. Now he hopes that he has left Chicken Street and the backpacker cafés of Kabul for good, that he is on his own again. He and his red Hero bike. It rides well, but after the first day's cycling he has a headache from pounding over the seams between the cement plates of the road. How is he going to cope all the way to Kandahar? His thoughts hover in daydreams as his exhausted body works on auto-pilot. Only Lotta's letters, the words she always uses, drum in his chest. My dearest, my dearest, my dearest.

Kandahar

PK meets another Belgian in one of the Kandahar's luxury hotels. PK tells him that he has come from Kabul and is on his way to Borås. On a bike.

'You've cycled all the way from Kabul?' the Belgian asks.

'Do you think that's far?' PK answers with a question.

'Yes, it's five hundred kilometres. That's a long way by bike. And you're going to ride several thousand kilometres further to...? What was it called? Borås? Where's that? In... Switzerland?'

'Yes.'

'Are you sure?'

'Yes, Borås is in Switzerland,' PK says.

The Belgian looks at him questioningly.

'Are you sure?'

'One hundred per cent.'

But the Belgian is not so certain. PK shows him Lotta's letter.

He reads, then takes out a map. 'Here!' he says after a while and points to a spot on the paper. 'This is Borås.'

'Yes. In Switzerland, no?'

'No, Sweden,' says the Belgian and laughs.

'You pronounce it a little differently, but aren't they the same place?'

'They are two different countries,' the Belgian says firmly.

Now it is PK's turn to look sceptical. 'Are you sure?'

The Belgian shows him on the map. He's right. How stupid could he be? She told him she was Swedish. But he had thought Swedes lived in a country called Switzerland. And then he remembers her words:

'No, we don't make watches in my country. My city is famous for weaving fabric.'

He is thoroughly embarrassed, and puts it down to never having examined such a detailed map before. The Belgian's had every road marked and labelled with a number, and it was overlaid with a grid that gave exact latitudes and longitudes. PK had only ever read those crude atlases for sale in the markets of India. They were completely useless for a cyclist wanting to find his way between New Delhi and Borås. He had got this far by asking.

At least he is going in the right direction.

'Aren't I?'

'Yes,' the Belgian confirms.

But PK cannot just blame bad maps.

He had most definitely believed that the inhabitants of Switzerland called themselves Swedes and anything from Switzerland was Swedish. But no, Swedish people came from Sweden. But why come up with two such similar sounding names? It was a recipe for confusion.

Maybe this whole plan was a stupid mistake. How could he not even know where he was going? It was more hopeless than he had first thought.

'How much further is Sweden from Switzerland?' he asks the Belgian.

'About one and a half thousand kilometres more,' he replies.

PK goes to the post office and asks to look through the cardboard box of poste restante. A light blue aerogram is waiting for him. Rejoicing, he opens it.

'My dearest PK...'

He drinks in her words like a thirsty camel drinks water.

> Time is almost 9.30 p.m. I've been horse
> riding continuously for six hours. PK, to be

> honest, I'm a bit worried to learn about your plans to go by road all alone from India. We were four adults travelling together, when something happened to us or the car we could always defence each other, but if you go on your own, who will help to defence you when your self-defence isn't enough?

He thinks about her warning. He should be travelling with someone. The route from India to Europe is no game, especially not for the solo traveller. She's right. But he does not have anyone to do the journey with, that is the problem. He has only his sleeping bag and his bike for companionship. But he is sure it will work out. He has his easel, a smile and an ability to make friends even among his worst critics.

And yet, he wants the trip to be tough. It should not come too easy. The road to Lotta must be paved with adversity. Only then will it feel authentic. Aches from the saddle, exhaustion every time he puts his bicycle down in the afternoon, relief to fill his belly with food and lay his body in a hammock, to stretch his legs, dispel negative thoughts and fight to keep the doubt and homesickness at bay.

It is too expensive to fly, but more than that, it would be too easy. That is how the rich travel, but not him. He is a drifter, a vagabond. So far, he has overcome all the obstacles put in his way. Sword in hand, Alexander the Great had made his way along the same route, admittedly in the opposite direction. But PK is travelling with a pencil. His battering ram.

'I understand that you have met many helpful people along the way. You are able to reach people with your paper and pencil. When I think about that, I'm not so worried,' writes Lotta.

PK decides to keep focused on the end goal. Soon, we will be reunited.

Kandahar – Delaram

Afghanistan feels both modern and ancient at the same time. The roads are neat and straight, something he has never seen in India before. Even the Grand Trunk Road is just rubble compared to this, he thinks. But Afghanistan is a strange place. He sees almost only men out on the streets, and the women who do venture out are hidden underneath a thick layer of material.

As is his way, he quickly makes new friends. It comes naturally to him; he does not need to think about it. He jokes with the people he meets. It always breaks the ice; a laugh bridges language and cultural differences. And then he draws them. He works fast, first just a sketch, which he shows them. It never fails. Even policemen and soldiers break out in smiles when they see his drawings.

He is invited home by one of the head doctors at Kandahar hospital. He has seen PK's portraits on the streets of the city and wants him to draw one of his four wives.

'Of course!' PK responds, and cycles there the following day with a stick of charcoal, a bundle of pencils and a pad of paper in a bag dangling from the handlebars.

The doctor's house is palatial. He must be immensely rich, PK thinks as the butler opens the door. He is let in and shown around by the doctor himself, who is at pains to explain that the furniture has been imported from Paris and no luxury is too much for him and his wives.

PK walks into a circular room crowned by an immense semi-circular sofa. This is where the doctor's first, second and third wives are sitting. Their faces are uncovered, a rare sight in Afghanistan. Perhaps they only need to wear burqas when going outside, PK reflects. He greets them in turn, putting his hands together and bowing: 'Namaste.'

The three wives return the greeting with curious looks and mumbled hellos.

Then, a figure enters. A walking tent, but somewhere deep inside the burqa there is, PK assumes, a person. The doctor points to the fabric and he understands: this is his fourth wife, and PK will be drawing her.

PK is left alone in a side room, facing her. He is petrified, unable to bring himself to draw a piece of cloth. But then she starts talking. He is flabbergasted. The voice speaks perfect English with a clear American accent. If he closes his eyes he would have assumed she was an American tourist.

She removes the burqa. He is even more surprised. She is wearing a tight T-shirt, jeans and high-heeled shoes. A thick layer of make-up has been painted on her face and the sweet smell of perfume hangs like a cloud around her. But she cannot be older than fifteen. She is beautiful, very beautiful even, in complete contrast to the dull, heavy fabric of her covering. But her age saddens him. He thinks of her husband, the head doctor. Sixty-four, wrinkled, bald and with a fat belly. The poor girl! What a miserable future!

His sorrow then turns to anger. These outdated traditions, polygamy and arranged marriages, they have to be stopped. Love cannot be planned and controlled. Love must be free. In the future, the people of Afghanistan and India must be able to choose for themselves who they will marry.

He tells himself that he is the happiest Indian in the world. Unlike the girl sitting opposite him, he took his chance and broke with tradition. But then the uncertainty of it all comes back to him. His separation from Lotta, the unbearable longing, the journey. Is he really happy?

At least the doctor's young wife knows her lot. What is he heading towards? Will he ever reach the remote town of Borås and be reunited with Lotta? And will he ever see his father and siblings again?

He is free, he is unburdened. But he is also driven to pedal every day until he almost collapses with exhaustion. In fact, he is also one of the loneliest Indians in the world. The anxiety is physical, a constant tingling sensation just below his lower left rib. The more he thinks about how vulnerable he really is, the more it eats at his sense of freedom and his hopes for future happiness. Maybe Lotta was right. This journey is far too dangerous to undertake alone.

The girl's husband keeps popping his head in, asking when he will be done. He should really start now. But he cannot, his mind is spinning and he feels paralysed. Instead, he asks the beautiful fourth wife:

'Are you happy?'

'Yes, I'm happy,' she answers quickly.

'But your husband, do you really love him?'

'Yes.'

'In your heart?'

'I really love him.'

'But do you think he loves you?'

'Yes.'

'But he has three other wives.'

'He loves me most.'

'How do you know that?'

'I get whatever I want. I just have to point. If I want a new perfume from Paris, he makes a call and then a week later it arrives in the mail.'

'But wouldn't it be better to marry a boy your own age?'

'I don't trust men my age, they say all kinds of pretty things, tell you they love you, but they never keep their promises.'

She sounds brainwashed, he thinks, but he does not say this.

'He only sleeps with me, not the other three,' she says.

PK turns to the work at hand. And yet he keeps thinking about her life choices. Maybe she sees something he cannot. He thinks of a story his mother used to tell him as a boy about six blind men and their encounter with an elephant. The first man approaches the elephant and grabs hold of one of the animal's legs. 'Ah, the elephant is a tree, this is the trunk,' he says.

The next blind man goes round the back and takes hold of the tail. 'You fool, the elephant is a kind of rope.'

The third blind man stretches out his hands and feels the trunk. 'You're both wrong. The elephant is a type of snake.'

The fourth man reaches for the tusks. 'What nonsense. The elephant is a kind of spear.'

The fifth man grabs the elephant's ear. 'No, no, the elephant is a type of fan for when the weather gets hot.'

Finally, the last blind man approaches the belly. 'You are all wrong. The elephant is a wall.'

The six blind men turn to the elephant keeper.

'Which of us is right?' they ask.

'You are all right, and you are all wrong,' says the elephant keeper.

We're both blind, the doctor's wife and I, PK reflects. We only see and understand what is right in front of us.

The next morning, he starts out west again. He has the address of the rich man's friend, also a doctor, who lives in Delaram, halfway to Herat.

This friend receives him warmly at the city border, invites him to his home and offers him tea. As they sit drinking, the doctor reaches under his bed.

'Do you want a look?' asks the doctor, still a bachelor, and passes PK a bundle of American *Playboy* magazines.

PK flips through them and gives them back. No wonder Afghan men have to resort to these kinds of magazines when all the women in their country are hidden from view. The bare breasts are like the pieces of an elephant's body, he thinks. Surely the young doctor would be more satisfied with a real woman?

He can feel the tiredness come, the nagging headache, the aching in his thigh muscles. He sips his tea and stares outside. But instead of Afghanistan, he sees his village by the river at the edge of the forest. The images still live in his memory.

The next day, he cycles on under a tall sky, a chill caressing his cheeks, his mind empty of thoughts.

Delaram – Herat – Islam Qala

After Delaram, the East–West A1 turns north towards Herat. This is the route everyone takes, and therefore the route PK takes. There is no real alternative. It is the main road for hippies and locals alike.

PK rides from dawn to dusk with just an hour's break for lunch. The same light grey concrete slabs with the irritating joins between them. The bike jumps with each seam. Not something the Russians thought about when they built the road, clearly. What was wrong with asphalt?

He does not worry too much about where he will sleep. Something always turns up. But of the hundreds of addresses in his notebook, none of them can be found along this road. The majority are in Europe. Yet, the people of rural Afghanistan are extremely hospitable, he is discovering. They invite him in for tea and food, and often offer him a bed to sleep in. Of course they can provide shelter for the night. He is welcomed without reservation. He does not even have to draw in exchange for something to eat.

He keeps pedalling, his eyes fixed on the horizon. He is overtaken by trucks loaded with hay, mattresses and goats heading west, and once or twice a day he meets an imaginatively painted bus full of Europeans heading east. He knows that most of them will be sitting in the cafés of Chicken Street within a week, and then outside the Indian Coffee House a few weeks after that, sharing tips and experiences from the road.

The budget hostel in Herat is one of the dirtiest he has ever stayed in. He lies in a bed with a base made of braided rope but with no mattress. His sleep is fitful and broken by nightmares. Horrible nightmares. Beggars approach him in groups, ten, twenty, thirty of them. Hands outstretched. He looks down at their calloused palms, raises his eyes and sees they have no heads. An army of headless beggars, closing in on him. Their demands are a hoarse whisper, but he can hear their threats clearly nonetheless.

The next morning, he wakes to the sun shining through a small opening above his head. He is sweaty and dirty; he has not washed in days. His body is sticky. His mouth is dry. The floor is gravelly and the painted concrete floor is flaking. *Rudolf was murdered in this bed*, has been rather ominously scrawled on the wall beside him. Who was Rudolf, how was he murdered, and by whom? His dreams are echoes of the images of famine and suffering he used to paint when he lived under the bridges of New Delhi.

The day is beginning, and he heads out onto the streets of Herat to make some money. He wants to add to the thick wad of notes stuffed into the cloth bag that hangs around his neck and in the hidden pockets sewn into his trousers. Then he will eat his fill and continue on west. Only once his pockets and stomach are satisfied will he think of Lotta.

But less than one hundred metres from the hotel, a car stops in front of him and a man jumps out from the passenger seat. He introduces himself and explains that he is an adviser to the district governor.

'Get in the car, please,' he says.

'Okay,' PK says.

'The governor has a PhD in political science, he is a very important and intelligent man,' explains the adviser in the back seat of the car as it zooms through Herat's narrow streets.

'We have noticed that you are offering your services as an artist. The governor wants a portrait.'

The governor lives in a grand house protected by fences and guards at the front entrance. PK greets the governor, who is waiting for them. He examines PK, squints. PK knows what this means. They sit down in the courtyard and PK works quickly. Before long his concentrated pencil marks have conjured away the squint. The governor is delighted.

'The best portrait I have ever seen,' he exclaims, and then asks if there is anything he can do for the Indian artist.

PK tells him his Afghan visa expired two weeks ago and that he will have problems when he reaches the border with Iran.

'No, you won't,' the governor replies confidently.

'No?'

'I will take care of it.'

Indeed, when PK shows the border police at Islam Qala his passport and the expired visa inside, they merely smile and wave him on.

Islam Qala – Taybad – Farhadgerd – Mashhad – Bojnurd – Azadshahr – Sari – Amol – Tehran

In Iran, he suffers setbacks. He sleeps for two nights by the side of the road, with nothing more than fruit in his belly. He has money in the cloth bag around his neck – that is not the problem – but he is too far from civilization to buy anything. From the border, he hitchhikes with a truck, but is dropped again after an hour. He continues to cycle, but he has ridden more days in a row than he really has the energy for, and his legs and bottom are so sore he can barely sit down in the saddle. He feels his ribs and knows he has lost weight. When he looks at his reflection, he sees a hippy staring back at him.

He decides to rest in a white beach pavilion in the small resort town of Sari, on the Caspian Sea. They sell ice cream here during the day, he thinks. Now it is night, the beach is deserted. He rolls out a sleeping bag, settles himself gently on the floor, careful not to hurt his backside. His stomach aches from hunger. He falls into an exhausted state half-way between wakefulness and sleep. The beach is so light, the sea so calm, the sky so blue. It is a beautiful place to drift away.

Every time he has sunk this far, been this close to rock bottom, something has happened to pull him back up again. As the sun rises over the pavilion the next morning, he rouses gently from his torpor. He would happily never open his eyes again. That is his first thought. He wants to remain on the edge a while longer, then plunge into the dreamless sleep of eternal darkness.

Just then, he hears laughter. He is woken properly and

opens his eyes. He is surrounded by ten girls lifting their veils and smiling at him. Such pleasant expressions on their sweet Persian faces, he thinks. They look as if they want to eat him. He sits up and reflexively reaches for his sketchbook to show them his drawings. It's the best way to communicate. It usually works.

But one of them speaks English.

'I'm an artist,' PK says.

They are not figments of his famished imagination. The girl tells him they are students from Tehran who have come to spend the day by the beach. They have brought a picnic. He flips through the sketchbook and tells them about his journey from India. They laugh and ply him with food. Bread, yogurt, dates and olives. Such a sweet feeling as they line his stomach.

He has ridden all the way from India, via Afghanistan's snow-topped mountains and through the Shah's Promised Land, on his way to Europe and the woman he loves. A murmur runs through his audience.

'How wonderful!' exclaims the English-speaking girl.

They give him food to pack in his backpack.

If there is one thing he has learned about life, it is that sometimes it pays to come close to the abyss.

After Sari, he feels lighter on his bike again. The villages arrive faster, he meets more people and is often invited into people's homes for food and shelter. Some Iranians are disparaging about the shoddy bike he bought in Afghanistan, so he buys a new one in a market he passes on the way.

Refreshed, excited, carrying a full bottle of water and with a newly oiled bike chain, he continues along Highway 79 towards Tehran, where he hopes a letter from Lotta will be waiting.

The spring sun warms his thighs during the afternoon while the evening chills his cheeks after dusk. He stops at teahouses, drinks and draws the other guests, and is thus invited home. He has not stayed one night in a hotel since Herat in Afghanistan.

Before he goes to sleep he thinks of Lotta. He is still confident she will welcome him with open arms. It has not occurred to him yet that she might have changed her mind or met another man. He is so convinced of the steadfastness of their love that doubt does not have a chance.

There was nothing keeping him in India now his mother was gone. Sure, he still had his father and brothers and sister in Orissa, and all his friends from art school and the Congress Party in Delhi, but he has only ever really loved his mother. And now Lotta. He cannot travel to Kalabati. Lotta, however, is waiting for him just beyond the horizon.

His mind obsesses over one thought for hours as he rides: he must be reunited with Lotta. It is either that or die. And this idea wipes away all fear. Whatever will be will be, it's best if I don't overthink it, he philosophizes as he pedals past villages and towns with names like Qaemshahr, Shirgah and Pol-e-Sefid.

He is being driven by emotion not rational thought, he knows that. He is listening to his heart, his gut. A bicycle trip this long is foolish. The dangers are many, the risk of major setbacks constant. Perhaps the plan is downright impossible. But it is only by refusing to think logically that he can continue on.

And yet so far no one he has met has told him the trip to Sweden is foolish. In fact, when PK tells people he is riding to Scandinavia, they react as if it is perfectly normal. The route is full of romantics like him. Tireless travellers. Cultural refugees. Seekers. Besides all the hippies, he also meets migrants; poor Asians on the way to wealthy Europe. With these companions, he shares the feeling that anything is possible.

Back in India, he was met with a different reaction. His

friends warned him not to undertake the journey. It's impossible, they said. Bicycles are for poor people. Bicycles are dangerous. Bicycles are slow. You can't. You'll never make it. You're going to die.

But how wrong they were.

So far he has not met a single unfriendly person. He has been lulled into a sense that everyone along the hippy trail is curious, positive, generous and kind. Maybe he could live his whole life in motion, he thinks, every day made up of first encounters with interesting people.

In Iran the hospitality continues. He sleeps less and less outside and after leaving the Caspian Sea, he is almost never alone or hungry. He receives water, dried fish, apples, oranges and dates along the way. He sleeps every night in a bed without having to pay a single rial. His ticket to the bountiful Promised Land is the fact that he is Indian.

'Oh, India,' they say. 'A very good country.'

'You think so?'

Until his recent death, the Indian President was a Muslim by the name of Fakhruddin Ali Ahmed. Iranian newspapers devoted pages to his obituary, the Muslim who reached the top in a Hindu country.

People repeat the same speech he has heard so many times since he crossed the border. So generous of the Hindus to make a Muslim president, they say. PK does not see it in terms of generosity. In truth, it was a way to appease the country's minorities, a clever gesture that involved no real sacrifice. The office of president was largely meaningless; the Prime Minister was really the one in charge.

But the Iranians are impressed nevertheless. Muslims in PK's country have the same rights as everyone else, they say. And yes, it is true, on paper at least. An old man tells him about the historian al-Biruni who travelled from Persia to India a thousand years ago. The Hindus told him

India was the most perfect country, with the most powerful kings, the finest religion and the most advanced science. To this old man, India shimmered in gold and silver.

Even if that was the case back then, the India of today is no paradise on earth, PK thinks to himself. The capital's slums reek. But he does not say so. He makes no objection. It is easier that way. He does not want to disappoint his hosts. Such illusions are the basis for an easy friendship.

In contrast, everything about Iran is rich and orderly; the change was noticeable as soon as he crossed the border. The Afghan border guards were dressed in dirty, worn uniforms, their border stations dilapidated. On the Iranian side, everything is new and clean, the people are better dressed and look healthier, the cars are modern, roadside stops are equipped with luxurious sofas and vending machines delivering cold, clean water for free. A border can make all the difference.

He rides west along the Caspian Sea and then south towards Tehran. Another, more southerly, road is actually closer, but the hippy buses usually take this one, and he does not dare deviate. As long as he stays on the hippy trail, he will meet other travellers whom he can draw, and therefore continue to make money. They are also generous with their advice and offer assistance when he gets into trouble.

He needs rest. By now he has taken on the appearance of a wandering holy man, his hair is matted and his body smeared with dirt. He rents a tent at a camping ground outside Mashhad and unpacks everything he has, peels off his filthy clothes and scrubs them with a bar of soap. He shaves, trims his nasal hair, lathers up and lets the hot water wash over him. It has been a long time since he felt this clean.

A small lake occupies the middle of the campsite, alongside the grave of a famous Iranian poet. A mosque sits nestled on an island in the middle of the water, illuminated by coloured lights once dusk falls. In the evenings, people come from the city to enjoy the tranquillity and visit these sites of pilgrimage. They bring food and blankets and picnic until late.

PK understands that this is a golden opportunity. He sets up his easel and gets his sign translated into Persian. Then he sits and waits.

By the first day, a queue has already formed. He draws all evening and the next, earning himself good money. Iranians are rich. PK notices they arrive in big, expensive cars.

He puts no price on his sign. When people ask how much, he answers only, 'Whatever you think it's worth.'

Iranians gladly pay five, sometimes even ten times more for a portrait than he is accustomed to, in addition to giving him food, fruit, tea and rose water.

Iran has been so welcoming, but now his thoughts turn to the road ahead, and Europe. He has heard so many warnings that doubt has begun to creep in; he worries that things might not continue as smoothly once he makes it out of Asia and into this new continent.

Tehran – Qazvin

But first comes Tehran, and it's chaos. Cars are everywhere, jostling for space in the narrow streets with trucks, buses, carts loaded with goods, as well as cyclists trying not to get crushed, their faces wrapped in shawls to avoid swallowing too much dust and grit.

PK adjusts his backside on the saddle and continues pedalling hard, signalling several times with an extra large horn that he has mounted on the handlebar to make himself heard in the traffic. The horn emits a loud, penetrating sound. He notices how the motorcyclists turn their heads to see who, or what, is making the noise. It is his only weapon against the thundering trucks.

Despite the cacophony around him, he is reflecting on the person he has become, who he used to be and the person he might turn into once he arrives in Sweden. He pedals to shut out any other thoughts.

He is a hybrid. Sometimes he thinks all cultures and beliefs coexist inside him.

He is one of India's oppressed indigenous people, a symbol for the injustices of the caste system, and at the same time a man on his way out into the world. He is a poor village boy and a successful city man. He owns nothing and everything at once. He is knowledgeable about art history, romanticism and the colours of Turner's English landscapes, and yet he hardly knows where Sweden is. Already, he has had a more eventful life than he ever dreamed possible as a child, yet he still feels inexperienced, believes literally what people tell him and is curious to learn new things. He has attempted suicide three times, almost starved to death, and yet he is a lighthearted and, dare he say it, happy human being. He believes in destiny and tradition, but also in the liberty that comes from rejecting such ideas.

I am a chameleon. I can blend in anywhere. I can be an outcast among outcasts, important among important people.

But he knows his limitations. He has never demanded to be noticed, he does not know how to affect others or his surroundings.

In Tehran, he acquires a white piece of cardboard that he secures via a wooden stick to his luggage carrier. On it, he writes, *I am an Indian artist on my way to Sweden*. He attaches his portfolio as well, including everything he has done since he left Kabul. Now, he is a rolling advertisement for himself.

As he rides through Tehran, he notices another portrait, this time not by him. Wherever he goes, on lamp posts and the façades of houses, hangs the same picture.

'Who's that?' he asks eventually, pointing to the ubiquitous young man.

'The son of the King of Kings,' people tell him. 'The Prince of Princes.'

The King of Kings? The Prince of Princes?

'Don't you know who the Shah is?' says a fruit seller. 'The Shah of Iran? That's his son. One day he will take over,' says the man, pointing to the portrait.

He likes it. The young man looks friendly. He makes a drawing of the Prince of Princes and fastens it to the placard that has become a sail on the back of his bike.

The drawing attracts attention. A queue develops in one of Tehran's squares as people watch him work and wait to be drawn themselves.

He cycles out of the Iranian capital, and heads west along Highway 2 towards Tabriz. Someone tells him he has cycled over three thousand kilometres since his start in New Delhi. He never thinks in kilometres. What can a number tell you about a journey? It means such different things depending on your method of transportation, whether on a plane, a bus or a bike. He has been going for almost two months, and he must have at least as long ahead of him. This has more meaning than three thousand kilometres.

The sun is hot without burning his skin and the wind fans him without slowing him down. A good day for cycling. The question, as always, is where is he going to sleep tonight? But he is not worried. It is one of the uncertainties he has learned to live with, and even appreciate. He has slept in tents, gazebos and among cattle in their sheds. The standard of his accommodation has varied, but it has always been sufficient for his needs.

Either he collapses, or reaches his goal. Arrive or die trying. Had his mother still been alive, it would have been different. She was the love that could have kept him in India. But now he is leaving all that ridiculousness behind. He presses on, trying to resurrect the feeling Lotta gave him back in India, that life is not meaningless.

But what if she has changed her mind? What if she no longer wants him?

Qazvin – Zanjan – Tabriz

As PK pedals through Iran, news has spread back home in Orissa about his big trip west. He has been sending regular excerpts from his diary to a local newspaper, and they are published unedited. His older brother sends PK the newspaper clippings, and tells everyone he knows about PK's journey. He has become the talk of the entire state.

He may be the furthest he has ever been from home, but he feels utterly present. From this distance, so many thousands of miles from the Brahmins, his untouchability means nothing. Everybody loves success. The Brahmins can only treat you badly as long as you stay in your home village, working in a simple job, making no money. Then their talk of ritual purity carries weight. But when you make a name for yourself, a career, suddenly your low caste melts into insignificance. The higher castes bow to you. Oh, the falsehood, the hypocrisy!

One of the articles he sends from Iran causes a particular stir. His brother writes to say everyone has been talking about it.

The story arises from the most basic of human activities, and goes like this. One day he squats behind a tuft of high dry grass in the Iranian desert and relieves himself. His bicycle with his placards and portfolio is parked on the hard shoulder and looks like a beached sailboat in the distance. The sun is shining and a slight breeze makes the yellow blades of grass sway. As he sits, his mind wanders to an event that occurred when he was no more than six or maybe seven years old. He had gone to the outskirts of the village to find a place to relieve himself. A tree: that looked good. He climbed it. There was nothing strange about that. People did so in thousands of villages all over India; the countryside was the toilet. PK was smart to do his business from a height: that way he could avoid the smell and the flies.

Suddenly, he heard a roar. A roar that indicated surprise as much as anger. Terrified, PK glanced down. Beneath him he saw an old man, and on his head were the contents of PK's bowels. And not just any man. He was a Brahmin. PK jumped down and ran. The Brahmin ran after him, but PK was young and quick and the Brahmin was old and slow and dressed in an unwieldy ankle-length piece of cloth. PK escaped.

Never again did he defecate in the trees.

He looks around, out across the Iranian desert. There is no soul in sight, no risk of contaminating any holy men out here. He sits face to face with the long grass. His friends, he thinks.

'Dear grass,' he begins after checking no one can hear him.

'Here you are, struggling in the heat,' he says to one straw in particular, 'as many of your friends have succumbed from dehydration in the desert.'

The blade of grass answers with a polite tremble.

'You once had a big family, but you are almost the only one left... But you are needed. Without you, the desert would be impossible to live in. Here, even the slightest gust of wind grows into a storm and the sand is like a million needles lodging themselves into your face. You and your few remaining friends fight on, and it is thanks to you that the sand doesn't blow away completely.

'Where I come from, Athmallik in the state of Orissa in India, we have other kinds of grasses. And they are our happiness. Rice, our main staple, is also a type of grass. Your cousin. Did you know that?'

A snap of wind snatches hold of the blade and it bends, as if bowing to his wise words.

'I love you, little grass. You are man's peacemaker and Earth's protector. Without you, there would be chaos.'

But the blade of grass says nothing.

'We humans pull you up by your roots. You are our treasure. We use you to build our houses. But we have no right to hurt you like this. Man has his place, as does the wind, the sand and you, blade of grass; you too have yours.'

He pours a few drops of water from his canteen onto the dry grass as a gesture of his appreciation. The earth trembles in gratitude, he imagines.

He mounts his bicycle and is back on the road, but as he rides he decides to record the conversation and send it home to his brother.

And now it has been published in the newspaper. To think people would enjoy it so much! The people of Orissa must have recognized themselves in his words. Surely everyone has turned philosopher while squatting in the bushes, he thinks. Nature has a soul that deserves respect, or else we humans must face the karmic consequences.

He shakes his head and smiles, and travels on faster than usual towards Tabriz, hoping to find a letter waiting for him there.

Tabriz – Marand – Dogubayazit – Erzurum – Ankara – Istanbul

He pedals, hitchhikes, daydreams, and with tired legs arrives into Tabriz on his new Iranian cycle, his third since leaving Delhi.

Tabriz, Prophet Zoroaster's birthplace. A letter from Lotta is waiting for him. *My dearest,* she begins. And a letter from Linnea, the Austrian girl who was so badly injured in Afghanistan and whom he took to hospital in Kabul. She has arrived safely back home in Vienna. *My dearest*, she also begins. Only later does he think that perhaps Linnea had been in love with him. Or maybe not. His friends in India almost always wrote in such florid prose. All sugar sweet affection, it was the Indian way. So he thinks nothing of it when Linnea writes:

> Dearest PK
>
> Hope you are fine. PK, *my baby*, soon you will come to me in Vienna. I believe you should arrive last week. I was waiting for a long time. I hope you come soon. I think about you a lot and when I do that I feel happy. We will have such a wonderful time together. There is so much I want to show you. Now I finish this letter, but I wait patiently for you to arrive.
>
> Ihr treuer Freund.
>
> Linnea.

He jumps back on his bike and continues towards Turkey.

Iran was vast. So is Turkey. The world is vast. He is very tired of all this cycling now. Where is Europe? Will I be in Borås soon?

More often now, he picks up rides with trucks. It is easy to hitchhike in Turkey.

PK never promised anyone he was going to ride all the way. The trip to Europe was never about proving his physical strength or stamina; it was not some challenge of the body. He promised he would arrive by any means, that was all. Had he enough money, he might have bought a plane ticket. He chose to ride a bike because it was the only option available to him. It was all he could afford. He made a virtue out of necessity. The journey was always going to be difficult and laborious.

He sits next to the driver and his friend, dozing as the landscape slowly changes, thoughts of all that has happened in the past year flickering through his mind. Everything about his life is different now, not just the surrounding geography.

Yes, I have changed.

He was awoken from a slumber in a greater sense: meeting Lotta was the alarm that brought everything into focus. Before her, he had trouble distinguishing his own desires from the wishes of others. It was as if he saw no boundary between what he thought of himself and what others thought of him. But she made him aware of the line between his sense of self and his circumstances.

Now, memories from the time before Lotta are already hazy. Had he ever made a decision for himself, taken ownership of his own choices, before he met her? No, he had allowed himself to float, to be led by others. He had been afraid to be seen and heard, and rarely said what he really thought. He listened and imitated. He had been a guest in other people's lives. Curious, sure, but ultimately submissive.

He has always tried to please others. Lotta used to tell him he was too naïve, almost like a child. But she also liked that about him. 'The fact that you do not feel the need to keep asserting yourself is your strength', she said.

He also takes the occasional bus ride. With his bike on the roof, he settles into his seat at the front. The vehicle jolts into life and starts along the rough, straight road between Van and Ankara.

People spoke good English in Iran, but in Turkey it is impossible to make himself understood. In the absence of words, he draws. Everyone understands the pictures, regardless of their lack of a common tongue. He draws quick caricatures of other passengers. The entire bus bursts into laughter when he reveals the results. The moustached men and scarf-wearing women offer up bread, cheese and fruit. He sits cross-legged, eating sweet apples and plump, bitter olives, and looks out over the plains. They understand each other somehow.

The story is repeated on several buses and in cafés, restaurants and shelters. The Turkish people love to laugh. He receives invitations to their homes, where he draws in return for shelter and something to eat. You are such kind, warm-hearted people, he tells them. They are flattered and ply him with more food.

Once in Istanbul, he gets up early. The minarets are making their supplications as he hurries to the main post office to see if there are any letters waiting for him. One from Lotta with dense rows of her characteristically squiggly handwriting. One from his father. And one from Linnea in Vienna. Hers is thick and has been sent by recorded mail. Out falls a train ticket: the Trans Balkan Express from Istanbul to Vienna.

***

He walks along the Golden Horn and looks out over the blue water and the covered Galata Bridge with all its shops and restaurants. Istanbul smells like Asia, but somehow feels different. He cannot put his finger on what it is exactly. He walks through the streets towards the Topkapi Palace and breathes in the chilly morning air thick with wood smoke, pine and the taste of the sea. Cigarette smoke wafts out of the teahouses. Steamboat horns blast as he climbs up the hills, and at the top he can still hear the muffled sounds of old 1950s American Chevrolets and Buicks cruising along the streets of Istanbul below. The cars are even older than the ones back home. But the women dress in the latest fashions, unlike in Afghanistan and Iran. Blouses, skirts, jeans, and hair worn down around their shoulders. Nowhere does he see them covered by scarves, niqab or any other form of concealment.

He senses that Istanbul is a premonition of his future.

So many domes and bridges, and so solidly built. In school, PK read about Tamerlane, the warlord who razed Delhi and executed large portions of the town's male population. Was he Turkish? He was born near Samarkand, which is now part of the Soviet Union. Anyway, he only had one eye, PK thinks as he sits on a stool near the Blue Mosque, drinking a cold glass of salty ayran.

He stays in a small budget hotel near Sirkeci, the railway station on the European side. There, he feels lonely and sad. He sits on his narrow bed in the eight-bed dorm room and reads his letters over and over again to remind himself that there are people in the world who care about him. He is surrounded by millions of people and yet he is so very small and so very alone. Everyone is on their way somewhere else, but he is stuck, spinning.

He goes to the bank to cash a cheque given as payment for a picture. As he sits behind a desk waiting for the money, he takes out his sketchbook and a pencil – as habit dictates – and starts drawing one of the bankers. After a few minutes, a crowd has gathered around him. The staff stop what they are doing and join the circle.

'It looks just like me!' the banker laughs when he sees the portrait. 'You are very talented, Mr Indian!' and shows it to his colleagues.

One of the women working at the bank would like to have her portrait done too. She is so beautiful and PK wants to capture her face. But he is nervous about drawing women, in case they take offence at the results. Men are more relaxed. No, he does not want to take the risk, they might throw him out. Especially with such a pretty face.

'I'm sorry, I don't have time,' he says, bowing politely.

Eager to get away, PK writes *Best wishes!* in a corner of the portrait, tears the paper from the pad and hands it to the banker. He wants to pay.

'How much?' he asks.

'Whatever you like.' This is PK's standard response these days.

He pays well, enough for PK to afford to eat out every day for at least a week.

Feeling upbeat and flush with cash, he takes a taxi to Istiklal Avenue, a shopping street on the other side of the Bosphorus. He wants to buy a gift for Lotta. While in the taxi, he takes out his sketchbook and draws the driver as the car struggles up one of the city's hills in its lowest gear. It only takes PK a few minutes to complete and he hands the picture to the driver as soon as they reach his destination. The driver's sullen expression suddenly breaks and a smile bursts across his face. PK wonders for a moment if the man might be about to embrace him. Instead the driver refuses payment for the trip and invites PK to his home. PK accepts, because it means he can save a little more money for Europe.

***

He wanders around the covered Grand Bazaar, which reminds him of the streets of Old Delhi, with its small shops and shelves crammed with spices, leather, gold and meerschaum pipes. The basic formula for a market, it has been the same since the beginning of time. Part trade, part theatre. Vendors pull and tug at his clothes, just like back home.

He feels safe. The intrusiveness feels familiar.

In Kabul, he bought leather shoes and a handbag for Lotta. Now he purchases a necklace with turquoise stones strung on a leather strap. Then he goes to The Pudding Shop, not a shop selling desserts but a café serving Turkish cuisine. It's the preferred hangout for hippies at the beginning, or the end, of the road between East and West. He sits in the back of the oblong room and rereads the letters from Lotta and Linnea. Then he stares at the train ticket.

At times he has felt as if this journey was going to last for all eternity. Pedal, hitchhike, bus and bike again. The near death experiences. The muggy heat, the stubborn midday sun. Blisters have come and gone, his buttocks are now permanently numb, and his stomach is almost always crying with hunger. Even his head feels like a steaming, freshly baked sponge. The train ticket is a gift from heaven. The angels have sent it through their messenger on Earth, Linnea, via the international postal service.

He almost cannot believe it is true. He will ride the train to Vienna. The last leg to Europe does not have to be done by bike.

Europe, he thinks. He wonders if he'll ever fit in.

He looks around at essentially the same scene as the Indian Coffee House in Delhi: backpackers, just like him, and a bulletin board full of hastily written notes.

VW van to India, we leave on Friday, one vacancy.

Magic Bus London–Kathmandu. Five vacant seats.

Has anyone found my Pentax Spot Matic?

What should he do with his bicycle? Take it with him on the train? He tucks the ticket inside his waistband and decides to sell the bike and buy a new one in Vienna. He writes in his notebook: *Steady modern men's bicycle for sale, purchased in Tehran. Only twenty dollars!* He tears out the page and pins it to the bulletin board.

Istanbul – Vienna

He gets off the train at Westbahnhof in Vienna. Is this what Europe looks like? Hefty houses, clean streets and neatly dressed people. A reserved calm. But somehow also strained. It is beautiful. A dreamscape. Like stepping out onto a stage in a puppet theatre. Vienna is a storybook.

Linnea's sister Silvia meets him at the station. Linnea, who so longed for PK and wrote such loving letters, left Vienna for India only two days ago. She waited and waited, but finally gave up, says Silvia. PK never came. Perhaps she thought he had turned around and gone back. And her hunger to return to India had overcome her.

Silvia takes him to the family business, Gallery 10, located in the city centre. Silvia's mother greets him, but also wrinkles her nose and pulls him into the bathroom in the back. There, a tall, old-fashioned bathtub on lion's feet awaits. She fills it with steaming water and bath bubbles, tells him to undress and get in. He is shy, but she is insistent, so he strips naked. Only then does he realize how bad he smells, how filthy his clothes are lying on the floor and how wild his beard and hair have grown.

He bathes and thinks of Europe. Its scent of soap. A far cry from Asia's teeming dirt and kaleidoscopic quotidian life. His heart is more uncertain than ever. The damned worry begins to grow inside him again; he feels a long way from home now.

He stays with Silvia and her boyfriend. An artist and his wheelchair-bound wife also live in the same apartment.

Silvia tells PK about Europe. The truths of her own culture. She wants him to develop thick skin, to be prepared, not to be so naïve.

'People aren't as friendly here, not like in Asia. Europeans are individualists and think only of themselves,' she says, adding that kind, gullible people get into trouble in Europe.

'Watch out, Europeans are racists. You can get beaten at any moment just because you have dark skin,' she continues, explaining in detail how he should greet people, initiate conversations and behave.

PK is grateful for her good advice.

She cares about me, he thinks, as Silvia pours her counsel over him.

In just one week, he has learned a lot about the exotic, foreign culture of Europe.

The artist in Silvia's apartment smokes incessantly. He is kind but always drunk and his behaviour is erratic. One moment he is despondent, gloomy, the next he laughs, or is so overtaken by emotion that he pulls PK into his arms. One night he gets up, embraces PK and tells him that he is welcome to kiss his wife.

'Be my guest,' he says.

But PK does not touch her. He does not dare. He does not want to. They do not know each other. They have only ever said hello. Why would he kiss a woman he does not know? Instead, he puts his palms together and bows, a humble gesture to the artist's wheelchair-bound wife, and steps out into the chill of the spring rain.

He walks the glistening, empty streets, along the Danube and towards the lush green of the Town Hall and city parks, thinking about the heat, the dust, the dirt and crowds of Delhi. And the freedom of Europe. It will take some time to get used to it.

In Vienna, he looks up some of the people he met on the hippy trail. His notebook is full of the addresses of fellow travellers who told him to make contact. He drinks tea with them, goes to beer halls with them, draws them. They pay handsomely and his travel funds grow.

Now, he thinks, I'll buy myself a nice, expensive bike with lots of gears and ride the last stretch towards my goal.

'You can't ride to Sweden,' says Silvia.

'Yes, I can,' he insists.

Silvia takes him to the Prater, where they walk under the shade of the horse chestnut trees on Hauptallee and ride the Ferris wheel. They take the metro to drab old cafés and drink coffee with whipped cream, travel by tram to gloomy basement restaurants enveloped in a thick fog of tobacco. They are friendly, these people, but why do they keep warning him about the realities of living in Europe? It is as if the kindness and ease of the trip so far have been replaced by stress, irritation and callousness. In Europe, rules not feelings prevail, he learns from these friends. Europeans are less humane than the rest of the world – is that what they mean? He struggles to comprehend it. Tries to believe them.

'PK,' they say, 'you're a good man, you make people good. But you can't change Europe. In Europe, empathy is dying out. Fear is what drives people, not love.'

Love? If they are so attached to rules and regulations, maybe they cannot believe in love? Did that mean Lotta was not really in love with him?

He understands that Europe is hard. At the same time, here, his ideas come to life. He reflects, problematizes, twists the obvious, complicates. He has been swept on in a current of emotion but now he can feel the momentum slowing, becoming a narrower, slower stream. He has hit the riverbed. And now he is breaking through the surface, gasping in oxygen-rich, rational thoughts.

Maybe Lotta does not want him any more?

He lies in the guest room in Silvia's apartment, sinking

into the overly soft mattress and wrapped in the excessively thick duvet, and is beset with doubts. But somehow he is able to gather his strength to counter them. In the darkness he sees his mother. She is sitting on the floor beside the bed and watching him. She is the counterforce. In the flow of his dark memories, she is the small, bright spot. He falls asleep in her glow.

Before he has time to buy a new bicycle, he meets the gallery owner, who introduces himself as Herr Manfred Scheer and tells PK he admires his determination.

'To make a sacrifice for someone you love is a wonderful and enviable thing. Imagine if more people let themselves be guided by love,' Herr Scheer thinks aloud. 'The world would be a much more beautiful place,' he continues, before telling PK he has something for him.

They go into his office and the man hands PK an oblong envelope. He opens it and takes out a ticket. No, two tickets. Two train tickets.

'It's too much,' PK says, wanting to pay for himself.

The gallery owner refuses, but after some hesitation accepts two of PK's artworks instead.

Wien Westbahnhof–Copenhagen Central

Copenhagen Central–Gothenburg Central

Vienna – Passau

He sits, slumped in the plush seat. The stuffing is so soft it feels as if he has no skeleton and is made only of soft tissue. He spent his childhood sleeping on a straw mat on the floor. In his rented room in New Delhi, he had only a bed with a mattress of thin, braided rope. The second-class carriages had only unreserved seats consisting of wooden benches. His bicycle, a hard, tautly sprung leather saddle; the buses in western Asia, unyielding, shiny padded vinyl seats. He was used to feeling his shoulder blades, tailbone and pelvis. He wants to know where his body ends and things begin. Sinking into something so utterly forgiving, with no resistance, feels unreal.

Why do Europeans wrap their bodies in thick layers of pillows, feather cushions and mattresses? Is it the cold, or because they feel lost? Is it fear? Are they afraid of the hardness of their own bodies?

Wien, Melk, Linz, Wels. European cities have peculiar, monosyllabic names.

He is approaching yet another border. The train brakes, screeches to a halt. A damp smell of cold steel, burnt asbestos and wool affronts his nostrils. The corridor fills with uniformed men.

The interior door is flung open.

'*Reispass, bitte!*'

He holds out his green Indian passport.

The West German border guards flip back and forth through the pages of the exotic document. It is not every day they get to check an Indian passport in Passau.

'*Unmöglich, mein Herr*. We are so sorry. Follow here!' the man says in a mixture of German and English.

PK is forced off the train and follows them to a room on the other side of the platform.

'*Scheisse*,' PK mumbles as he steps down from the train. Silvia taught him this useful word as he was leaving Vienna that morning.

This is it, he thinks. They think he is an illegal immigrant coming to settle in their rich and beautiful country. He is going to take their jobs, steal their girls and be a burden on their society. Except that all he wants is to pass through; he has no interest in West Germany.

They ask him to open his worn bag. Their eyes are hard, their expressions unmoving. They think he is carrying illegal goods. No discussion is to be had; they will lock him up for a few days while they organize his deportation back the thousands of miles he has come. They root around among his dirty clothes and find bicycle tubing and bundles of light blue aerogram letters tied together with a length of thin, grubby rope.

'We will contact the Indian Embassy in West Germany and they will buy a ticket for you so you can go home again,' says one of the officers as he lifts up a blue shirt and holds it at arm's length between his thumb and index finger, as if it were contagious.

PK's grandfather used to say that if you use only two fingers to do your work, the results can only dissatisfy you. Of course, the shirt smelled bad: it had been a long time since he had been able to wash it. But the officer is clearly unhappy with his job; he is on autopilot. Or so his grandfather would have said had he been there.

The officer unfolds a wrinkled newspaper article. It is written in English and has been torn from the Indian magazine *Youth Times*. At least so it says at the top of the page. He starts reading.

'Oh, it says here he's married.'

Eight policemen gather around the brown Indian hippy with the long curly hair and the dirty bag. One of them unfolds one of the blue aerograms and reads. It is written by a woman, he gathers when he looks at the sender. He is satisfied that the Indian and the woman are more than just friends.

'Yes, it seems so. He's married,' says the other man. 'With a Swedish woman,' he adds.

'Her name is Lotta,' says the officer with the newspaper article, who then folds it again.

PK begins to tell the German passport police about his journey's beginning, back in New Delhi, India, his homeland, and the bicycle ride through deserts and over mountains, across seven countries and two continents, all the hundreds of stops along the way to drink, eat and sleep in villages and towns. Despite the incredible hospitality he has encountered, he very nearly did not make it this far, he says. He switched to train travel in Istanbul and there are now only two countries remaining between him and—

'Get to the point,' one of the men interrupts.

'I'm not smuggling drugs and I have no plans to settle in West Germany.'

He sees the scepticism in their eyes and grows despondent. One of the officers says it's time to call the Indian Embassy and arrange transportation. A police car will take him to a detention centre for illegal immigrants or perhaps directly to the airport in Munich for immediate departure. The police explain that West Germany cannot let everyone in who comes knocking on their door. Then he starts conferring in German with one of his colleagues. PK cannot understand, but he feels as if something is squeezing him around the chest. An evil force. He wails, weeps and moans.

'You can't stop me now! You can't possibly be so heartless!' PK complains in an ever louder falsetto.

Everything is exploding. His voice, his self-confidence, his conviction. He looks out the window and sees the train still standing on the tracks, waiting to continue north towards Munich. The green carriages are enveloped in a grey mist. A light rain is falling and he is cold.

But Europeans are motivated by rules, not cries from the heart.

The adventure has come to an end. Hope is lost. His future is shattered. All the dreams, all the longing, everything he has been fighting for, everything. All in vain!

Up until this moment, he has been convinced that he would reach his destination eventually. Doubts had come but were driven away, faith has pushed him forward on his mad plan. But after the warnings of friends in Vienna, he is no longer so sure. And now: the officers in Passau, at the border station between Austria and West Germany, do not look happy.

'*Ein moment, bitte!*' says one of the officers, looking at him with an equally rehearsed expression, one designed to reveal no emotion or clue as to what he is thinking.

PK tries to appear as newly in love as possible, but suspects the battle is lost. He prepares to take his bag, go to the waiting room and wait for the next train back to Vienna.

The border guards look again at the letters from Lotta and the article from the *Youth Times*. The article is illustrated with a picture of PK, his cheek pressed against Lotta's.

'He's telling the truth. He's married,' one of the border police says.

PK's façade breaks. Tears pour down his cheeks. Weeping, he tells them the story of the fountain, his art, the prophecy, the meeting, the blessing and the bicycle trip.

The officer, whose expression only moments ago had been so hard, so serious, relaxes. Then he laughs and suddenly seems quite cheerful.

'And you're going to Sweden?' he asks with a new tone.

'To my Lotta.'

'Oh well, so it seems,' he says to his colleague and turns to PK again.

'And she lives in Sweden?' he asks for the fifth time.

'In Borås.'

Passau – Munich – Hamburg – Puttgarden – Rodby – Copenhagen – Helsingborg

It has been a month since he left Istanbul and his third bicycle behind him. His friends were worried about him, refused to let him continue his pedalling, and insisted that he should travel the last part of his journey by safer and faster means. There are many things more dangerous than riding a bicycle through Europe. People are so anxious, so pessimistic, he thinks, tucked up inside the cabin as the train rushes northward, to the cold air that blankets the northern hemisphere. How is he going to survive this far north?

But why be discouraged? The border guards let him in, he was not sent home, he had a ticket all the way to Gothenburg. Surely nothing could go wrong now?

Again and again he reminds himself of what he is, where he comes from, and the emotions that have driven him from India. The anger at the priests who threw stones at him and the teacher who refused to let him sit inside the classroom. The bittersweet feeling at the thought of getting his revenge. Frustration at being born untouchable, and therefore worthless.

Without that frustration, he would not be where he is now, sitting on a train on his way to Sweden. Frustration is his driving force. The feelings of worthlessness are the ones that are leading him to happiness. Without that sense of inferiority, he would never have become an artist. Exclusion is the engine that pushes him along the road and beyond his imagination.

As a child, he was always full of questions. When they worshipped cows and threw stones at him, he asked himself how it was possible that a boy was worth less than an ox. Did his veins not pump with the same blood as the Brahmins? When his classmates refused to play with him, he asked himself what would really happen if he touched them. Aside from their shock and anger. Would the world collapse, the sky fall in, the divine cycle of the universe be knocked out of whack?

'The sun is blocked by many dark clouds, but one day the wind will blow them away.' These were his grandfather's words of comfort when he was in his blackest moods.

Grandfather said other things too, but he did not understand all of it. Words of wisdom like 'We come from love, and it is to love we return: that is the meaning of life' were easy enough to understand, but 'We can't know love if we don't know ourselves' was more obscure. He struggled with that one for a long time.

He sits in a German train compartment remembering Grandpa's wise words, and now, finally, he understands. All he meant was that the precondition of love is self-knowledge.

The black clouds disappeared when he met Lotta. What is it, exactly, that happens when you fall in love? Such a powerful force. Forgiveness. She gave me the power to forgive. That was what happened.

On the platform in Copenhagen, he sees a girl and a boy locked in a tight embrace. She is about to board the train, her suitcase stands by her side. The boy is not going with her. They kiss. Long and deep. Oh my God, they are using tongues! No one is stopping them! In India, someone would have shouted at them, pulled them apart.

So this is Europe, he thinks. My future!

The train creaks through the gears at the ferry terminal in Helsingborg. The Norwegian woman sitting diagonally opposite him looks worried, and then suddenly speaks.

'Do you have a return ticket?'

'No,' he replies. 'Why?'

'They won't let you in if you don't.'

The Swedish border police are on their way. He hears them open the door to the next cabin and ask for passports. The Norwegian woman opens her purse, takes out several bills and stuffs them into PK's shirt pocket.

'Three thousand Swedish kronor,' she says simply.

The police enter. He shows his passport. They look at him sceptically.

'Indian citizen?'

'Yes.'

'And you're visiting Sweden?'

'Is there a problem, sir?'

'What is the purpose of your trip?' the police continue.

'I am married to a Swedish woman.'

Bewildered, the police look at each other as if to determine who is going to have to deal with this mess. One of them asks if he has papers to prove it. PK's heart is cold. They have been blessed by his father, but he does not have one single official document, stamp or signature that actually *says* they are married.

He is at the border, so close now. And yet so far away.

The Norwegian woman gestures to him and points at his shirt pocket. Then he understands. He takes out the wad of notes she thrust upon him and shows them to the police.

Astonishment is followed by a visible relaxation in their demeanour. They smile at each other, back out of the compartment and close the door. PK returns the money to the woman. His own funds have dwindled to almost nothing since leaving Vienna. Most certainly not enough to convince the police to let him in.

'You are an angel,' he says to the woman sitting opposite. He would never have got this far without a whole world full of angels just like her.

***

As a child, he had learned to use his creativity to overcome obstacles. His mother used to tell him a story about the crow who could not reach the water in the pot. The bird gathered stones in its beak and dropped them inside, one by one. It took the crow a long time, but eventually it filled the pot with enough gravel to raise the water to a level at which it could drink.

'Think like a crow,' said his mother.

But sometimes obstacles are still insurmountable. If everything had depended upon his own individual means, his ability and talent, he would never have met so many benefactors, the selfless people who helped him on his way. They have been there for him since those days under Minto Bridge in New Delhi, when his stomach ached from hunger and he warmed his cold hands over bonfires of rubbish. Of this he is convinced.

Helsingborg – Gothenburg – Borås

He is cold. Confused and anxious. Expectant. What is he doing here? A bearded Indian, medium height, matted hair, filthy clothes, among all these tall, clean people. The light outside the carriage window dazzles him. A brushstroke of red has been applied across the horizon but the sky is still light, despite the fact that it is the middle of the night. How is that possible?

He falls asleep. By the time he awakes the sun is high and streaming into the compartment. The train is stationary. Sweating, he pulls down the window and leans out. White flowers – a type of anemone, he learns later – line the tracks, and the cheerful song of a black bird with a yellow beak fills his ears. The sound is as beautiful as Lata Mangeshkar's voice, the soundtrack to his youth back home in India.

The train stops at Gothenburg Central.

He breathes in the clean, cool air through his nostrils and steps cautiously out onto the newly resurfaced platform. Everything is so different to all the other cities he has passed through. Nothing like Asia. No sweaty bodies pressing against him. No porters, no bells as the tea sellers pass, and definitely no beggars. But also different from Istanbul and Vienna. No chimneys with sooty black smoke, no minaret cries, no crumbling façades, none of the stench of petrol or coal.

Everything is so quiet, clean and empty. At home in India, he often wondered where all the people came from. How could so many squeeze into one place? Here, however, he asks himself where they have all gone. Hello? Where are you hiding?

On the square in front of the train station, he asks a passer-by for the nearest youth hostel. Then a backpacker whom he met on his way from New Delhi appears. He lives in Gothenburg, and can take him to the Salvation Army Guesthouse. He is grateful for the continued help of the friends he made on the hippy trail.

He stands in the youth hostel's shared bathroom shaving, having just finished his shower. Beside him a white man is also washing, his clothes as dirty as PK's. His skin is scarred and his eyes are bloodshot. Suddenly, he removes his teeth and lifts off his hair. Fear grips hold of PK. He screams. Black magic!

The magician turns and, in broken English, asks why he is screaming.

PK does not answer, but gathers his razor, stuffs it into his toilet bag and runs to the front desk to tell them about the fakir in the bathroom.

'Watch out, he could be dangerous,' he tells the young man on reception. 'Believe me, I'm from India, I know the harm black magic can do.'

'How much have you had to drink exactly?' the receptionist replies.

He finds a payphone and calls Lotta.

'I can't believe it, you're in Gothenburg!' she says.

Fear drowns out any pleasure he feels in finally hearing her voice. He tells her he has just met a magician, but no one believes him. And neither does she apparently. She laughs and asks if PK has ever seen false teeth or a toupee before.

She'll be there soon, very soon, to fetch him.

He is standing by the reception desk of the Salvation Army Guesthouse for young men in Gothenburg, when he sees her. She is wearing a dark blue blazer with gold buttons.

Neither of them speak. It has been sixteen months since they parted at the railway station in New Delhi.

PK has been on the verge of a breakdown, standing there in the lobby waiting for Lotta. The last few days have been exhausting. But all tiredness is gone, obliterated by the rush of anticipation pumping through his body.

He shakes himself, tries to give words to his feelings, but nothing makes sense. He looks at her. And starts to cry.

Lotta knows that he is often overcome by the power of his emotions. So she suggests they take a walk. To the Garden Society, she says.

'A café in the midst of flowers.'

They stop for coffee. The sun is big, the air is warm. The sky a crisp light blue. The wood anemones are in flower all along the canal.

So big this year! Lotta is thinking. She has never seen such large anemones. As big as Ferris wheels! she says to herself as they walk hand in hand. PK has no idea what size wood anemones usually are, and anyway, his mind is somewhere else.

PK looks down at the canal and marvels at the clarity of the water. Not at all black and viscous.

They ride the very last bit of his journey together, in her yellow car, past places he cannot pronounce.

Landvetter, Bollebygd, Sandared, Sjömarken.

Suddenly, fear surges through him again. That she might have changed her mind, that her father might disapprove, that he might not fit in.

But they are already on their way to Borås.

He is approaching his final stop. It must have been predetermined. It must be fate. His fate.

28 May 1977. Finally, he is home.

Homecoming

The apartment with the pink plaster façade on Ulvensgatan consists of three rooms and belongs to Lotta's family. Her mother and father live in another apartment on the floor above. It is PK's first summer in Sweden. He spends most of it in a knitted turtleneck and a wool jacket, sitting on a wooden chair in the living room with the window open, listening to the singing of birds and the rustling of birch trees. Now and then a car drives past. Borås is a world away from the cities he had cycled through, where you had to concentrate to distinguish individual sounds in the thundering cacophony of rumbling and screeching.

He likes the silence: it gives him a sense of peace. But sometimes it is too much of a good thing, and he shudders. Everyone on the bus, for example, looks away. When he ventures a few words to his fellow passengers they answer politely, cordially even. But no one initiates contact. They sit shoulder to shoulder, and yet each is encased in his own refrigerator, always cold.

Sometimes it feels like he has passed into another world altogether, away from all the suffering. It is as if this is a reward for his devoted struggle out in the real world. Sweden is emotionally cool and physically comfortable at the same time. It makes his skin itch.

But he will get used to it.

Outside the open window, he sees two men run past in the direction of the forest. They are in a hurry. Danger, he senses. PK rushes outside and follows them into the woods. A fire, he thinks, and these men are going to extinguish it. They can use the water from the nearby lake, soon they'll be passing buckets to each other. They need help.

But there is no smoke. He sees no flames between the trees, no panic in the two men's faces. Dressed in blue tracksuits, they have stopped and are talking calmly to each other, their hands against two nearby tree trunks as if trying to push them over.

PK stares at them.

'What are you doing?' he asks in English.

'Stretching,' they respond.

'Why?'

'We are orienteering.'

PK doesn't know what that means.

'We orienteer.'

PK has no compass to guide him through this strange new world.

There is another man in Sweden. He has not cycled several thousand kilometres over mountains and through deserts, nor was he told as a baby that he will marry a musical woman born under the sign of Taurus. But he always has enough to eat, never sleeps under bridges, and certainly never thinks of suicide. Nor has he drawn portraits of presidents and prime ministers. But he is blond, fair-skinned and Swedish, looks neat and friendly, plays the flute, speaks perfect Swedish, and never misunderstands what is going on around him. And he knows Lotta very well. They have been singing in the same choir for years.

His name is Bengt. It is much easier to pronounce than Pradyumna Kumar.

One evening Bengt comes to visit. He talks and talks, studying PK and Lotta as they sit beside each other on the couch. His speech is rushed and his looks are strange. PK begins to wonder if he is unwell.

Hours pass, evening turns to night, but Bengt refuses to go home.

'Why is he staying so long?' PK asks Lotta as the clock turns three and Bengt is in the bathroom.

In the end PK is too tired to stay up any longer, trying to follow their guest's monologue in Swedish. He goes out and takes a walk, thinking it might encourage Bengt to go home.

But when PK returns Bengt is still there, his eyes red and puffy, his cheeks stained with tears. Suddenly their guest rises to his feet, slams the door and disappears down the stairs. Finally, they are alone. PK hears the main door slam again. Then all is quiet.

'Why was he crying?' PK asks.

'We've known each other a long time,' Lotta begins,

'we're friends, nothing more. But I realize now that he's in love with me. He can't take it that you're here, living with me.' Bengt thinks PK is a nice man, but that he should not be staying with Lotta.

PK lies down in bed next to Lotta and watches the shadows from the street dance on the ceiling. But sleep is impossible. His mind is spinning, obsessing on the same thought: *There should be two Lottas, one for me and one for Bengt.*

The next morning he gets up and announces that he is going to the bicycle shop.

'Why?'

'I want to buy a bike.'

She looks at him, puzzled.

'A good, sturdy bike that can take me all the way back to India.'

Lotta starts to cry, and PK leaves.

PK can think of nothing but Bengt for the rest of the day. It pains PK to think that he would be a perfect match for Lotta. He chooses a bicycle and tells the owner he will return the next day to pick it up. On his way back to Lotta's apartment, he bumps into many of his new Swedish friends. 'I'm going to ride home to India,' he tells them. They laugh. But PK is serious, they quickly realize. They have nothing to say to this.

'What am I doing here if there is no love?' PK demands.

The return journey would go faster. This time, he would take the more direct route. He will not stop and hang out on the hippy trail. No, he will ride all day, from morning to nightfall, straight for New Delhi and the India Post main office to see if the job is still available. If that fails, he will take the bus into the Himalayas, find a Buddhist monastery tucked away in some remote and beautiful location, and become a monk.

He wants a home. He does not care about the house, the furnishings or the way it looks. It is security he needs, a place to build a life.

The following night, Lotta and PK are sitting at home on the couch.

'I haven't changed my mind,' he is saying. 'I'm going to ride back to New Delhi.'

Tears continue down Lotta's cheeks.

'Why are you crying?'

'Because I don't want you to buy a bicycle and leave.' She leans closer, hugs him. He lets her. Maybe it is a farewell.

'Should I go now?'

'No, I don't want you to go,' Lotta sniffs. 'I don't care about Bengt. I didn't even know he was in love with me. I want to be with you, together in one big mess. For life.'

Sweden is a strange country. People go around thanking each other for nothing. Not to mention the constant meaningless phrases, like 'What nice weather we're having.' Why bother saying it? All you have to do is look up at the sky to see for yourself if the weather is good or not.

'If your friends and relatives went to Orissa,' he says to Lotta, 'and walked around the main street of my village saying things like "What nice weather we're having, Mr Pravat," people would shake their heads and keep walking. They'd think the foreigners had gone mad.'

But he will probably get used to it.

He is more in tune with social protocol when he meets Lotta's mother for the first time. At least he thinks he is. All he has to do is greet her with the polite phrases in Swedish Lotta has nagged him about.

Ask how she's feeling, then talk about the weather. How are you? Beautiful weather we're having today! he repeats to himself under his breath as the doorbell rings.

But it is cold outside, so he will have to make a change to his speech: How are you? It's cold today! Really cold! Something like that.

Standing eye to eye with his mother-in-law, the moment has arrived.

'How are you?' he begins, and then, 'Very old.'

It's almost right, but not quite. On top of this, his mother-in-law's hearing is bad. She says nothing in return. She must be a melancholy soul, PK thinks.

But later that evening, Lotta is not pleased with his performance. 'Why did you call my mother old? She was very upset.'

'It was a misunderstanding,' he tries to explain.

The meeting with Lotta's father does not go much better.

PK drops onto his knees to touch the old man's feet. That is how you show respect to your elders in India. But apparently not in Sweden. 'Where did the little Indian go?' Lotta's father says later, when describing the meeting.

And then there are the cows. During his first summer in Sweden, they go to visit the family summerhouse in the nearby countryside. That's when PK sees them, out in their pasture. Someone's forgotten to open the gate, PK thinks. Cows should roam free. So he opens it. Before long, the animals have strolled out and into the road.

Cars start honking irritably. PK waves cheerfully back. That is how you get the cows to move out of the way in India too! It turns out they're not so different here after all.

But the farmer is furious.

'Who let the cows out?' he demands in a temper.

'That was *me*,' PK replies proudly.

He takes a four-month course in Swedish for immigrants and works hard at fitting into his new home country. He is used to going everywhere barefoot and sometimes forgets to put on his shoes when he goes outside, even though it is winter. Often it takes the feeling of icy slush between his toes to make him realize his mistake.

A temporary teaching position in the art department of a local high school opens up and PK applies, even though his Swedish is still rudimentary. But art needs no language, everyone understands a picture, he reflects. He receives an invitation to attend an interview at the municipal department of education. He wears shoes and brushes his hair. So civilized, so Swedish. Almost.

The red light flashes to green and he enters the interview room, still trying to slow his breathing to mask his anxiety. The interviewer is pacing back and forth, his thumbs hooked in his braces. He rocks on his toes, but says nothing. PK's nerves intensify. He does not understand what the man is doing or what it means.

Then, suddenly, the interviewer speaks.

'And what have you *sysslat* with?'

He has learned the Swedish word for work, *arbeta*, and even *jobba*, but he has never heard this word *sysslat* before. Later he would learn it meant 'to be occupied'. The Swedish Employment Service's favourite term; it is not a job, it is an 'occupation', you do not work, you are 'occupied with your career'.

The first Swedish person PK had ever met was Jan Lindblad, the famous director of wildlife films. He came to PK's home village in the jungle in 1968 to film the animals of Tikarpada Wildlife Reserve. The teenaged PK served as a runner for the crew and watched in fascination as they dragged their heavy equipment through the undergrowth, rigged up their cameras and connected their devices with long electrical vines.

Jan Lindblad liked PK and called him Jungle Boy. He was so funny and friendly and he treated the untouchables as if they were just like everyone else.

PK observed as Jan Lindblad crept through the vegetation, whistling to attract birds. He was very good at it. He produced melodies and mimicked the animals so that PK laughed until his stomach ached.

That is it! PK realizes in the middle of his interview. The man is asking if PK can whistle. That makes sense! Clearly whistling is a very important skill in Sweden. Teachers whistle to the children to call them in from their break, after all. That is how they do things here in Sweden.

PK takes a deep yogic breath and begins whistling, producing a strong and full sound. I too can be like Jan Lindblad, I too can be Swedish, PK thinks. This will prove I am qualified to teach art in a local school.

But the man does not look happy. He freezes, then raises his palm. Later, PK would learn this was a signal meaning 'stop'. But right now, PK has no idea. In India, a raised palm means 'Great, keep it up!' So he continues, louder and with even greater gusto.

He whistles until his cheeks hurt and then stops. That should be enough.

The interviewer looks away. Then he looks straight into PK's eyes and asks ten short questions about his education and background. Nothing more. Then he goes to the door and opens it. PK gathers his papers.

'Thank you, goodbye!' the man says firmly.

He sounds almost angry.

After the interview, PK tortures himself with questions about the man's behaviour. Why had he been so abrupt? Was he not good enough for the job? Did he whistle the wrong tune?

Yet a few days later, PK receives a call from the headmaster of Engelbrecht School. Would Pradyumna Kumar Mahanandia be willing to take a temporary job as an art teacher and report to work early the next morning?

People think their love will never last. He will find it too hard to adapt. The darkness, the cold, the growing racism, even the way Swedes socialize, it will all break him sooner or later, they say. 'Oh God, how can an Indian village boy learn to live in modern Sweden?' they whisper to each other, shaking their heads. 'Before long he will realize just how different it is here and go back to the jungle.'

But PK never longs to return to India. 'Mentally, I have escaped India entirely,' he writes in the red and black diary Lotta has given him. He fills it quickly – and then another, and another – with musings about his new life in Sweden. For the first year he spends his evenings on the couch in the apartment on Ulvensgatan and writes down all his disappointments, new experiences, the people who believe in them and those who do not. He writes as the autumn rain splashes against the façade of the apartment building, as the shards of ice glisten in the winter sun and the blackbirds sing through the open window in the first warmth of the following spring. He lets himself absorb it all, and processes his thoughts in these pages. Sweden and the culture shock have made him a more reflective man.

With every passing day he becomes more Swedish and less Indian. But Lotta is taking an opposite path. She immerses herself in yoga and meditation. She recites mantras as the first rays of morning sun light the sky. PK hates mantras. The monotonous purr reminds him of all that he has escaped: the power of the Brahmins, the alienation and the suicide attempts. But he learns to overcome even those feelings, which still sometimes manifest themselves in physical nausea. He must mute the memories and live with them.

Other aspects of Indian culture he recalls with more fondness, so long as they have nothing to do with religion.

After first arriving, PK painted postcards and posters with Indian motifs, which he sold to friends and colleagues. He had pictures published in several Swedish newspapers. His proudest moment was when the culture section of one of Sweden's biggest newspapers, *Aftonbladet,* published a full-length feature about his art and organized an exhibition of his drawings in its newsroom, just as *The Kabul Times* had done previously. The *Aftonbladet* article led to more shows in the capital.

It is difficult to escape his place of origin, however. People keep telling him to teach yoga, despite his protests that he barely knows enough about it to practise himself, let alone teach. And yet, expectations are high. Offers to lead courses become ever more frequent.

'I've never even taken a yoga class, all I know was taught to me by my big brother,' PK tells the residents of Borås.

'So much the better,' they answer.

When the local community college advertises the city's first ever yoga course taught by a real Indian, places are snapped up fast. Nearly all his students are female.

PK goes through the movements his brother had shown him. It's not much, he thinks. But they seem happy, asking him questions about yoga's deeper philosophical meaning and significance, things Lotta ought to have answered, because he does not really know the answers. And yet, strangely, the women seem satisfied with his confused and partial responses that are neither insightful nor profound, based as they are on fragments he had heard as a young man.

'I smile and teach my yoga classes. At least it's work and earns me money,' PK writes in his diary.

Sometimes his thoughts turn to what would have become of him had he never met Lotta, bought that first bike in New Delhi or started riding west. He daydreams about what life would have been like had he not fallen in love and been charged with the 'energy of forgiveness', and had instead remained in his homeland, an India paralysed by caste conflict. I would have become a politician and fought for the rights of the untouchables, he concludes. Politics would have been my only weapon.

Maybe he would have been elected to Parliament for Indira Gandhi's Congress Party. Then he would have presumably started taking bribes just like everyone else. Power corrupts. That is the way it is. Very few people can resist and remain clean.

Maybe politics would have proved insufficient to quell his anger. Thoughts of revenge had been a feature of his childhood and had even lasted into adulthood. Despite the best efforts of his parents to dissuade and calm him, they have been a part of him ever since he can remember: thoughts of horrific acts of revenge. Until he met Lotta, that is.

'You must forgive,' his mother and father had said.

It has been a long time since PK last thought of revenge. Now, if the anger ever starts to fizz and burn, he understands that the object of his rage is nothing more than a mirror image of himself.

PK wants to be Swedish. He ignores the fact that the people around them remain sceptical. The more friends and colleagues doubt his ability to cope in Sweden, the more he fights to fit in. And it is this struggle to embrace all things Swedish that changes everything. It drives him forward. Learning the language is not easy. He understands most of what is said, but often his pronunciation holds him back. Misunderstandings occur because of misplaced emphasis, a wrong consonant or vowel sound. But each mistake only makes him more determined. He is going to succeed! It is going to work out! As long as he does not give up!

During his first year in Sweden, a teenage student approaches him in the corridor and asks why he has not married an Indian woman instead.

'It would suit you better,' she declares.

'Love knows no borders,' PK responds brusquely and goes out into the schoolyard, where Lotta is waiting for him.

He will overcome these obstacles. He starts teacher training in outdoor education at Mullsjö College outside Jönköping, learns to ski both cross-country and downhill. He takes mountaineering courses in Tarnaby and climbs Sweden's highest peak. He gets a job as a recreational leader at Elfsborg, the largest sports club in Borås, puts on events at the church and for the local chapter of the Red Cross, learns to like cinnamon buns and to ride the family horse. He gains ever more skills and experiences specific to Swedish culture, hoping that eventually Swedes will start treating him as a person and not as a representative of the place where he happened to be born.

Lotta and PK continue living in the apartment in Borås, but every summer they move out to the old family farm at Kroksjöås that used to belong to Lotta's grandparents. There, they grow cauliflowers and potatoes, take walks in the woods and discuss the possibility of eventually moving out to the forest permanently.

Late in the summer of 1985, Emelie is born. Not any old day. 15 August. The same day, thirty-eight years earlier, that India had gained independence from the British. What a coincidence! 'Today I feel freer than ever,' he writes in his diary.

His father, brothers and the rest of the family back home in Orissa see it as an omen.

'Now your roots are firmly planted in your new country,' his father writes in a letter, adding that he hopes PK has not forgotten his Indian ancestry completely. 'I am looking forward to hearing about Emelie's naming ceremony,' he writes.

PK is forced to disguise his aversion to religion. His family in India would be disappointed if he did not organize a *Namkarana* ceremony, the Hindu equivalent of a Christian baptism. Eleven days after their daughter is born, PK and Lotta perform the ritual according to Hindu tradition. They gather the Swedish part of the family – PK's family in India could not afford to come – and they shave the thin tufts of Emelie's hair as PK reads out loud all the auspicious names and honorific titles his father has sent.

'The Swedish side of the family didn't much appreciate the ritual. They looked at Emelie's shaven head as if she was a prisoner in a concentration camp,' he writes in his diary.

But by the time Emelie's brother Karl-Siddhartha is born three years later, they are used to these strange Indian rituals.

After several years of substitute teaching, courses in Swedish for immigrants and further studying, PK sends his transcript from the art school in New Delhi to the Swedish National Board of Education to have it approved. The Swedish authorities accept the qualification and he is now able to take a permanent position as an art teacher at Engelbrecht School.

At the beginning of every semester, he clears away the chairs and benches and tells the students to sit cross-legged on the floor. He wants them to know that as well as being another adult, a responsible, conscientious and composed authority figure, he is also just a kid like them. He imitates jungle birds and animals, lies down on his back and waves his legs in the air. He does headstands, taken from his morning yoga practice in the living room. The children laugh and understand they need not fear a teacher so willing to make a fool of himself.

The cobra had protected him from the rain as a baby in the basket in the hut with the broken roof, and it had also ensured his safe arrival in Borås. Now it continues to protect him in his new country. The students at Engelbrecht School like to pour sugar into the headmaster and other teachers' petrol tanks. But PK is spared. No one touches his white Volvo 242. A rumour circulates among the school's troublemakers that PK keeps a cobra in the boot.

'Never touch the Indian's car, you might get bitten!'

As PK stands in front of his students, his thoughts often return to his own school days, and all the times in primary school when he had been bullied by his classmates and the teacher. The untouchable pariah. Such bullying en masse is not possible in Sweden, which reassures him.

But it does happen on a smaller scale, even in Borås. When PK sees Swedish students harassing each other he bursts with an uncontrollable anger. One of the school's known bullies makes the mistake of tormenting one of his victims right before PK's eyes. PK's reaction is instinctive. He roars. Swedish turns to English and then to Oriya, the language of his childhood. He is overwhelmed by feelings difficult to explain to the Swedish kids. He connects to a deeper anger, rooted in that classroom in Athmallik, and it explodes right here in his classroom in Sweden.

'Get down on your knees!' he bellows.

A string of Oriya follows, incomprehensible to everyone but PK.

For the first time, the bully obeys and kneels down, as he can feel the meaning of PK's words, even if he does not understand them. The boy bends his head and keeps his eyes on the floor; he is too scared to move. PK lets his captive stay there for the rest of the lesson, defeated and humiliated.

Forcing a student to kneel for more than half an hour is not an acceptable punishment in a Swedish school. PK knows that, but that day, he does not care. The memory of his own vulnerability is still raw. The rage that has been sitting just below the surface for so long takes precedence. He feels ashamed about it afterwards. But many years later, he receives a call from the young bully, now a grown man, drunk and crying. He is ringing to thank PK. A letter follows repeating the sentiment, claiming that his Indian teacher had 'taken the devil out of him'. The victim later tells PK that the experience had also been transformative for him.

'No one ever bullied me again after that; you broke a pattern in a way that everyone else was scared to try,' he said.

Kroksjöås Farm, thirty-five years after the first time he saw a wood anemone. Såken Lake laps against the shore, fir trees rustle in the wind and the laughter of children rolls over the dark surface of the water from the beach on the other side. He loves the sounds of the Scandinavian forest.

He sits on a white garden chair, his feet tickled by the high, yellow grass interspersed with poppies and daisies, and reflects on his life in Sweden. Almost a whole lifetime has passed.

He would not have survived without Lotta.

Now he has taken early retirement to make time to paint. During all those years as a teacher, he found it next to impossible to create anything in the studio tucked into their small apartment in the centre of Borås and then, after they moved to the forest permanently, in the red barn next to the yellow wooden house. Any spare time he once had disappeared entirely when the school started demanding he write long reports for each student using the school's new computer system. It was the perfect excuse to withdraw.

He has already been up for hours, completed his daily yoga practice that, paradoxically, has long been an indispensable part of his morning routine since he was forced to teach it as a newly arrived immigrant. He has had his ginger tea in the conservatory and finally eaten breakfast, a masala omelette on toasted bread. Afternoon is fast approaching in the house by the lake and the children have just woken up.

They are adults now.

Emelie has finished her studies in fashion management with a focus on marketing, and is about to head out into the world of work. She has interned in Copenhagen, rummaged in London's markets, spent a spring in Bombay and has recently been to Orissa to sign contracts with artisans who specialize in weaving ikat scarves.

Karl-Siddhartha, otherwise known as Kid Sid, has been touring Sweden and the rest of Europe as a DJ since he was a teenager. He even won the DMC World DJ Championships at the age of sixteen. He has used the money he has earned to study for a helicopter licence. His dream is to work as a professional helicopter pilot in India, and perhaps fly politicians and businessmen from inaccessible parts of Orissa.

Both children feel a strong attraction to their father's home country.

Their first contact with India was through their cousin Ranjita, who came on a visit to Borås from Athmallik before Emelie and Karl-Siddhartha started school. Emelie thought that their Indian cousin was very strange. Even though she was in her teens, she did not know how to use cutlery. That alone was enough to mark her out as odd to the little Swedes.

The following year PK and Lotta took the children to India for the first time. PK was worried about how it would all go. During his lessons in Swedish for immigrants, he had been taught that children should wear helmets when riding a bicycle. He embraced the Swedish love of safety as if it were written in stone. No more the Indian 'whatever' mentality, from now on it was Swedish helmets, always. Even though they had no plans to ride bikes in India, they packed helmets into their luggage. India is so dangerous, he realized.

Emelie wore a blue styrofoam helmet virtually the whole trip, in small towns as well as large cities, while playing with her cousins in the fields and on dirt paths. The villagers in Athmallik had never seen anything like it.

'Hello, little girl,' they said, laughing and tapping their

fingers on her head. The five-year-old Emelie was furious.

'You never know what could happen,' PK countered when she begged to take it off. It was sweaty and itched.

It is summer and PK is sitting out in the garden by the outhouse they have built for guests, swatting away a stubborn fly. He is trying to formulate his ideas as if explaining them to a Swede who knows nothing about India. Imagine, he will say, that the nobility and clergy occupy all the important positions in society and that you, who belong to neither group, are ostracized wherever you go. Imagine that the people are at first cheerful and open, but quickly frown and turn away as soon as you tell them your name. Imagine that all of Sweden's priests are born to this position, and they stand in front of the churches and yell at you to go away and worship elsewhere. That they will even bend down, gather handfuls of gravel and throw it at you so that you will run, before slamming the door and locking it. And then consider, he continues to his imaginary Swedish friend, these experiences are repeated every day, year after year, even though the law says you have the same rights as everyone else and that it is illegal for you to face such discrimination.

Then he recalls a book he read about in both the Indian and Swedish newspapers that tells the story of an oppressed and exploited low-caste girl called Phoolan Devi who ends up in a criminal gang, becomes a bandit queen and takes bloody revenge on her former tormentors. She was put in prison, but later released and became a Member of Parliament and celebrity all over India, the world even, all because of the book and film made about her life. And yet, in the end, she was murdered by the relatives of her former bullies: revenge by the ones she took revenge upon.

That's what happens if you give an eye for an eye. Continued hatred is the only outcome of a blood feud.

Reprisals prolong suffering. No, revenge is good for no one, PK thinks, breathing in the scent of freshly mown grass.

A gust of wind gently rattles a nearby birch. He looks out over the lake and the ripples shimmering across the water's surface.

PK cannot understand why the government of India does not outlaw the caste system once and for all, relegate it to the history books. Sure, discrimination based on caste is technically illegal. And there are reservations and quotas so that low castes are given a little helping hand. But it is an outright ban that is required. In England, the Church condemned slavery and serfdom as early as 1102, and in Sweden slavery was declared illegal in 1335 by King Magnus Erikson. India's untouchables are not enslaved, but just as serfs in medieval Europe were not allowed into the church, there are still Hindu priests that deny untouchables entry to their temples to this very day. Untouchables are still commonly thought to defile all that is pure and holy.

PK feels the anger swell inside him when he thinks of the injustice. His grandfather, who lived under British colonial rule and attended the Victoria Vernacular School, at least had the dignity of being treated the same as his high-caste schoolmates. But PK, who grew up in the newly liberated and independent India, was forced to sit out on the veranda, to be separated from his classmates and endure the fiercest and subtlest forms of discrimination.

'It was a concerted campaign of oppression, that's what it was,' he mumbles to himself and begins along the path by the lake and up through the pines.

The sun is shining for once over the rain-saturated hamlet. He walks through the drowsy forest, around the mounds of rock and earth wrapped in soft, damp moss. It is as if someone has placed a giant green marzipan blanket over everything, making a traditional Swedish *prinsesstårta,* princess cake, out of nature.

The tall fir trees form a roof over his head. He leaps from stone to stone across a gurgling stream. He emerges on the other side and into a clearing where the dew glistens like silver in the tall grass. A long, slippery footbridge crosses the marshy meadow, and then the trees fold away. There it is, the lake, today smooth and shiny. Dead trunks lie on the sandy beach as if abandoned in a giant game of Mikado. The water is dark brown, almost like Coca-Cola.

'What nice weather we've been having,' PK says as he meets a neighbour on the gravel road that leads back to the cottage.

He thinks about the contradictory feelings that are stirred up inside him every time he returns to his village in India. A few years previously, state politicians in Orissa ordered a helicopter to collect PK, Lotta and their two children and fly them from the state capital to the village where the locals had gathered in what was billed as an official visit. They were to worship PK's resurrection, the successful untouchable boy. To say it had been overwhelming would be an understatement. The Brahmin girls whose fathers had once thrown stones at him kneeled down and touched his feet, before decorating him with garlands of marigolds. But while the Brahmins may now admire him, he was still careful not to challenge their power overtly. Otherwise it could have caused trouble after his return to Sweden.

His older brother Pramod, the one who was a successful railway manager in Bokaro, hired several untouchables to work for him in accordance with the government's edict. And yet, one day, he was found lifeless on the floor of his bungalow. The servant looked down at his face, which had mysteriously grown whiter with each passing year. At the corner of his mouth, a blue foam bubble popped.

'Death by natural causes,' the police said. But his family and friends doubted it.

He had challenged the Brahmins too forcefully, was their conclusion. A law-abiding civil servant who followed the new anti-discrimination laws was still too much for the higher castes. They poisoned him. And the perpetrators, whoever they were, went free.

PK goes down to the shore and skims a flat stone over the smooth surface of the lake. He can physically feel the grief and nausea that come over him every time he smells incense, or hears Hindu temple music, or even prayers or other ritual texts being read aloud in Sanskrit. But in these situations he has a weapon. These feelings are nothing more than passing clouds; before long the wind will blow them on again.

He draws the air into his lungs. It smells of fresh water and reeds. And he listens to the distant splashes and children's laughter from the beach on the other side. The forest makes him calm. The thick tree trunks, pine needles, moss, the heather and stubby blueberry bushes. Our kingdom, for Lotta and me, he thinks.

Autumn arrives and the rain clouds sweep through Borås. PK puts on his rubber boots and goes out into the woods where the rain is streaming down from the towering branches above, causing the moss to swell and glisten. He knows how precarious his memories are. When he thinks of his life in India and the bicycle trip that brought him to Sweden it feels as if it happened to another PK. These days he prefers to stay at home, painting in his studio in the barn, taking walks in the forest, going out with his chainsaw to do some gardening and then returning to their little cottage to look out over the lake.

PK recalls a speech he made only a couple of years ago to Lotta's relatives, the members of the von Schedvin family.

The talk took place in the symbolic heart of the Swedish nobility, Riddarhuset in Stockholm. He was dressed in a dark blue collarless suit and a sand-coloured Indian raw-silk shirt. His moustache was dyed and his hair combed flat.

He had given talks about his life many times before, for study groups and in schools, for civil servants, local associations and pensioner clubs, but here, at the so-called House of the Nobility, he was more nervous than usual. The pompous surroundings, the paintings, the crests and all the fine hand-painted china, it made him feel small and insignificant. But he gathered his courage, stepped up to the microphone and began to talk about his childhood, about the jungle and the elephants, the snakes and the temples, and of course the caste system. He wanted to take this opportunity to make a comparison between the Indian caste system and the Swedish class structure. Priests, warriors, merchants and workers, said the Indians. Nobles, clergy, burghers and peasants, said the Swedes.

Then he told them about the prophecy, his falling in love with Lotta and the bicycle trip to Sweden. Fate, love, his journey.

'I have no power over the direction of my life, and neither do you, dear audience. Look at me! Everything turned out as the prophecy predicted and not how my father, teachers or anyone else planned.'

Yet PK is sure that man has free will, and that destiny is only a framework. The prophets can only predict the contours of a human life. His mother, Kalabati, phrased it in hopeful terms: 'No one is doomed to be untouchable forever and nobody of the highest caste can expect to decide for eternity who can or cannot enter the temples or perform the sacred rituals.'

He went on to explain that laws already existed that made discrimination illegal and quotas were in place to help low castes get an education and jobs, but that India still needed to go further if it wanted to be rid of the caste system.

'A ban! That's my vision.'

More speeches followed. The Utkal University of Culture in Bhubaneswar called and wanted to grant him an honorary doctorate. He could not resist. He was flattered, and proud.

When he was little, they kicked him into the dirt; now they're brushing him down and dressing him with garlands – PK found this amusing. For an untouchable to be granted a doctorate had to mean the world was making some kind of progress, despite all the wars and continued misery.

Once again, he dresses in his dark bluc suit, takes a deep breath and steps out onto the stage. The lights are hot, beads of sweat gather on his forehead, and hundreds of pairs of eyes stare back at him. He is given flowers, and an orange cape with a gold fringe is draped over his shoulders. The speech made in his honour is pompous and over-the-top, in good Indian tradition.

'I have not always been so happy in my life as I am now. When I was a young student, I tried many times to end my own life. Every day I struggled to find food to eat and I was always hungry,' PK says when it is his turn.

'Everything starts with the family we grow up in. If the family isn't working, society cannot work.' He continues with one of his grandfather's sayings: with righteousness in your heart, your home will be harmonious, with harmony at home comes order in society, and with order in society comes peace on earth.

And he would not have got this far – to the yellow house in the woods of Sweden – if it had not been for the inspiring example set by the people of Orissa, he adds out of politeness.

'Do not thank me, say thank you to yourselves,' he says, repeating the words of the late Swedish Prime Minister, Olof Palme.

One frostbitten December morning, Lotta, Emelie, Karl-Siddhartha and I board a plane in Gothenburg. We are going to the former kingdom of Athmallik. We fly over Denmark's powder-white fields and Vienna's oxidized copper roofs. We cross over Iran's arid plains and Afghanistan's rocky mountains, where thirty years previously I struggled on my bike in the opposite direction. We pass high above the sun-scorched Ganges plains, where a train once carried me away from the village along gleaming rails, over jungles dark and curly like broccoli, before making a turn at the Bay of Bengal, the Black Pagoda and the temple of the sun god with the magic wheel. Finally, we land in the fields where I grew up.

We rent a car and drive along bumpy roads past the market towns of Dhenkanal and Angul, before turning off the main road down an even narrower track edged by increasingly dense jungle. All the way back to my childhood.

We enter the village to the sound of an orchestra. Eight men walk in front of our four-wheel-drive Chevrolet, which crawls rather than drives for fear of crushing the musicians. I received the same welcome the last time I came to visit, with exactly the same melody, played by the same drums, clarinet, tuba. Villagers line the main street, waving at us as we pass.

We live in the house between the mountains and the river. The house that we built so that we have a place to return to now that both my father and mother are dead and my childhood home is long gone. From here I can coordinate my charitable work: water wells, the school and the activity centre that holds workshops for the women.

I want to help those who have not been as fortunate as myself, even if my work is only a drop in the ocean. There is so much to do. A crowd gathers every morning outside our door, they have come for advice.

We go down to the Mahanadi River, where women wash clothes by the beach, buffaloes and cows wade in the knee-high currents and crocodiles bask on the protruding sandbanks. A procession of men, women and children from the village follows behind us. My personal bodyguard, dressed in a black military-style beret and camouflage, sits beside me, sent and paid for by the state government.

Among the procession is the village bard, a Brahmin who raises his stick to the heavens and shouts his tribute to God, 'Hari Bol!' He laughs, his teeth rattling and red from years of chewing betel nut.

I have two bodyguards then, a Brahmin and a soldier. The best protection a man could hope for.

The Brahmin tells me he has performed this ritual, the laughter and the 'Hari Bol!', every day since 1962 and has not been sick once. God rewards the devout. But Karl-Siddhartha quickly tires of the monotonous chanting and teaches the old man instead to shout out 'Hey you!' in Gothenburg-heavy Swedish.

Halfway to the river, the Brahmin invites us into his home. There, in the darkness, he has erected an altar, as in most Hindu homes. But instead of the usual images of Shiva or Vishnu, he has placed a picture of... Lotta and me.

We stand and watch as the Brahmin falls to his knees, raising his hands to worship the photograph.

I look at Lotta, who shakes her head and smiles. We can hardly believe our eyes.

Postscript

The Indian Caste System

As PK says, the caste system in India is not that hard to understand on the surface. It's when you start to delve more deeply into its divisions and subdivisions that it seems as chaotic and bewildering as a busy Indian street market.

The word caste is derived from the Portuguese *casta*, meaning 'race, breed or ancestry', and originally from the Latin *casto,* meaning 'pure or chaste'. There is no precise translation in Indian languages, but varna and jati are the two most proximate terms. These two concepts represent different levels of social identity within the caste system.

According to Brahminical books like the *Rigveda*, varna in Sanskrit means 'colour, type, or order', inferring the colour of one's skin. Historically there were four main varna existing in a rigid hierarchy. At the top were the Brahmins (teachers, intellectuals, priests), then the Kshatriya (warriors and rulers), followed by the Vaishya (traders, merchants, artisans) and finally the Shudra (labourers, servants).

Some groups of people were banished from the varna system and were referred to as 'untouchables', now known as Dalits. They are socially excluded to this day.

Jati refers to birth and is typically associated with a job

or occupation. The jati belong to one of the four varna, and it's at this point that PK's Western friends throw their hands in the air and change the conversation, because there are thousands of jati. These complex social groups defy clear definition.

The *Rigveda* verses that PK mentions are a collection of ancient Indian Sanskrit hymns dedicated to Rigvedic deities, one of whom is Purusha, the 'cosmic being'. He inhabits everything universally conscious and unconscious and is depicted as a being with a thousand heads, eyes and legs.

The untouchable or Dalit caste to which PK belongs was traditionally involved in occupations that were regarded as impure, such as leatherwork, butchering or removal of animal carcasses, or disposal of rubbish and human waste. They were generally outcasts, banned from everyday social life, physically separated from the rest of the community and forbidden to enter temples or schools. As PK describes, untouchables are social pariahs from the moment of birth, outlawed, vagrant and undesirable, categorized as unpersons by dint of an accident of fate.

Although the Indian caste system has ancient origins, the British Raj exacerbated the problems by making caste organization legally binding, thereby enabling a divide and rule means of government. Between 1860 and 1920, the British segregated Indians by caste, giving the top administrative jobs to the upper castes. However, protests during the 1920s forced the colonial administration to begin a policy of positive discrimination by offering a percentage of government jobs to the lower castes.

The British, on the whole, did not consider untouchables to be subhuman or ritually unclean but useful manpower, and many were recruited into the army. During the Raj rule untouchables were treated with a degree of pragmatic benevolence and they achieved some small emancipation. PK's family did well by the British.

Even so, Mahatma Gandhi started a nationwide movement against untouchability and named the so-called lower classes *Harijan* or 'Children of God'. He started the All-India Anti-Untouchability League and the weekly newspaper *Harijan*. He also undertook a Harijan tour of India between November 1933 and August 1934, which helped spread the message down to the lowest and most oppressed sections of society. However, by renaming untouchables with the seemingly elevated word Harijan, many believed Gandhi papered over the deep-set issue of the persecution of the underclasses. They claimed it only removed 'the offence to the ear' and little else changed. Nowadays Harijan is considered by many to be a derogatory and insulting term. PK himself really dislikes the word, as it can be taken to imply a denial of true parentage.

Untouchables were later called 'Scheduled Castes' and 'Scheduled Tribes' under the India Act of 1935, and the later Indian Constitution of 1950. The constitution also banned discrimination on the basis of caste and announced quotas in government jobs and educational institutions for Scheduled Castes and Tribes. The Untouchability (Offences) Act (1955) provides penalties for discrimination on the grounds that an individual is from a Scheduled Caste.

Despite these measures the divisions between caste groups persist and violence and intolerance continue, especially in rural areas. In the early 21st century, Scheduled Castes or Dalits numbered 170 million people in India.

A recent Human Rights Watch statement says:

> Despite commitments to end caste and descent-based discrimination, the practice persists due to poor enforcement of laws and policies. Affected communities face severe restrictions and limited access to resources,

> services and development, keeping most in severe poverty. In India atrocities and violence against Dalits are on a double-digit rise, whereas acquittal rates for these crimes remain extremely high. The attacks are brutal and inhumane, ranging from gang-rapes to the recent burning alive of two children in India's Haryana state.[1]

PK regards caste as a serious disease, like cancer, and discrimination is merely the symptom. We must focus on curing the disease (the root of the problem) rather than the symptom, and love and compassion are the appropriate medicines to do this. In Sanskrit, the word Dalit means 'suppressed, smashed, broken to pieces'. Legislation can achieve only so much. As PK says: 'laws are useless if left unenforced. Ancient prejudices are embedded in people's minds like layers of bedrock. Change must come from within, from the heart.'

1 Human Rights Watch statement: 11 March 2016, General Debate on Ending Discrimination Based on Caste and Descent

PK's Acknowledgments

First of all, I would like to express my deepest gratitude to Juliet, Novin and everyone at Oneworld for their love, warmth and constant support, as well as for their hard work on this story. When I first met them at their publishing house in London I immediately felt at home, and they and all their colleagues have made a great impression on me. As my son commented: 'We have found the best publishing house in the world.' The name 'Oneworld' is very appropriate to their ethos, and we share the same vision for the future of mankind.

This book was born from the story of two individuals, Charlotte and myself. We came from completely different backgrounds, from different continents and different worlds, which eventually became one world! I never dreamed that one day people would be inspired to write, publish and read a book about us.

I would like to thank my mother, who brought me into the world. Although she could not read or write, she was able to use her fingers to count the days, weeks and months, she kept track of Indian tribal festivals and understood the sun, moon and the movements of the planets. My mother taught me how to forgive and how to live in harmony, while my father taught me how to survive. As a child, I spent a lot of time wondering how I could make my mother happy. Today, I can feel her looking down at me from heaven, and I know she is glad that this book has been written about her son.

I am also indebted to Swedish author Per J Andersson and his beloved wife Pernilla for their relentless research over the last six years, during which time Per visited my village in East India and interviewed many of the people mentioned in the book. Special thanks are also due to Liselott and Adam at Forum, and all those involved. I would also like to thank Martin Fletcher for his editorial assistance, and for his postscript on the Indian caste system.

Very special thanks to my dear British friend Anne, who many years ago agreed to type out my old diaries on my typewriter. She felt a strong emotional attachment to my story and gave me a great deal of encouragement, and she is a very loyal friend to me and all my family.

Finally, neither this story nor the book would have been possible without Charlotte's warmth and unconditional love. As well as my wife, life partner and best friend, she is my goddess – I not only love her, but I worship her.

I must also give my deepest thanks to my beloved wife for being infinitely patient with me, for letting me talk endlessly and for listening to all my ideas. Special thanks to our daughter Emelie, a sympathetic soul and a great flute player like my dad, for her true moral support, and to our son, the prince Karl Siddhartha – he is the real businessman of the family and has many other wonderful talents. I am also very grateful to Charlotte´s dear mother AnnMarie for her invaluable advice on how to live in the Swedish countryside in an eco-friendly way, and for affectionately calling me Mowgli for the last 40 years, just like my grandfather always did. I am also thankful to Charlotte´s sister Ulla who is an excellent horse rider, is always brutally honest, and who has been cutting my hair better than a professional barber since I arrived in Sweden.

Last but not the least, I beg the forgiveness of all those who helped me, fed me and gave me valuable advice during my long overland journey on the hippie trail from the east to the west and whose names I have failed to mention here.

Photo Album

Shridhar, PK's father

PK, standing between his father and mother, with his younger brother Prabir and a cousin sitting in front

Kalabati, PK's mother

Self-portrait entitled 'Love to my Lotta'

A portrait of PK by his friend Tarique

PK doing portraits by Connaught Place in New Delhi

Drawing a Swedish lady

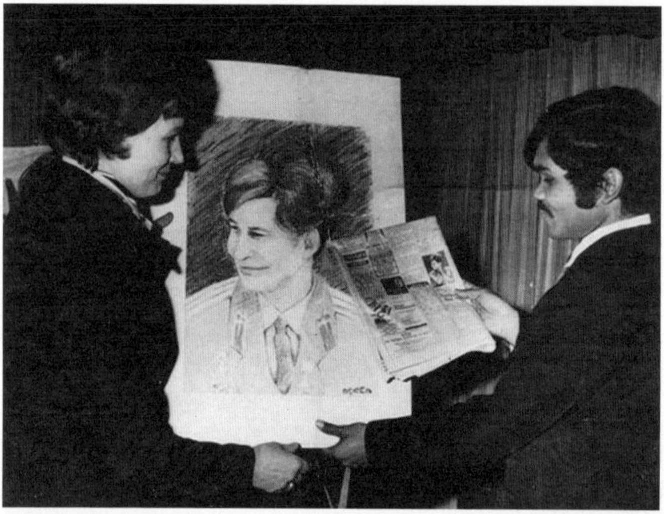

PK meeting the Soviet cosmonaut Valentina Teresjkova, whom he had just drawn

B.D. Jatti was the third president to be drawn by PK in just a few short years

Visiting Prime Minister Indira Ghandi with friends from Orissa

Lotta and a friend in Varanasi

The first photo of PK and Lotta together, taken in New Delhi in January 1976

PK in his home in New Delhi

PK and Lotta in Lodi Colony in New Delhi

Together again after the long bicycle ride

PK and Lotta's wedding in Borås on 28 May 1979, exactly two years after they were reunited in Sweden

Upside-down yoga at a conference for the blind at Mullsjö College

A Mahanadia-von Schedvin family portrait taken at a studio in Sandared

The family: Emelie, Lotta, PK, Karl-Siddharta

PK and Lotta at home in Kroksjöås

Morning Prayer at a school in Baghmunda, where PK's niece Ranjita is a teacher

PK talks to students at Kalinga Institute of Social Sciences (KISS), Odisha

About PK and Lotta

PK and LOTTA have been happily married since 1979. They have two children and live in Borås, Sweden. PK is an Art and Culture Adviser for the Swedish Government, and also the Oriya Cultural Ambassador to Sweden.

About the Author

PER J ANDERSSON is a writer and journalist. He is the co-founder of travel magazine *Vagabond*, and has been visiting India for the last 30 years.

About the Translator

ANNA HOLMWOOD translates literature from Swedish and Chinese to English.

PRAISE FOR
WHERE THE CRAWDADS SING

'Owens combines high tension with precise detail about how people dress, sound, live and eat – the case studies in her book are both human and natural . . . Surprise bestsellers are often works that chime with the times. Though set in the 1950s and 60s, *Where the Crawdads Sing* is, in its treatment of racial and social division and the fragile complexities of nature, obviously relevant to contemporary politics and ecology. But these themes will reach a huge audience though the writer's old-fashioned talents for compelling character, plotting and landscape description'

THE GUARDIAN

'The strength of the story comes from the sympathetic portrait of its heroine who cannot fail to captivate, right up until the surprising end'

***i* NEWSPAPER**

'A painfully beautiful first novel that is at once a murder mystery, a coming-of-age narrative and a celebration of nature . . . Owens here surveys the desolate marshlands of the North Carolina coast through the eyes of an abandoned child. And in her isolation that child makes us open our own eyes to the secret wonders – and dangers of her private world'

NEW YORK TIMES BOOK REVIEW

'Unsettling and tinged with sadness, yet astonishingly fresh, powerful and mesmerising – with a surprising ending that will haunt you. I couldn't put it down'

THE LADY

'Heart-wrenching . . . A fresh exploration of isolation and nature from a female perspective along with a compelling love story'

ENTERTAINMENT WEEKLY

'Both a coming-of-age story and a mysterious account of a murder investigation told from the perspective of a young girl . . . Through Kya's story, Owens explores how isolation affects human behaviour, and the deep effect that rejection can have on our lives'

VANITY FAIR

'A stunningly beautiful novel. Owens brings the North Carolina marshlands to lush, exquisite life'

***THE BOOKSELLER*, 'BOOK OF THE MONTH'**

'A lush debut novel, Owens delivers her mystery wrapped in gorgeous, lyrical prose. It's clear she's from this place – the land of the southern coasts, but also the emotional terrain – you can feel it in the pages. A magnificent achievement, ambitious, credible and very timely'

ALEXANDRA FULLER, *NEW YORK TIMES* BESTSELLING AUTHOR OF *DON'T LET'S GO TO THE DOGS TONIGHT*

'This is a heart-wrenching coming-of-age story, perfect for book clubs'

CANDIS

'A story that's evocative and sad and with a remarkable heroine'

IMAGE

'A nature-infused romance with a killer twist'

REFINERY29

Delia Owens is the co-author of three internationally bestselling nonfiction books about her life as a wildlife scientist in Africa. She holds a BS in Zoology from the University of Georgia and a PhD in Animal Behaviour from the University of California at Davis. She has won the John Burroughs Award for Nature Writing and has been published in *Nature, The African Journal of Ecology* and *International Wildlife,* among many others. She lives in the mountains of North Carolina. *Where the Crawdads Sing* is her first novel.

WHERE THE CRAWDADS SING

DELIA OWENS

corsair

CORSAIR

First published in the US in 2018 by GP Putnam's Sons
First published in Great Britain in 2019 by Corsair
This paperback edition published in 2019

A CIP catalogue record for this book is available from the British Library.

ISBN: 978-1-4721-5466-8

Printed and bound in Great Britain by
Clays Ltd, Elcograf S.p.A.

Papers used by Corsair are from well-managed forests and other responsible sources.

MIX
Paper from
responsible sources
FSC® C104740

Corsair
An imprint of
Little, Brown Book Group
Carmelite House
50 Victoria Embankment
London EC4Y 0DZ

An Hachette UK Company
www.hachette.co.uk

www.littlebrown.co.uk

To Amanda, Margaret, and Barbara

Here's to'd ya
If I never see'd ya
I never knowed ya.
I see'd ya
I knowed ya
I loved ya,
Forever.

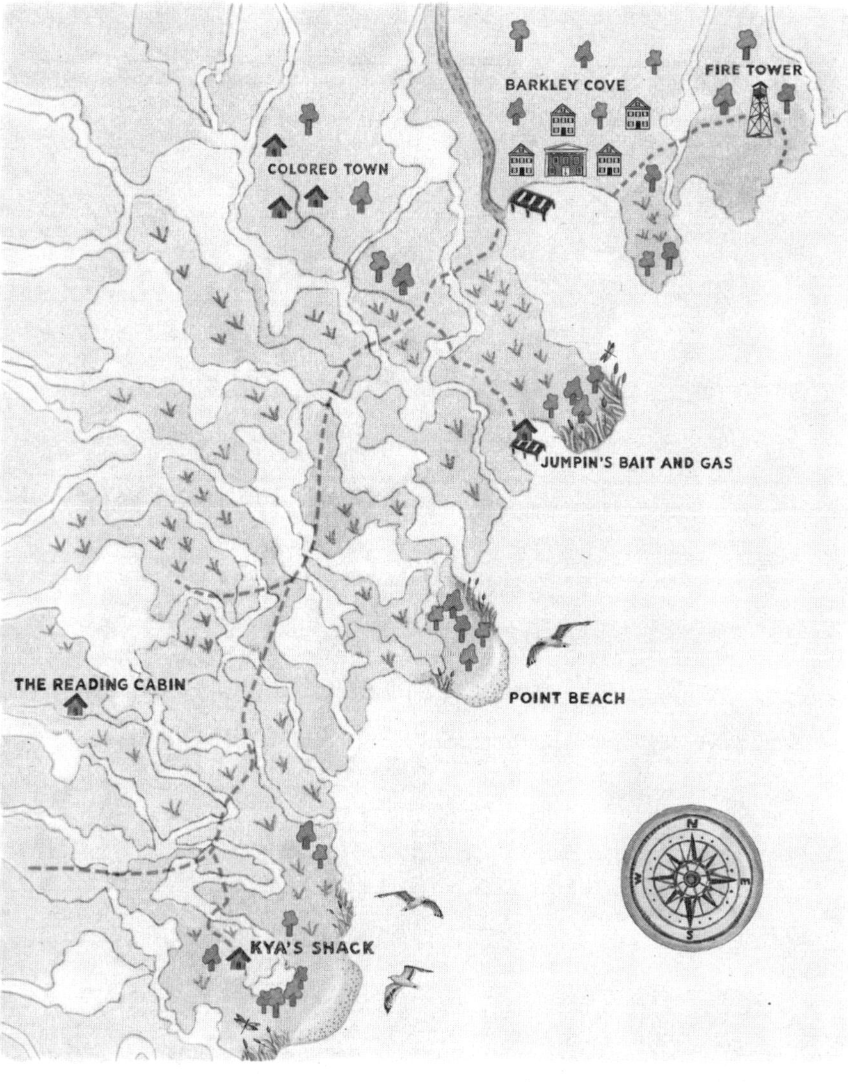
BARKLEY COVE
FIRE TOWER
COLORED TOWN
JUMPIN'S BAIT AND GAS
THE READING CABIN
POINT BEACH
KYA'S SHACK
N
E
S
W

WHERE
THE
CRAWDADS
SING

PART 1

The Marsh

Prologue

1969

Marsh is not swamp. Marsh is a space of light, where grass grows in water, and water flows into the sky. Slow-moving creeks wander, carrying the orb of the sun with them to the sea, and long-legged birds lift with unexpected grace—as though not built to fly—against the roar of a thousand snow geese.

Then within the marsh, here and there, true swamp crawls into low-lying bogs, hidden in clammy forests. Swamp water is still and dark, having swallowed the light in its muddy throat. Even night crawlers are diurnal in this lair. There are sounds, of course, but compared to the marsh, the swamp is quiet because decomposition is cellular work. Life decays and reeks and returns to the rotted duff; a poignant wallow of death begetting life.

On the morning of October 30, 1969, the body of Chase Andrews lay in the swamp, which would have absorbed it silently, routinely. Hiding it for good. A swamp knows all about death, and doesn't necessarily define it as tragedy, certainly not a sin. But this morning two boys from the village rode their bikes out to the old fire tower and, from the third switchback, spotted his denim jacket.

1.

Ma

1952

The morning burned so August-hot, the marsh's moist breath hung the oaks and pines with fog. The palmetto patches stood unusually quiet except for the low, slow flap of the heron's wings lifting from the lagoon. And then, Kya, only six at the time, heard the screen door slap. Standing on the stool, she stopped scrubbing grits from the pot and lowered it into the basin of worn-out suds. No sounds now but her own breathing. Who had left the shack? Not Ma. She never let the door slam.

But when Kya ran to the porch, she saw her mother in a long brown skirt, kick pleats nipping at her ankles, as she walked down the sandy lane in high heels. The stubby-nosed shoes were fake alligator skin. Her only going-out pair. Kya wanted to holler out but knew not to rouse Pa, so opened the door and stood on the brick-'n'-board steps. From there she saw the blue train case Ma carried. Usually, with the confidence of a pup, Kya knew her mother would return with meat wrapped in greasy brown paper or with a chicken, head dangling down. But she never wore the gator heels, never took a case.

Ma always looked back where the foot lane met the road, one arm held high, white palm waving, as she turned onto the track, which wove through bog forests, cattail lagoons, and maybe—if the tide obliged—eventually into town. But today she walked on, unsteady in the ruts. Her tall figure emerged now and then through the holes of the forest until only swatches of white scarf flashed between the leaves. Kya sprinted to the spot she knew would bare the road; surely Ma would wave from there, but she arrived only in time to glimpse the blue case—the color so wrong for the woods—as it disappeared. A heaviness, thick as black-cotton mud, pushed her chest as she returned to the steps to wait.

Kya was the youngest of five, the others much older, though later she couldn't recall their ages. They lived with Ma and Pa, squeezed together like penned rabbits, in the rough-cut shack, its screened porch staring big-eyed from under the oaks.

Jodie, the brother closest to Kya, but still seven years older, stepped from the house and stood behind her. He had her same dark eyes and black hair; had taught her birdsongs, star names, how to steer the boat through saw grass.

"Ma'll be back," he said.

"I dunno. She's wearin' her gator shoes."

"A ma don't leave her kids. It ain't in 'em."

"You told me that fox left her babies."

"Yeah, but that vixen got 'er leg all tore up. She'd've starved to death if she'd tried to feed herself 'n' her kits. She was better off to leave 'em, heal herself up, then whelp more when she could raise 'em good. Ma ain't starvin', she'll be back." Jodie wasn't nearly as sure as he sounded, but said it for Kya.

Her throat tight, she whispered, "But Ma's carryin' that blue case like she's goin' somewheres big."

. . .

The shack sat back from the palmettos, which sprawled across sand flats to a necklace of green lagoons and, in the distance, all the marsh beyond. Miles of blade-grass so tough it grew in salt water, interrupted only by trees so bent they wore the shape of the wind. Oak forests bunched around the other sides of the shack and sheltered the closest lagoon, its surface so rich in life it churned. Salt air and gull-song drifted through the trees from the sea.

Claiming territory hadn't changed much since the 1500s. The scattered marsh holdings weren't legally described, just staked out natural—a creek boundary here, a dead oak there—by renegades. A man doesn't set up a palmetto lean-to in a bog unless he's on the run from somebody or at the end of his own road.

The marsh was guarded by a torn shoreline, labeled by early explorers as the "Graveyard of the Atlantic" because riptides, furious winds, and shallow shoals wrecked ships like paper hats along what would become the North Carolina coast. One seaman's journal read, "rang'd along the Shoar . . . but could discern no Entrance . . . A violent Storm overtook us . . . we were forced to get off to Sea, to secure Ourselves and Ship, and were driven by the Rapidity of a strong Current . . .

"The Land . . . being marshy and Swamps, we return'd towards our Ship . . . Discouragement of all such as should hereafter come into those Parts to settle."

Those looking for serious land moved on, and this infamous marsh became a net, scooping up a mishmash of mutinous sailors, castaways, debtors, and fugitives dodging wars, taxes, or laws that they didn't take to. The ones malaria didn't kill or the swamp didn't swallow bred into a woodsmen tribe of several races and multiple cultures, each of whom could fell a small forest with a hatchet and pack a buck for miles. Like river rats, each had his own territory, yet had to fit into the fringe or simply disappear some day in the swamp. Two hundred years later, they were joined by runaway slaves, who escaped into the marsh and were called maroons, and freed slaves, penniless and beleaguered, who dispersed into the water-land because of scant options.

Maybe it was mean country, but not an inch was lean. Layers of life—squiggly sand crabs, mud-waddling crayfish, waterfowl, fish, shrimp, oysters, fatted deer, and plump geese—were piled on the land or in the water. A man who didn't mind scrabbling for supper would never starve.

It was now 1952, so some of the claims had been held by a string of disconnected, unrecorded persons for four centuries. Most before the Civil War. Others squatted on the land more recently, especially after the World Wars, when men came back broke and broke-up. The marsh did not confine them but defined them and, like any sacred ground, kept their secrets deep. No one cared that they held the land because nobody else wanted it. After all, it was wasteland bog.

Just like their whiskey, the marsh dwellers bootlegged their own laws—not like those burned onto stone tablets or inscribed on documents, but deeper ones, stamped in their genes. Ancient and natural, like those hatched from hawks and doves. When cornered, desperate, or isolated, man reverts to those instincts that aim straight at survival. Quick and just. They will always be the trump cards because they are passed on more frequently from one generation to the next than the gentler genes. It is not a morality, but simple math. Among themselves, doves fight as often as hawks.

Ma didn't come back that day. No one spoke of it. Least of all Pa. Stinking of fish and drum likker, he clanked pot lids. "Whar's supper?"

Eyes downcast, the brothers and sisters shrugged. Pa dog-cussed, then limp-stepped out, back into the woods. There had been fights before; Ma had even left a time or two, but she always came back, scooping up whoever would be cuddled.

The two older sisters cooked a supper of red beans and cornbread, but no one sat to eat at the table, as they would have with Ma. Each dipped beans from the pot, flopped cornbread on top, and wandered off to eat on their floor mattresses or the faded sofa.

Kya couldn't eat. She sat on the porch steps, looking down the lane. Tall for her age, bone skinny, she had deep-tanned skin and straight hair, black and thick as crow wings.

Darkness put a stop to her lookout. Croaking frogs would drown the sounds of footsteps; even so, she lay on her porch bed, listening. Just that morning she'd awakened to fatback crackling in the iron skillet and whiffs of biscuits browning in the wood oven. Pulling up her bib overalls, she'd rushed into the kitchen to put the plates and forks out. Pick the weevils from the grits. Most dawns, smiling wide, Ma hugged her—"Good morning, my special girl"—and the two of them moved about the chores, dancelike. Sometimes Ma sang folk songs or quoted nursery rhymes: "This little piggy went to market." Or she'd swing Kya into a jitterbug, their feet banging the plywood floor until the music of the battery-operated radio died, sounding as if it were singing to itself at the bottom of a barrel. Other mornings Ma spoke about adult things Kya didn't understand, but she figured Ma's words needed somewhere to go, so she absorbed them through her skin, as she poked more wood in the cookstove. Nodding like she knew.

Then, the hustle of getting everybody up and fed. Pa not there. He had two settings: silence and shouting. So it was just fine when he slept through, or didn't come home at all.

But this morning, Ma had been quiet; her smile lost, her eyes red.

She'd tied a white scarf pirate style, low across her forehead, but the purple and yellow edges of a bruise spilled out. Right after breakfast, even before the dishes were washed, Ma had put a few personals in the train case and walked down the road.

The next morning, Kya took up her post again on the steps, her dark eyes boring down the lane like a tunnel waiting for a train. The marsh beyond was veiled in fog so low its cushy bottom sat right on the mud. Barefoot, Kya drummed her toes, twirled grass stems at doodlebugs, but a six-year-old can't sit long and soon she moseyed onto the tidal flats, sucking sounds pulling at her toes. Squatting at the edge of the clear water, she watched minnows dart between sunspots and shadows.

Jodie hollered to her from the palmettos. She stared; maybe he was coming with news. But as he wove through the spiky fronds, she knew by the way he moved, casual, that Ma wasn't home.

"Ya wanta play explorers?" he asked.

"Ya said ya're too old to play 'splorers."

"Nah, I just said that. Never too old. Race ya!"

They tore across the flats, then through the woods toward the beach. She squealed as he overtook her and laughed until they reached the large oak that jutted enormous arms over the sand. Jodie and their older brother, Murph, had hammered a few boards across the branches as a lookout tower and tree fort. Now, much of it was falling in, dangling from rusty nails.

Usually if she was allowed to crew at all it was as slave girl, bringing her brothers warm biscuits swiped from Ma's pan.

But today Jodie said, "You can be captain."

Kya raised her right arm in a charge. "Run off the Spaniards!" They broke off stick-swords and crashed through brambles, shouting and stabbing at the enemy.

Then—make-believe coming and going easily—she walked to a mossy log and sat. Silently, he joined her. He wanted to say something to get her mind off Ma, but no words came, so they watched the swimming shadows of water striders.

Kya returned to the porch steps later and waited for a long time, but, as she looked to the end of the lane, she never cried. Her face was still, her lips a simple thin line under searching eyes. But Ma didn't come back that day either.

2.

Jodie

1952

After Ma left, over the next few weeks, Kya's oldest brother and two sisters drifted away too, as if by example. They had endured Pa's red-faced rages, which started as shouts, then escalated into fist-slugs, or backhanded punches, until one by one, they disappeared. They were nearly grown anyway. And later, just as she forgot their ages, she couldn't remember their real names, only that they were called Missy, Murph, and Mandy. On her porch mattress, Kya found a small pile of socks left by her sisters.

On the morning when Jodie was the only sibling left, Kya awakened to the *clatter-clank* and hot grease of breakfast. She dashed into the kitchen, thinking Ma was home frying corn fritters or hoecakes. But it was Jodie, standing at the woodstove, stirring grits. She smiled to hide the letdown, and he patted the top of her head, gently shushing her to be quiet: if they didn't wake Pa, they could eat alone. Jodie didn't know how to make biscuits, and there wasn't any bacon, so he cooked grits and scrambled eggs in lard, and they sat down together, silently exchanging glances and smiles.

They washed their dishes fast, then ran out the door toward the marsh, he in the lead. But just then Pa shouted and hobbled toward them. Impossibly lean, his frame seemed to flop about from poor gravity. His molars yellow as an old dog's teeth.

Kya looked up at Jodie. "We can run. Hide in the mossy place."

"It's okay. It'll be okay," he said.

Later, near sunset, Jodie found Kya on the beach staring at the sea. As he stepped up beside her, she didn't look at him but kept her eyes on the roiling waves. Still, she knew by the way he spoke that Pa had slugged his face.

"I hafta go, Kya. Can't live here no longer."

She almost turned to him, but didn't. Wanted to beg him not to leave her alone with Pa, but the words jammed up.

"When you're old enough you'll understand," he said. Kya wanted to holler out that she may be young, but she wasn't stupid. She knew Pa was the reason they all left; what she wondered was why no one took her with them. She'd thought of leaving too, but had nowhere to go and no bus money.

"Kya, ya be careful, hear. If anybody comes, don't go in the house. They can get ya there. Run deep in the marsh, hide in the bushes. Always cover yo' tracks; I learned ya how. And ya can hide from Pa, too." When she still didn't speak, he said good-bye and strode across the beach to the woods. Just before he stepped into the trees, she finally turned and watched him walk away.

"This little piggy stayed home," she said to the waves.

Breaking her freeze, she ran to the shack. Shouted his name down the hall, but Jodie's things were already gone, his floor bed stripped bare.

She sank onto his mattress, watching the last of that day slide down the wall. Light lingered after the sun, as it does, some of it pooling in the room, so that for a brief moment the lumpy beds and piles of old clothes took on more shape and color than the trees outside.

A gnawing hunger—such a mundane thing—surprised her. She walked to the kitchen and stood at the door. All her life the room had been warmed from baking bread, boiling butter beans, or bubbling fish stew. Now, it was stale, quiet, and dark. "Who's gonna cook?" she asked out loud. Could have asked, *Who's gonna dance?*

She lit a candle and poked at hot ashes in the woodstove, added kindling. Pumped the bellows till a flame caught, then more wood. The Frigidaire served as a cupboard because no electricity came near the shack. To keep the mold at bay, the door was propped open with the flyswatter. Still, greenish-black veins of mildew grew in every crevice.

Getting out leftovers, she said, "I'll tump the grits in lard, warm 'em up," which she did and ate from the pot, looking through the window for Pa. But he didn't come.

When light from the quarter moon finally touched the shack, she crawled into her porch bed—a lumpy mattress on the floor with real sheets covered in little blue roses that Ma had got at a yard sale—alone at night for the first time in her life.

At first, every few minutes, she sat up and peered through the screen. Listening for footsteps in the woods. She knew the shapes of all the trees; still some seemed to dart here and there, moving with the moon. For a while she was so stiff she couldn't swallow, but on cue, the familiar songs of tree frogs and katydids filled the night. More comforting than three blind mice with a carving knife. The darkness held an odor of sweetness, the earthy breath of frogs and salamanders who'd made it through one more stinky-hot day. The marsh snuggled in closer with a low fog, and she slept.

. . .

For three days Pa didn't come and Kya boiled turnip greens from Ma's garden for breakfast, lunch, and dinner. She'd walked out to the chicken coop for eggs but found it bare. Not a chicken or egg anywhere.

"Chicken shits! You're just a bunch of chicken shits!" She'd been meaning to tend them since Ma left but hadn't done much of anything. Now they'd escaped as a motley flock, clucking far in the trees beyond. She'd have to scatter grits, see if she could keep them close.

On the evening of the fourth day, Pa showed up with a bottle and sprawled across his bed.

Walking into the kitchen the next morning, he hollered, "Whar's ev'body got to?"

"I don't know," she said, not looking at him.

"Ya don't know much as a cur-dawg. Useless as tits on a boar hog."

Kya slipped quietly out the porch door, but walking along the beach searching for mussels, she smelled smoke and looked up to see a plume rising from the direction of the shack. Running as fast as she could, she broke through the trees and saw a bonfire blazing in the yard. Pa was throwing Ma's paintings, dresses, and books onto the flames.

"No!" Kya screamed. He didn't look at her, but threw the old battery-operated radio into the fire. Her face and arms burned as she reached toward the paintings, but the heat pushed her back.

She rushed to the shack to block Pa's return for more, locking eyes with him. Pa raised his backhand toward Kya, but she stood her ground. Suddenly, he turned and limp-stepped toward his boat.

Kya sank onto the brick 'n' boards, watching Ma's watercolors of the marsh smolder into ash. She sat until the sun set, until all the buttons glowed as embers and the memories of dancing the jitterbug with Ma melted into the flames.

Over the next few days, Kya learned from the mistakes of the others, and perhaps more from the minnows, how to live with him. Just keep out of the way, don't let him see you, dart from sunspots to shadows. Up and out of the house before he rose, she lived in the woods and water, then padded into the house to sleep in her bed on the porch as close to the marsh as she could get.

Pa had fought Germany in the Second World War, where his left femur caught shrapnel and shattered, their last source of pride. His weekly disability checks, their only source of income. A week after Jodie left, the Frigidaire stood empty and hardly any turnips remained. When Kya walked into the kitchen that Monday morning, Pa pointed to a crumpled dollar and loose coins on the kitchen table.

"This here'll get ya food fer the week. Thar ain't no such thang as handouts," he said. "Ever'thang cost sump'm, and fer the money ya gotta keep the house up, stove wood c'lected, and warsh the laundree."

For the first time ever Kya walked alone toward the village of Barkley Cove to buy groceries—*this little piggy went to market.* She plodded through deep sand or black mud for four miles until the bay glistened ahead, the hamlet on its shore.

Everglades surrounded the town, mixing their salty haze with that of the ocean, which swelled in high tide on the other side of Main Street. Together the marsh and sea separated the village from the rest of the world, the only connection being the single-lane highway that limped into town on cracked cement and potholes.

There were two streets: Main ran along the oceanfront with a row of shops; the Piggly Wiggly grocery at one end, the Western Auto at the other, the diner in the middle. Mixed in there were Kress's Five and Dime, a Penney's (catalog only), Parker's Bakery, and a Buster Brown Shoe Shop. Next to the Piggly was the Dog-Gone Beer Hall, which offered roasted hot dogs, red-hot chili, and fried shrimp served in folded paper boats. No ladies or children stepped inside because it wasn't considered proper, but a take-out window had been cut out of the wall so they could order hot dogs and Nehi cola from the street. Coloreds couldn't use the door or the window.

The other street, Broad, ran from the old highway straight toward the ocean and into Main, ending right there. So the only intersection in town was Main, Broad, and the Atlantic Ocean. The stores and businesses weren't joined together as in most towns but were separated by small, vacant lots brushed with sea oats and palmettos, as if overnight the marsh had inched in. For more than two hundred years, sharp salty winds had weathered the cedar-shingled buildings to the color of rust, and the window frames, most painted white or blue, had flaked and cracked. Mostly, the village seemed tired of arguing with the elements, and simply sagged.

The town wharf, draped in frayed ropes and old pelicans, jutted into the small bay, whose water, when calm, reflected the reds and yellows of shrimp boats. Dirt roads, lined with small cedar houses, wound through the trees, around lagoons, and along the ocean on either end of the shops. Barkley Cove was quite literally a backwater town, bits scattered here and there among the estuaries and reeds like an egret's nest flung by the wind.

Barefoot and dressed in too-short bib overalls, Kya stood where the marsh track met the road. Biting her lip, wanting to run home. She couldn't reckon what she'd say to people; how she'd figure the grocery money. But hunger was a pushing thing, so she stepped onto Main and walked, head down, toward the Piggly Wiggly on a crumbling sidewalk that appeared now and then between grass clumps. As she approached the Five and Dime, she heard a commotion behind her and jumped to the side just as three boys, a few years older than she, sped by on bikes. The lead boy looked back at her, laughing at the near miss, and then almost collided with a woman stepping from the store.

"CHASE ANDREWS, you get back here! All three of you boys." They pedaled a few more yards, then thought better of it and returned to the woman, Miss Pansy Price, saleslady in fabric and notions. Her family had once owned the largest farm on the outskirts of the marsh and, although they were forced to sell out long ago, she continued her role as genteel landowner. Which wasn't easy living in a tiny apartment above the diner. Miss Pansy usually wore hats shaped like silk turbans, and this morning her headwear was pink, setting off red lipstick and splotches of rouge.

She scolded the boys. "I've a mind to tell y'all's mamas about this. Or better, yo' papas. Ridin' fast like that on the sidewalk, nearly runnin' me over. What ya got to say for yo'self, Chase?"

He had the sleekest bike—red seat and chrome handlebars, raised up. "We're sorry, Miss Pansy, we didn't see ya 'cause that girl over yonder got in the way." Chase, tanned with dark hair, pointed at Kya, who had stepped back and stood half inside a myrtle shrub.

"Never mind her. You cain't go blamin' yo' sins on somebody else, not even swamp trash. Now, you boys gotta do a good deed, make up fer this. There goes Miss Arial with her groceries, go help carry 'em to her truck. And put yo' shirttails in."

"Yes, ma'am," the boys said as they biked toward Miss Arial, who had taught them all second grade.

Kya knew that the parents of the dark-haired boy owned the Western Auto store, which was why he rode the snazziest bike. She'd seen him unloading big cardboard boxes of merchandise from the truck, packing it in, but she had never spoken a word to him or the others.

She waited a few minutes, then, head low again, walked toward the grocery. Inside the Piggly Wiggly, Kya studied the selection of grits and chose a one-pound bag of coarse ground yellow because a red tag hung from the top—a *special of the week*. Like Ma taught her. She fretted in the aisle until no other customers stood at the register, then walked up and faced the checkout lady, Mrs. Singletary, who asked, "Where's ya mama at?" Mrs. Singletary's hair was cut short, curled tight, and colored purple as an iris in sunlight.

"Doin' chores, ma'am."

"Well, ya got money for the grits, or don't ya?"

"Yes'm." Not knowing how to count the exact amount, she laid down the whole dollar.

Mrs. Singletary wondered if the child knew the difference in the coins, so as she placed the change into Kya's open palm she counted slowly, "Twenty-five, fifty, sixty, seventy, eighty, eighty-five and three pennies. 'Cause the grits cost twelve cents."

Kya felt sick to her stomach. Was she supposed to count something back? She stared to the puzzle of coins in her palm.

Mrs. Singletary seemed to soften. "Okay, then. Git on with ya."

Kya dashed from the store and walked as fast as she could toward the marsh track. Plenty of times, Ma had told her, "Never run in town or people'll think you stole something." But as soon as Kya reached the sandy track, she ran a good half mile. Then speed-walked the rest.

Back home, thinking she knew how to fix grits, she threw them into boiling water like Ma had done, but they lumped up all together in one big ball that burned on the bottom and stayed raw in the middle. So rubbery she could only eat a few bites, so she searched the garden again and found a few more turnip greens between the goldenrod. Then boiled them up and ate them all, slurping down the pot likker.

In a few days she got the hang of fixing grits, although no matter how hard she stirred, they lumped up some. The next week she bought backbones—marked with a red tag—and boiled them with grits and collard greens in a mush that tasted fine.

Kya had done the laundry plenty with Ma, so knew how to scrub clothes on the rub board under the yard spigot with bars of lye soap. Pa's overalls were so heavy wet she couldn't wring them out with her tiny hands, and couldn't reach the line to hang them, so draped them sopping over the palmetto fronds at the edge of the woods.

She and Pa did this two-step, living apart in the same shack, sometimes not seeing each other for days. Almost never speaking. She tidied up after herself and after him, like a serious little woman. She wasn't near enough of a cook to fix meals for him—he usually wasn't there anyway—but she made his bed, picked up, swept up, and washed the dishes most of the time. Not because she'd been told, but because it was the only way to keep the shack decent for Ma's return.

Ma had always said the autumn moon showed up for Kya's birthday. So even though she couldn't remember the date of her birth, one evening when the moon rose swollen and golden from the lagoon, Kya said to herself, "I reckon I'm seven." Pa never mentioned it; certainly there was no cake. He didn't say anything about her going to school either, and she, not knowing much about it, was too afraid to bring it up.

Surely Ma would come back for her birthday, so the morning after the harvest moon she put on the calico dress and stared down the lane. Kya willed Ma to be walking toward the shack, still in her alligator shoes and long skirt. When no one came, she got the pot of grits and walked through the woods to the seashore. Hands to her mouth, she held her head back and called, "*Kee-ow, kee-ow, kee-ow.*" Specks of silver appeared in the sky from up and down the beach, from over the surf.

"Here they come. I can't count as high as that many gulls are," she said.

Crying and screeching, the birds swirled and dived, hovered near her face, and landed as she tossed grits to them. Finally, they quieted and stood about preening, and she sat on the sand, her legs folded to the side. One large gull settled onto the sand near Kya.

"It's my birthday," she told the bird.

3.

Chase

1969

The rotted legs of the old abandoned fire tower straddled the bog, which created its own tendrils of mist. Except for cawing crows, the hushed forest seemed to hold an expectant mood as the two boys, Benji Mason and Steve Long, both ten, both blond, started up the damp staircase on the morning of October 30, 1969.

"Fall ain't s'posed to be this hot," Steve called back to Benji.

"Yeah, and everythang quiet 'cept the crows."

Glancing down between the steps, Steve said, "Whoa. What's that?"

"Where?"

"See, there. Blue clothes, like somebody's lyin' in the mud."

Benji called out, "Hey, you! *Whatchadoin'?*"

"I see a face, but it ain't movin'."

Arms pumping, they ran back to the ground and pushed their way to the other side of the tower's base, greenish mud clinging to their boots. There lay a man, flat on his back, his left leg turned grotesquely forward from the knee. His eyes and mouth wide open.

"Jesus Christ!" Benji said.

"My God, it's Chase Andrews."

"We better git the sheriff."

"But we ain't s'posed to be out here."

"That don't matter now. And them crows'll be snooping 'round anytime now."

They swung their heads toward the cawing, as Steve said, "Maybe one of us oughta stay, keep them birds off him."

"Ya're crazy if you think I'm gonna stick 'round here by maself. And I'm bettin' a Injun-head you won't either."

With that, they grabbed their bikes, pedaled hard down the syrupy sand track back to Main, through town, and ran inside the low-slung building where Sheriff Ed Jackson sat at his desk in an office lit with single lightbulbs dangling on cords. Hefty and of medium height, he had reddish hair, his face and arms splotched with pale freckles, and sat thumbing through a *Sports Afield*.

Without knocking, the boys rushed through the open door.

"Sheriff . . ."

"Hey, Steve, Benji. You boys been to a fire?"

"We seen Chase Andrews flat out in the swamp under the fire tower. He looks dead. Ain't movin' one bit."

Ever since Barkley Cove had been settled in 1751, no lawman extended his jurisdiction beyond the saw grass. In the 1940s and '50s, a few sheriffs set hounds on some mainland convicts who'd escaped into the marsh, and the office still kept dogs just in case. But Jackson mostly ignored crimes committed in the swamp. Why interrupt rats killing rats?

But this was Chase. The sheriff stood and took his hat from the rack. "Show me."

Limbs of oak and wild holly screeched against the patrol truck as the sheriff maneuvered down the sandy track with Dr. Vern Murphy, lean and fit with graying hair, the town's only physician, sitting beside him. Each man swayed to the tune of the deep ruts, Vern's head almost banging against the window. Old friends about the same age, they fished together some and were often thrown onto the same case. Both silent now at the prospect of confirming whose body lay in the bog.

Steve and Benji sat in the truck bed with their bikes until the truck stopped.

"He's over there, Mr. Jackson. Behind them bushes."

Ed stepped from the truck. "You boys wait here." Then he and Dr. Murphy waded the mud to where Chase lay. The crows had flown off when the truck came, but other birds and insects whirred above. Insolent life thrumming on.

"It's Chase, all right. Sam and Patti Love won't survive this." The Andrewses had ordered every spark plug, balanced every account, strung every price tag at the Western Auto for their only child, Chase.

Squatting next to the body, listening for a heartbeat with his stethoscope, Vern declared him dead.

"How long ya reckon?" Ed asked.

"I'd say at least ten hours. The coroner'll know for sure."

"He must've climbed up last night, then. Fell from the top."

Vern examined Chase briefly without moving him, then stood next to Ed. Both men stared at Chase's eyes, still looking skyward from his bloated face, then glanced at his gaping mouth.

"How many times I've told folks in this town something like this was bound to happen," the sheriff said.

They had known Chase since he was born. Had watched his life ease from charming child to cute teen; star quarterback and town hot shot to working for his parents. Finally, handsome man wedding the prettiest girl. Now, he sprawled alone, less dignified than the slough. Death's crude pluck, as always, stealing the show.

Ed broke the silence. "Thing is, I can't figure why the others didn't run for help. They always come up here in a pack, or at least a couple of 'em, to make out." The sheriff and doctor exchanged brief but knowing nods that even though he was married, Chase might bring another woman to the tower. "Let's step back out of here. Get a good look at things," Ed said, as he lifted his feet, stepping higher than necessary. "You boys stay where you are; don't go making any more tracks."

Pointing to some footprints that led from the staircase, across the bog, to within eight feet of Chase, Ed asked them, "These your prints from this morning?"

"Yessir, that's as far as we went," Benji said. "Soon as we seen it was Chase, we backed up. You can see there where we backed up."

"Okay." Ed turned. "Vern, something's not right. There's no footprints near the body. If he was with his friends or whoever, once he fell, they would've run down here and stepped all around him, knelt next to him. To see if he was alive. Look how deep our tracks are in this mud, but there're no other fresh tracks. None going toward the stairs or away from the stairs, none around the body."

"Maybe he was by himself, then. That would explain everything."

"Well, I'll tell you one thing that doesn't explain. Where're *his* footprints? How did Chase Andrews walk down the path, cross this muck to the stairs so he could climb to the top, and not leave any footprints himself?"

4.

School

1952

A few days after her birthday, out alone barefooting in mud, Kya bent over, watching a tadpole getting its frog legs. Suddenly she stood. A car churned through deep sand near the end of their lane. No one ever drove here. Then the murmur of people talking—a man and a woman—drifted through the trees. Kya ran fast to the brush, where she could see who was coming but still have ways to escape. Like Jodie taught her.

A tall woman emerged from the car, unsteadily maneuvering in high heels just like Ma had done along the sandy lane. They must be the orphanage people come to get her.

I can outrun her for sure. She'd fall nose-first in them shoes. Kya stayed put and watched the woman step to the porch's screen door.

"Yoo-hoo, anybody home? Truant officer here. I've come to take Catherine Clark to school."

Now this was something. Kya sat mute. She was pretty sure she was supposed to go to school at six. Here they were, a year late.

She had no notion how to talk to kids, certainly not to a teacher, but she wanted to learn to read and what came after twenty-nine.

"Catherine, dear, if ya can hear me, please come on out. It's the law, hon; ya gotta go to school. But 'sides that, you'll like it, dear. Ya get a hot lunch every day for free. I think today they're havin' chicken pie with crust."

That was something else. Kya was very hungry. For breakfast she'd boiled grits with soda crackers stirred in because she didn't have any salt. One thing she already knew about life: you can't eat grits without salt. She'd eaten chicken pie only a few times in her life, but she could still see that golden crust, crunchy on the outside, soft inside. She could feel that full gravy taste, like it was round. It was her stomach acting on its own that made Kya stand up among the palmetto fronds.

"Hello, dear, I'm Mrs. Culpepper. You're all grown up and ready to go to school, aren't ya?"

"Yes'm," Kya said, head low.

"It's okay, you can go barefoot, other chillin do, but 'cause you're a li'l girl, you have to wear a skirt. Do you have a dress or a skirt, hon?"

"Yes'm."

"Okay then, let's go get ya dressed up."

Mrs. Culpepper followed Kya through the porch door, having to step over a row of bird nests Kya had lined up along the boards. In the bedroom Kya put on the only dress that fit, a plaid jumper with one shoulder strap held up with a safety pin.

"That's fine, dear, you look just fine."

Mrs. Culpepper held out her hand. Kya stared at it. She hadn't touched another person in weeks, hadn't touched a stranger her whole life. But she put her small hand in Mrs. Culpepper's and was led down the path to the Ford Crestliner driven by a silent man wearing a gray fedora. Sitting in the backseat, Kya didn't smile and didn't feel like a chick tucked under its mother's wing.

Barkley Cove had one school for whites. First grade through twelfth went to a brick two-story at the opposite end of Main from the sheriff's office. The black kids had their own school, a one-story cement block structure out near Colored Town.

When she was led into the school office, they found her name but no date of birth in the county birth records, so they put her in the second grade, even though she'd never been to school a day in her life. Anyhow, they said, the first grade was too crowded, and what difference would it make to marsh people who'd do a few months of school, maybe, then never be seen again. As the principal walked her down a wide hallway that echoed their footsteps, sweat popped out on her brow. He opened the door to a classroom and gave her a little push.

Plaid shirts, full skirts, shoes, lots of shoes, some bare feet, and eyes—all staring. She'd never seen so many people. Maybe a dozen. The teacher, the same Mrs. Arial those boys had helped, walked Kya to a desk near the back. She could put her things in the cubbyhole, she was told, but Kya didn't have any things.

The teacher walked back to the front and said, "Catherine, please stand and tell the class your full name."

Her stomach churned.

"Come now, dear, don't be shy."

Kya stood. "Miss Catherine Danielle Clark," she said, because that was what Ma once said was her whole name.

"Can you spell *dog* for us?"

Staring at the floor, Kya stood silent. Jodie and Ma had taught her some letters. But she'd never spelled a word aloud for anybody.

Nerves stirred in her stomach; still, she tried. "*G-o-d.*"

Laughter let loose up and down the rows.

"Shh! Hush, y'all!" Mrs. Arial called out. "We never laugh, ya hear me, we never laugh at each other. Y'all know better'n that."

Kya sat down fast in her seat at the back of the room, trying to disappear like a bark beetle blending into the furrowed trunk of an oak. Yet nervous as she was, as the teacher continued the lesson, she leaned forward, waiting to learn what came after twenty-nine. So far all Miss Arial had talked about was something called phonics, and the students, their mouths shaped like O's, echoed her sounds of *ah, aa, o,* and *u,* all of them moaning like doves.

About eleven o'clock the warm-buttery smell of baking yeast rolls and pie pastry filled the halls and seeped into the room. Kya's stomach panged and fitted, and when the class finally formed a single file and marched into the cafeteria, her mouth was full of saliva. Copying the others, she picked up a tray, a green plastic plate, and flatware. A large window with a counter opened into the kitchen, and laid out before her was an enormous enamel pan of chicken pie crisscrossed with thick, crispy pastry, hot gravy bubbling up. A tall black woman, smiling and calling some of the kids by name, plopped a big helping of pie on her plate, then some pink-lady peas in butter and a yeast roll. She got banana pudding and her own small red-and-white carton of milk to put on her tray.

She turned into the seating area, where most of the tables were full of kids laughing and talking. She recognized Chase Andrews and his friends, who had nearly knocked her off the sidewalk with their bikes, so she turned her head away and sat at an empty table. Several times in quick succession, her eyes betrayed her and glanced at the boys, the only faces she knew. But they, like everyone else, ignored her.

Kya stared at the pie full of chicken, carrots, potatoes, and little peas. Golden brown pastry on top. Several girls, dressed in full skirts fluffed out wide with layers of crinolines, approached. One was tall, skinny, and blond, another round with chubby cheeks. Kya wondered how they could climb a tree or even get in a boat wearing those big skirts. Certainly couldn't wade for frogs; wouldn't even be able to see their own feet.

As they neared, Kya stared at her plate. What would she say if they sat next to her? But the girls passed her by, chirping like birds, and joined their friends at another table. For all the hunger in her stomach, she found her mouth had gone dry, making it difficult to swallow. So after eating only a few bites, she drank all the milk, stuffed as much pie as she could into the milk carton, carefully so nobody would see her do it, and wrapped it and the roll in her napkin.

The rest of the day, she never opened her mouth. Even when the teacher asked her a question, she sat mute. She reckoned she was supposed to learn from them, not them from her. *Why put maself up for being laughed at?* she thought.

At the last bell, she was told the bus would drop her three miles from her lane because the road was too sandy from there, and that she had to walk to the bus every morning. On the way home, as the bus swayed in deep ruts and passed stretches of cord grass, a chant rose from the front: "MISS Catherine Danielle Clark!" Tallskinnyblonde and Roundchubbycheeks, the girls at lunch, called out, "Where ya been, marsh hen? Where's yo' hat, swamp rat?"

The bus finally stopped at an unmarked intersection of tangled tracks way back in the woods. The driver cranked the door open, and Kya scooted out and ran for nearly half a mile, heaved for breath, then jogged all the way to their lane. She didn't stop at the shack but ran full out through the palmettos to the lagoon and down the trail that led through dense, sheltering oaks to the ocean. She broke out onto the barren beach, the sea opening its arms wide, the wind tearing loose her braided hair as she stopped at the tide line. She was as near to tears as she had been the whole day.

Above the roar of pounding waves, Kya called to the birds. The ocean sang bass, the gulls sang soprano. Shrieking and crying, they circled over the marsh and above the sand as she threw piecrust and yeast rolls onto the beach. Legs hanging down, heads twisting, they landed.

A few birds pecked gently between her toes, and she laughed from the tickling until tears streamed down her cheeks, and finally great, ragged sobs erupted from that tight place below her throat. When the carton was empty she didn't think she could stand the pain, so afraid they would leave her like everybody else. But the gulls squatted on the beach around her and went about their business of preening their gray extended wings. So she sat down too and wished she could gather them up and take them with her to the porch to sleep. She imagined them all packed in her bed, a fluffy bunch of warm, feathered bodies under the covers together.

Two days later she heard the Ford Crestliner churning in the sand and ran into the marsh, stepping heavily across sandbars, leaving footprints as plain as day, then tiptoeing into the water, leaving no tracks, doubling back, and taking off in a different direction. When she got to mud, she ran in circles, creating a confusion of clues. Then, when she reached hard ground, she whispered across it, jumping from grass clump to sticks, leaving no trace.

They came every two or three days for a few more weeks, the man in the fedora doing the search and chase, but he never even got close. Then one week no one came. There was only the cawing of crows. She dropped her hands to her sides, staring at the empty lane.

Kya never went back to school a day in her life. She returned to heron watching and shell collecting, where she reckoned she could learn something. "I can already coo like a dove," she told herself. "And lots better than them. Even with all them fine shoes."

One morning, a few weeks after her day at school, the sun glared white-hot as Kya climbed into her brothers' tree fort at the beach and searched for sailing ships hung with skull-and-crossbones flags. Proving that imagination grows in the loneliest of soils, she shouted, "Ho! Pirates ho!" Brandishing her sword, she jumped from the tree to attack. Suddenly pain shot through her right foot, racing like fire up her leg. Knees caving in, she fell on her side and shrieked. She saw a long rusty nail sticking deep in the bottom of her foot. "Pa!" she screamed. She tried to remember if he had come home last night. "HELP me, Pa," she cried out, but there was no answer. In one fast move, she reached down and yanked the nail out, screaming to cover the pain.

She moved her arms through the sand in nonsensical motions, whimpering. Finally, she sat up and looked at the bottom of her foot. There was almost no blood, just the tiny opening of a small, deep wound. Right then she remembered the lockjaw. Her stomach went tight and she felt cold. Jodie had told her about a boy who stepped on a rusty nail and didn't get a tetanus shot. His jaws jammed shut, clenched so tight he couldn't open his mouth. Then his spine cramped backward like a bow, but there was nothing anybody could do but stand there and watch him die from the contortions.

Jodie was very clear on one point: you had to get the shot within two days after stepping on a nail, or you were doomed. Kya had no idea how to get one of those shots.

"I gotta do sump'm. I'll lock up for sure waitin' for Pa." Sweat rolling down her face in beads, she hobbled across the beach, finally entering the cooler oaks around the shack.

Ma used to soak wounds in salt water and pack them with mud mixed with all kinds of potions. There was no salt in the kitchen, so Kya limped into the woods toward a brackish slipstream so salty at low tide, its edges glistened with brilliant white crystals. She sat on the ground, soaking her foot in the marsh's brine, all the while moving her mouth: open, close, open, close, mocking yawns, chewing motions, anything to keep it from jamming up. After nearly an hour, the tide receded enough for her to dig a hole in the black mud with her fingers, and she eased her foot gently into the silky earth. The air was cool here, and eagle cries gave her bearing.

By late afternoon she was very hungry, so went back to the shack. Pa's room was still empty, and he probably wouldn't be home for hours. Playing poker and drinking whiskey kept a man busy most of the night. There were no grits, but rummaging around, she found an old greasy tin of Crisco shortening, dipped up a tiny bit of the white fat, and spread it on a soda cracker. Nibbled at first, then ate five more.

She eased into her porch bed, listening for Pa's boat. The approaching night tore and darted and sleep came in bits, but she must have dropped off near morning for she woke with the sun fully on her face. Quickly she opened her mouth; it still worked. She shuffled back and forth from the brackish pool to the shack until, by tracking the sun, she knew two days had passed. She opened and closed her mouth. Maybe she had made it.

That night, tucking herself into the sheets of the floor mattress, her mud-caked foot wrapped in a rag, she wondered if she would wake up dead. No, she remembered, it wouldn't be that easy: her back would bow; her limbs twist.

A few minutes later, she felt a twinge in her lower back and sat up. "Oh no, oh no. Ma, Ma." The sensation in her back repeated itself and made her hush. "It's just an itch," she muttered. Finally, truly exhausted, she slept, not opening her eyes until doves murmured in the oak.

She walked to the pool twice a day for a week, living on saltines and Crisco, and Pa never came home the whole time. By the eighth day she could circle her foot without stiffness and the pain had retreated to the surface. She danced a little jig, favoring her foot, squealing, "I did it, I did it!"

The next morning, she headed for the beach to find more pirates.

"First thing I'm gonna do is boss my crew to pick up all them nails."

Every morning she woke early, still listening for the clatter of Ma's busy cooking. Ma's favorite breakfast had been scrambled eggs from her own hens, ripe red tomatoes sliced, and cornbread fritters made by pouring a mixture of cornmeal, water, and salt onto grease so hot the concoction bubbled up, the edges frying into crispy lace. Ma said you weren't really frying something unless you could hear it crackling from the next room, and all her life Kya had heard those fritters popping in grease when she woke. Smelled the blue, hot-corn smoke. But now the kitchen was silent, cold, and Kya slipped from her porch bed and stole to the lagoon.

Months passed, winter easing gently into place, as southern winters do. The sun, warm as a blanket, wrapped Kya's shoulders, coaxing her deeper into the marsh. Sometimes she heard night-sounds she didn't know or jumped from lightning too close, but whenever she stumbled, it was the land that caught her. Until at last, at some unclaimed moment, the heart-pain seeped away like water into sand. Still there, but deep. Kya laid her hand upon the breathing, wet earth, and the marsh became her mother.

5.

Investigation

1969

Overhead, cicadas squealed against a mean sun. All other life-forms cowered from the heat, emitting only a vacant hum from the undergrowth.

Wiping his brow, Sheriff Jackson said, "Vern, there's more to do here, but it doesn't feel right. Chase's wife and folks don't know he's passed."

"I'll go tell them, Ed," Dr. Vern Murphy replied.

"I appreciate that. Take my truck. Send the ambulance back for Chase, and Joe with my truck. But don't speak a word about this to anybody else. I don't want everybody in this town out here, and that's just what'll happen if you mention it."

Before moving, Vern stared for a long minute at Chase, as though he had overlooked something. As a doctor, he should fix this. Heavy swamp air stood behind them, waiting patiently for its turn.

Ed turned to the boys. "Y'all stay right here. I don't need anybody yapping about this in town, and don't put your hands on anything or make any more tracks in the mud."

"Yessir," Benji said. "Ya think somebody killed Chase, don't ya? 'Cause there's no footprints. Pushed him off, maybe?"

"I didn't say any such thing. This is standard police work. Now, you boys just keep out of the way and don't repeat anything you hear out here."

Deputy Joe Purdue, a small man with thick sideburns, showed up in the patrol truck in less than fifteen minutes.

"Just can't take it in. Chase dead. He was the best quarterback this town ever saw. This is plumb outta kilter."

"You got that right. Well, let's get to work."

"What ya got so far?"

Ed moved farther from the boys. "Well, obviously, on the surface, it looks like an accident: he fell from the tower and was killed. But so far I haven't found any of his footprints walking toward the steps or prints from anybody else either. Let's see if we can find any evidence that somebody covered 'em up."

The two lawmen combed the area for a full ten minutes. "You're right, not one print 'cept for the boys," Joe said.

"Yeah, and no signs of somebody brushing them out. I just don't get it. Let's move on. I'll work on this later," Ed said.

They took pictures of the body, of its position relative to the steps, close-ups of head wounds, the leg bent wrong. Joe made notes as Ed dictated. As they measured the distance from the body to the trail, they heard the sides of the ambulance scratching the thick bushes along the lane. The driver, an old black man who'd taken the wounded, ill, dying, and dead under his charge for decades, bowed his head in respect and whispered suggestions: "A'right den, his'n arms ain't gwine tuck in much, so cain't roll 'im onta the gunny; hafta lift 'im and he's gwine be heavy; Sheriff, sir, ya cradle Mr. Chase's head. Dat's good. My, my." By late morning, they'd loaded him, complete with clinging sludge, into the back.

Since Dr. Murphy had by now informed Chase's parents of his death, Ed told the boys they could go on home, and he and Joe started up the stairs, which switched to the top, narrowing at each level. As they climbed, the round corners of the world moved out farther and farther, the lush, rounded forests and watery marsh expanding to the very rims.

When they reached the last step, Jackson lifted his hands and pushed open an iron grate. After they climbed onto the platform, he eased it down again because it was part of the floor. Wooden planks, splintered and grayed with age, formed the center of the platform, but around the perimeter, the floor was a series of see-through square grates that could be opened and closed. As long as they were down you could walk on them safely, but if one was left open, you could fall to the earth sixty feet below.

"Hey, look at that." Ed pointed to the far side of the platform, where one of the grates stood open.

"What the hell?" Joe said as they walked to it. Peering down, they saw the perfect outline of Chase's misshapen form embedded in the mud. Yellowish goo and duckweed had splashed to the sides like a splatter painting.

"This doesn't figure," Ed said. "Sometimes folks forget to close the grate over the stairs. You know, on their way back down. We've found it open a few times, but the others are almost never left open."

"Why would Chase open this one in the first place? Why would anybody?"

"Unless somebody planned to push somebody else to their death," Ed said.

"Then why didn't they close it afterward?"

"Because if Chase had fallen through on his own, he couldn't have closed it. Had to be left open to look like an accident."

"Look at that support beam below the hole. It's all bashed in and splintered."

"Yeah, I see. Chase must've banged his head on it when he fell."

"I'll climb out there, look for blood or hair samples. Collect some splinters."

"Thanks, Joe. And take some close-ups. I'll go get a rope to spot you. We don't need two bodies in this muck in one day. And we have to take fingerprints off this grate, the grate by the stairs, the railing, the banisters. Everything anybody would've touched. And collect any hair samples, threads."

More than two hours later, they stretched their backs from the leaning and stooping. Ed said, "I'm not saying there was foul play. Way too early. But besides that, I can't think of anyone who'd want to kill Chase."

"Well, I'd say there'd be quite a list," the deputy said.

"Like who? What're you talking about?"

"C'mon, Ed. Ya know how Chase was. Tom-cattin', ruttin' 'round like a penned bull let out. 'Fore he was married, after he was married, with single girls, married women. I seen randy dogs at a bitch fest better behaved."

"C'mon, he wasn't that bad. Sure. He had a reputation as a ladies' man. But I don't see anybody in this town committin' murder over it."

"I'm just sayin' there's people didn't like him. Some jealous husband. It'd have to be somebody he knew. Somebody we all know. Not likely Chase'd climb up here with some stranger," Joe said.

"Unless he was up to his navel in debt with some out-of-towner. Something like that we didn't know about. And a man strong enough to push Chase Andrews. No small task."

Joe said, "I can already think of a few guys up to it."

6.

A Boat and a Boy

1952

One morning, Pa, shaved fresh and dressed in a wrinkled button-down shirt, came into the kitchen and said he was leaving on the Trailways bus for Asheville to discuss some issues with the army. He figured he had more disability due him and was off to see about it and wouldn't be back for three or four days. He'd never told Kya his business, where he was going, or when he was coming back, so, standing there in her too-short bib overalls, she stared up at him, mute.

"Ah b'leeve ya deaf and dumb as all git-out," he said, the porch door slapping behind him.

Kya watched him gimp along the path, left leg swinging to the side, then forward. Her fingers knotted. Maybe they were all going to leave her, one by one down this lane. When he reached the road and unexpectedly looked back, she threw her hand up and waved hard. A shot to keep him tethered. Pa lifted an arm in a quick, dismissive salutation. But it was something. It was more than Ma had done.

From there, she wandered to the lagoon, where early light caught the glimmer of hundreds of dragonfly wings. Oaks and thick brush encircled the water, darkening it cavelike, and she stopped as she eyed Pa's boat drifting there on the line. If she took it into the marsh and he found out, he'd take his belt to her. Or the paddle he kept by the porch door; the "welcome bat," Jodie had called it.

Perhaps a yearning to reach out yonder pulled her toward the boat—a bent-up, flat-bottomed metal skiff Pa used for fishing. She'd been out in it all her life, usually with Jodie. Sometimes he'd let her steer. She even knew the way through some of the intricate channels and estuaries that wandered through a patchwork of water and land, land and water, finally to the sea. Because even though the ocean was just beyond the trees surrounding the shack, the only way to get there by boat was to go in the opposite direction, inland, and wind through miles of the maze of waterways that eventually hooked back to the sea.

But, being only seven and a girl, she'd never taken the boat out by herself. It floated there, tied by a single cotton line to a log. Gray grunge, frayed fishing tackle, and half-crushed beer cans covered the boat floor. Stepping in, she said out loud, "Gotta check the gas like Jodie said, so Pa won't figure I took it." She poked a broken reed into the rusted tank. "'Nough for a short ride, I reckon."

Like any good robber, she looked around, then flicked the cotton line free of the log and poled forward with the lone paddle. The silent cloud of dragonflies parted before her.

Not able to resist, she pulled the starter rope and jerked back when the motor caught the first time, sputtering and burping white smoke. Grabbing the tiller, she turned the throttle too far, and the boat turned sharply, the engine screaming. She released the throttle, threw her hands up, and the boat eased to a drift, purring.

When in trouble, just let go. Go back to idle.

Accelerating now more gently, she steered around the old fallen cypress, *putt, putt, putt* beyond the piled sticks of the beaver lodge. Then, holding her breath, she steered toward the lagoon entrance, almost hidden by brambles. Ducking beneath the low-hanging limbs of giant trees, she churned slowly through thicket for more than a hundred yards, as easy turtles slid from water-logs. A floating mat of duckweed colored the water as green as the leafy ceiling, creating an emerald tunnel. Finally, the trees parted, and she glided into a place of wide sky and reaching grasses, and the sounds of cawing birds. The view a chick gets, she reckoned, when it finally breaks its shell.

Kya tooled along, a tiny speck of a girl in a boat, turning this way and that as endless estuaries branched and braided before her. *Keep left at all the turns going out,* Jodie had said. She barely touched the throttle, easing the boat through the current, keeping the noise low. As she broke around a stand of reeds, a whitetail doe with last spring's fawn stood lapping water. Their heads jerked up, slinging droplets through the air. Kya didn't stop or they would bolt, a lesson she'd learned from watching wild turkeys: if you act like a predator, they act like prey. Just ignore them, keep going slow. She drifted by, and the deer stood as still as a pine until Kya disappeared beyond the salt grass.

She entered a place with dark lagoons in a throat of oaks and remembered a channel on the far side that flowed to an enormous estuary. Several times she came upon dead ends, had to backtrack to take another turn. Keeping all these landmarks straight in her mind so she could get back. Finally the estuary lay ahead, water stretching so far it captured the whole sky and all the clouds within it.

The tide was going out, she knew by water lines along the creek shores. When it receded enough, any time from now, some channels would shallow up and she'd run aground, get stranded. She'd have to head back before then.

As she rounded a stand of tall grass, suddenly the ocean's face—gray, stern, and pulsing—frowned at her. Waves slammed one another, awash in their own white saliva, breaking apart on the shore with loud booms—energy searching for a beachhead. Then they flattened into quiet tongues of foam, waiting for the next surge.

The surf taunted her, daring her to breach the waves and enter the sea, but without Jodie, her courage failed. Time to turn around anyway. Thunderheads grew in the western sky, forming huge gray mushrooms pressing at the seams.

There'd been no other people, not even distant boats, so it was a surprise when she entered the large estuary again, and there, close against the marsh grass, was a boy fishing from another battered rig. Her course would take her only twenty feet from him. By now, she looked every bit the swamp child—hair blown into tangles, dusty cheeks streaked with wind-tears.

Neither low gas nor storm threat gave her the same edgy feeling as seeing another person, especially a boy. Ma had told her older sisters to watch out for them; if you look tempting, men turn into predators. Squishing her lips tight, she thought, *What am I gonna do? I gotta go right by him.*

From the corner of her eye, she saw he was thin, his golden curls stuffed under a red baseball cap. Much older than she, eleven, maybe twelve. Her face was grim as she approached, but he smiled at her, warm and open, and touched the brim of his hat like a gentleman greeting a fine lady in a gown and bonnet. She nodded slightly, then looked ahead, increasing the throttle and passing him by.

All she could think of now was getting back to familiar footing, but somewhere she must have turned wrong, for when she reached the second string of lagoons, she couldn't find the channel that led home. Round and round, near oak knees and myrtle thickets, she searched. A slow panic eased in. Now, the grass banks, sandbars, and bends all looked the same. She cut the engine and stood smack-dab in the middle of the boat, balancing with feet spread wide, trying to see over the reeds, but couldn't. She sat. Lost. Low on gas. Storm coming.

Stealing Pa's words, she cussed her brother for leaving. "Damn ya, Jodie! Shit fire an' fall in. You just shit fire an' fall in it."

She whimpered once as the boat drifted in soft current. Clouds, gaining ground against the sun, moved weighted but silent overhead, pushing the sky and dragging shadows across the clear water. Could be a gale any minute. Worse, though: if she wandered too long, Pa would know she took the boat. She eased ahead; maybe she could find that boy.

Another few minutes of creek brought a bend and the large estuary ahead, and on the other side, the boy in his boat. Egrets took flight, a line of white flags against the mounting gray clouds. She anchored him hard with her eyes. Afraid to go near him, afraid not to. Finally, she turned across the estuary.

He looked up when she neared.

"Hey," he said.

"Hey." She looked beyond his shoulder into the reeds.

"Which way you headed, anyhow?" he asked. "Not out, I hope. That storm's comin'."

"No," she said, looking down at the water.

"You okay?"

Her throat tightened against a sob. She nodded but couldn't speak.

"You lost?"

She bobbed her head again. Wasn't going to cry like a girl.

"Well, then. I git lost all the time," he said, and smiled. "Hey, I know you. You're Jodie Clark's sister."

"I used ta be. He's gone."

"Well, you're still his . . ." But he let it drop.

"How'd you know me?" She threw a quick, direct look at his eyes.

"Oh, I've been fishin' with Jodie some. I saw you a couple a' times. You were just a little kid. You're Kya, right?"

Someone knew her name. She was taken aback. Felt anchored to something; released from something else.

"Yeah. You know my place? From here?"

"Reckon I do. It's 'bout time anyhow." He nodded at the clouds. "Follow me." He pulled his line, put tackle in the box, and started his outboard. As he headed across the estuary, he waved, and she followed. Cruising slowly, he went directly to the right channel, looked back to make sure she'd made the turn, and kept going. He did that at every bend to the oak lagoons. As he turned into the dark waterway toward home, she could see where she'd gone wrong, and would never make the mistake again.

He guided her—even after she waved that she knew her way—across her lagoon, up to the shore where the shack squatted in the woods. She motored up to the old waterlogged pine and tied up. He drifted back from her boat, bobbing in their contrary wakes.

"You okay now?"

"Yeah."

"Well, storm's comin', I better git."

She nodded, then remembered how Ma taught her. "Thank ya."

"All right, then. My name's Tate 'case ya see me again."

She didn't respond, so he said, "Bye now."

As he headed out, slow raindrops splattered the lagoon beach, and she said, "It's gonna rain bullfrogs; that boy'll get soaked through."

She stooped to the gas tank and stuck in her reed dipstick, cupping her hands around the rim, so rain wouldn't drop in. Maybe she couldn't count coins, but she knew for sure, you can't let water get in gas.

It's way low. Pa's gonna know. I gotta tote a can to the Sing Oil 'fore Pa gits back.

She knew the owner, Mr. Johnny Lane, always referred to her family as swamp trash, but dealing with him, the storms, and tides would be worth it, because all she could think of now was getting back into that space of grass and sky and water. Alone, she'd been scared, but that was already humming as excitement. There was something else, too. The calmness of the boy. She'd never known anybody to speak or move so steady. So sure and easy. Just being near him, and not even that close, had eased her tightness. For the first time since Ma and Jodie left, she breathed without pain; felt something other than the hurt. She needed this boat and that boy.

That same afternoon, holding his bike by the handlebars, Tate Walker strolled through town, nodding at Miss Pansy in the Five and Dime, and past the Western Auto to the tip of the town wharf. He scanned the sea for his dad's shrimp boat, *The Cherry Pie,* and spotted its bright red paint far out, the wide net-wings rocking with the swells. As it neared, escorted by its own cloud of gulls, he waved, and his father, a large man with mountain shoulders and thick red hair and a beard, threw his hand in the air. Scupper, as everyone in the village called him, tossed the line to Tate, who tied up, then jumped on board to help the crew unload the catch.

Scupper tousled Tate's hair. "How's it, son? Thanks for coming by."

Tate smiled, nodded. "Sure." They and the crew busied about, loading shrimp into crates, toting them to the wharf, calling out to one another about grabbing beers at the Dog-Gone, asking Tate about school. Taller by a hand than the other men, Scupper scooped up three wire crates at a time, carrying them across the plank, going back for more. His fists were bear-sized, knuckles chapped and split. In less than forty minutes the deck was hosed, nets tied, lines secured.

He told the crew he'd join them another day for beer; he had to do some tuning up before going home. In the wheelhouse, Scupper put a 78 record of Miliza Korjus on the player strapped to the counter and turned the volume up. He and Tate went below and squeezed into the engine hold, where Tate handed tools to his dad as he greased parts and tightened bolts by a dim lightbulb. All the while the soaring, sweet opera lifted higher into the sky.

Scupper's great-great-grandfather, emigrating from Scotland, had shipwrecked off the coast of North Carolina in the 1760s and was the only survivor. He swam to shore, landing on the Outer Banks, found a wife, and fathered thirteen children. Many could trace their roots back to that one Mr. Walker, but Scupper and Tate stayed mostly to themselves. Didn't join the Sunday picnic spreads of chicken salad and deviled eggs with their relatives often, not like they had when his mother and sister were still there.

Finally, in the graying dusk, Scupper slapped Tate on the shoulders. "All done. Let's get home, get supper on."

They walked up the wharf, down Main, and out a winding road to their house, a two-story with weathered cedar-shake siding, built in the 1800s. The white window trim had been painted fresh, and the lawn running almost to the sea was cut neat. But the azaleas and rosebushes next to the house sulked in weeds.

Pulling off yellow boots in the mudroom, Scupper asked, "You tired of burgers?"

"Never tired of burgers."

Tate stood at the kitchen counter, picking up globs of hamburger meat, forming patties, and placing them on a plate. His mother and sister, Carianne, both wearing baseball caps, grinned at him from a picture hanging next to the window. Carianne loved that Atlanta Crackers cap, had worn it everywhere.

He looked away from them, started slicing tomatoes, stirring baked beans. If not for him, they'd be here. His mother basting a chicken, Carianne cutting biscuits.

As usual Scupper got the burgers a bit black, but they were juicy inside and thick as a small city phone book. Both hungry, they ate in silence for a while, and then Scupper asked Tate about school.

"Biology's good; I like it, but we're doing poetry in English class. Can't say I like it much. We each gotta read one out loud. You used to recite some, but I don't remember them."

"I got the poem for you, son," Scupper said. "My favorite—'The Cremation of Sam McGee' by Robert Service. Used to read it out to y'all. Was your mama's favorite. She laughed every time I read it, never got tired of it."

Tate looked down at the mention of his mother, pushed his beans around.

Scupper went on. "Don't go thinking poetry's just for sissies. There's mushy love poems, for sure, but there's also funny ones, lots about nature, war even. Whole point of it—they make ya feel something." His dad had told him many times that the definition of a real man is one who cries without shame, reads poetry with his heart, feels opera in his soul, and does what's necessary to defend a woman. Scupper walked to the sitting room, calling back, "I used to know most of it by heart, but not anymore. But here it is, I'll read it to ya." He sat back down at the table and began reading. When he got to this segment:

> "And there sat Sam, looking cool and calm, in the heart of
> the furnace roar;
> And he wore a smile you could see a mile, and he said,
> 'Please close that door.

It's fine in here, but I greatly fear you'll let in the cold
    and storm—
Since I left Plumtree down in Tennessee, it's the first time
    I've been warm.'"

Scupper and Tate chuckled.

"Your mom always laughed at that."

They smiled, remembering. Just sat there a minute. Then Scupper said he'd wash up while Tate did his homework. In his room, scanning through the poetry book for one to read in class, Tate found a poem by Thomas Moore:

. . . she's gone to the Lake of the Dismal Swamp,
Where, all night long, by a fire-fly lamp,
She paddles her white canoe.

And her fire-fly lamp I soon shall see,
And her paddle I soon shall hear;
Long and loving our life shall be,
And I'll hide the maid in a cypress tree,
When the footstep of death is near.

The words made him think of Kya, Jodie's little sister. She'd seemed so small and alone in the marsh's big sweep. He imagined his own sister lost out there. His dad was right—poems made you feel something.

7.

The Fishing Season

1952

That evening, after the fishing boy led her home through the marsh, Kya sat cross-legged on her porch bed. Mist from the downpour eased through the patched-up screen, touching her face. She thought about the boy. Kind yet strong, like Jodie. The only people she ever spoke to were Pa now and then and, even less often, the cash-register lady at the Piggly Wiggly, Mrs. Singletary, who had recently taken to teaching Kya the difference between quarters, nickels, and dimes—she already knew about pennies. But Mrs. Singletary could also get nosey.

"Dahlin', what's yo' name, anyhow? And why don't yo' ma come in anymore? Haven't seen 'er since the turnips put out."

"Ma's got lots of chores, so she sends me to the store."

"Yeah, dear, but ya never buy nears enough for yo' family."

"Ya know, ma'am, I gotta go. Ma needs these grits right away."

When possible, Kya avoided Mrs. Singletary, using the other checkout lady, who didn't show any interest except to say kids shouldn't come to the market barefoot. She thought of telling the lady she didn't plan to pick grapes with her toes. Who could afford grapes, anyhow?

More and more Kya didn't talk to anybody but the gulls. She wondered if she could strike some bargain with Pa to use his boat. Out in the marsh, she could collect feathers and shells and maybe see the boy sometimes. She'd never had a friend, but she could feel the use of it, the pull. They could boat around in the estuaries some, explore the fens. He might think of her as a little kid, but he knew his way around the marsh and might teach her.

Pa didn't have a car. He used the boat to fish, to go to town, to maneuver through the swamp to the Swamp Guinea, a weathered bar and poker joint connected to solid ground by a rickety boardwalk through cattails. Made of rough-cut clapboard under a tin roof, it rambled from one add-on to the next, the floor at different levels depending on how high the brick chicken-legs perched it above the swamp. When Pa went there or anywhere, he took the boat, only rarely walked, so why would he lend it to her?

But he'd let her brothers use it when he wasn't, probably because they caught fish for supper. She had no interest in fishing, but maybe she could trade something else, figuring that was the way to reach him. Cook maybe, do more around the house, until Ma came back.

The rain eased. A single drop, here then there, shook a leaf like the flick of a cat's ear. Kya hopped up, cleaned out the Frigidaire-cupboard, mopped the stained plywood kitchen floor, and scraped off months of caked-on grits from the woodstove burners. Early the next morning, she scrubbed Pa's sheets, reeking of sweat and whiskey, and draped them over the palmettos. She went through her brothers' room, not much bigger than a closet, dusting and sweeping. Dirty socks were piled in the back of the closet and yellowed comic books strewn next to the two soiled mattresses on the floor. She tried to see the boys' faces, the feet that went with the socks, but the details blurred. Even Jodie's face was fading; she'd see his eyes for an instant, then they'd slip away, closing.

The next morning, carrying a gallon can, she walked the sandy tracks to the Piggly and bought matches, backbone, and salt. Saved out two dimes. "Can't get milk, gotta get gas."

She stopped by the Sing Oil filling station just outside Barkley Cove, which stood in a grove of pines surrounded by rusted-out trucks and jalopy cars stacked on cement blocks.

Mr. Lane saw Kya coming. "Git on outta here, ya little beggar-hen. Marsh trash."

"I got cash money, Mr. Lane. I need gas and oil for Pa's boat motor." She held out two dimes, two nickels, and five pennies.

"Well, it ain't hardly worth ma trouble for such a piddly sum, but c'mon, give it here." He reached for the bent-up, square container.

She thanked Mr. Lane, who grunted again. The groceries and gas weighed more with every mile, and it took some time to get home. Finally in the shade of the lagoon, she emptied the can into the gas tank and scrubbed the boat with rags and wet sand for grist until the metal sides showed through the grime.

On the fourth day after Pa left, she started keeping a lookout. By late afternoon a cold dread set in and her breathing shallowed up. Here she was again, staring down the lane. Mean as he was, she needed him to come back. Finally, in the early evening, there he came, walking the sandy ruts. She ran to the kitchen and laid out a goulash of boiled mustard greens, backbone, and grits. She didn't know how to make gravy, so poured the backbone stock—floating with morsels of white fat—into an empty jelly jar. The plates were cracked and didn't match, but she had the fork on the left, the knife on the right like Ma taught her. Then she waited, flattened up against the Frigidaire like a roadkill stork.

He banged the front door open against the wall and walked through the sitting room to his bedroom in three strides, without calling her or looking in the kitchen. That was normal. She heard him putting his case on the floor, pulling out drawers. He'd notice the fresh bedding, the clean floor for sure. If not his eyes, his nose would catch the difference.

In a few minutes he stepped out, straight into the kitchen, and looked at the set table, at the steaming bowls of food. He saw her standing against the fridge, and they stared at each other like they'd never seen each other before.

"Ah swannee, girl, what's a' this? Looks like ya went an' got all growed up. Cookin' and all." He didn't smile, but his face was calm. He was unshaven, with dark unwashed hair hanging across his left temple. But he was sober; she knew the signs.

"Yessir. I fixed cornbread too, but it didn't come out."

"Well, ah thankee. That's a mighty good girl. Ah'm plumb wore out and hungry as a wallow-hog." He pulled out a chair and sat, so she did the same. In silence they filled their plates and picked stringy meat from the stingy backbones. He lifted a vertebra and sucked out the marrow, fatty juice glistening on his whiskered cheeks. Gnawed on those bones till they were slick as silk ribbons.

"This here's better'n a cold collard sandwich," he said.

"I wish the cornbread'd come out. Maybe shoulda put more soda in, less eggs." Kya couldn't believe she was talking on so, but couldn't stop herself. "Ma made it so good, but I guess I didn't pay enough mind to the details . . ." Then thought she shouldn't be talking about Ma, so hushed up.

Pa pushed his plate toward her. "'Nough for a dab more?"

"Yessir, there's aplenty."

"Oh, and tump some of that cornbread right in tha stew. Ah got a hankerin' for soppin' up the stock, and my bet is that bread's just fine, mushy like spoonbread."

She smiled to herself as she filled his plate. Who would've thought they'd find cornbread as a footing.

But now, after thinking about it, she worried that if she asked to use the boat, he would think she'd cooked and cleaned only for the favor, which was how it started out, but now seemed somehow different. She liked sitting down and eating like a family. Her need to talk to somebody felt urgent.

So she didn't mention using the boat by herself, instead asked, "Can I go out fishin' with ya sometime?"

He laughed hard, but it was kind. The first time he'd laughed since Ma and the others left. "So ya wanta go fishin'?"

"Yessir, I do."

"You're a girl," he said, looking at his plate, chewing backbone.

"Yessir, I'm your girl."

"Well, Ah might could take ya out sometime."

The next morning, as Kya careened down the sandy lane, her arms held straight out, she sputtered wet noises from her lips, spittle spraying. She would lift off and sail over the marsh, looking for nests, then rise and fly wing to wing with eagles. Her fingers became long feathers, splayed against the sky, gathering the wind beneath her. Then suddenly she was jerked back to Earth by Pa hollering to her from the boat. Her wings collapsed, stomach pitched; he must have figured out she'd used it. She could already feel the paddle on her bottom and the backs of her legs. She knew how to hide, wait until he was drunk, and he'd never find her. But she was too far down the lane, in full view, and there he was standing with all his poles and rods, motioning for her to come. She walked over, quiet, scared. The fishing tackle was strewn about, a poke of corn likker tucked under his seat.

"Git in" was all he said as invitation. She started to express glee or gratitude, but his blank expression kept her quiet, as she stepped to the bow and sat on the metal seat facing forward. He pull-cranked and they headed up the channel, ducking the overgrowth as they cruised up and down the waterways, Kya memorizing broken trees and old stump signposts. He eased the motor down in a backwater and motioned for her to sit on the center seat.

"Go on now, scratch some worms from the can," he said, a hand-rolled cigarette hanging at the corner of his mouth. He taught her to snag the bait, to cast and reel. It seemed he contorted his body in odd postures to avoid brushing against her. They only talked fishing; never ventured to other subjects, neither smiled often, but on common ground they were steady. He drank some likker but then got busy and didn't drink more. At late day, the sun sighed, fading to the color of butter, and they may not have noticed, but their own shoulders finally rounded and their necks slacked.

Secretly Kya hoped not to catch a fish, but she felt a tug, jerked her line, and raised a thick bream, flashing silver and blue. Pa leaned out and snatched it in the net, then sat back, slapping his knee and yahooing like she'd never seen. She grinned wide and they looked into each other's eyes, closing a circuit.

Before Pa strung it up, the bream flopped around in the boat bottom and Kya had to watch a distant string of pelicans, study the cloud forms, anything but look into dying fish eyes staring at a world without water, wide mouth sucking worthless air. But what it cost her and what it cost that fish was worth it to have this little shred of family. Perhaps not for the fish, but still.

They went out in the boat again the next day, and in a dark lagoon, Kya spotted the soft breast feathers of a great horned owl floating on the surface. Each curled at both ends, so that they drifted around like tiny orange boats. She scooped them up and put them in her pocket. Later she found an abandoned hummingbird nest woven onto an outstretched branch, and tucked it safely in the bow.

That evening, Pa cooked up a supper of fried fish—coated in cornmeal and black pepper—served with grits and greens. As Kya washed up after, Pa walked into the kitchen, carrying his old World War II–issue knapsack. Standing near the door, he flung it roughly onto one of the chairs. It slid to the floor with a thud, which made her jump and whirl around.

"Thought ya could use that fer yo' feathers, bird nests, and all that other stuff ya c'lect."

"Oh," Kya said. "Oh, thank ya." But he was already out the porch door. She picked up the frayed knapsack, made of canvas tough enough for a lifetime and covered in small pockets and secret compartments. Heavy-duty zips. She stared out the window. He had never given her anything.

Every warmish day of winter and every day of spring, Pa and Kya went out, far up and down the coast, trolling, casting, and reeling. Whether in estuary or creek, she scanned for that boy Tate in his boat, hoping to see him again. She thought about him sometimes, wanted to be his friend, but had no idea how to go about it or even how to find him. Then, just like that, one afternoon she and Pa came around a bend, and there he was fishing, almost in that same spot where she first saw him. Right off, he grinned and waved. Without thinking, she threw her hand up and waved back, almost smiling. Then dropped her hand just as quick when Pa looked at her, surprised.

"One a' Jodie's friends, before he left," she said.

"Ya gotta watch out for folks 'round here," he said. "Woods're full a' white trash. Pert near ever'body out here's a no-'count."

She nodded. Wanted to look back at the boy, but didn't. Then worried he would think her unfriendly.

Pa knew the marsh the way a hawk knows his meadow: how to hunt, how to hide, how to terrorize intruders. And Kya's wide-eyed questions spurred him to explain goose seasons, fish habits, how to read weather in the clouds and riptides in the waves.

Some days she packed a picnic supper in the knapsack and they ate crumbly cornbread, which she had almost mastered, with sliced onions, as the setting sun posed over the marsh. Occasionally, he forgot the bootleg and they drank tea from jelly jars.

"My folks weren't always po', ya know," Pa blurted out one day as they sat in oak shadows, casting lines across a brown lagoon buzzing with low-flying insects.

"They had land, rich land, raised tobaccy and cott'n and such. Over near Asheville. Yo' gramma on my side wore bonnets big as wagon wheels and long skirts. We lived in a house wit a verander that went a' the way around, two stories high. It wa' fine, mighty fine."

A gramma. Kya's lips parted. Somewhere, there was or had been a grandmother. Where was she now? Kya longed to ask what happened to everybody. But was afraid.

Pa continued on his own. "Then it all went wrong together. Ah was a young'un through most of it, so don't know, but there was the D'pression, cott'n weevils, Ah don't know what all, and it was gone. Only thang left was debts, lotsa debts."

With these sketchy details, Kya struggled to visualize his past. There was nothing of Ma's history. Pa would go into a rage if any of them talked about their lives before Kya was born. She knew her family had lived somewhere far away before the marsh, near her other grandparents, a place where Ma wore store-bought dresses with small pearly buttons, satin ribbons, and lace trim. After they moved into the shack, Ma kept the dresses in trunks, taking one out every few years and stripping it down for a work smock because there was no money for anything new. Now those fine clothes along with their story were gone, burned in the bonfire Pa started after Jodie left.

Kya and Pa cast some more, their lines swishing over soft yellow pollen floating on the still water, and she thought that was the end of it, but he added, "Someday Ah'll take ya to Asheville, show ya the land that was our'n, shoulda been your'n."

After a bit he jerked his line. "Looky here, hon, Ah got us a big un, big as Alabamee!"

Back in the shack they fried the fish and hush puppies "fat as goose aigs." Then she displayed her collections, carefully pinning the insects to pieces of cardboard and the feathers to the wall of the back bedroom in a soft, stirring collage. Later she lay in her bed on the porch listening to the pines. She closed her eyes, and then opened them wide. He had called her "hon."

8.

Negative Data

1969

After finishing their morning's investigative work at the fire tower, Sheriff Ed Jackson and Deputy Joe Purdue escorted Chase's widow, Pearl, and his parents, Patti Love and Sam, to see him lying on a steel table under a sheet in a chilled lab at the clinic, which served as a morgue. To say good-bye. But it was too cold for any mother; unbearable for any wife. Both women had to be helped from the room.

Back at the sheriff's office, Joe said, "Well, that was as bad as it gets . . ."

"Yeah. Don't know how anybody gets through it."

"Sam didn't say a word. He never was a talker, but this'll do him in."

Saltwater marsh, some say, can eat a cement block for breakfast, and not even the sheriff's bunker-style office could keep it at bay. Watermarks, outlined with salt crystals, waved across the lower walls, and black mildew spread like blood vessels toward the ceiling. Tiny dark mushrooms hunkered in the corners.

The sheriff pulled a bottle from the bottom drawer of his desk and poured them both a double in coffee mugs. They sipped until the sun, as golden and syrupy as the bourbon, slipped into the sea.

Four days later, Joe, waving documents in the air, entered the sheriff's office. "I got the first of the lab reports."

"Let's have a look."

They sat on opposite sides of the sheriff's desk, scanning. Joe, now and then, swatted at a single housefly.

Ed read out loud, "Time of death between midnight and two A.M., October 29 to 30, 1969. Just what we thought."

After a minute of reading, he continued. "What we have is negative data."

"You got that right. There ain't a thing here, Sheriff."

"Except for the two boys going up to the third switchback, there're no fresh fingerprints on the railing, the grates, nothing. None from Chase or anybody else." Afternoon whiskers shadowed the sheriff's otherwise ruddy complexion.

"So somebody wiped 'em clean. Everything. If nothing else, why aren't his fingerprints on the railing, the grate?"

"Exactly. First we had no footprints—now no fingerprints. There's no evidence at all that he walked across the mud to the steps, walked up the steps, or opened the two grates at the top—the one above the stairs and the one he fell through. Or that anybody else did either. But negative data's still data. Somebody cleaned up real good or killed him somewhere else and moved his body to the tower."

"But if his body was hauled to the tower, there'd be tire tracks."

"Right, we need to go back out there, look for tread marks besides ours and the ambulance. May have overlooked something."

After a minute more of reading, Ed said, "Anyway, I'm confident now, this was no accident."

Joe said, "I agree, and not just anybody can wipe up tracks this good."

"I'm hungry. Let's go by the diner on the way out there."

"Well, get ready for an ambush. Everybody in town's pretty riled up. Chase Andrews's murder's the biggest thing's happened 'round here, maybe ever. Gossip's goin' up like smoke signals."

"Well, keep an ear out. We might pick up a tidbit or two. Most ne'er-do-wells can't keep their mouths shut."

A full bank of windows, framed by hurricane shutters, covered the front of the Barkley Cove Diner, which overlooked the harbor. Only the narrow street stood between the building, constructed in 1889, and the soggy steps of the village pier. Discarded shrimp baskets and wadded-up fishing nets lined the wall under the windows, and here and there, mollusk shells littered the sidewalk. Everywhere: seabird cries, seabird dung. The aroma of sausage and biscuits, boiled turnip greens, and fried chicken thankfully overtook the high smell of fish barrels lining the dock.

A mild bustle spilled out when the sheriff opened the door. Every booth—high-backed with red padded upholstery—was taken, as were most of the tables. Joe pointed to two empty stools at the soda fountain counter, and the two walked toward them.

On the way they heard Mr. Lane from the Sing Oil saying to his diesel mechanic, "I reckon it was Lamar Sands. Ya r'member, he caught his wife doin' a number wif Chase right on the deck of his fancy ski boat. There's motive, and Lamar's had other run-ins wif tha law."

"What run-ins?"

"He was wif that bunch that slit the sheriff's tars."

"They were just kids back then."

"Thar was sump'm else too, I just cain't r'member."

Behind the counter, owner-cook Jim Bo Sweeny darted from flipping crab cakes on the griddle to stirring a pot of creamed corn on the burner to poking chicken thighs in the deep fryer, then back again. Putting piled-high plates in front of customers in between. People said he could mix biscuit dough with one hand while filleting a catfish with the other. He offered up his famous specialty—grilled flounder stuffed with shrimp served on pimento-cheese grits—only a few times a year. No advertising needed; word got out.

As the sheriff and deputy wove among the tables toward the counter, they heard Miss Pansy Price of Kress's Five and Dime say to a friend, "It coulda been that woman lives out in the marsh. Crazy 'nough for the loony bin. I jus' bet she'd be up to this kinda thing . . ."

"What d'ya mean? What'd she have to do with anything?"

"Well, for a while thar, she was got herself involved wif . . ."

As the sheriff and deputy stepped up to the counter, Ed said, "Let's just order take-out po'boys and get out of here. We can't get dragged into all this."

9.

Jumpin'

1953

Sitting in the bow, Kya watched low fingers of fog reaching for their boat. At first, torn-off cloud bits streamed over their heads, then mist engulfed them in grayness, and there was only the *tick, tick, tick* of the quiet motor. Minutes later, small splotches of unexpected color formed as the weathered shape of the marina gas station eased into view, as though it and not them was moving. Pa motored in, bumping gently against the dock. She'd only been here once. The owner, an old black man, sprang up from his chair to help them—the reason everybody called him Jumpin'. His white sideburns and salt-and-pepper hair framed a wide, generous face and owl eyes. Tall and spare, he seemed to never stop talking, smiling, or throwing his head back, lips shut tight in his own brand of laugh. He didn't dress in overalls, like most workmen around, but wore an ironed blue button-down shirt, too-short dark trousers, and work boots. Not often, but now and then on the meanest summer days, a tattered straw hat.

His Gas and Bait teetered on its own wobbly wharf. A cable ran from the closest oak on shore, about forty feet across the backwater, and held on with all its might. Jumpin's great-grandpa had built the wharf and shack of cypress planks way back before anybody could remember, sometime before the Civil War.

Three generations had nailed bright metal signs—Nehi Grape Soda, Royal Crown Cola, Camel Filters, and twenty years' worth of North Carolina automobile license plates—all over the shack, and that burst of color could be seen from the sea through all but the thickest fog.

"Hello, Mister Jake. How ya doin'?"

"Well, Ah woke up on the right side of dirt," Pa answered.

Jumpin' laughed as if he'd never heard the worn-out phrase. "Ya got your li'l daughter with you an' all. That's mighty fine."

Pa nodded. Then, as an afterthought, "Yep, this here's ma daughter, Miz Kya Clark."

"Well, I'm mighty proud to know ya, Miss Kya."

Kya searched her bare toes but found no words.

Jumpin' wasn't bothered and kept talking about the good fishing lately. Then he asked Pa, "Fill 'er up then, Mister Jake?"

"Yeah, slam 'er right up to tha top."

The men talked weather, fishing, then more weather till the tank was full.

"Good day to y'all, now," he said, as he tossed off the line.

Pa cruised slowly back onto a bright sea—the sun taking less time to devour the fog than it took Jumpin' to fill a tank. They chugged around a piney peninsula for several miles to Barkley Cove, where Pa tied to the deeply etched beams of the town wharf. Fishermen busied about, packing fish, tying line.

"Ah reckon we can git us some rest'rant vittles," Pa said, and led her along the pier toward the Barkley Cove Diner. Kya had never eaten restaurant food; had never set foot inside. Her heart thumped as she brushed dried mud from her way-too-short overalls and patted down her tangled hair. As Pa opened the door, every customer paused mid-bite. A few men nodded faintly at Pa; the women frowned and turned their heads. One snorted, "Well, they prob'ly can't read the *shirt and shoes required.*"

Pa motioned for her to sit at a small table overlooking the wharf. She couldn't read the menu, but he told her most of it, and she ordered fried chicken, mashed potatoes, gravy, white acre peas, and biscuits fluffy as fresh-picked cotton. He had fried shrimp, cheese grits, fried "okree," and fried green tomatoes. The waitress put a whole dish of butter pats perched on ice cubes and a basket of cornbread and biscuits on their table, and all the sweet iced tea they could drink. Then they had blackberry cobbler with ice cream for dessert. So full, Kya thought she might get sick, but figured it'd be worth it.

As Pa stood at the cash register paying the bill, Kya stepped out onto the sidewalk, where the ripe smell of fishing boats hung over the bay. She held a greasy napkin wrapped around the leftover chicken and biscuits. Her overalls pockets were stuffed with packages of saltines, which the waitress had left right on the table for the taking.

"Hi." Kya heard a tiny voice behind her and turned to see a girl of about four years with blond ringlets looking up at her. She was dressed in a pale blue frock and reached out her hand. Kya stared at the little hand; it was puffy-soft and maybe the cleanest thing Kya had ever seen. Never scrubbed with lye soap, certainly no mussel mud beneath the nails. Then she looked into the girl's eyes, in which she herself was reflected as just another kid.

Kya shifted the napkin to her left hand and extended her right slowly toward the girl's.

"Hey there, get away!" Suddenly Mrs. Teresa White, wife of the Methodist preacher, rushed from the door of the Buster Brown Shoe Shop.

Barkley Cove served its religion hard-boiled and deep-fried. Tiny as it was, the village supported four churches, and those were just for the whites; the blacks had three more.

Of course, the pastors and preachers, and certainly their wives, enjoyed highly respected positions in the village, always dressing and behaving accordingly. Teresa White often wore pastel skirts and white blouses, matching pumps and purse.

Now she hurried toward her daughter and lifted her in her arms. Stepping away from Kya, she put the girl back on the sidewalk and squatted next to the child.

"Meryl Lynn, dahlin', don't go near that girl, ya hear me. She's dirty."

Kya watched the mother run her fingers through the curls; didn't miss how long they held each other's eyes.

A woman came out of the Piggly Wiggly and walked quickly up to them. "Ya all right, Teresa? What happened here? Was that girl botherin' Meryl Lynn?"

"I saw her in time. Thank you, Jenny. I wish those people wouldn't come to town. Look at her. Filthy. Plumb nasty. There's that stomach flu goin' around and I just know for a fact it came in with them. Last year they brought in that case of measles, and that's serious." Teresa walked away, clutching the child.

Just then Pa, carrying some beer in a brown paper bag, called behind her, "Whatcha doin'? C'mon, we gotta git outta here. Tide's goin' out." Kya turned and followed, and as they steered home to the marsh, she saw the curls and eyes of mother and child.

Pa still disappeared some, not coming back for several days, but not as often as before. And when he did show up, he didn't collapse in a stupor but ate a meal and talked some. One night they played gin rummy, he guffawing when she won, and she giggling with her hands over her mouth like a regular girl.

Each time Kya stepped off the porch, she looked down the lane, thinking that even though the wild wisteria was fading with late spring and her mother had left late the previous summer, she might see Ma walking home through the sand. Still in her fake alligator heels. Now that she and Pa were fishing and talking, maybe they could try again to be a family. Pa had beat all of them, mostly when he was drunk. He'd be all right for a few days at a time—they would eat chicken stew together; once they flew a kite on the beach. Then: drink, shout, hit. Details of some of the bouts were sharp in her mind. Once Pa shoved Ma into the kitchen wall, hitting her until she slumped to the floor. Kya, sobbing for him to quit, touched his arm. He grabbed Kya by the shoulders, shouted for her to pull down her jeans and underpants, and bent her over the kitchen table. In one smooth, practiced motion he slid the belt from his pants and whipped her. Of course, she remembered the hot pain slicing her bare bottom, but curiously, she recalled the jeans pooled around her skinny ankles in more vivid detail. And Ma crumpled into the corner by the cookstove, crying out. Kya didn't know what all the fighting was about.

But if Ma came back now, when Pa was acting decent, maybe they could start over. Kya never thought it would be Ma who left and Pa who stayed. But she knew her mother wouldn't leave her forever; if she was out there somewhere in the world, she'd come back. Kya could still see the full, red lips as Ma sang to the radio, and hear her words, "Now listen close to Mr. Orson Welles; he speaks proper like a gentleman. Don't ever say *ain't*, it isn't even a word."

Ma had painted the estuaries and sunsets in oils and watercolors so rich they seemed peeled from the earth. She had brought some art supplies with her and could buy bits and pieces at Kress's Five and Dime. Sometimes Ma had let Kya paint her own pictures on brown paper bags from the Piggly Wiggly.

In early September of that fishing summer, on one afternoon that paled with heat, Kya walked to the mailbox at the end of the lane. Leafing through the grocery ads, she stopped dead when she saw a blue envelope addressed in Ma's neat hand. A few sycamore leaves were turning the same shade of yellow as when she left. All that time without a trace and now a letter. Kya stared at it, held it to the light, ran her fingers across the slanted, perfect script. Her heart banged against her chest.

"Ma's alive. Living somewhere else. Why hasn't she come home?" She thought of tearing the letter open, but the only word she could read for sure was her name, and it was not on the envelope.

She ran to the shack, but Pa had motored somewhere in the boat. So she propped the letter against the saltshaker on the table where he'd see it. As she boiled black-eyed peas with onions, she kept an eye on the letter lest it disappear.

Every few seconds, she ducked to the kitchen window to listen for the boat's *whirr.* Then suddenly Pa was limp-walking up the steps. All courage left her, and she dashed past him, hollering that she was going to the outhouse; supper would be ready soon. She stood inside the smelly latrine, her heart running races to her stomach. Balancing on the wooden bench, she watched through the quarter-moon slit in the door, not knowing exactly what she expected.

Then the porch door slammed, and she saw Pa walking fast toward the lagoon. He went straight to the boat, a poke in his hand, and motored away. She ran back to the house, into the kitchen, but the letter was gone. She flung open his dresser drawers, rummaged through his closet, searching. "It's mine, too! It's mine as much as yours." Back in the kitchen, she looked in the trash can and found the letter's ashes, still fringed in blue. With a spoon she dipped them up and laid them on the table, a little pile of black and blue remains. She picked, bit by bit, through the garbage; maybe some words had drifted to the bottom. But there was nothing but traces of cinder clinging to onionskin.

She sat at the table, the peas still singing in the pot, and stared at the little mound. "Ma touched these. Maybe Pa'll tell me what she wrote. Don't be stupid—that's as likely as snow fallin' in the swamp."

Even the postmark was gone. Now she'd never know where Ma was. She put the ashes in a little bottle and kept it in her cigar box next to her bed.

Pa didn't come home that night or the next day, and when he finally did, it was the old drunk who staggered through the door. When she mounted the courage to ask about the letter, he barked, "It ain't none a' yo' bidness." And then, "She ain't comin' back, so ya can just forget 'bout that." Carrying a poke, he shuffled toward the boat.

"That isn't true," Kya hollered at his back, her fists bunched at her sides. She watched him leaving, then shouted at the empty lagoon, "*Ain't* isn't even a word!"

Later she would wonder if she should have opened the letter on her own, not even shown it to Pa. Then she could have saved the words to read someday, and he'd have been better off not knowing them.

Pa never took her fishing again. Those warm days were just a thrown-in season. Low clouds parting, the sun splashing her world briefly, then closing up dark and tight-fisted again.

Kya couldn't remember how to pray. Was it how you held your hands or how hard you squinted your eyes that mattered? "Maybe if I pray, Ma and Jodie will come home. Even with all the shouting and fussing, that life was better than this lumpy-grits."

She sang mis-snippets of hymns—"and He walks with me when dew is still on the roses"—all she remembered from the little white church where Ma had taken her a few times. Their last visit had been Easter Sunday before Ma left, but all Kya remembered about the holiday was shouting and blood, somebody falling, she and Ma running, so she dropped the memory altogether.

Kya looked through the trees at Ma's corn and turnip patch, all weeds now. Certainly there were no roses.

"Just forget it. No god's gonna come to this garden."

10.

Just Grass in the Wind

1969

Sand keeps secrets better than mud. The sheriff parked his rig at the beginning of the fire tower lane so they wouldn't drive over any evidence of someone driving the night of the alleged murder. But as they walked along the track, looking for vehicle treads other than their own, sand grains shifted into formless dimples with every step.

Then, at the mud holes and swampy areas near the tower, a profusion of detailed stories revealed themselves: a raccoon with her four young had trailed in and out of the muck; a snail had woven a lacy pattern interrupted by the arrival of a bear; and a small turtle had lain in the cool mud, its belly forming a smooth shallow bowl.

"Clear as a picture, but besides our rigs, not a thing man-made."

"I dunno," Joe said. "See this straight edge, then a little triangle. That could be a tread."

"No, I think that's a bit of turkey print, where a deer stepped on top, made it look geometrical like that."

After another quarter hour, the sheriff said, "Let's hike out to that little bay. See if somebody boated over here instead of coming by truck." Pushing pungent myrtle from their faces, they walked to the tiny inlet. The damp sand revealed prints of crabs, herons, and pipers, but no humans.

"Well, but look at this." Joe pointed to a large pattern of disturbed sand crystals that fanned into an almost perfect half circle. "Could be the imprint of a round-bowed boat that was pulled on shore."

"No. See where the wind blew this broken grass stalk back and forth through the sand. Drawing this half circle. That's just grass in the wind."

They stood looking around. The rest of the small half-moon beach was covered in a thick layer of broken shells, a jumble of crustacean parts, and crab claws. Shells the best secret-keepers of all.

11.

Croker Sacks Full

1956

In the winter of 1956, when Kya was ten, Pa came hobbling to the shack less and less often. Weeks passed with no whiskey bottle on the floor, no body sprawled on the bed, no Monday money. She kept expecting to see him limping through the trees, toting his poke. One full moon, then another had passed since she'd seen him.

Sycamore and hickories stretched naked limbs against a dull sky, and the relentless wind sucked any joy the winter sun might have spread across the bleakness. A useless, drying wind in a sea-land that couldn't dry.

Sitting on the front steps, she thought about it. A poker-game fight could have ended with him beat up and dumped in the swamp on a cold, rainy night. Or maybe he just got fall-down drunk, wandered off into the woods, and fell face-first in the backwater bog.

"I guess he's gone for good."

She bit her lips until her mouth turned white. It wasn't like the pain when Ma left—in fact, she struggled to mourn him at all. But being completely alone was a feeling so vast it echoed, and the authorities were sure to find out and take her away. She'd have to pretend, even to Jumpin', that Pa was still around.

And there would be no Monday money. She'd stretched the last few dollars for weeks, surviving on grits, boiled mussels, and the occasional remnant egg from the rangy hens. The only remaining supplies were a few matches, a nubbin of soap, and a handful of grits. A fistful of Blue Tips wouldn't make a winter. Without them she couldn't boil the grits, which she fixed for herself, the gulls, and the chickens.

"I don't know how to do life without grits."

At least, she thought, wherever Pa had disappeared to this time, he had gone on foot. Kya had the boat.

Of course, she'd have to find another way to get food, but for right now she pushed the thought to a far corner of her mind. After a supper of boiled mussels, which she had learned to smash into a paste and spread on soda crackers, she thumbed through Ma's beloved books, play-reading the fairy tales. Even at ten she still couldn't read.

Then the kerosene light flickered, faded, and died. One minute there was a soft circle of a world, and then darkness. She made an *oh* sound. Pa had always bought the kerosene and filled the lamp, so she hadn't thought much about it. Until it was dark.

She sat for a few seconds, trying to squeeze light from the leftovers, but there was almost nothing. Then the rounded hump of the Frigidaire and the window frame began to take shape in the dimness, so she touched her fingers along the countertop until she found a candle stub. Lighting it would take a match and there were only five left. But darkness was a right-now thing.

Swish. She struck the match, lit the candle, and the blackness retreated to the corners. But she'd seen enough of it to know she had to have light, and kerosene cost money. She opened her mouth in a shallow pant. "Maybe I oughta walk to town and turn myself in to the authorities. At least they'd give me food and send me to school."

But after thinking a minute she said, "No, I cain't leave the gulls, the heron, the shack. The marsh is all the family I got."

Sitting in the last of the candlelight, she had an idea.

Earlier than usual, she got up the next morning when the tide was low, pulled on her overalls, and slipped out with a bucket, claw knife, and empty tow bags. Squatting in mud, she collected mussels along the sloughs like Ma had taught her, and in four hours of crouching and kneeling had two croker sacks full.

The slow sun pulled from the sea as she motored through dense fog up to Jumpin's Gas and Bait. He stood as she neared.

"Hello, Miss Kya, ya wantin' some gas?"

She tucked her head. Hadn't spoken a word to anyone since her last trip to the Piggly Wiggly, and her speech was slipping some. "Maybe gas. But that depends. I hear tell you buy mussels, and I got some here. Can you pay me cash money and some gas throwed in?" She pointed to the bags.

"Yessiree, you sho' do. They fresh?"

"I dug 'em 'fore dawn. Just now."

"Well, then. I can give ya fifty cent for one bag, a full tank for the other."

Kya smiled slightly. Real money she made herself. "Thank ya" was all she said.

As Jumpin' filled the tank, Kya walked into his tiny store there on the wharf. She'd never paid it much mind because she shopped at the Piggly, but now she saw that besides bait and tobacco, he sold matches, lard, soap, sardines, Vienna sausages, grits, soda crackers, toilet paper, and kerosene. About everything she needed in the world was right here. Lined up on the counter were five one-gallon jars filled with penny candy—Red Hots, jawbreakers, and Sugar Daddys. It seemed like more candy than would be in the world.

With the mussel money she bought matches, a candle, and grits. Kerosene and soap would have to wait for another croker full. It took all her might not to buy a Sugar Daddy instead of the candle.

"How many bags you buy a week?" she asked.

"Well now, we striking up a bidness deal?" he asked as he laughed in his particular way—mouth closed, head thrown back. "I buy 'bout forty pounds ever' two-three days. But mind, others bring 'em in, too. If ya bring 'em in, and I already got some, well, you'd be out. It's first come, first serve. No other way of doing it."

"Okay. Thank you, that'd be fine. Bye, Jumpin'." Then she added, "Oh, by the way, my pa sends his regards to ya."

"That so, well then. Ya do the same from me, if ya please. Bye yourself, Miss Kya." He smiled big as she motored away. She almost smiled herself. Buying her own gas and groceries surely made her a grown-up. Later, at the shack when she unpacked the tiny pile of supplies, she saw a yellow-and-red surprise at the bottom of the bag. Not too grown-up for a Sugar Daddy Jumpin' had dropped inside.

To stay ahead of the other pickers, Kya slipped down to the marsh by candle or moon—her shadow wavering around on the glistening sand—and gathered mussels deep in the night. She added oysters to her catch and sometimes slept near gullies under the stars to get to Jumpin's by first light. The mussel money turned out to be more reliable than the Monday money ever had, and she usually managed to beat out other pickers.

She stopped going to the Piggly, where Mrs. Singletary always asked why she wasn't in school. Sooner or later they'd grab her, drag her in. She got by with her supplies from Jumpin's and had more mussels than she could eat. They weren't that bad tossed into the grits, mashed up beyond recognition. They didn't have eyes to look at her like the fish did.

12.

Pennies and Grits

1956

For weeks after Pa left, Kya would look up when ravens cawed; maybe they'd seen him swing-stepping through the woods. At any strange sound in the wind, she cocked her head, listening for somebody. Anybody. Even a mad dash from the truant lady would be good sport.

Mostly she looked for the fishing boy. A few times over the years, she'd seen him in the distance, but hadn't spoken to him since she was seven, three years ago when he showed her the way home through the marsh. He was the only soul she knew in the world besides Jumpin' and a few salesladies. Wherever she glided through the waterways, she scanned for him.

One morning, as she motored into a cord grass estuary, she saw his boat tucked in the reeds. Tate wore a different baseball cap and was taller now, but even from more than fifty yards, she recognized the blond curls. Kya idled down, maneuvered quietly into long grass, and peered out at him. Working her lips, she thought of cruising over, maybe asking if he had caught any fish. That seemed to be what Pa and anybody else in the marsh said when they came across somebody: "Anythang bitin'? Had any nibbles?"

But she only stared, didn't move. She felt a strong pull toward him and a strong push away, the result being stuck firmly in this spot. Finally, she eased toward home, her heart pushing against her ribs.

Every time she saw him it was the same: watching him as she did the herons.

She still collected feathers and shells, but left them, salty and sandy, strewn around the brick-'n'-board steps. She dallied some of each day while dishes piled up in the sink, and why wash overalls that got muddied up again? Long ago she'd taken to wearing the old throwaway overalls from gone-away siblings. Her shirts full of holes. She had no more shoes at all.

One evening Kya slipped the pink-and-green flowery sundress, the one Ma had worn to church, from the wire hanger. For years now she had fingered this beauty—the only dress Pa didn't burn—had touched the little pink flowers. There was a stain across the front, a faded brown splotch under the shoulder straps, blood maybe. But it was faint now, scrubbed out like other bad memories.

Kya pulled the dress over her head, down her thin frame. The hem came almost to her toes; that wouldn't do. She pulled it off, hung it up to wait for another few years. It'd be a shame to cut it up, wear it to dig mussels.

A few days later Kya took the boat over to Point Beach, an apron of white sand several miles south of Jumpin's. Time, waves, and winds had modeled it into an elongated tip, which collected more shells than other beaches, and she had found rare ones there. After securing her boat at the southern end, she strolled north, searching. Suddenly distant voices—shrill and excited—drifted on the air.

Instantly, she ran across the beach toward the woods, where an oak, more than eighty feet from one side to the other, stood knee-deep in tropical ferns. Hiding behind the tree, she watched a band of kids strolling down the sand, now and then dashing around in the waves, kicking up sea spray. One boy ran ahead; another threw a football. Against the white sand, their bright madras shorts looked like colorful birds and marked the changing season. Summer was walking toward her down the beach.

As they moved closer, she flattened herself against the oak and peered around. Five girls and four boys, a bit older than she, maybe twelve. She recognized Chase Andrews throwing the ball to those boys he was always with.

The girls—Tallskinnyblonde, Ponytailfreckleface, Shortblackhair, Alwayswearspearls, and Roundchubbycheeks—hung back in a little covey, walking slower, chattering and giggling. Their voices lifted up to Kya like chimes. She was too young to care much about the boys; her eyes fixed on the troop of girls. Together they squatted to watch a crab skittering sideways across the sand. Laughing, they leaned against one another's shoulders until they flopped on the sand in a bundle.

Kya bit her bottom lip as she watched. Wondering how it would feel to be among them. Their joy created an aura almost visible against the deepening sky. Ma had said women need one another more than they need men, but she never told her how to get inside the pride. Easily, she slipped deeper into the forest and watched from behind the giant ferns until the kids wandered back down the beach, until they were little spots on the sand, the way they came.

Dawn smoldered beneath gray clouds as Kya pulled up to Jumpin's wharf. He walked out of the little shop shaking his head.

"I'm sorry as can be, Miss Kya," he said. "But they beatcha to it. I got my week's quota of mussels, cain't buy no mo'."

She cut the engine and the boat banged against a piling. This was the second week she'd been beat out. Her money was gone and she couldn't buy a single thing. Down to pennies and grits.

"Miss Kya, ya gotta find some udder ways to bring cash in. Ya can't git all yo' coons up one tree."

Back at her place, she sat pondering on the brick 'n' boards, and came up with another idea. She fished for eight hours straight, then soaked her catch of twenty in saltwater brine through the night. At daybreak she lined them up on the shelves of Pa's old smokehouse—the size and shape of an outhouse—built a fire in the pit, and poked green sticks into the flames like he'd done. Blue-gray smoke billowed and puffed up the chimney and through every crack in the walls. The whole shack huffing.

The next day she motored to Jumpin's and, still standing in her boat, held up her bucket. In all it was a pitiful display of small bream and carp, falling apart at the seams. "Ya buy smoked fish, Jumpin'? I got some here."

"Well, I declare, ya sho' did, Miss Kya. Tell ya what: I'll take 'em on consignment like. If I sell 'em, ya get the money; if I don't, ya get 'em back like they is. That do?"

"Okay, thanks, Jumpin'."

That evening Jumpin' walked down the sandy track to Colored Town—a cluster of shacks and lean-tos, and even a few real houses squatting about on backwater bogs and mud sloughs. The scattered encampment was in deep woods, back from the sea, with no breeze, and "more skeeters than the whole state of Jawja."

After about three miles he could smell the smoke from cookfires drifting through the pines and hear the chatter of some of his grandchillin. There were no roads in Colored Town, just trails leading off through the woods this way and that to different family dwellings. His was a real house he and his pa had built with pine lumber and a raw-wood fence around the hardpan dirt yard, which Mabel, his good-sized wife, swept clean as a whistle just like a floor. No snake could slink within thirty yards of the steps without being spotted by her hoe.

She came out of the house to meet him with a smile, as she often did, and he handed her the pail with Kya's smoked fish.

"What's this?" she asked. "Looks like sump'm even dogs wouldn't drag in."

"It's that girl again. Miss Kya brung 'em. Sometimes she ain't the first one with mussels, so she's gone to smokin' fish. Wants me to sell 'em."

"Lawd, we gotta do something 'bout that child. Ain't nobody gonna buy them fish; I can cook 'em up in stew. Our church can come up wif some clothes, other things for her. We'll tell 'er there's some family that'll trade jumpers for carpies. What size is she?"

"Ya askin' me? Skinny. All's I know is she's skinny as a tick on a flagpole. I 'spect she'll be there first thing in the mornin'. She's plumb broke."

After eating a breakfast of warmed-up mussels-in-grits, Kya motored over to Jumpin's to see if any money'd come in from the smoked fish. In all these years it had just been him there or customers, but as she approached slowly she saw a large black woman sweeping the wharf like it was a kitchen floor. Jumpin' was sitting in his chair, leaning back against the store wall doing figures in his ledger. Seeing her, he jumped up, waved.

"G'mornin'," she called quietly, drifting expertly up to the dock.

"Hiya, Miss Kya. Got somebody here for ya to meet. This here's ma wife, Mabel." Mabel walked up and stood next to Jumpin', so that when Kya stepped onto the wharf, they were close.

Mabel reached out and took Kya's hand, held it gently in hers, and said, "It's mighty fine to meet ya, Miss Kya. Jumpin's told me what a fine girl ya are. One a' de best oryster pickers."

In spite of hoeing her garden, cooking half of every day, and scrubbing and mending for whites, Mabel's hand was supple. Kya kept her fingers in that velvet glove but didn't know what to say, so stood quiet.

"Now, Miss Kya, we got a family who'll trade clothes and other stuff ya need for yo' smoked fish."

Kya nodded. Smiled at her feet. Then asked, "What about gas for ma boat?"

Mabel turned question eyes at Jumpin'.

"Well now," he said, "I'll give ya some today 'cause I know you're short. But ya keep bringin' in mussels and such when ya can."

Mabel said in her big voice, "Lawd, child, let's don't worry none about the details. Now let me look atcha. I gotta calculate yo' size to tell 'em." She led her into the tiny shop. "Let's sit right here, and ya tell me what clothes and what-all else ya need."

After they discussed the list, Mabel traced Kya's feet on a piece of brown paper bag, then said, "Well, come back tomorrer and there'll be a stack here for ya."

"I'm much obliged, Mabel." Then, her voice low, said, "There's something else. I found these old packages of seeds, but I don't know about gardenin'."

"Well now." Mabel leaned back and laughed deep in her generous bosom. "I can sure do a garden." She went over every step in great detail, then reached into some cans on the shelf and brought out squash, tomato, and pumpkin seeds. She folded each kind into some paper and drew a picture of the vegetable on the outside. Kya didn't know if Mabel did this because she couldn't write or because she knew Kya couldn't read, but it worked fine for both of them.

She thanked them as she stepped into her boat.

"I'm glad to help ya, Miss Kya. Now come back tomorrer for yo' things," Mabel said.

That very afternoon, Kya started hoeing the rows where Ma's garden used to be. The hoe made clunking sounds as it moved down the rows, releasing earthy smells and uprooting pinkish worms. Then a different *clink* sounded, and Kya bent to uncover one of Ma's old metal-and-plastic barrettes. She swiped it gently against her overalls until all the grit fell clear. As if reflected in the cheap artifact, Ma's red mouth and dark eyes were clearer than they'd been in years. Kya looked around; surely Ma was walking up the lane even now, come to help turn this earth. Finally home. Such stillness was rare; even the crows were quiet, and she could hear her own breathing.

Sweeping up bunches of her hair, she pinned the barrette above her left ear. Maybe Ma was never coming home. Maybe some dreams should just fade away. She lifted the hoe and clobbered a chunk of hard clay into smithereens.

When Kya motored up to Jumpin's wharf the next morning, he was alone. Perhaps the large form of his wife and her fine ideas had been an illusion. But there, sitting on the wharf, were two boxes of goods that Jumpin' was pointing to, a wide grin on his face.

"G'mornin', Miss Kya. This here's for ya."

Kya jumped onto the wharf and stared at the overflowing crates.

"Go on, then," Jumpin' said. "It's all your'n."

Gently she pulled out overalls, jeans, and real blouses, not just T-shirts. A pair of navy blue lace-up Keds and some Buster Brown two-tone saddle shoes, polished brown and white so many times they glowed. Kya held up a white blouse with a lace collar and a blue satin bow at the neck. Her mouth opened a little bit.

The other box had matches, grits, a tub of oleo, dried beans, and a whole quart of homemade lard. On top, wrapped in newspaper, were fresh turnips and greens, rutabagas, and okra.

"Jumpin'," she said softly, "this is more than those fish woulda cost. This could be a month's fish."

"Well now, what'a folks gonna do with old clothes layin' 'round the house? If they got these things extra, and ya need 'em, and ya got fish, and they need fish, then that's the deal. Ya gotta take 'em now, 'cause I ain't got room for that junk 'round here."

Kya knew that was true. Jumpin' had no extra space, so she'd be doing him a favor to take them off his wharf.

"I'll take 'em, then. But you tell 'em thank you, will you? And I'll smoke more fish and bring it in soon as I can."

"Okay then, Miss Kya. That'll be fine. Ya bring in fish when ya git 'em."

Kya chugged back into the sea. Once she rounded the peninsula, out of sight of Jumpin's, she idled down, dug in the box, and pulled out the blouse with the lace collar. She put it on right over her scratchy bib overalls with patched knees, and tied the little satin ribbon into a bow at her neck. Then, one hand on the tiller, the other on lace, she glided across ocean and estuaries toward home.

13.

Feathers

1960

Lanky yet brawny for fourteen, Kya stood on an afternoon beach, flinging crumbs to gulls. Still couldn't count them; still couldn't read. No longer did she daydream of winging with eagles; perhaps when you have to paw your supper from mud, imagination flattens to that of adulthood. Ma's sundress fit snugly across her breasts and fell just below her knees; she reckoned she had caught up, and then some. She walked back to the shack, got a pole and line, and went straight to fishing from a thicket on the far side of her lagoon.

Just as she cast, a stick snapped behind her. She jerked her head around, searching. A footfall in brush. Not a bear, whose large paws squished in debris, but a solid *clunk* in the brambles. Then the crows cawed. Crows can't keep secrets any better than mud; once they see something curious in the forest they have to tell everybody. Those who listen are rewarded: either warned of predators or alerted to food. Kya knew something was up.

She pulled in the line, wrapped it around the pole even as she pushed silently through the brush with her shoulders. Stopped again, listened.

A dark clearing—one of her favorite places—spread cavernlike under five oaks so dense only hazy streams of sunlight filtered through the canopy, striking lush patches of trillium and white violets. Her eyes scanned the clearing but saw no one.

Then a shape slunk through a thicket beyond, and her eyes swung there. It stopped. Her heart pumped harder. She hunkered down, stoop-running fast and quiet into the undergrowth on the edge of the clearing. Looking back through the branches, she saw an older boy walking fast through the woods, his head moving to and fro. He stopped as he saw her.

Kya ducked behind a thorn bush, then squeezed into a rabbit run that twisted through brambles thick as a fort wall. Still bent, she scrambled, scratching her arms on prickly scrub. Paused again, listening. Hid there in burning heat, her throat racking from thirst. After ten minutes, no one came, so she crept to a spring that pooled in moss, and drank like a deer. She wondered who that boy was and why he'd come. That was the thing about going to Jumpin's—people saw her there. Like the underbelly of a porcupine, she was exposed.

Finally, between dusk and dark, that time when the shadows were unsure, she walked back toward the shack by way of the oak clearing.

"'Cause of him sneaking 'round, I didn't catch any fish ta smoke."

In the center of the clearing was a rotted-down stump, so carpeted in moss it looked like an old man hiding under a cape. Kya approached it, then stopped. Lodged in the stump and sticking straight up was a thin black feather about five or six inches long. To most it would have looked ordinary, maybe a crow's wing feather. But she knew it was extraordinary for it was the "eyebrow" of a great blue heron, the feather that bows gracefully above the eye, extending back beyond her elegant head. One of the most exquisite fragments of the coastal marsh, right here. She had never found one but knew instantly what it was, having squatted eye to eye with herons all her life.

A great blue heron is the color of gray mist reflecting in blue water. And like mist, she can fade into the backdrop, all of her disappearing except the concentric circles of her lock-and-load eyes. She is a patient, solitary hunter, standing alone as long as it takes to snatch her prey. Or, eyeing her catch, she will stride forward one slow step at a time, like a predacious bridesmaid. And yet, on rare occasions she hunts on the wing, darting and diving sharply, swordlike beak in the lead.

"How'd it get stuck straight up in the stump?" Whispering, Kya looked around. "That boy must've put it here. He could be watchin' me right now." She stood still, heart pounding again. Backing away, she left the feather and ran to the shack and locked the screen door, which she seldom did since it offered scant protection.

Yet as soon as dawn crept between the trees, she felt a strong pull toward the feather, at least to look at it again. At sunrise she ran to the clearing, looked around carefully, then walked to the stump and lifted the feather. It was sleek, almost velvety. Back at the shack, she found a special place for it in the center of her collection—from tiny hummingbird feathers to large eagle tails—that winged across the wall. She wondered why a boy would bring her a feather.

The next morning, Kya wanted to rush to the stump to see if another one had been left, but she made herself wait. She must not run into the boy. Finally, in late morning she walked to the clearing, approaching slowly, listening. She didn't hear or see anybody, so she stepped forward, and a rare, brief smile lit her face when she saw a thin white feather stuck into the top of the stump. It reached from her fingertips to her elbow, and curved gracefully to a slender point. She lifted it and laughed out loud. A magnificent tail feather of a tropicbird. She'd never seen these seabirds because they didn't occur in this region, but on rare occasions they were blown over land on hurricane wings.

Kya's heart filled with wonder that someone had such a collection of rare feathers that he could spare this one.

Since she couldn't read Ma's old guidebook, she didn't know the names for most of the birds or insects, so made up her own. And even though she couldn't write, Kya had found a way to label her specimens. Her talent had matured and now she could draw, paint, and sketch anything. Using chalks or watercolors from the Five and Dime, she sketched the birds, insects, or shells on grocery bags and attached them to her samples.

That night she splurged and lit two candles and set them in saucers on the kitchen table so she could see all the colors of the white; so she could paint the tropicbird feather.

For more than a week there was no feather on the stump. Kya went by several times a day, cautiously peeping through ferns, but saw nothing. She sat in the cabin in midday, something she rarely did.

"Shoulda soaked beans for supper. Now it's too late." She walked through the kitchen, rummaging through the cupboard, drumming her fingers on the table. Thought of painting, but didn't. Walked again to the stump.

Even from some distance she could see a long, striped tail feather of a wild turkey. It caught her up. Turkeys had been one of her favorites. She'd watched as many as twelve chicks tuck themselves under the mother's wings even as the hen walked along, a few tumbling out of the back, then scrambling to catch up.

But about a year ago, as Kya strolled through a stand of pines, she'd heard a high-pitched shriek. A flock of fifteen wild turkeys—mostly hens, a few toms and jakes—rushed about, pecking what looked like an oily rag crumpled in the dirt. Dust stirred from their feet and shrouded the woods, drifting up through branches, caught there. As Kya had crept closer, she saw it was a hen turkey on the ground, and the birds of her own flock were pecking and toe-scratching her neck and head. Somehow she'd managed to get her wings so tangled with briars, her feathers stuck out at strange angles and she could no longer fly. Jodie had said that if a bird becomes different from the others—disfigured or wounded—it is more likely to attract a predator, so the rest of the flock will kill it, which is better than drawing in an eagle, who might take one of them in the bargain.

A large female clawed at the bedraggled hen with her large, horny feet, then pinned her to the ground as another female jabbed at her naked neck and head. The hen squealed, looked around with wild eyes at her own flock assaulting her.

Kya ran into the clearing, throwing her arms around. "Hey, what ya doing? Git outta here. Stop it!" The flurry of wings kicked up more dust as the turkeys scattered into brush, two of them flying heavy into an oak. But Kya was too late. The hen, her eyes wide open, lay limp. Blood ran from her wrinkled neck, bent crooked on the dirt.

"Shoo, go on!" Kya chased the last of the large birds until they shuffled away, their business complete. She knelt next to the dead hen and covered the bird's eye with a sycamore leaf.

That night after watching the turkeys, she ate a supper of leftover cornbread and beans, then lay on her porch bed, watching the moon touch the lagoon. Suddenly, she heard voices in the woods coming toward the shack. They sounded nervous, squeaky. Boys, not men. She sat straight up. There was no back door. It was get out now or still be sitting on the bed when they came. Quick as a mouse, she slipped to the door, but just then candles appeared, moving up and down, their light jiggling in halos. Too late to run.

The voices got louder. "Here we come, Marsh Girl!"

"Hey—ya in thar? Miss Missin' Link!"

"Show us yo' teeth! Show us yo' swamp grass!" Peals of laughter.

She ducked lower behind the half wall of the porch as the footsteps moved closer. The flames flickered madly, then went out altogether as five boys, maybe thirteen or fourteen years old, ran across the yard. All talking stopped as they galloped full speed to the porch and tagged the door with their palms, making slapping sounds.

Every smack a stab in the turkey hen's heart.

Against the wall, Kya wanted to whimper but held her breath. They could break through the door easy. One hard yank, and they'd be in.

But they backed down the steps, ran into the trees again, hooting and hollering with relief that they had survived the Marsh Girl, the Wolf Child, the girl who couldn't spell *dog*. Their words and laughter carried back to her through the forest as they disappeared into the night, back to safety. She watched the relit candles, bobbing through the trees. Then sat staring into the stone-quiet darkness. Shamed.

Kya thought of that day and night whenever she saw wild turkeys, but she was thrilled to see the tail feather on the stump. Just to know the game was still on.

14.

Red Fibers

1969

Muggy heat blurred the morning into a haze of no sea, no sky. Joe walked out of the sheriff's building and met Ed getting out of the patrol truck. "C'mon over here, Sheriff. Got more from the lab on the Chase Andrews case. Hot as a boar's breath inside." He led the way to a large oak, its ancient roots punching through the bare dirt like fists. The sheriff followed, crunching acorns, and they stood in the shade, faces to the sea breeze.

He read out loud. "'Bruising on the body, interior injuries, consistent with an extensive fall.' He did bang the back of his head on that beam—the blood and hair samples matched his—which caused severe bruising and damage to the posterior lobe but didn't kill him.

"There you have it; he died where we found him, had not been moved. The blood and hair on the crossbeam prove it. 'Cause of death: sudden impact on occipital and parietal lobe of the posterior cerebral cortex, severed spine'—from falling off the tower."

"So somebody did destroy all the foot- and fingerprints. Anything else?"

"Listen to this. They found lots of foreign fibers on his jacket. Red wool fibers that didn't come from any of his clothes. Sample included." The sheriff shook a small plastic bag.

Both men peered at the fuzzy red threads flattened against the plastic like spider webbing.

"Wool, it says. Could be a sweater, scarf, hat," Joe said.

"Shirt, skirt, socks, cape. Hell, it could be anything. And we have to find it."

15.

The Game

1960

The next noon, hands on her cheeks, Kya approached the stump slowly, almost in prayer. But no feather on the stump. Her lips pinched.

"A' course. I gotta leave something for him."

Her pocket brought a tail feather from an immature bald eagle she'd found that morning. Only someone who knew birds well would know this splotchy, tatty feather was eagle. A three-year-old, not yet crowned. Not as precious as the tail feather of the tropicbird, but still a dear thing. She laid it carefully on the stump with a little rock on top, pinned from the wind.

That night, arms folded under her head, she lay on her porch bed, a slight smile on her face. Her family had abandoned her to survive a swamp, but here was someone who came on his own, leaving gifts for her in the forest. Uncertainty lingered, but the more she thought about it, the less likely it seemed the boy meant her harm. It didn't fit that anyone who liked birds would be mean.

The next morning, she sprang from bed and went about doing what Ma had called a "deep clean." At Ma's dresser, Kya meant only to cull the remnants of the drawers, but as she picked up her mother's brass-and-steel scissors—the finger holes curled and shaped with intricate patterns of lilies—she suddenly pulled back her hair, not trimmed since Ma left more than seven years ago, and cut off eight inches. Now it fell just below her shoulders. She looked at herself in the mirror, tossed her head a bit, smiled. Scrubbed her fingernails and brushed her hair till it shone.

Replacing the brush and scissors, she looked down among some of Ma's old cosmetics. The liquid foundation and rouge had dried and cracked, but the shelf life of lipstick must be decades because when she opened a tube, it looked fresh. For the first time, never having played dress-up as a little girl, she put some on her lips. Smacked, then smiled again in the mirror. Thought she looked a bit pretty. Not like Ma, but pleasing enough. She giggled, then wiped it off. Just before closing the drawer, she saw a bottle of dried-up Revlon fingernail polish—Barely Pink.

Kya lifted the little jar, remembering how Ma had walked back from town one day with this bottle of fingernail polish, of all things. Ma said it would look real good with their olive skin. She lined up Kya and her two older sisters in a row on the faded sofa, told them to stick out their bare feet, and painted all those toes and then their fingernails. Then she did her own, and they laughed and had a fine time flouncing around the yard, flashing their pink nails. Pa was off somewhere, but the boat was moored at the lagoon. Ma came up with the idea of all the girls going out in the boat, something they had never done.

They climbed into the old skiff, still cavorting like they were tipsy. It took a few pulls to get the outboard cranked, but finally it jumped to, and off they went, Ma steering across the lagoon and into the narrow channel that led to the marsh. They breezed along the waterways, but Ma didn't know all that much about it, and when they went into a shallow lagoon, they got stuck in gummy black mud, thick as tar. They poled this way and that but couldn't budge. There was nothing left to do but climb over the side, skirts and all, sinking in the muck up to their knees.

Ma hollering, "Now don't turn it over, girls, don't turn it over," they hauled on the boat until it was free, squealing at one another's muddy faces. It took some doing to get back in, flopping over the side like so many landed fish. And, instead of sitting on the seats, the four of them squinched up on the bottom of the boat all in a line, holding their feet to the sky, wiggling their toes, their pink nails gleaming through the mud.

Lying there Ma said, "You all listen now, this is a real lesson in life. Yes, we got stuck, but what'd we girls do? We made it fun, we laughed. That's what sisters and girlfriends are all about. Sticking together even in the mud, 'specially in mud."

Ma hadn't bought any polish remover, so when it began to peel and chip, they had faded, patchy pink nails on all their fingers and toes, reminding them of the good time they'd had, and that real-life lesson.

Looking at the old bottle, Kya tried to see her sisters' faces. And said out loud, "Where're you now, Ma? Why didn't you stick?"

As soon as she reached the oak clearing the next afternoon, Kya saw bright, unnatural colors against the muted greens and browns of the forest. On the stump was a small red-and-white milk carton and next to it another feather. It seemed the boy had upped the ante. She walked over and picked up the feather first.

Silver and soft, it was from the crest of a night heron, one of the most beautiful of the marsh. Then she looked inside the milk carton. Rolled up tight were some packages of seeds—turnips, carrots, and green beans—and, at the bottom of the carton, wrapped in brown paper, a spark plug for her boat engine. She smiled again and turned a little circle. She had learned how to live without most things, but now and then she needed a spark plug. Jumpin' had taught her a few minor engine repairs, but every part meant a walk to town and cash money.

And yet here was an extra spark plug, to be set aside until needed. A surplus. Her heart filled up. The same feeling as having a full tank of gas or seeing the sunset under a paint-brushed sky. She stood absolutely still, trying to take it in, what it meant. She had watched male birds wooing females by bringing them gifts. But she was pretty young for nesting.

At the bottom of the carton was a note. She unfolded it and looked at the words, written carefully in simple script that a child could read. Kya knew the time of the tides in her heart, could find her way home by the stars, knew every feather of an eagle, but even at fourteen, couldn't read these words.

She had forgotten to bring anything to leave. Her pockets yielded only ordinary feathers, shells, and seedpods, so she hurried back to the shack and stood in front of her feather-wall, window-shopping. The most graceful were the tail feathers from a tundra swan. She took one from the wall to leave at the stump next time she passed.

As evening fell, she took her blanket and slept in the marsh, close to a gully full of moon and mussels, and had two tow bags filled by dawn. Gas money. They were too heavy to tote, so she dragged the first one back toward the lagoon. Even though it wasn't the shortest route, she went by way of the oak clearing to leave the swan feather. She walked into the trees without looking, and there, leaning against the stump, was the feather boy. She recognized him as Tate, who had shown her the way home through the marsh when she was a little girl. Tate, who, for years, she had watched from a distance without the courage to go near. Of course, he was taller and older, probably eighteen. His golden hair stuck out from his cap in all manner of curls and loose bits, and his face was tan, pleasing. He was calm, smiled wide, his whole face beaming. But it was his eyes that caught her up; they were golden brown with flecks of green, and fixed on hers the way heron eyes catch a minnow.

She halted, shaken by the sudden break in the unwritten rules. That was the fun of it, a game where they didn't have to talk or even be seen. Heat rose in her face.

"Hey, Kya. Please . . . don't . . . run. It's . . . just me . . . Tate," he said very quietly, slowly, like she was dumb or something. That was probably what the townspeople said of her, that she barely spoke human.

Tate couldn't help staring. She must be thirteen or fourteen, he thought. But even at that age, she had the most striking face he'd ever seen. Her large eyes nearly black, her nose slender over shapely lips, painted her in an exotic light. She was tall, thin, giving her a fragile, lithesome look as though molded wild by the wind. Yet young, strapping muscles showed through with quiet power.

Her impulse, as always, was to run. But there was another sensation. A fullness she hadn't felt for years. As if something warm had been poured inside her heart. She thought of the feathers, the spark plug, and the seeds. All of it might end if she ran. Without speaking, she lifted her hand and held the elegant swan feather toward him. Slowly, as though she might spring like a startled fawn, he walked over and studied it in her hand. She watched in silence, looking only at the feather, not his face, nowhere near his eyes.

"Tundra swan, right? Incredible, Kya. Thank you," he said. He was much taller and bent slightly as he took it from her. Of course, this was the time for her to thank him for his gifts, but she stood silent, wishing he would go, wishing they could stick to their game.

Trying to fill the silence, he continued. "My dad's the one who taught me birds."

Finally she looked up at him and said, "I can't read yo' note."

"Well, sure, since you don't go to school. I forgot. All it said was, I saw you a couple of times when I was fishing, and it got me thinking that maybe you could use the seeds and the spark plug. I had extra and thought it might save you a trip to town. I figured you'd like the feathers."

Kya hung her head and said, "Thank you for them; that was mighty fine of you."

Tate noticed that while her face and body showed early inklings and foothills of womanhood, her mannerisms and turns of phrase were somewhat childlike, in contrast to the village girls whose mannerisms—overdoing their makeup, cussing, and smoking—outranked their foothills.

"You're welcome. Well, I better be going, getting late. I'll drop by now and then, if that's okay."

Kya didn't say a word to that. The game must be over. As soon as he realized she wasn't going to speak again, he nodded to her, touched his hat, and turned to go. But just as he ducked his head to step into the brambles, he looked back at her.

"You know, I could teach you to read."

16.

Reading

1960

For days, Tate didn't return for the reading lessons. Before the feather game, loneliness had become a natural appendage to Kya, like an arm. Now it grew roots inside her and pressed against her chest.

Late one afternoon, she struck out in her boat. "I cain't just sit 'round waitin'."

Instead of docking at Jumpin's, where she'd be seen, she stashed her rig in a small cove just south and, carrying a croker sack, walked down the shaded path toward Colored Town. A soft rain had fallen most of the day, and now as the sun neared the horizon, the forest formed its own fog that drifted through succulent glades. She'd never gone to Colored Town, but knew where it was and figured she could find Jumpin' and Mabel's place once she got there.

She wore jeans and a pink blouse from Mabel. In the croker sack were two pint jars of real runny blackberry jam she'd made herself to return Jumpin' and Mabel's kindness. A need to be with someone, a chance to talk with a woman friend urged her toward them. If Jumpin' wasn't home yet, maybe she could sit down with Mabel and visit a spell.

Then, nearing a bend in the road, Kya heard voices coming toward her. She stopped, listened carefully. Quickly she stepped off the path into the woods and hid behind a myrtle thicket. A minute later, two white boys, dressed in raggedy bib overalls, came around the bend, toting fishing tackle and a string of catfish long as her arm. She froze behind the thicket and waited.

One of the boys pointed down the lane. "Lookee up thar."

"Ain't we lucky. Here comes a nigger walkin' to Nigger Town." Kya looked down the path, and there, walking home for the evening, was Jumpin'. Quite close, he had surely heard the boys, but he simply dropped his head, stepped into the woods to give them a berth, and moved on.

What's the matter with 'im, why don't he do sump'm? Kya raged to herself. She knew *nigger* was a real bad word—she knew by the way Pa had used it like a cussword. Jumpin' could have knocked the boys' heads together, taught them a lesson. But he walked on fast.

"Jest an ol' nigger walkin' to town. Watch out, nigger-boy, don't fall down," they taunted Jumpin', who kept his eyes on his toes. One of the boys reached down, picked up a stone, and slung it at Jumpin's back. It hit just under his shoulder blade with a thud. He lurched over a bit, kept walking. The boys laughed as he disappeared around the bend, then they picked up more rocks and followed him.

Kya stalked through brush until she was ahead of them, her eyes glued on their caps bobbing above the branches. She crouched at a spot where thick bushes grew next to the lane, where in seconds they would pass within a foot of her. Jumpin' was up ahead, out of sight. She twisted the cloth bag with the jam so that it was wrung tight and knotted against the jars. As the boys drew even with the thicket, she swung the heavy bag and whacked the closest one hard across the back of his head. He pitched forward and fell on his face. Hollering and screeching, she rushed the other boy, ready to bash his head too, but he took off. She slipped about fifty yards into the trees and watched until the first boy stood, holding his head and cussing.

Toting the bag of jam jars, she turned back toward her boat and motored home. Thought she'd probably never go viztin' again.

The next day, when the sound of Tate's motor chugged through the channel, Kya ran to the lagoon and stood in the bushes, watching him step out of his boat, holding a rucksack. Looking around, he called out to her, and she stepped slowly forward dressed in jeans that fit and a white blouse with mismatched buttons.

"Hey, Kya. Sorry I couldn't get here sooner. Had to help my dad, but we'll get you reading in no time."

"Hey, Tate."

"Let's sit here." He pointed to an oak knee in deep shade of the lagoon. From the rucksack he pulled out a thin, faded book of the alphabet and a lined writing pad. With a careful slow hand, he formed the letters between the lines, *a A, b B*, asking her to do the same, patient with her tongue-between-lips effort. As she wrote, he said the letters out loud. Softly, slowly.

She remembered some of the letters from Jodie and Ma but didn't know much at all about putting them into proper words.

After only minutes, he said, "See, you can already write a word."

"What d'ya mean?"

"*C-a-b*. You can write the word *cab*."

"What's *cab*?" she asked. He knew not to laugh.

"Don't worry if you don't know it. Let's keep going. Soon you'll write a word you know."

Later he said, "You'll have to work lots more on the alphabet. It'll take a little while to get it, but you can already read a bit. I'll show you." He didn't have a grammar reader, so her first book was his dad's copy of Aldo Leopold's *A Sand County Almanac*. He pointed to the opening sentence and asked her to read it back to him. The first word was *There* and she had to go back to the alphabet and practice the sound of each letter, but he was patient, explaining the special sound of *th*, and when she finally said it, she threw her arms up and laughed. Beaming, he watched her.

Slowly, she unraveled each word of the sentence: "'There are some who can live without wild things, and some who cannot.'"

"Oh," she said. "Oh."

"You can read, Kya. There will never be a time again when you can't read."

"It ain't just that." She spoke almost in a whisper. "I wadn't aware that words could hold so much. I didn't know a sentence could be so full."

He smiled. "That's a very good sentence. Not all words hold that much."

Over the coming days, sitting on the oak knee in shade or the shore in sun, Tate taught her how to read the words, which sang of the geese and cranes, real all around them. "What if there be no more goose music?"

In between helping his dad or pitching baseball with his friends, he came to Kya's place several times a week and, now, no matter what she was doing—weeding the garden, feeding the chickens, searching for shells—she listened for the sound of his boat humming up the channel.

On the beach one day, reading about what chickadees eat for lunch, she asked him, "You live with yo' family in Barkley Cove?"

"I live with my dad. Yes, in Barkley."

Kya didn't ask if he had more family, now gone. His ma must have left him, too. Part of her longed to touch his hand, a strange wanting, but her fingers wouldn't do it. Instead she memorized the bluish veins on the inside of his wrist, as intricate as those sketched on the wings of wasps.

At night, sitting at the kitchen table, she went over the lessons by kerosene lamp, its soft light seeping through the shack windows and touching the lower branches of the oaks. The only light for miles and miles of blackness except for the soft glow of fireflies.

Carefully, she wrote and said each word over and over. Tate said long words were simply little ones strung together—so she wasn't afraid of them, went straight to learning *Pleistocene* along with *sat*. Learning to read was the most fun she'd ever had. But she couldn't figure why Tate had offered to teach po' white trash like her, why he'd come in the first place, bringing exquisite feathers. But she didn't ask, afraid it might get him thinking on it, send him away.

Now at last Kya could label all her precious specimens. She took each feather, insect, shell, or flower, looked up how to spell the name in Ma's books, and wrote it carefully on her brown-paper-bag painting.

. . .

"What comes after twenty-nine?" she asked Tate one day.

He looked at her. She knew more about tides and snow geese, eagles and stars than most ever would, yet she couldn't count to thirty. He didn't want to shame her, so didn't show surprise. She was awfully good at reading eyes.

"Thirty," he said simply. "Here, I'll show you the numbers and we'll do some basic arithmetic. It's easy. I'll bring you some books about it."

She went around reading everything—the directions on the grits bag, Tate's notes, and the stories from her fairy-tale books she had pretended to read for years. Then one night she made a little *oh* sound, and took the old Bible from the shelf. Sitting at the table, she turned the thin pages carefully to the one with the family names. She found her own at the very bottom. There it was, her birthday: *Miss Catherine Danielle Clark, October 10, 1945*. Then, going back up the list, she read the real names of her brothers and sisters:

Master Jeremy Andrew Clark, January 2, 1939. "Jeremy," she said out loud. "Jodie, I sure never thought a' you as Master Jeremy."

Miss Amanda Margaret Clark, May 17, 1937. Kya touched the name with her fingers. Repeated it several times.

She read on. *Master Napier Murphy Clark, April 4, 1936*. Kya spoke softly, "Murph, ya name was Napier."

At the top, the oldest, *Miss Mary Helen Clark, September 19, 1934*. She rubbed her fingers over the names again, which brought faces before her eyes. They blurred, but she could see them all squeezed around the table eating stew, passing cornbread, even laughing some. She was ashamed that she had forgotten their names, but now that she'd found them, she would never let them go again.

Above the list of children she read: *Mister Jackson Henry Clark married Miss Julienne Maria Jacques, June 12, 1933.* Not until that moment had she known her parents' proper names.

She sat there for a few minutes with the Bible open on the table. Her family before her.

Time ensures children never know their parents young. Kya would never see the handsome Jake swagger into an Asheville soda fountain in early 1930, where he spotted Maria Jacques, a beauty with black curls and red lips, visiting from New Orleans. Over a milkshake he told her his family owned a plantation and that after high school he'd study to be a lawyer and live in a columned mansion.

But when the Depression deepened, the bank auctioned the land out from under the Clarks' feet, and his father took Jake from school. They moved down the road to a small pine cabin that once, not so long ago really, had been occupied by slaves. Jake worked the tobacco fields, stacking leaves with black men and women, babies strapped on their backs with colorful shawls.

One night two years later, without saying good-bye, Jake left before dawn, taking with him as many fine clothes and family treasures—including his great-grandfather's gold pocket watch and his grandmother's diamond ring—as he could carry. He hitchhiked to New Orleans and found Maria living with her family in an elegant home near the waterfront. They were descendants of a French merchant, owners of a shoe factory.

Jake pawned the heirlooms and entertained her in fine restaurants hung with red velvet curtains, telling her that he would buy her that columned mansion. As he knelt under a magnolia tree, she agreed to marry him, and they wed in 1933 in a small church ceremony, her family standing silent.

By now, the money was gone, so he accepted a job from his

father-in-law in the shoe factory. Jake assumed he would be made manager, but Mr. Jacques, a man not easily taken in, insisted Jake learn the business from the bottom up like any other employee. So Jake labored at cutting out soles.

He and Maria lived in a small garage apartment furnished with a few grand pieces from her dowry mixed with flea-market tables and chairs. He enrolled in night classes to finish high school but usually skipped out to play poker and, stinking of whiskey, came home late to his new wife. After only three weeks, the teacher dropped him from the classes.

Maria begged him to stop drinking, to show enthusiasm for his job so that her father would promote him. But the babies started coming and the drinking never stopped. Between 1934 and 1940 they had four children, and Jake was promoted only once.

The war with Germany was an equalizer. Boiled down to the same uniform-hue as everyone else, he could hide his shame, once again play proud. But one night, sitting in a muddy foxhole in France, someone shouted that their sergeant was shot and sprawled bleeding twenty yards away. Mere boys, they should have been sitting in a dugout waiting to bat, nervous about some fastball. Still, they jumped at once, scrambling to save the wounded man—all but one.

Jake hunched in a corner, too scared to move, but a mortar exploded yellow-white just beyond the hole, shattering the bones of his left leg into fragments. When the soldiers tumbled back into the trench, dragging the sergeant, they assumed Jake had been hit while helping the others rescue their comrade. He was declared a hero. No one would ever know. Except Jake.

With a medal and a medical discharge, he was sent home. Determined not to work again in the shoe factory, Jake stayed only a few nights in New Orleans. With Maria standing by silently, he sold all her fine furniture and silver, then packed his family onto the train and moved them to North Carolina. He discovered from an old friend that his mother and father had died, clearing the way for his plan.

He'd convinced Maria that living in a cabin his father had built as a fishing retreat on the coast of North Carolina would be a new start. There would be no rent and Jake could finish high school. He bought a small fishing boat in Barkley Cove and motored through miles of marsh waterways with his family and all their possessions piled around them—a few fine hatboxes perched on top. When they finally broke into the lagoon, where the ratty shack with rusted-out screens hunkered under the oaks, Maria clutched her youngest child, Jodie, fighting tears.

Pa assured her, "Don't ya worry none. I'll get this fixed up in no time."

But Jake never improved the shack or finished high school. Soon after they arrived, he took up drinking and poker at the Swamp Guinea, trying to leave that foxhole in a shot glass.

Maria did what she could to make a home. She bought sheets from rummage sales for the floor mattresses and a stand-alone tin bathtub; she washed the laundry under the yard spigot, and figured out on her own how to plant a garden, how to keep chickens.

Soon after they arrived, dressed in their best, she hiked the children to Barkley Cove to register them in school. Jake, however, scoffed at the notion of education, and more days than not, told Murph and Jodie to skip school and bring in squirrels or fish for supper.

Jake took Maria for only one moonlit boat ride, the result of which was their last child, a daughter named Catherine Danielle; later nicknamed Kya because, when first asked, that's what she said her name was.

Now and then, when sober, Jake dreamed again of completing school, making a better life for them all, but the shadow of the foxhole would move across his mind. Once sure and cocky, handsome and fit, he could no longer wear the man he had become and he'd take a swig from his poke. Blending in with the fighting, drinking, cussing renegades of the marsh was the easiest thing Jake ever did.

17.

Crossing the Threshold

1960

One day during the reading summer when she motored to Jumpin's, he said, "Now, Miss Kya, there's sump'm else. Some men been pokin' 'round, askin' 'bout ya."

She looked right at him instead of off to the side. "Who, what d'they want?"

"I b'lieve they're from the Sochul Services. They askin' all kinds of questions. Is yo' pa still 'round, where ya ma is, if ya goin' to school this fall. An when ya come here; they 'specially wanta know what times ya come here."

"What'd you tell 'em, Jumpin'?"

"Well, I done ma best to put 'em off ya. Told 'em ya pa just fine, out fishin's all." He laughed, threw his head back. "Then I told 'em I neva know when ya boat in here. Now, don't ya worry none, Miss Kya. Jumpin'll send 'em on a snipe hunt if they come again."

"Thank ya." After filling her tank, Kya headed straight home. She'd have to be on guard more now, maybe find a place in the marsh where she could hide out some until they gave up on her.

Late that afternoon, as Tate pulled up to the shore, the hull crunching softly on sand, she said, "Can we meet somewheres else, 'sides here?"

"Hey, Kya, good to see you." Tate greeted her, still sitting at the tiller.

"What d'ya think?"

"It's *besides*, not *'sides*, and it's polite to greet people before asking a favor."

"You say *'sides* sometimes," she said, almost smiling.

"Yeah, we all got magnolia mouth, being from the North Carolina sticks, but we have to try."

"Good afternoon, Mr. Tate," she said, making a little curtsy. He caught a glimpse of the spunk and sass somewhere inside. "Now, can we meet somewhere besides here? Please."

"Sure, I guess, but why?"

"Jumpin' said the Social Services are lookin' for me. I'm scared they'll pull me in like a trout, put me in a foster home or sump'm."

"Well, we better hide way out there where the crawdads sing. I pity any foster parents who take you on." Tate's whole face smiled.

"What d'ya mean, where the crawdads sing? Ma used to say that." Kya remembered Ma always encouraging her to explore the marsh: "Go as far as you can—way out yonder where the crawdads sing."

"Just means far in the bush where critters are wild, still behaving like critters. Now, you got any ideas where we can meet?"

"There's a place I found one time, an old fallin'-down cabin. Once you know the turnoff, ya can get there by boat; I can walk there from here."

"Okay then, get in. Show me this time; next time we'll meet there."

"If I'm out there I'll leave a little pile of rocks right here by the tyin'-up log." Kya pointed to a spot on the lagoon beach. "Otherwise, I'm 'round here somewhere and will come out when I hear yo' motor."

They puttered slowly through the marsh, then planed off south through open sea, away from town. She bounced along in the bow, wind-tears streaming across her cheeks and tickling cool in her ears. When they reached a small cove, she guided him up a narrow freshwater creek hung low with brambles. Several times the creek seemed to peter out, but Kya motioned that it was okay to go on, and they crashed through more brush.

Finally they broke into a wide meadow where the stream ran by an old one-room log cabin, collapsed on one end. The logs had buckled, some lying around the ground like pick-up sticks. The roof, still sitting on the half wall, sloped down from high end to low like a lopsided hat. Tate pulled the boat up onto the mud and they silently walked to the open door.

Inside was dark and reeked of rat urine. "Well, I hope you don't plan on living here—the whole thing could collapse on your head." Tate pushed at the wall. It seemed sturdy enough.

"It's just a hideout. I can stash some food 'case I have to go on the run awhile."

Tate turned and looked at her as their eyes adjusted to the dark.

"Kya, you ever thought of just going back to school? It wouldn't kill you, and they might leave you alone if you did."

"They must've figured out I'm alone, and if I go, they'll grab me, put me in a home. Anyway, I'm too old for school now. Where would they put me, first grade?" Her eyes widened at the notion of sitting in a tiny chair, surrounded by little kids who could pronounce words, count to fifty.

"What, so you plan to live alone in the marsh forever?"

"Better than going to a foster home. Pa used to say he'd farm us out to one if we were bad. Told us they're mean."

"No, they're not. Not always. Most of them are nice people who like kids," he said.

"You sayin' you'd go to a foster home 'fore you'd live in the marsh?" she asked, chin jutted out, hand on her hip.

He was silent a minute. "Well, bring some blankets out, matches in case it gets cold. Maybe some tins of sardines. They last forever. But don't keep fresh food; it'll bring the bears in."

"I ain't scared of bears."

"I'm not scared of bears."

For the rest of the summer Kya and Tate did the reading lessons at the tumbledown cabin. By mid-August they had read through *A Sand County Almanac,* and although she couldn't read every word, she got most of it. Aldo Leopold taught her that floodplains are living extensions of the rivers, which will claim them back any time they choose. Anyone living on a floodplain is just waiting in the river's wings. She learned where the geese go in winter, and the meaning of their music. His soft words, sounding almost like poetry, taught her that soil is packed with life and one of the most precious riches on Earth; that draining wetlands dries the land for miles beyond, killing plants and animals along with the water. Some of the seeds lie dormant in the desiccated earth for decades, waiting, and when the water finally comes home again, they burst through the soil, unfolding their faces. Wonders and real-life knowledge she would've never learned in school. Truths everyone should know, yet somehow, even though they lay exposed all around, seemed to lie in secret like the seeds.

They met at the log cabin several times a week, but she slept most nights in her shack or on the beach with the gulls. She had to collect firewood before winter, so made a mission of it, toting loads from near and far and stacking them somewhat neatly between two pines. The turnips in her garden barely poked their heads above the goldenrod; still she had more vegetables than she and the deer could eat. She harvested the last of the late-summer crop and stored the squash and beets in the cool shade of the brick-'n'-board steps.

But all the while, she kept her ears out for the lugging sounds of an automobile, filled with men come to take her away. Sometimes the listening was tiresome and creepy, so she'd walk to the log cabin and sleep the night on the dirt floor, wrapped in her spare blanket. She timed her mussel collecting and fish smoking so that Tate could take them to Jumpin's and bring back her supplies. Keeping her underbelly less exposed.

"Remember when you read your first sentence, you said that some words hold a lot?" Tate said one day, sitting on the creek bank.

"Yeah, I remember, why?"

"Well, especially poems. The words in poems do more than say things. They stir up emotions. Even make you laugh."

"Ma used to read poems, but I don't remember any."

"Listen to this; it's by Edward Lear." He took out a folded envelope and read,

> "Then Mr. Daddy Long-legs
> And Mr. Floppy Fly
> Rushed downward to the foamy sea
> With one sponge-taneous cry;

And there they found a little boat,
Whose sails were pink and gray;
And off they sailed among the waves,
Far, and far away."

Smiling, she said, "It makes a rhythm like waves hitting the beach."

After that she went into a poem-writing phase, making them up as she boated through the marsh or looked for shells—simple verses, singsong and silly. "There's a mama blue jay lifting from a branch; I'd fly too, if I had a chance." They made her laugh out loud; filled up a few lonely minutes of a long, lonely day.

One late afternoon, reading at the kitchen table, she remembered Ma's book of poetry and scrounged until she found it. The volume so worn, the covers had long since gone, the pages held together by two frayed rubber bands. Kya carefully took them off and thumbed through the pages, reading Ma's notes in the margins. At the end was a list of page numbers of Ma's favorites.

Kya turned to one by James Wright:

Suddenly lost and cold,
I knew the yard lay bare,
I longed to touch and hold
My child, my talking child,
Laughing or tame or wild . . .

Trees and the sun were gone,
Everything gone but us.
His mother sang in the house,
And kept our supper warm,

And loved us, God knows how,
The wide earth darkened so.

And this one by Galway Kinnell.

I did care. . . .
I did say everything I thought
In the mildest words I knew. And now, . . .
I have to say I am relieved it is over:
At the end I could feel only pity
For that urge toward more life.
. . . Goodbye.

Kya touched the words as if they were a message, as though Ma had underlined them specifically so her daughter would read them someday by this dim kerosene flame and understand. It wasn't much, not a handwritten note tucked in the back of a sock drawer, but it was something. She sensed that the words clinched a powerful meaning, but she couldn't shake it free. If she ever became a poet, she'd make the message clear.

After Tate started his senior year in September, he couldn't come to Kya's place as often, but when he did, he brought her discarded textbooks from school. He didn't say a word about the biology books being too advanced for her, so she plowed through chapters she wouldn't have seen for four years in school. "Don't worry," he'd say, "you'll get a little more every time you read it." And that was true.

As the days grew shorter, again they met near her shack because there wasn't enough daylight to get to the reading cabin. They had always studied outside, but when a crazed wind blew one morning, Kya built up the fire in the woodstove. No one had crossed the shack's threshold since Pa disappeared more than four years ago, and to ask anybody inside would seem unthinkable. Anyone but Tate.

"Wanta sit in the kitchen by the stove?" she said when he dragged his rig onto the lagoon shore.

"Sure," he said, knowing not to make a big deal of the invitation.

As soon as he stepped inside the porch, he took nearly twenty minutes to explore and exclaim over her feathers and shells and bones and nests. When they finally settled at the table, she pulled her chair close to his, their arms and elbows nearly touching. Just to feel him near.

With Tate so busy helping his dad, the days dragged slow from nose to tail. Late one evening she took her first novel, *Rebecca* by Daphne du Maurier, from Ma's bookshelf and read about love. After a while she closed the book and walked to the closet. She slipped on Ma's sundress and swished around the room, flipping the skirt about, whirling in front of the mirror. Her mane and hips swaying, she imagined Tate asking her to dance. His hand on her waist. As if she were Mrs. de Winter.

Abruptly she caught herself and bent over, giggling. Then stood very still.

"Come on up here, child," Mabel sang out one afternoon. "I got ya some things." Jumpin' usually brought the boxes of goods for Kya, but when Mabel showed up, there was usually something special.

"Go on then, pick up yo' stuff. I'll fill yo' tank," Jumpin' said, so Kya hopped onto the wharf.

"Look here, Miss Kya," Mabel said, as she lifted a peach-colored dress with a layer of chiffon over the flowered skirt, the most beautiful piece of clothing Kya had ever seen, prettier than Ma's sundress. "This dress is fit for a princess like you." She held it in front of Kya, who touched it and smiled. Then, facing away from Jumpin', Mabel leaned over at the middle with some effort and lifted a white bra from the box.

Kya felt heat all over.

"Now, Miss Kya, don't be shy, hon. Ya be needin' this 'bout now. And, child, if there's ever anything ya need to talk to me about, anything ya don't understand, ya let ol' Mabel know. Ya heah?"

"Yes'm. Thank you, Mabel." Kya tucked the bra deep in the box, under some jeans and T-shirts, a bag of black-eyed peas, and a jar of put-up peaches.

A few weeks later, watching pelicans float and feed in the sea, her boat riding up and down waves, Kya's stomach suddenly cramped up. She'd never been seasick, and this felt different from any pain she'd ever had. She pulled her boat ashore at Point Beach and sat on the sand, legs folded to one side like a wing. The pain sharpened, and she grimaced, made a little moan. She must have the runs coming.

Suddenly she heard the purr of a motor and saw Tate's rig cutting through the white-capped surf. He turned inland the instant he saw her and made for shore. She spat out some of Pa's cussing. She always liked seeing Tate, but not when she might have to run to the oak woods any second with diarrhea. After dragging his boat next to hers, he plopped down on the sand beside her.

"Hey, Kya. What're you doing? I was just going out to your place."

"Hey, Tate. It's good to see you." She tried to sound normal, but her stomach twisted tightly.

"What's wrong?" he asked.

"What do you mean?"

"You don't look good. What's wrong?"

"I think I'm sick. My stomach's cramping real hard."

"Oh." Tate looked out over the sea. Dug his bare toes in the sand.

"Maybe you should go," she said, head down.

"Maybe I should stay till you're better. Suppose you can't get yourself home?"

"I might have to go to the woods. I might be sick."

"Maybe. But I don't think that's going to help," he said quietly.

"What do you mean? You don't know what's wrong with me."

"Does this feel different from other stomachaches?"

"Yes."

"You're almost fifteen, right?"

"Yes. What's that got to do with it?"

He was quiet a minute. Shuffled his feet, digging his toes deeper in the sand. Looking away from her, he said, "It might be, you know, what happens to girls your age. Remember, a few months ago I brought you a pamphlet about it. It was with those biology books." Tate glanced at her briefly, his face blazing, and looked away again.

Kya dropped her eyes as her whole body blushed. Of course, there'd been no Ma to tell her, but indeed a school booklet Tate had brought explained some. Now her time had come, and here she was sitting on the beach becoming a woman right in front of a boy. Shame and panic filled her. What was she supposed to do? What exactly would happen? How much blood would there be? She imagined it leaking into the sand around her. She sat silent as a sharp pain racked her middle.

"Can you get yourself home?" he asked, still not looking at her.

"I think so."

"It'll be okay, Kya. Every girl goes through this just fine. You go on home. I'll follow way back to make sure you get there."

"You don't have to."

"Don't worry about me. Now get going." He stood and walked to his boat, not looking at her. He motored out and waited quite far offshore until she headed up coast toward her channel. So far back he was just a speck, he followed until she reached her lagoon. Standing on the bank, she waved briefly to him, her face down, not meeting his eyes.

Just as she had figured out most things, Kya figured out how to become a woman on her own. But the next morning at first light, she boated over to Jumpin's. A pale sun seemed suspended in thick fog as she approached his wharf and looked for Mabel, knowing there was little chance she'd be there. Sure enough, only Jumpin' walked out to greet her.

"Hi, Miss Kya. Ya needin' gas a'ready?"

Still sitting in the boat, Kya answered quietly, "I need to see Mabel."

"I'm sorry as can be, child, Mabel ain't here today. Can I help ya?"

Head down low, she said, "I need to see Mabel bad. Soon."

"Well then." Jumpin' looked across the small bay out to sea and saw no more boats coming in. Anybody needing gas at any time of day and every day including Christmas could count on Jumpin' being here—he hadn't missed a single day in fifty years, except when their baby angel, Daisy, died. He couldn't leave his post. "Ya hang on there, Miss Kya, I gonna run up the lane a ways, get some chillin to fetch Mabel. Any boat come in, ya tell 'em I'll be right back."

"I will. Thank you."

Jumpin' hurried up the wharf and disappeared as Kya waited, glancing out in the bay every few seconds, dreading another boat coming in. But in no time he was back, saying some kids had gone to get Mabel; Kya should "just wait a spell."

Jumpin' busied himself unpacking packets of chewing tobacco on the shelves and generally doing around. Kya stayed in her boat. Finally Mabel hurried across the boards, which shook with her swing as if a small piano were being pushed down the wharf. Carrying a paper bag, she didn't bellow out a greeting, as she would have otherwise, but stood on the wharf above Kya and said quietly, "Mornin', Miss Kya, what's all this 'bout, child? What's wrong, hon?"

Kya dropped her head more, mumbled something Mabel couldn't hear.

"Can ya get out of that boat, or should I get in there with ya?"

Kya didn't answer, so Mabel, almost two hundred pounds' worth, stepped one foot, then the other into the small boat, which complained by bumping against the piling. She sat down on the center bench, facing Kya at the stern.

"Now, child, tell me what's wrong."

The two leaned their heads together, Kya whispering, and then Mabel pulled Kya right over to her full bosom, hugging and rocking her. Kya was rigid at first, not accustomed to yielding to hugs, but this didn't discourage Mabel, and finally Kya went limp and slumped against the comfort of those pillows. After a while, Mabel leaned back and opened the brown paper bag.

"Well, I figured what's wrong, so I brought ya some things." And there, sitting in the boat at Jumpin's wharf, Mabel explained the details to Kya.

"Now, Miss Kya, this ain't nothin' to be 'shamed of. It ain't no curse, like folks say; this here's the startin' of all life, and only a woman can do it. You're a woman now, baby."

When Kya heard Tate's boat the next afternoon, she hid in thick brambles and watched him. For anyone to know her at all seemed strange enough, but now he knew about the most personal and private occurrence of her life. Her cheeks burned at the thought of it. She would hide until he left.

As he pulled onto the lagoon shore and stepped out of the boat, he carried a white box tied up with string. "Yo! Kya, where are you?" he called. "I brought petite cakes from Parker's."

Kya had not tasted anything like cake for years. Tate lifted some books out of the boat, so Kya moseyed out of the bushes behind him.

"Oh, there you are. Look at this." He opened the box, and there, arranged neatly, were little cakes, each only an inch square, covered in vanilla icing with a tiny pink rose perched on the top. "Come on, dig in."

Kya lifted one and, still not looking at Tate, bit into it. Then pushed the rest of it into her mouth. Licked her fingers.

"Here." Tate set the box next to their oak. "Have all you want. Let's get started. I brought a new book." And that was that. They went into the lessons, never uttering a word about the other thing.

Autumn was coming; the evergreens might not have noticed, but the sycamores did. They flashed thousands of golden leaves across slate-gray skies. Late one afternoon, after the lesson, Tate lingering when he should have left, he and Kya sat on a log in the woods. She finally asked the question she'd wanted to ask for months. "Tate, I appreciate your teaching me to read and all those things you gave me. But why'd you do it? Don't you have a girlfriend or somebody like that?"

"Nah—well, sometimes I do. I had one, but not now. I like being out here in the quiet and I like the way you're so interested in the marsh, Kya. Most people don't pay it any attention except to fish. They think it's wasteland that should be drained and developed. People don't understand that most sea creatures—including the very ones they eat—need the marsh."

He didn't mention how he felt sorry for her being alone, that he knew how the kids had treated her for years; how the villagers called her the Marsh Girl and made up stories about her. Sneaking out to her shack, running through the dark and tagging it, had become a regular tradition, an initiation for boys becoming men. What did that say about men? Some of them were already making bets about who would be the first to get her cherry. Things that infuriated and worried him.

But that wasn't the main reason he'd left feathers for Kya in the forest, or why he kept coming to see her. The other words Tate didn't say were his feelings for her that seemed tangled up between the sweet love for a lost sister and the fiery love for a girl. He couldn't come close to sorting it out himself, but he'd never been hit by a stronger wave. A power of emotions as painful as pleasurable.

Poking a grass stalk down an ant hole, she finally asked, "Where's your ma?"

A breeze wandered through the trees, gently shaking branches. Tate didn't answer.

"You don't have to say nothing," she said.

"Anything."

"You don't have to say anything."

"My mother and little sister died in a car wreck over in Asheville. My sister's name was Carianne."

"Oh. I'm so sorry, Tate. I bet your ma was real nice and pretty."

"Yes. Both of them were." He spoke to the ground, between his knees. "I've never talked about it before. To anybody."

Me neither, Kya thought. Out loud she said, "My ma walked off one day and didn't come back. The mama deer always come back."

"Well, at least you can hope she does. Mine won't come back for sure."

They were silent a moment, then Tate continued. "I think . . ." But he stopped, looked away.

Kya looked at him, but he stared at the ground. Quiet.

She said, "What? You think what? You can say anything to me."

Still he said nothing. From a patience born from knowing, she waited.

Finally, very softly he said, "I think they went to Asheville to buy my birthday present. There was this certain bike I wanted, had to have it. The Western Auto didn't carry them, so I think they went to Asheville to buy that bike for me."

"That doesn't make it your fault," she said.

"I know, but it feels like my fault," Tate said. "I don't even remember what kind of bike it was."

Kya leaned closer to him, not enough to touch. But she felt a sensation—almost like the space between their shoulders had shifted. She wondered if Tate felt it. She wanted to lean in closer, just enough so their arms would gently brush together. To touch. And wondered if Tate would notice.

And just at that second, the wind picked up, and thousands upon thousands of yellow sycamore leaves broke from their life support and streamed across the sky. Autumn leaves don't fall; they fly. They take their time and wander on this, their only chance to soar. Reflecting sunlight, they swirled and sailed and fluttered on the wind drafts.

Tate sprang from the log and called to her, "See how many leaves you can catch before they hit the ground!" Kya jumped up, and the two of them leapt and skipped through curtains of falling leaves, reaching their arms wide, snatching them before they fell to the earth. Laughing, Tate dived toward a leaf only inches from the ground, caught it, and rolled over, holding his trophy in the air. Kya threw her hands up, releasing all the leaves she had rescued back into the wind. As she ran back through them, they caught like gold in her hair.

Then, as she whirled around, she bumped into Tate, who had stood, and they froze, staring into each other's eyes. They stopped laughing. He took her shoulders, hesitated an instant, then kissed her lips, as the leaves rained and danced around them as silently as snow.

She knew nothing about kissing and held her head and lips stiff. They broke away and looked at each other, wondering where that had come from and what to do next. He lifted a leaf gently from her hair and dropped it to the ground. Her heart beat wildly. Of all the ragged loves she'd known from wayward family, none had felt like this.

"Am I your girlfriend now?" she asked.

He smiled. "Do you want to be?"

"Yes."

"You might be too young," he said.

"But I know feathers. I bet the other girls don't know feathers."

"All right, then." And he kissed her again. This time she tilted her head to the side and her lips softened. And for the first time in her life, her heart was full.

18.

White Canoe

1960

Now, every new word began with a squeal, every sentence a race. Tate grabbing Kya, the two of them tumbling, half childlike, half not, through sourweed, red with autumn.

"Be serious a second," he said. "The only way to get multiplication tables is to memorize them." He wrote $12 \times 12 = 144$ in the sand, but she ran past him, dived into the breaking surf, down to the calm, and swam until he followed into a place where gray-blue light beams slanted through the quiet and highlighted their forms. Sleek as porpoises. Later, sandy and salty, they rolled across the beach, arms tight around each other as if they were one.

The next afternoon he motored into her lagoon but stayed in his boat after beaching. A large basket covered in a red-checkered cloth sat at his feet.

"What's that? What'd you bring?" she asked.

"A surprise. Go on, get in."

They flowed through the slow-moving channels into the sea, then south to a tiny half-moon bay. After wrist-flicking the blanket onto the sand, he placed the covered basket on it, and as they sat, he lifted the cloth.

"Happy birthday, Kya," he said. "You're fifteen." A two-tiered bakery cake, tall as a hatbox and decorated with shells of pink icing, rose from the basket. Her name scripted on top. Presents, wrapped in colorful paper and tied with bows, surrounded the cake.

She stared, flabbergasted, her mouth open. No one had wished her happy birthday since Ma left. No one had ever given her a store-bought cake with her name on it. She'd never had presents in real wrapping paper with ribbons.

"How'd you know my birthday?" Having no calendar, she had no idea it was today.

"I read it in your Bible."

While she pleaded for him not to cut through her name, he sliced enormous pieces of cake and plopped them on paper plates. Staring into each other's eyes, they broke off bites and stuffed them in their mouths. Smacking loudly. Licking fingers. Laughing through icing-smeared grins. Eating cake the way it should be eaten, the way everybody wants to eat it.

"Want to open your presents?" He smiled.

The first: a small magnifying glass, "so you can see the fine details of insect wings." Second: a plastic clasp, painted silver and decorated with a rhinestone seagull, "for your hair." Somewhat awkwardly, he pulled some locks behind her ear and clipped the barrette in place. She touched it. More beautiful than Ma's.

The last present was in a larger box, and Kya opened it to find ten jars of oil paint, tins of watercolors, and different-sized brushes: "for your paintings."

Kya picked up each color, each brush. "I can get more when you need them. Even canvas, from Sea Oaks."

She dipped her head. "Thank you, Tate."

"Easy does it. Go slow, now," Scupper called out as Tate, surrounded by fishing nets, oil rags, and preening pelicans, powered the winch. The bow of *The Cherry Pie* bobbled on the cradle, gave a shudder, then glided onto the underwater rails at Pete's Boat Yard, the lopsided pier and rusted-out boathouse, the only haul-out in Barkley Cove.

"Okay, good, she's on. Bring her out." Tate eased more power to the winch, and the boat crawled up the track and into dry dock. They secured her in cables and set about scraping blotchy barnacles from her hull as crystal-sharp arias of Miliza Korjus rose from the record player. They'd have to apply primer, then the annual coat of red paint. Tate's mother had chosen the color, and Scupper would never change it. Once in a while Scupper stopped scraping and waved his large arms to the music's sinuous shape.

Now, early winter, Scupper paid Tate adult wages to work for him after school and on weekends, but Tate couldn't get out to Kya's as much. He didn't mention this to his dad; he'd never mentioned anything about Kya to his dad.

They hacked at barnacles until dark, until even Scupper's arms burned. "I'm too tired to cook, and I reckon you are, too. Let's grab some grub at the diner on the way home."

Nodding at everyone, there not being one person they didn't know, they sat at a corner table. Both ordered the special: chicken-fried steak, mash and gravy, turnips, and coleslaw. Biscuits. Pecan pie with ice cream. At the next table, a family of four joined hands and lowered their heads as the father said a blessing out loud. At "Amen" they kissed the air, squeezed hands, and passed the cornbread.

Scupper said, "Now, son, I know this job's keeping ya from things. That's the way it is, but you didn't go to the homecoming dance or anything last fall, and I don't want you to miss all of it, this being your last year. There's that big dance at the pavilion coming up. You asking a girl?"

"Nah. I might go, not sure. But there's nobody I want to ask."

"There's not one single girl in school you'd go with?"

"Nope."

"Well then." Scupper leaned back as the waitress put down his plate of food. "Thank you, Betty. You sure heaped it up good." Betty moved around and set down Tate's plate, piled even higher.

"Y'all eat up now," she said. "Thar's more where this come from. The special's all-you-can-eat." She smiled at Tate before walking with an extra hip-swing back to the kitchen.

Tate said, "The girls at school are silly. All they talk about is hair-dos and high heels."

"Well now, that's what girls do. Sometimes you gotta take things as they are."

"Maybe."

"Now, son, I don't pay much mind to idle talk, never have done. But there's a regular riptide of gossip saying you've got something going with that girl in the marsh." Tate threw up his hands. "Now hold on, hold on," Scupper continued. "I don't believe all the stories about her; she's probably nice. But take a care, son. You don't want to go starting a family too early. You get my meaning, don't you?"

Keeping his voice low, Tate hissed, "First you say you don't believe those stories about her, then you say I shouldn't start a family, showing you do believe she's that kind of girl. Well, let me tell you something, she's not. She's more pure and innocent than any of those girls you'd have me go to the dance with. Oh man, some of the girls in this town, well, let's just say they hunt in packs, take no prisoners. And yes, I've been going out to see Kya some. You know why? I'm teaching her how to read because people in this town are so mean to her she couldn't even go to school."

"That's fine, Tate. That's good of you. But please understand it's my job to say things like this. It may not be pleasant and all for us to talk about, but parents have to warn their kids about things. That's my job, so don't get huffy about it."

"I know," Tate mumbled while buttering a biscuit. Feeling very huffy.

"Come on now. Let's get another helping, then some of that pecan pie."

After the pie came, Scupper said, "Well, since we've talked about things we never mention, I might as well say something else on my mind."

Tate rolled his eyes at his pie.

Scupper continued. "I want you to know, son, how proud I am of you. All on your own, you've studied the marsh life, done real well at school, applied for college to get a degree in science. And got accepted. I'm just not the kind to speak on such things much. But I'm mighty proud of you, son. All right?"

"Yeah. All right."

Later in his room, Tate recited from his favorite poem:

"Oh when shall I see the dusky Lake,
And the white canoe of my dear?"

. . .

Around the work, as best he could, Tate got out to Kya's, but could never stay long. Sometimes boating forty minutes for a ten-minute beach walk, holding hands. Kissing a lot. Not wasting a minute. Boating back. He wanted to touch her breasts; would kill just to look at them. Lying awake at night, he thought of her thighs, how soft, yet firm, they must be. To think beyond her thighs sent him roiling in the sheets. But she was so young and timid. If he did things wrong, it might affect her somehow, then he'd be worse than the boys who only talked about snagging her. His desire to protect her was as strong as the other. Sometimes.

On every trip to Kya's, Tate took school or library books, especially on marsh creatures and biology. Her progress was startling. She could read anything now, he said, and once you can read anything you can learn everything. It was up to her. "Nobody's come close to filling their brains," he said. "We're all like giraffes not using their necks to reach the higher leaves."

Alone for hours, by the light of the lantern, Kya read how plants and animals change over time to adjust to the ever-shifting earth; how some cells divide and specialize into lungs or hearts, while others remain uncommitted as stem cells in case they're needed later. Birds sing mostly at dawn because the cool, moist air of morning carries their songs and their meanings much farther. All her life, she'd seen these marvels at eye level, so nature's ways came easily to her.

Within all the worlds of biology, she searched for an explanation of why a mother would leave her offspring.

. . .

One cold day, long after all the sycamore leaves had fallen, Tate stepped out of his boat with a present wrapped in red-and-green paper.

"I don't have anything for you," she said, as he held the present out for her. "I didn't know it's Christmas."

"It's not." He smiled. "Not by a long shot," he lied. "Come on, it's not much."

Carefully she took the paper off to find a secondhand Webster's dictionary. "Oh, Tate, thank you."

"Look inside," he said. Tucked in the *P* section was a pelican feather, forget-me-not blossoms pressed between two pages of the *F*s, a dried mushroom under *M*. So many treasures were stashed among the pages, the book would not completely close.

"I'll try to come back the day after Christmas. Maybe I can bring a turkey dinner." He kissed her good-bye. After he left, she swore out loud. Her first chance since Ma left to give a gift to someone she loved, and she'd missed it.

A few days later, shivering in the sleeveless, peach-colored chiffon dress, she waited for Tate on the lagoon shore. Pacing, she clutched her present for him—a head tuft from a male cardinal—wrapped in the paper he had used. As soon as he stepped out of his boat, she stuck the present into his hands, insisting he open it there, so he did. "Thank you, Kya. I don't have one."

Her Christmas complete.

"Now let's get you inside. You must be freezing in that dress." The kitchen was warm from the woodstove, but still he suggested she change into a sweater and jeans.

Working together they heated the food he'd brought: turkey,

cornbread dressing, cranberry sauce, sweet potato casserole, and pumpkin pie—all leftovers from Christmas dinner at the diner with his dad. Kya had made biscuits, and they ate at the kitchen table, which she had decorated with wild holly and seashells.

"I'll wash up," she said, as she poured hot water from the woodstove into the basin.

"I'll help you." And he came up behind her and put his arms around her waist. She leaned her head back against his chest, eyes closed. Slowly his fingers moved under her sweater, across her sleek stomach, toward her breasts. As usual, she wore no bra, and his fingers circled her nipples. His touch lingered there, but a sensation spread down her body as though his hands had moved between her legs. A hollowness that urgently needed filling pulsed through her. But she didn't know what to do, what to say, so pushed back.

"It's okay," he said. And just held her there. Both of them breathing deep.

The sun, still shy and submissive to winter, peeped in now and then between days of mean wind and bitter rain. Then one afternoon, just like that, spring elbowed her way in for good. The day warmed, and the sky shone as if polished. Kya spoke quietly, as she and Tate walked along the grassy bank of a deep creek, overhung with tall sweetgum trees. Suddenly he grabbed her hand, shushing her. Her eyes followed his to the water's edge, where a bullfrog, six inches wide, hunkered under foliage. A common enough sight, except this frog was completely and brilliantly white.

Tate and Kya grinned at each other and watched until he disappeared in one silent, big-legged leap. Still, they were quiet as they backed away into the brush another five yards. Kya put her hands over her mouth and giggled. Bounced away from him in a girlish jig in a body not quite so girlish.

Tate watched her for a second, no longer thinking about frogs. He stepped toward her purposely. His expression stopped her in front of a broad oak. He took her shoulders and pushed her firmly against the tree. Holding her arms along her sides, he kissed her, his groin pushing against hers. Since Christmas they had kissed and explored slowly; not like this. He had always taken the lead but had watched her questioningly for signs to desist; not like now.

He pulled away, the deep golden-brown layers of his eyes boring into hers. Slowly he unbuttoned her shirt and pulled it off, exposing her breasts. He took his time to examine them with his eyes and fingers, circling her nipples. Then he unzipped her shorts and pulled them down, until they dropped to the ground. Almost naked for the first time in front of him, she panted and moved her hands to cover herself. Gently he moved her hands away and took his time looking at her body. Her groin throbbed as if all her blood had surged there. He stepped out of his shorts and, still staring at her, pushed his erection against her.

When she turned away in shyness, he lifted her chin and said, "Look at me. Look me in the eyes, Kya."

"Tate, Tate." She reached out, trying to kiss him, but he held her back, forcing only her eyes to take him in. She didn't know raw nakedness could bring such want. He whispered his hands against her inner thighs, and instinctively she stepped each foot to the side slightly. His fingers moved between her legs and slowly massaged parts of her she never knew existed. She threw her head back and whimpered.

Abruptly, he pushed away from her and stepped back. "God, Kya, I'm sorry. I'm sorry."

"Tate, please, I want to."

"Not like this, Kya."

"Why not? Why not like this?"

She reached for his shoulders and tried to pull him back to her.

"Why not?" she said again.

He picked up her clothes and dressed her. Not touching her where she wanted, where parts of her body still pounded. Then he lifted her and carried her to the creek bank. Put her down, and sat beside her.

"Kya, I want you more than anything. I want you forever. But you're too young. You're only fifteen."

"So what? You're only four years older. It's not like you're suddenly mister know-it-all adult."

"Yes, but I can't get pregnant. And I can't be damaged as easily by this. I won't do it, Kya, because I love you." Love. There was nothing about the word she understood.

"You still think I'm a little girl," she whined.

"Kya, you're sounding more and more like a little girl every second." But he smiled as he said it, and pulled her closer.

"When, then, if not now? When can we?"

"Just not yet."

They were quiet for a moment, and then she asked, "How did you know what to do?" Head down, shy again.

"The same way you did."

One afternoon in May as they walked from the lagoon, he said, "You know, I'm going away soon. To college."

He had spoken of going to Chapel Hill, but Kya had pushed it from her mind, knowing at least they had summer.

"When? Not now."

"Not long. A few weeks."

"But why? I thought college started in the fall."

"I got accepted for a job in a biology lab on campus. I can't pass that up. So I'm starting summer quarter."

Of all the people who left her, only Jodie had said good-bye. Everyone else had walked away forever, but this didn't feel any better. Her chest burned.

"I'll come back as much as I can. It's not that far, really. Less than a day by bus."

She sat quiet. Finally she said, "Why do you have to go, Tate? Why can't you stay here, shrimp like your dad?"

"Kya, you know why. I just can't do that. I want to study the marsh, be a research biologist." They had reached the beach and sat on the sand.

"Then what? There're no jobs like that here. You'll never come home again."

"Yes, I will. I won't leave you, Kya. I promise. I'll come back to you."

She jumped to her feet, startling the plovers, who flew up, squawking. She ran from the beach into the woods. Tate ran after her, but as soon as he reached the trees, he stopped, looked around. She had already lost him.

But just in case she stood in earshot, he called out, "Kya, you can't run from every whipstitch. Sometimes you have to discuss things. Face things." Then with less patience, "Damn it, Kya. Damn it to hell!"

A week later, Kya heard Tate's boat whirring across her lagoon and hid behind a bush. As he eased through the channel, the heron lifted on slow silver wings. Some part of her wanted to run, but she stepped onto the shore, waiting.

"Hey," he said. For once he didn't wear a cap, and his wild blond curls wafted about his tanned face. It seemed that in the last few months, his shoulders had widened into those of a man.

"Hey."

He stepped from the boat, took her hand, and led her to the reading-log, where they sat.

"Turns out I'm leaving sooner than I thought. I'm skipping the graduation ceremonies so I can start my job. Kya, I've come to say good-bye." Even his voice seemed manlike, ready for a more serious world.

She didn't answer, but sat looking away from him. Her throat pulled in tight. He placed two bags of school and library rejects, mostly science books, at her feet.

She wasn't sure she could speak. She wanted him to take her again to the place of the white frog. In case he never came back, she wanted him to take her there now.

"I'm going to miss you, Kya. Every day, all day."

"You might forget me. When you get busy with all that college stuff and see all those pretty girls."

"I'll never forget you. Ever. You take care of the marsh till I get back, you hear? And be careful."

"I will."

"I mean it now, Kya. Watch out for folks; don't let strangers get near you."

"I think I can hide or outrun anybody."

"Yes, I believe you can. I'll come home in about a month, I promise. For the Fourth of July. I'll be back before you know it."

She didn't answer, and he stood, jammed his hands into his jeans pockets. She stood next to him, but they both looked away, into the trees.

He took her shoulders and kissed her for a long time.

"Good-bye, Kya." For a moment she looked somewhere over his shoulder and then into his eyes. A chasm she knew to its greatest depths.

"Good-bye, Tate."

Without another word, he got in his boat and motored across the lagoon. Just before entering the thick brambles of the channel, he turned and waved. She lifted her hand high above her head, and then touched it to her heart.

19.

Something Going On

1969

The morning after reading the second lab report, the eighth day since finding Chase Andrews's body in the swamp, Deputy Purdue pushed open the door to the sheriff's office with his foot and stepped inside. He carried two paper cups of coffee and a bag of hot donuts—just pulled from the fryer.

"Oh man, the smell of Parker's," Ed said as Joe placed the goods on the desk. Each man dug an enormous donut from the brown paper bag splotched with grease stains. Smacked loudly, licked glazed fingers.

Speaking over each other, both men announced, "Well, I got something."

"Go ahead," Ed said.

"I got it from several sources that Chase had something goin' on in the marsh."

"Going on? What do you mean?"

"Not sure, but some guys at the Dog-Gone say 'bout four years ago he started goin' out to the marsh a lot by himself, was real secretive about it. He'd still go fishin' or boatin' with his friends, but made a lot of trips alone. I was thinkin' maybe he got himself mixed up with some potheads or worse. Got over his head with some nasty drug thug. Ya lie down with dogs, ya get up with fleas. Or in this case, not get up at all."

"I don't know. He was such an athlete; hard to picture him getting mixed up in drugs," the sheriff said.

"Former athlete. And anyhow, lots of 'em get tangled up in drugs. When the grand days of hero dry up, they gotta get a high from somewheres else. Or maybe he had a woman out there."

"I just don't know of any ladies out there that'd be his type. He only hung out with the so-called Barkley elite. Not trash."

"Well, if he thought of himself as slummin', maybe that's why he was so quiet about it."

"True," the sheriff said. "Anyway, whatever he had going on out there, it opens up a whole new side of his life we didn't know about. Let's do some snooping, see what he was up to."

"Ya said you got something, too?"

"Not sure what. Chase's mother called, said she had something important to tell us about the case. Something to do with a shell necklace he wore all the time. She's sure it's a clue. Wants to come in here to tell us about it."

"When's she coming?"

"This afternoon, pretty soon."

"It'd be nice to have a real clue. Beats walkin' around looking for some guy wearin' a red wool sweater with a motive attached. We gotta admit, if this was a murder, it was a clever one. The marsh chewed up and swallowed all the evidence, if there was any. Do we have time for lunch before Patti Love gets here?"

"Sure. And the special's fried pork chops. Blackberry pie."

20.

July 4

1961

Dressed in the now too-short peach chiffon, Kya walked barefoot to the lagoon on July 4 and sat on the reading-log. Cruel heat shrugged off the last wisps of fog, and a dense humidity she could barely breathe filled the air. Now and then she knelt to the lagoon and splashed cool water on her neck, all the while listening for the hum of Tate's boat. She didn't mind waiting; she read the books he'd given her.

The day dragged itself by minutes, the sun getting stuck in the middle. The log hardened, so she settled on the ground, her back against a tree. Finally, hungry, she rushed back to the shack for a leftover sausage and biscuit. Ate fast, afraid he would come while she quit her post.

The muggy afternoon rallied mosquitoes. No boat; no Tate. At dusk, she stood straight and still and silent as a stork, staring at the empty-quiet channel. Breathing hurt. Stepping out of the dress, she eased into the water and swam in the dark coolness, the water sliding over her skin, releasing heat from her core. She pulled from the lagoon and sat on a mossy patch of the bank, nude until she dried, until the moon slipped beneath the earth. Then, carrying her clothes, walked inside.

She waited the next day. Each hour warmed until noon, blistered after midday, throbbed past sunset. Later, the moon threw hope across the water, but that died, too. Another sunrise, another white-hot noon. Sunset again. All hope gone to neutral. Her eyes shifted listlessly, and though she listened for Tate's boat, she was no longer coiled.

The lagoon smelled of life and death at once, an organic jumbling of promise and decay. Frogs croaked. Dully she watched fireflies scribbling across the night. She never collected lightning bugs in bottles; you learn a lot more about something when it's not in a jar. Jodie had taught her that the female firefly flickers the light under her tail to signal to the male that she's ready to mate. Each species of firefly has its own language of flashes. As Kya watched, some females signed *dot, dot, dot, dash,* flying a zigzag dance, while others flashed *dash, dash, dot* in a different dance pattern. The males, of course, knew the signals of their species and flew only to those females. Then, as Jodie had put it, they rubbed their bottoms together like most things did, so they could produce young.

Suddenly Kya sat up and paid attention: one of the females had changed her code. First she flashed the proper sequence of dashes and dots, attracting a male of her species, and they mated. Then she flickered a different signal, and a male of a different species flew to her. Reading her message, the second male was convinced he'd found a willing female of his own kind and hovered above her to mate. But suddenly the female firefly reached up, grabbed him with her mouth, and ate him, chewing all six legs and both wings.

Kya watched others. The females got what they wanted—first a mate, then a meal—just by changing their signals.

Kya knew judgment had no place here. Evil was not in play, just life pulsing on, even at the expense of some of the players. Biology sees right and wrong as the same color in different light.

She waited another hour for Tate, and finally walked toward the shack.

The next morning, swearing at the shreds of cruel hope, she went back to the lagoon. Sitting at the water's edge, she listened for the sound of a boat chugging down the channel or across the distant estuaries.

At noon she stood and screamed, "TATE, TATE, NO, NO." Then dropped to her knees, her face against the mud. She felt a strong pull out from under her. A tide she knew well.

21.
Coop

1961

Hot wind rattled the palmetto fronds like small dry bones. For three days after giving up on Tate, Kya didn't get out of bed. Drugged by despair and heat, she tossed in clothes and sheets damp from sweat, her skin sticky. She sent her toes on missions to scout for cool spots between the sheets, but they found none.

She didn't note the time of moonrise or when a great horned owl took a diurnal dive at a blue jay. From bed, she heard the marsh beyond in the lifting of blackbird wings, but didn't go to it. She hurt from the crying songs of the gulls above the beach, calling to her. But for the first time in her life, did not go to them. She hoped the pain from ignoring them would displace the tear in her heart. It did not.

Listless, she wondered what she had done to send everyone away. Her own ma. Her sisters. Her whole family. Jodie. And now Tate. Her most poignant memories were unknown dates of family members disappearing down the lane. The last of a white scarf trailing through the leaves. A pile of socks left on a floor mattress.

Tate and life and love had been the same thing. Now there was no Tate.

"Why, Tate, why?" She mumbled into the sheets, "You were supposed to be different. To stay. You said you loved me, but there is no such thing. There is no one on Earth you can count on." From somewhere very deep, she made herself a promise never to trust or love anyone again.

She'd always found the muscle and heart to pull herself from the mire, to take the next step, no matter how shaky. But where had all that grit brought her? She drifted in and out of thin sleep.

Suddenly, the sun—full, bright, and glaring—struck her face. Never in her life had she slept until midday. She heard a soft rustling sound and, raising herself onto her elbows, saw a raven-sized Cooper's hawk standing on the other side of the screen door, peering in. For the first time in days, an interest stirred in her. She roused herself as the hawk took wing.

Finally, she made a mush of hot water and grits and headed to the beach to feed the gulls. When she broke onto the beach, all of them swirled and dived in flurries, and she dropped to her knees and tossed the food on the sand. As they crowded around her, she felt their feathers brushing her arms and thighs, and threw her head back, smiling with them. Even as tears streamed her cheeks.

For a month after July 4, Kya did not leave her place, did not go into the marsh or to Jumpin's for gas or supplies. She lived on dried fish, mussels, oysters. Grits and greens.

When all her shelves were empty, she finally motored to Jumpin's for supplies but didn't chat with him as usual. Did her business and left him standing, staring after her. Needing people ended in hurt.

A few mornings later, the Cooper's hawk was back on her steps, peering at her through the screen. *How odd,* she thought, cocking her head at him. "Hey, Coop."

With a little hop, he lifted, made a flyby, then soared high into the clouds. Watching him, at last, Kya said to herself, "I have to get back into the marsh," and she took the boat out, easing along the channels and slipstreams, searching for bird nests, feathers, or shells for the first time since Tate abandoned her. Even so, she couldn't avoid thoughts of him. The intellectual fascinations or the pretty girls of Chapel Hill had drawn him in. She couldn't imagine college women, but whatever form they took would be better than a tangled-haired, barefoot mussel-monger who lived in a shack.

By the end of August, her life once more found its footing: boat, collect, paint. Months passed. She only went to Jumpin's when low supplies demanded, but spoke very little to him.

Her collections matured, categorized methodically by order, genus, and species; by age according to bone wear; by size in millimeters of feathers; or by the most fragile hues of greens. The science and art entwined in each other's strengths: the colors, the light, the species, the life; weaving a masterpiece of knowledge and beauty that filled every corner of her shack. Her world. She grew with them—the trunk of the vine—alone, but holding all the wonders together.

But just as her collection grew, so did her loneliness. A pain as large as her heart lived in her chest. Nothing eased it. Not the gulls, not a splendid sunset, not the rarest of shells.

Months turned into a year.

The lonely became larger than she could hold. She wished for someone's voice, presence, touch, but wished more to protect her heart.

Months passed into another year. Then another.

PART 2

The Swamp

22.

Same Tide

1965

Nineteen years old, legs longer, eyes larger and seemingly blacker, Kya sat on Point Beach, watching sand crabs bury themselves backward into the swash. Suddenly, from the south, she heard voices and jumped to her feet. The group of kids—now young adults—she'd watched occasionally through the years ambled toward her, tossing a football, running and kicking the surf. Anxious they would see her, she loped to the trees, sand tearing from her heels, and hid behind the broad trunk of an oak tree. Knowing how odd this made her.

Not much has changed, she thought, *them laughing, me holing up like a sand crab.* A wild thing ashamed of her own freakish ways.

Tallskinnyblonde, Ponytailfreckleface, Alwayswearspearls, and Roundchubbycheeks romped the beach, tangled in laughs and hugs. On her rare trips to the village, she'd heard their slurs. "Yeah, the Marsh Girl gits her clothes from colored people; has to trade mussels for grits."

Yet after all these years, they were still a group of friends. That was something. Silly-looking on the outside, yes, but as Mabel had said several times, they were a sure troop. "Ya need some girlfriends, hon, 'cause they're furever. Without a vow. A clutch of women's the most tender, most tough place on Earth."

Kya found herself laughing softly with them as they kicked salt water on one another. Then, shrieking, they rushed as one into the deeper surf. Kya's smile faded when they pulled themselves out of the water and into their traditional group hug.

Their squeals made Kya's silence even louder. Their togetherness tugged at her loneliness, but she knew being labeled as marsh trash kept her behind the oak tree.

Her eyes shifted to the tallest guy. Wearing khaki shorts and no shirt, he threw the football. Kya watched the cords of muscles bunching on his back. His tan shoulders. She knew he was Chase Andrews, and over the years, ever since he nearly ran her over on his bicycle, she'd seen him with these friends on the beach, walking into the diner for milk shakes, or at Jumpin's buying gas.

Now, as the group came closer, she watched only him. When another tossed the ball, he ran to catch it and came close to her tree, his bare feet digging in the hot sand. As he raised his arm to throw, he happened to glance back and caught Kya's eyes. After passing the ball, without giving any sign to the others, he turned and held her gaze. His hair was black, like hers, but his eyes were pale blue, his face strong, striking. A shadow-smile formed on his lips. Then he walked back to the others, shoulders relaxed, sure.

But he had noticed her. Had held her eyes. Her breath froze as a heat flowed through her.

She tracked them, mostly him, down the shore. Her mind looking one way, her desire the other. Her body watched Chase Andrews, not her heart.

The next day she returned—same tide, different time, but no one was there, just noisy sandpipers and wave-riding sand crabs.

She tried to force herself to avoid that beach and stick to the marsh, searching for bird nests and feathers. Stay safe, feeding grits to gulls. Life had made her an expert at mashing feelings into a storable size.

But loneliness has a compass of its own. And she went back to the beach to look for him the next day. And the next.

Late one afternoon, after watching for Chase Andrews, Kya walks from her shack and lies back on a sliver of beach, slick from the last wave. She stretches her arms over her head, brushing them against the wet sand, and extends her legs, toes pointed. Eyes closed, she rolls slowly toward the sea. Her hips and arms leave slight indentions in the glistening sand, brightening and then dimming as she moves. Rolling nearer the waves, she senses the ocean's roar through the length of her body and feels the question: *When will the sea touch me? Where will it touch me first?*

The foamy surge rushes the shore, reaching toward her. Tingling with expectancy, she breathes deep. Turns more and more slowly. With each revolution, just before her face sweeps the sand, she lifts her head gently and takes in the sun-salt smell. *I am close, very close. It is coming. When will I feel it?*

A fever builds. The sand wetter beneath her, the rumble of surf louder. Even slower, by inches she moves, waiting for the touch. Soon, soon. Almost feeling it before it comes.

She wants to open her eyes to peek, to see how much longer. But she resists, squinting her lids even tighter, the sky bright behind them, giving no hints.

Suddenly she shrieks as the power rushes beneath her, fondles her thighs, between her legs, flows along her back, swirling under her head, pulling her hair in inky strands. She rolls faster into the deepening wave, against streaming shells and ocean bits, the water embracing her. Pushing against the sea's strong body, she is grasped, held. Not alone.

Kya sits up and opens her eyes to the ocean foaming around her in soft white patterns, always changing.

Since Chase had glanced at her on the beach, she'd already gone to Jumpin's wharf twice in one week. Not admitting to herself that she hoped to see Chase there. Being noticed by someone had lit a social cord. And now, she asked Jumpin', "How's Mabel doing, anyway? Are any of your grandkids home?" like the old days. Jumpin' noticed the change, knew better than to comment. "Yessiree, got fou' wif us right now. House full up wif giggles and I don't know whut all."

But a few mornings later when Kya motored to the wharf, Jumpin' was nowhere to be seen. Brown pelicans, hunched up on posts, eyed her as though they were minding shop. Kya smiled at them.

A touch on her shoulder made her jump.

"Hi." She turned to see Chase standing behind her. She dropped her smile.

"I'm Chase Andrews." His eyes, ice-pack blue, pierced her own. He seemed completely comfortable to stare into her.

She said nothing, but shifted her weight.

"I've seen ya around some. Ya know, over the years, in the marsh. What's yo' name?" For a moment he thought she wasn't going to speak; maybe she was dumb or spoke a primal language, like some said. A less self-assured man might have walked away.

"Kya." Obviously, he didn't remember their sidewalk-bicycle encounter or know her in any way except as the Marsh Girl.

"Kya—that's different. But nice. You wanta go for a picnic? In my boat, this Sunday."

She looked past him, taking time to evaluate his words, but couldn't see them to an end. Here was a chance to be with someone.

Finally she said, "Okay." He told her to meet him at the oak peninsula north of Point Beach at noon. Then he stepped into his blue-and-white ski boat, metal bits gleaming from every possible surface, and accelerated away.

She turned at the sound of more footsteps. Jumpin' scurried up the dock. "Hi, Miss Kya. Sorry, I been totin' empty crates over yonder. Fill 'er up?"

Kya nodded.

On the way home, she cut the motor and drifted, the shore in sight. Leaning against the old knapsack, watching the sky, she recited poetry by heart, as she did sometimes. One of her favorites was John Masefield's "Sea Fever":

> . . . all I ask is a windy day with the white clouds flying,
> And the flung spray and the blown spume, and the
> sea-gulls crying.

Kya recalled a poem written by a lesser-known poet, Amanda Hamilton, published recently in the local newspaper she'd bought at the Piggly Wiggly:

> Trapped inside,
> Love is a caged beast,
> Eating its own flesh.

Love must be free to wander,
To land upon its chosen shore
And breathe.

The words made her think of Tate, and her breathing stopped. All he'd needed was to find something better and he was gone. Didn't even come to say good-bye.

Kya didn't know, but Tate had come back to see her.

The day before he was to bus home that Fourth of July, Dr. Blum, the professor who'd hired him, walked into the protozoology lab and asked Tate if he'd like to join a group of renowned ecologists for a birding expedition over the weekend.

"I've noticed your interest in ornithology and wondered if you'd like to come. I only have room for one student, and I thought of you."

"Yes, absolutely. I'll be there." After Dr. Blum left, Tate stood there, alone, amid lab tables, microscopes, and the hum of the autoclave, wondering how he'd folded so fast. How quickly he'd jumped to impress his professor. The pride of being singled out, the only student invited.

His next chance to go home—and only for one night—had been fifteen days later. He was frantic to apologize to Kya, who would understand after she learned of Dr. Blum's invitation.

He'd cut throttle as he left the sea and turned into the channel, where logs were lined with the glistening backs of sunbathing turtles. Almost halfway, he spotted her boat carefully hidden in tall cord grass. Instantly, he slowed and saw her up ahead, kneeling on a wide sandbar, apparently fascinated by some small crustacean.

Her head low to the ground, she hadn't seen him or heard his slow-moving boat. He quietly turned his skiff into reeds, out of view. He'd known for years that she sometimes spied on him, peeping through needle brush. On impulse, he would do the same.

Barefoot, dressed in cutoff jeans and a white T-shirt, she stood up, stretching her arms high. Showcasing her wasp-thin waist. She knelt again and scooped sand in her hands, sifting it through her fingers, examining organisms left squiggling in her palm. He smiled at the young biologist, absorbed, oblivious. He imagined her standing at the back of the birding group, trying not to be noticed but being the first to spot and identify every bird. Shyly and softly, she would have listed the precise species of grasses woven into each nest, or the age in days of a female fledgling based on the emerging colors of her wing-tips. Exquisite minutiae beyond any guidebook or knowledge of the esteemed ecology group. The smallest specifics on which a species spins. The essence.

Suddenly Tate startled as Kya sprang to her feet, sand spilling from her fingers, and looked upstream, away from Tate. He could barely hear the low churn of an outboard motor coming their way, probably a fisherman or marsh dweller headed to town. A purring sound, common and calm as doves. But Kya grabbed the knapsack, sprinted across the sandbar, and scrambled into tall grass. Squatting low to the ground and snatching glances to see if the boat had come into view, she duck-walked toward her boat. Knees lifting nearly to her chin. She was closer to Tate now, and he saw her eyes, dark and crazed. When she reached her boat, she hunkered beside its girth, head low.

The fisherman—a merry-faced, hatted old man—puttered into view, saw neither Kya nor Tate, and disappeared beyond the bend. But she remained frozen, listening until the motor whined away, then stood, dabbing her brow. Continued to look in the direction of the boat as a deer eyes the empty brush of a departed panther.

On some level he knew she behaved this way, but since the feather game, had not witnessed the raw, unpeeled core. How tormented, isolated, and strange.

He'd been at college less than two months but had already stepped directly into the world he wanted, analyzing the stunning symmetry of the DNA molecule as if he'd crawled inside a glistening cathedral of coiling atoms and climbed the winding, acidic rungs of the helix. Seeing that all life depends on this precise and intricate code transcribed on fragile, organic slivers, which would perish instantly in a slightly warmer or colder world. At last, surrounded by enormous questions and people as curious as he to find the answers, drawing him toward his goal of research biologist in his own lab, interacting with other scientists.

Kya's mind could easily live there, but she could not. Breathing hard, he stared at his decision hiding there in cord grass: Kya or everything else.

"Kya, Kya, I just can't do this," he whispered. "I'm sorry."

After she moved away, he got into his boat and motored back toward the ocean. Swearing at the coward inside who would not tell her good-bye.

23.

The Shell

1965

The night after seeing Chase Andrews on Jumpin's wharf, Kya sat at her kitchen table in the easy flicker of lantern light. She'd started cooking again, and she nibbled on a supper of buttermilk biscuits, turnips, and pinto beans, reading while she ate. But thoughts of the picnic-date with Chase the next day unraveled every sentence.

Kya stood and walked into the night, into the creamy light of a three-quarter moon. The marsh's soft air fell silklike around her shoulders. The moonlight chose an unexpected path through the pines, laying shadows about in rhymes. She strolled like a sleepwalker as the moon pulled herself naked from the waters and climbed limb by limb through the oaks. The slick mud of the lagoon shore glowed in the intense light, and hundreds of fireflies dotted the woods. Wearing a secondhand white dress with a flowing skirt and waving her arms slowly about, Kya waltzed to the music of katydids and leopard frogs. She slid her hands along her sides and up her neck. Then moved them along her thighs as she held Chase Andrews's face in her eyes. She wanted him to touch her this way. Her breathing deepened. No one had ever looked at her as he did. Not even Tate.

She danced among the pale wings of mayflies, fluttering above the bright moon-mud.

The next morning, she rounded the peninsula and saw Chase in his boat, just offshore. Here in daylight, reality drifted ahead, waiting, and her throat dried. Steering onto the beach, she stepped out and pulled her boat in, the hull crunching against the sand.

Chase drifted up alongside. "Hi."

Looking over her shoulder, she nodded. He stepped out of his boat and held out his hand to her—long tanned fingers, an open palm. She hesitated; touching someone meant giving part of herself away, a piece she never got back.

Even so, she placed her hand lightly in his. He steadied her as she stepped into the stern and sat on the cushioned bench. A warm, fine day beamed down, and Kya, wearing denim cutoffs and a white cotton blouse—an outfit she'd copied from the others—looked normal. He sat next to her, and she felt his sleeve slide gently across her arm.

Chase eased the boat toward the ocean. The open water tossed the boat more than the quiet marsh, and she knew the pitching motion of the sea would brush her arm against his. That anticipation of touch kept her eyes straight ahead, but she did not move away.

Finally, a larger wave rose and dipped, and his arm, solid and warm, caressed hers. Jarring away, then touching again with every rise and drop. And when a swell surged beneath them, his thigh brushed against hers and her breathing stopped.

As they headed south along the coast, theirs the only boat in this remoteness, he accelerated. Ten minutes on, several miles of white beach stretched along the tide line, protected from the rest of the world by a rounded, thick forest. Up ahead, Point Beach unfolded into the water like a brilliant white fan.

Chase had not said a word since his greeting; she had not spoken at all. He glided the boat onto shore and tucked the picnic basket in the boat's shadow on the sand.

"Wanta walk?" he asked.

"Yes."

They strolled along the water, each small wave rushing their ankles in little eddies and then sucking at their feet as it was pulled back into the sea.

He didn't hold her hand, but now and then, in natural movement, their fingers brushed. Occasionally they knelt to examine a shell or a strand of transparent seaweed spiraled into art. Chase's blue eyes were playful; he smiled easily. His skin was dark tan like hers. Together they were tall, elegant, similar.

Kya knew Chase had chosen not to go to college but to work for his dad. He was a standout in town, the tom turkey. And somewhere within, she worried she was also a piece of beach art, a curiosity to be turned over in his hands, then tossed back on the sand. But she walked on. She'd given love a chance; now she wanted simply to fill the empty spaces. Ease the loneliness while walling off her heart.

After a half mile he faced her and bowed low, sweeping his arm in an exaggerated invitation for them to sit on the sand, against a driftwood log. They dug their feet into the white crystals and leaned back.

From his pocket Chase pulled out a harmonica.

"Oh," she said, "you play." The words felt rough on her tongue.

"Not very good. But when I got an audience leanin' against driftwood on the beach . . ." Closing his eyes, he played "Shenandoah," his palm fluttering on the instrument like a bird trapped against glass. It was a lovely, plaintive sound, like a note from a faraway home. Then, abruptly, he stopped midsong and picked up a shell slightly larger than a nickel, creamy white with bright splotches of red and purple.

"Hey, look at this," he said.

"Oh, it's an ornate scallop, *Pecten ornatus*," Kya said. "I only see them rarely. There are many of that genus here, but this particular species usually inhabits regions south of this latitude because these waters are too cool for them."

He stared at her. Of all the gossip, no one ever mentioned that the Marsh Girl, the girl who couldn't spell *dog*, knew the Latin names of shells, where they occurred—and why, forchristsake.

"I don't know about that," he said, "but look here, it's twisted." The little wings flaring on either side of the hinge were crooked, and there was a perfect little hole at the base. He turned it over in his palm. "Here, you keep it. You're the shell girl."

"Thanks." She slid it into her pocket.

He played a few more songs, ending with a stampede of "Dixie," and then they walked back to the wicker picnic basket and sat on a plaid blanket eating cold fried chicken, salt-cured ham and biscuits, and potato salad. Sweet and dill pickles. Slices of four-layer cake with half-inch-thick caramel icing. All homemade, wrapped in wax paper. He opened two bottles of Royal Crown Cola and poured them into Dixie cups—her first drink of soda pop in her life. The generous spread was incredible to her, with the neatly arranged cloth napkins, plastic plates and forks. Even minuscule pewter salt and pepper shakers. His mother must have packed it, she thought, not knowing he was meeting the Marsh Girl.

They talked softly of sea things—pelicans gliding and sandpipers prancing—no touching, little laughing. As Kya pointed out a jagged cord of pelicans, he nodded and maneuvered closer to her, so their shoulders brushed lightly. When she looked at him, he lifted her chin with his hand and kissed her. He touched her neck lightly, then feathered his fingers over her blouse toward her breast. Kissing and holding her, more firmly now, he leaned back until they were lying on the blanket. Slowly he moved until he was on top of her, pushed his groin between her legs, and in one movement pulled up her blouse. She jerked her head away and squirmed out from under him, her blacker-than-night eyes blazing. Tugged her top down.

"Easy, easy. It's okay."

She lay there—hair strewn across the sand, face flushed, red mouth slightly parted—stunning. Carefully, he reached up to touch her face, but fast as a cat, she sprang away, and stood.

Kya breathed hard. Last night, dancing alone on the lagoon shore, swaying about with the moon and mayflies, she'd imagined she was ready. Thought she knew all about mating from watching doves. No one had ever told her about sex, and her only experience with foreplay had been with Tate. But she knew the details from her biology books and had seen more creatures copulating—and it wasn't merely "rubbing their bottoms together" like Jodie had said—than most people ever would.

But this was too abrupt—picnic, then mate the Marsh Girl. Even male birds woo the females for a while, flashing brilliant feathers, building bowers, staging magnificent dances and love songs. Yes, Chase had laid out a banquet, but she was worth more than fried chicken. And "Dixie" didn't count as a love song. She should've known it would be like this. Only time male mammals hover is when they're in the rut.

The silence grew as they stared at each other, broken only by the sound of their breathing and the breakers beyond. Chase sat up and reached for her arm, but she jerked it away.

"I'm sorry. It's okay," he said as he stood. True, he'd come here to snag her, to be the first, but watching those eyes firing, he was entranced.

He tried again. "C'mon, Kya. I said I'm sorry. Let's just forget it. I'll take you back to yo' boat."

At that she turned and walked across the sand toward the woods. Her long body swaying.

"What're ya doin'? You can't walk back from here. It's miles."

But she was already in the trees, and ran a crow-route, first inland, then across the peninsula, toward her boat. The area was new to her, but blackbirds guided her across the inland marsh. She didn't slow for bogs or gullies, splashed right through creeks, jumped logs.

Finally, she bent over and, heaving, fell to her knees. Cussing worn-out words. As long as she ranted, sobs couldn't surface. But nothing could stop the burning shame and sharp sadness. A simple hope of being with someone, of actually being wanted, of being touched, had drawn her in. But these hurried groping hands were only a *taking*, not a *sharing* or *giving*.

She listened for sounds of him coming after her, not sure whether she wanted him to break through the brush and hold her, begging for forgiveness, or not. Raging again at that. Then, spent, she stood and walked the rest of the way to her boat.

24.

The Fire Tower

1965

Thunderheads piled and pushed against the horizon as Kya motored into the afternoon sea. She hadn't seen Chase since their beach picnic ten days ago, but still felt the shape and firmness of his body pinning hers against the sand.

No other boats were in sight as she steered toward an inlet south of Point Beach, where she had once seen unusual butterflies—so powerfully white they might have been albino. But forty yards out, she suddenly released the throttle when she saw Chase's friends packing picnic baskets and bright towels into their boats. Kya turned quickly to speed away but, against a strong pull, turned back and searched for him. She knew that no part of this yearning made sense. Illogical behavior to fill an emptiness would not fulfill much more. How much do you trade to defeat lonesomeness?

And there, near the spot where he kissed her, she saw him walking with fishing rods toward his boat. Behind him, Alwayswearspearls carried a cooler.

Suddenly, Chase turned his head and looked directly at her drifting in her boat. She didn't turn away but stared back at him. As always shyness won, so she broke eye contact, sped off, and steered into a shadowy cove. She'd wait until their little navy left before going to the beach herself.

Ten minutes later, she motored back into the sea and, up ahead, saw Chase alone in his boat, bobbing waves. Waiting.

The old longing swelled. He was still interested in her. True, he'd come on too strong at the picnic, but he'd stopped when she brushed him away. Had apologized. Perhaps she should give him another chance.

He motioned her over and called, "Hi, Kya."

She didn't go toward him, but not away either. He motored closer.

"Kya, I'm sorry 'bout the other day. Okay? C'mon, I wanta show you the fire tower."

She said nothing, still drifting his way, knowing it was weakness.

"Look, if you've never climbed the tower, it's a great way to see the marsh. Follow me."

She increased throttle and turned her boat toward his, all the while scanning the sea to make sure his friends were out of sight.

Chase motioned her north past Barkley Cove—the village serene and colorful in the distance—and landed on the beach of a small bay tucked in deep forest. After securing the boats, he led her down an overgrown path of wax myrtle and prickly holly. She'd never been to this watery and rooty forest, because it stood on the other side of the village and was too close to people. As they walked, thin runnels of backwater seeped under the brush—slinky reminders that the sea owned this land.

Then a true swamp settled deep with its low-earth smell and fusty air. Sudden, subtle, and silent all at once, it stretched into the mouth of the dark receding forest.

Kya saw the weathered wooden platform of the abandoned fire tower above the canopy, and a few minutes later, they arrived at its straddle-legged base, made of rough-cut poles. Black mud oozed around the legs and under the tower, and damp rot ate its way along the beams. Stairs switched to the top, the structure narrowing at each level.

After crossing the sludge, they started the climb, Chase leading. By the fifth switchback, the rounded oak forests tumbled west as far as they could see. In every other direction, slipstreams, lagoons, creeks, and estuaries wove through brilliant green grass to the sea. Kya had never been this high above the marsh. Now all the pieces lay beneath her, and she saw her friend's full face for the first time.

When they reached the last step, Chase pushed open the iron grate covering the stairwell. After they climbed onto the platform, he eased it down again. Before stepping on it, Kya tested it by tapping it with her toes. Chase laughed lightly. "It's fine, don't worry." He led her to the railing, where they looked over the marshland. Two red-tailed hawks, the wind whistling through their wings, soared by at eye level, their heads cocked in surprise to see a young man and woman standing in their airspace.

Chase turned to her and said, "Thanks for comin', Kya. For giving me another chance to say I'm sorry 'bout the other day. I was way outta line and it won't happen again."

She said nothing. Parts of her wanted to kiss him now, to feel his strength against her.

Reaching into her jeans pocket, she said, "I made a necklace with the shell you found. You don't have to wear it if you don't want to." She'd strung the shell on the rawhide the night before, thinking to herself she would wear it, but knowing all along she hoped to see Chase again and would give it to him if she had the chance. But even her wistful daydream had not envisioned them standing together on top of the fire tower overlooking the world. A summit.

"Thank ya, Kya," he said. He looked at it, and then he put it on over his head, fingering the shell as it rested against his throat. "'Course I'll wear it."

He said nothing trite like *I'll wear it forever, till the day I die.*

"Take me to your house," Chase said. Kya imagined the shack hunkered under oaks, its gray boards stained with blood from the rusting roof. The screens more holes than mesh. A place of patches.

"It's far," is all she said.

"Kya, I don't care how far or what it's like. C'mon, let's go."

This chance of acceptance might go away if she said no.

"All right." They climbed down the tower, and he led her back to the bay, motioning for her to lead the way in her boat. She cruised south to the maze of estuaries and ducked her head as she slipped into her channel, overhung with green. His boat was almost too big to fit in the jungle growth, certainly too blue and white, but it squeezed through, limbs screeching along the hull.

When her lagoon opened before them, the delicate details of every mossy branch and brilliant leaf reflected in the clear dark water. Dragonflies and snowy egrets lifted briefly at his strange boat, then resettled gracefully on silent wings. Kya tied up as Chase motored up to the shore. The great blue heron, having long ago accepted those less wild, stood stork-still only feet away.

Her laundry of faded overalls and T-shirts hung tatty on the line, and so many turnips had spread into the forests, it was difficult to tell where the garden ended and the wilderness began.

Looking at the patched screen porch, he asked, "How long ya lived out here by yourself?"

"I don't know exactly when Pa left. But about ten years, I think."

"That's neat. Livin' out here with no parents to tell ya what to do."

Kya didn't respond except to say, "There's nothing to see inside." But he was already walking up the brick-'n'-board steps. The first things he saw were her collections lining homemade shelves. A collage of the shimmering life just beyond the screen.

"You did all this?" he said.

"Yes."

He looked at some butterflies briefly but quickly lost interest. Thought, *Why keep stuff you can see right outside your door?*

Her little mattress on the porch floor had a cover as worn as an old bathrobe, but it was made up neat. A few steps took them through the tiny sitting room, with its sagging sofa, and then he peeped into the back bedroom, where feathers in every color, shape, and size winged across the walls.

She motioned him into the kitchen, wondering what she could offer him. For sure she had no Coca-Cola or iced tea, no cookies or even cold biscuits. The leftover cornbread sat on the stovetop next to a pot of black-eyed peas, shelled and ready to boil for supper. Not one thing for a guest.

Out of habit she stuck a few pieces of wood into the stove's firebox. Stoking it just so with the poker; flames jumping to instantly.

"That's it," she said, keeping her back to him, as she pumped the hand crank and filled the dented-in kettle—a picture of the 1920s propped up here in the 1960s. No running water, no electricity, no bathroom. The tin bathtub, its rim bent and rusted, stood in the corner of the kitchen, the stand-alone pie chest held leftovers covered neatly with tea towels, and the humped refrigerator gaped open, a flyswatter in its mouth. Chase had never seen anything like it.

He cranked the pump, watched the water come out into the enamel basin that served as the sink. Touched the wood stacked neatly against the stove. The only lights were a few kerosene lanterns, their chimneys smoked gray.

Chase was her first visitor since Tate, who had seemed as natural and accepting as other marsh creatures. With Chase, she felt exposed, as if someone were filleting her like a fish. Shame welled up inside. She kept her back to him but felt him move around the room, followed by the familiar creaks of the floor. Then he came up behind her, turned her gently, and embraced her lightly. He put his lips against her hair, and she could feel his breath near her ear.

"Kya, nobody I know could've lived out here alone like this. Most kids, even the guys, would've been too scared."

She thought he was going to kiss her, but he dropped his arms and walked to the table.

"What do you want with me?" she asked. "Tell me the truth."

"Look, I'm not gonna lie. You're gorgeous, free, wild as a dang gale. The other day, I wanted to get as close as I could. Who wouldn't? But that ain't right. I shouldn't've come on like that. I just wanta be with ya, okay? Get to know each other."

"Then what?"

"We'll just find out how we feel. I won't do anything unless ya want me to. How's that?"

"That's fine."

"Ya said you had a beach. Let's go to the beach."

She cut off pieces of the leftover cornbread for the gulls and walked ahead of him down the path until it opened wide to the bright sand and sea. As she let out her soft cry, the gulls appeared and circled above and around her shoulders. The large male, Big Red, landed and walked back and forth across her feet.

Chase stood a little distance away, watching as Kya disappeared into the spiraling birds. He hadn't planned on feeling anything for this strange and feral barefoot girl, but watching her swirl across the sand, birds at her fingertips, he was intrigued by her self-reliance as well as her beauty. He'd never known anyone like Kya; a curiosity as well as desire stirred in him. When she came back to where he stood, he asked if he could come again the next day, promised he would not even hold her hand, that he just wanted to be near her. She simply nodded. The first hope in her heart since Tate left.

25.

A Visit from Patti Love

1969

A light knock sounded on the door of the sheriff's office. Joe and Ed looked up as Patti Love Andrews, Chase's mother, appeared shadowy and fractured through the frosted glass. Still, they could recognize her in a black dress and hat. Graying brown hair in a tidy bun. An appropriately dull shade of lipstick.

Both men stood, and Ed opened the door, "Patti Love, hello. Come on in. Sit down. Can I offer you some coffee?"

She glanced at the half-empty mugs, lip-drips running down the rims. "No, thank you, Ed." She sat in the chair Joe pulled up. "Do you have any leads yet? Any more information since the lab report?"

"No. No, we don't. We're going over everything with a fine-tooth comb, and you and Sam'll be the first to know if we come up with anything."

"But it wasn't an accident, Ed. Right? I know it wasn't an accident. Chase woulda never just fallen off the tower by himself. You know what an athlete he was. And smart."

"We agree there's evidence enough to suspect foul play. But it's an ongoing investigation and nothing definite yet. Now, you said you had something to tell us?"

"Yes, and I think it's important." Patti Love looked from Ed to Joe and back to Ed. "There was a shell necklace that Chase wore all the time. Had for years. I know he was wearin' it the night he went to the tower. Sam and I had him over for dinner, remember I told you that—Pearl couldn't come; it was her bridge night—and he had on the necklace right before he went out to the tower. And then after he . . . well, when we saw him at the clinic, he didn't have the necklace on. I assumed the coroner had taken it off him, so I didn't mention it then, and with the funeral and all, I had forgotten about it. Then, the other day I drove over to Sea Oaks and asked the coroner if I could see Chase's things, his personal effects. You know, they had kept them for the lab work, but I wanted to hold them, just to feel what he wore that last night. So they let me sit at a table and go through them, and, Sheriff, that shell necklace wasn't there. I asked the coroner if he had taken it off, and he said no, he had not. He said he never saw any necklace at all."

"That's very curious," Ed said. "What was it strung with? Maybe it came off when he fell."

"It was a single shell hung on a piece of rawhide that was just long enough to go over his head. It wasn't loose and was tied in a knot. I just don't see how it could've flung off."

"I agree. Rawhide's tough and makes a mean knot," Ed said. "Why did he wear it all the time? Did somebody special make it for him? Give it to him?"

Patti Love sat silent, looking off to the side of the sheriff's desk. She dreaded saying more because she'd never admitted that her son had been involved with marsh trash. Of course, there had been village rumors that Chase and the Marsh Girl had been involved for more than a year before his marriage. And Patti Love suspected even after, but when friends had asked about the stories, she'd always denied them. But now it was different. Now she had to speak out because she just knew that wench had something to do with his death.

"Yes, I know who made the necklace for Chase. It was that woman who boats around in that old rattletrap boat; has for years. She made it and gave it to him when they were seeing each other for a while."

"You talking about the Marsh Girl?" the sheriff asked.

Joe spoke up. "You seen her lately? She's not a girl anymore, probably mid-twenties and a real looker."

"The Clark woman? Just trying to be clear," Ed asked. Brows bunched.

Patti Love said, "I don't know her name. Or even if she has one. People do call her the Marsh Girl. You know, she sold mussels to Jumpin' for years."

"Right. We're talking about the same person. Go ahead."

"Well, I was shocked when the coroner said Chase didn't have on the necklace. And then it occurred to me that she's the only one who'd have any interest in taking it. Chase had broken off their relationship and married Pearl. She couldn't have him, so maybe she killed him and took the necklace from his neck."

Patti Love trembled slightly, then caught her breath.

"I see. Well, this is very important, Patti Love, and worth pursuing. But let's not get ahead of ourselves," Ed said. "You're sure she gave it to him?"

"Yes, I'm sure. I know because Chase didn't want to tell me, but he finally did."

"Do you know anything else about the necklace or their relationship?"

"Not much at all. I don't even know for sure how long they saw each other. Probably nobody does. He was very sneaky about it. Like I said, he didn't tell me for months. Then after he told me, I never knew whether he was going out in his boat with his other friends or with her."

"Well, we'll look into it. I promise you that."

"Thank you. I'm sure this is a clue." She rose to leave, and Ed opened the door for her.

"Come back anytime you want to talk, Patti Love."

"Bye, Ed, Joe."

After closing the door, Ed sat again, and Joe asked, "Well, what d'ya think?"

"If somebody took the necklace off Chase at the tower, that would at least put them at the scene, and I can see somebody from the marsh being involved in this thing. They got their own laws. But I just don't know if a woman could've pushed a big guy like Chase through that hole."

"She coulda lured him up there, opened the grate before he got there, then when he came toward her in the dark, she coulda pushed him in before he even saw her," Joe said.

"Seems possible. Not easy, but possible. It's not much of a lead. The *absence* of a shell necklace," the sheriff said.

"At this point it's our only lead. 'Cept for the *absence* of prints and some mysterious red fibers."

"Right."

"But what I can't figure," Joe said, "is why she'd bother to take the necklace off him? Okay, as the woman wronged, she was hell-bent on killin' him. Even that's a stretch for motive, but why take the necklace when it could connect her smack-dab to the crime?"

"You know how it is. Seems like there's something in every murder case that doesn't make sense. People mess up. Maybe she was shocked and furious that he still wore the necklace, and after committing murder, it didn't seem like a big deal to snatch it off his neck. She wouldn't have known anybody could link the necklace to her. Your sources said Chase had something going on out there. Maybe, like you said earlier, it wasn't drugs at all, but a woman. This woman."

Joe said, "'Nother kind of drug."

"And marsh folks know how to cover prints because they snare, track, trap, and such. Well, it won't hurt to go out there and have a talk with her. Ask her where she was that night. We can question her about the necklace and see if it shakes her up a bit."

Joe asked, "You know how ta get ta her place?"

"Not sure by boat, but I think I can find it in the truck. Down that real windy road that goes way past a long chain of lagoons. A while back, I had to make house calls to see her father a few times. Nasty piece of work, that one."

"When we going?"

"Crack of day, see if we can get there before she takes off. Tomorrow. But first, we better go out to the tower and search really good for that necklace. Maybe it's been there all along."

"I don't see how. We've searched all over that place, looking for tracks, treads, clues."

"Still, we gotta do it. Let's go."

Later, after combing through the muck under the tower with rakes and fingers, they declared no shell necklace present.

Pale light seeped under a low, heavy dawn as Ed and Joe drove down the marsh track, hoping to get to the Marsh Girl's place before she boated off somewhere. They took several wrong turns and ended up at dead ends or at some ramshackle dwelling. At one shack somebody yelled, "Sheriff!" and mostly naked bodies took off in all directions, charging through brambles. "Damn potheads," the sheriff said. "At least the moonshiners kept their clothes on."

But finally they came to the long lane that led to Kya's shack. "This is it," Ed said.

He turned his outsized pickup onto the track and cruised quietly toward the dwelling, easing to a stop fifty feet from the door. Both men got out without a sound. Ed knocked on the wooden frame of the screen door. "Hello! Anybody home?" Silence followed, so he tried again. They waited two to three minutes. "Let's have a look 'round back, see if her boat's there."

"Nope. Looks like that log's where she ties up. She's a'ready gone. Dag-nabit," Joe said.

"Yep, heard us coming. She can probably hear a rabbit sleeping."

The next time they went before dawn, parked way down the road, and found her boat tied to its log. Still no one answered the door.

Joe whispered, "I get this feelin' she's right here watchin' us. Don't you? She's squattin' right here in the damn palmettos. Purt' near. I just know it." His head swung, eyes scanning the brambles.

"Well, this isn't going to work. If we come up with anything else we can get a warrant. Let's get outta here."

26.

The Boat Ashore

1965

The first week they were together, Chase pulled into Kya's lagoon almost every day after his work at the Western Auto, and they explored remote oak-lined channels. On Saturday morning, he took her on an expedition far up the coast to a place she'd never been because it was too far for her little boat. Here—instead of the estuaries and enormous sweeps of grass as in her marsh—clear water flowed as far as she could see through a bright and open cypress forest. Brilliant white herons and storks stood among water lilies and floating plants so green they seemed to glow. Hunched up on cypress knees as large as easy chairs, they ate pimento-cheese sandwiches and potato chips, grinning as geese glided just below their toes.

Like most people, Chase knew the marsh as a thing to be used, to boat and fish, or drain for farming, so Kya's knowledge of its critters, currents, and cattails intrigued him. But he scoffed at her soft touch, cruising at slow speeds, drifting silently past deer, whispering near birds' nests. He had no interest in learning the shells or feathers himself and questioned her when she scribbled notes in her journal or collected specimens.

"Why're you painting grass?" he asked one day in her kitchen.

"I'm painting their flowers."

He laughed. "Grass doesn't have flowers."

"Of course they do. See these blossoms. They're tiny, but beautiful. Each grass species has a different flower or inflorescence."

"What're ya gonna do with all this stuff anyway?"

"I'm keeping records so I can learn about the marsh."

"All ya need to know is when and where the fish bite, and I can tell ya that," he said.

She laughed for his sake, something she'd never done. Giving away another piece of herself just to have someone else.

That afternoon, after Chase left, Kya motored into the marsh alone. But did not feel alone. She accelerated slightly faster than usual, her long hair trailing in the wind, a slight smile brushed on her lips. Just knowing she would see him again soon, be with someone, lifted her to a new place.

Then, rounding a bend of tall grass, up ahead she saw Tate. He was quite far, maybe forty yards, and had not heard her boat. Instantly, she dropped throttle and killed the engine. Grabbed the oar and rowed backward into the grass.

"Home from college, I guess," she whispered. She'd seen him a few times over the years, but never this close. But now there he was, his untamed hair struggling with another red cap. Tanned face.

Tate wore high-top waders and strode through a lagoon, scooping up water samples in tiny vials. Not old jelly jars as when they were barefoot kids but petite tubes clinking in a special carrying rack. Professorial. Out of her league.

She didn't row away, but watched him awhile, thinking that every girl probably remembers her first love. She let out a long breath, then rowed back the way she came.

The next day, as Chase and Kya cruised north along the coast, four porpoises moved into their wake and followed them. It was a gray-sky day, and fingers of fog flirted with the waves. Chase switched off the engine, and as the boat drifted, he took out his harmonica and played the old song "Michael Row the Boat Ashore," a yearning and melodic tune sung by slaves in the 1860s as they rowed boats to the mainland from the Sea Islands of South Carolina. Ma used to sing it while scrubbing, and Kya sort of remembered the words. As if inspired by the music, the porpoises swam closer and circled the boat, their keen eyes fixing on Kya's. Then, two of them eased up against the hull, and she bowed her face only inches from theirs, and sang softly:

"Sister, help to trim dat boat, hallelujah
Brudder lend a helpin' hand, hallelujah.
Ma fadder gone to unknown land, hallelujah.
Michael, row the boat ashore, hallelujah.

"Jordan's river is deep and wide,
Meet my mother on the other side, hallelujah.
Jordan's river is chilly and cold
Chills the body but not the soul, hallelujah."

The porpoises stared at Kya for a few more seconds and then slipped backward into the sea.

Over the next few weeks, Chase and Kya spent evenings lazing with the gulls on her beach, lying back on sand still warm from the sun. Chase didn't take her into town, to the picture show or sock hops; it was the two of them, the marsh, the sea, and the sky. He didn't kiss her, only held her hand or put his arm lightly around her shoulders in the coolness.

Then one night he stayed late into the dark, and they sat on the beach under the stars by a small fire, shoulders touching, a blanket around them. The flames threw light across their faces and dark across the shore behind them, as campfires do. Looking into her eyes, he asked, "Is it okay if I kiss you now?" She nodded, so he leaned down and kissed her softly at first, and then like a man.

They lay back on the blanket, and she wiggled in as close to him as she could get. Feeling his strong body. He held her tight with both of his arms, but only touched her shoulders with his hands. Nothing more. She breathed deep, breathed in the warmth, the scents of him and the sea, the togetherness.

Only a few days later, Tate, still home from graduate school, raced his boat toward Kya's marsh channel, the first time he'd done so in five years. He still couldn't explain to himself why he'd never gone back to her before now. Mostly he'd been a coward, ashamed. Finally, he was going to find her, tell her he'd never stopped loving her and beg her to forgive him.

Those four years at university, he'd convinced himself that Kya could not fit in the academic world he sought. All through undergraduate, he'd tried to forget her; after all, there were plenty of female distractions at Chapel Hill. He even had a few long-term relationships, but no one compared. What he'd learned right after DNA, isotopes, and protozoans was that he couldn't breathe without her. True, Kya couldn't live in the university world he had sought, but now he could live in hers.

He had it all figured out. His professor had said Tate could finish graduate school in the next three years because he'd been conducting his research for his PhD dissertation all through undergraduate and it was nearly complete. Then, recently Tate learned that a federal research lab was to be built near Sea Oaks, and that he would have an excellent chance of being hired as a full-time research scientist. No one on Earth was better qualified: he'd been studying the local marsh most of his life, and soon he would have the PhD to back it up. In just a few short years, he could live here in the marsh with Kya and work at the lab. Marry Kya. If she would have him.

Now, as he bounced across waves toward her channel, suddenly Kya's boat zoomed south, perpendicular to his course. Letting go of the tiller, he threw both arms above his head, waving frantically to get her attention. Shouted out her name. But she was looking east. Tate glanced in that direction and saw Chase's ski boat veering toward her. Tate idled back, watching as Kya and Chase spun around each other in the blue-gray waves, in ever-smaller circles like eagles courting in the sky. Their wakes crazed and swirling.

Tate stared as they met and touched fingers across the churning water. He'd heard the rumors from his old friends in Barkley Cove but hoped they weren't true. He understood why Kya would fall for such a man, handsome, no doubt romantic, whizzing her around in his fancy boat, taking her on fancy picnics. She wouldn't know anything of his life in town—dating and courting other young women in Barkley, even Sea Oaks.

And, Tate thought, *who am I to say anything? I didn't treat her any better. I broke a promise, didn't even have the guts to break up with her.*

He dipped his head, then stole another glance just in time to see Chase lean over to kiss her. *Kya, Kya,* he thought. *How could I have left you?* Slowly, he accelerated and turned back toward the town harbor to help his dad crate and carry the catch.

A few days later, never knowing when Chase might come, Kya once again found herself listening for the sound of his boat. Just as she had for Tate. So whether pulling weeds, chopping stove wood, or collecting mussels, she'd tilt her head just so to catch the sound. "Squint yo' ears," Jodie used to say.

Tired of being weighted down by hope, she threw three days' worth of biscuits, cold backstrap, and sardines in her knapsack and walked out to the old falling-down log cabin; the "reading cabin," as she thought of it. Out here, in the real remote, she was free to wander, collect at will, read the words, read the wild. Not waiting for the sounds of someone was a release. And a strength.

In a scrub-oak thicket, just around the bend from the cabin, she found the tiny neck feather of a red-throated loon and laughed out loud. Had wanted this feather for as long as she could remember, and here it was a stone's throw downstream.

Mostly she came to read. After Tate left her those years ago, she no longer had access to books, so one morning she'd motored beyond Point Beach and another ten miles to Sea Oaks, a slightly larger and much swankier town than Barkley Cove. Jumpin' had said anyone could borrow books from the library there. She'd doubted if that was true for someone who lived in a swamp, but she had been determined to find out.

She'd tied up at the town wharf and crossed the tree-lined square overlooking the sea. As she walked toward the library, no one looked at her, whispered behind her back, or shooed her away from a window display. Here, she was not the Marsh Girl.

She handed Mrs. Hines, the librarian, a list of college textbooks. "Could you please help me find *The Principles of Organic Chemistry* by Geissman, *Invertebrate Zoology of the Coastal Marsh* by Jones, and *Fundamentals of Ecology* by Odum . . ." She'd seen these titles referenced in the last of the books Tate had given before he left her for college.

"Oh, my. I see. We'll have to get a library loan from the University of North Carolina at Chapel Hill for these books."

So now, sitting outside the old cabin, she picked up a scientific digest. One article on reproductive strategies was titled "Sneaky Fuckers." Kya laughed.

As is well known, the article began, in nature, usually the males with the most prominent secondary sexual characteristics, such as the biggest antlers, deepest voices, broadest chests, and superior knowledge secure the best territories because they have fended off weaker males. The females choose to mate with these imposing alphas and are thereby inseminated with the best DNA around, which is passed on to the female's offspring—one of the most powerful phenomena in the adaptation and continuance of life. Plus, the females get the best territory for their young.

However, some stunted males, not strong, adorned, or smart enough to hold good territories, possess bags of tricks to fool the females. They parade their smaller forms around in pumped-up postures or shout frequently—even if in shrill voices. By relying on pretense and false signals, they manage to grab a copulation here or there. Pint-sized male bullfrogs, the author wrote, hunker down in the grass and hide near an alpha male who is croaking with great gusto to call in mates. When several females are attracted to his strong vocals at the same time, and the alpha is busy copulating with one, the weaker male leaps in and mates one of the others. The imposter males were referred to as "sneaky fuckers."

Kya remembered, those many years ago, Ma warning her older sisters about young men who overrevved their rusted-out pickups or drove jalopies around with radios blaring. "Unworthy boys make a lot of noise," Ma had said.

She read a consolation for females. Nature is audacious enough to ensure that the males who send out dishonest signals or go from one female to the next almost always end up alone.

Another article delved into the wild rivalries between sperm. Across most life-forms, males compete to inseminate females. Male lions occasionally fight to the death; rival bull elephants lock tusks and demolish the ground beneath their feet as they tear at each other's flesh. Though very ritualized, the conflicts can still end in mutilations.

To avoid such injuries, inseminators of some species compete in less violent, more creative methods. Insects, the most imaginative. The penis of the male damselfly is equipped with a small scoop, which removes sperm ejected by a previous opponent before he supplies his own.

Kya dropped the journal on her lap, her mind drifting with the clouds. Some female insects eat their mates, overstressed mammal mothers abandon their young, many males design risky or shifty ways to outsperm their competitors. Nothing seemed too indecorous as long as the tick and the tock of life carried on. She knew this was not a dark side to Nature, just inventive ways to endure against all odds. Surely for humans there was more.

After finding Kya gone three days in a row, Chase started asking if he could come on a certain day, at a given time to see her at her shack or this or that beach, and always arrived on time. From far off she would see his brightly colored boat—like vivid feathers of a male bird's breeding plumage—floating on the waves and know he'd come just for her.

Kya started to picture him taking her on a picnic with his friends. All of them laughing, running into the waves, kicking the surf. Him lifting her, swirling around. Then sitting with the others sharing sandwiches and drinks from coolers. Bit by bit, pictures of marriage and children formed in spite of her resistance. *Probably some biological urge to push me into reproducing*, she told herself. But why couldn't she have loved ones like everybody else? Why not?

Yet every time she tried to ask when he would introduce her to his friends and parents, the words stuck to her tongue.

Drifting offshore, on a hot day a few months after they met, he said it was perfect for a swim. "I won't look," he said. "Take off your clothes and jump in, then I will." She stood in front of him, balancing in the boat, but as she pulled her T-shirt over her head, he didn't turn away. He reached out and ran his fingers lightly across her firm breasts. She didn't stop him. Pulling her closer, he unzipped her shorts and slipped them easily from her slender hips. Then he took off his shirt and shorts and pushed her down gently onto the towels.

Kneeling at her feet, without saying a word, he ran his fingers like a whisper along her left ankle up to the inside of her knee, slowly along the inside of her thigh. She raised her body toward his hand. His fingers lingered at the top of her thigh, rubbed over her panties, then moved across her belly, light as a thought. She sensed his fingers moving up her stomach toward her breasts and twisted her body away from him. Firmly, he pushed her flat and slid his fingers to her breast, slowly outlining the nipple with one finger. He looked at her, unsmiling, as he moved his hand down and pulled at the top of her panties. She wanted him, all of him, and her body pushed against his. But seconds later, she put her hand on his.

"C'mon, Kya," he said. "Please. We've waited forever. I've been pretty patient, don't ya think?"

"Chase, you promised."

"Damn it, Kya. What're we waiting for?" He sat up. "Surely, I showed ya I care for you. Why not?"

Sitting up, she pulled down her T-shirt. "What happens next? How do I know you won't leave me?"

"How does anybody ever know? But, Kya, I'm not going anywhere. I'm falling in love with you. I want to be with you all the time. What else can I do to show you?"

He had never mentioned love. Kya searched his eyes for truth but found only a hard stare. Unreadable. She didn't know exactly how she felt about Chase, but she was no longer lonely. That seemed enough.

"Soon, okay?"

He pulled her close to him. "It's okay. C'mere." He held her and they lay under the sun, drifting on the sea, the *slosh, slosh, slosh* of the waves beneath them.

Day drained away and night settled heavily, the village lights dancing here and there on the distant shore. Stars twinkling above their world of sea and sky.

Chase said, "I wonder what makes stars twinkle."

"Disturbance in the atmosphere. You know, like high atmospheric winds."

"That so?"

"I'm sure you know that most stars are too far away for us to see. We see only their light, which can be distorted by the atmosphere. But, of course, the stars are not stationary, but moving very fast."

Kya knew from reading Albert Einstein's books that time is no more fixed than the stars. Time speeds and bends around planets and suns, is different in the mountains than in the valleys, and is part of the same fabric as space, which curves and swells as does the sea. Objects, whether planets or apples, fall or orbit, not because of a gravitational energy, but because they plummet into the silky folds of spacetime—like into the ripples on a pond—created by those of higher mass.

But Kya said none of this. Unfortunately, gravity holds no sway on human thought, and the high school text still taught that apples fall to the ground because of a powerful force from the Earth.

"Oh, guess what," Chase said. "They've asked me to help coach the high school football team."

She smiled at him.

Then thought, *Like everything else in the universe, we tumble toward those of higher mass.*

The next morning, on a rare trip to the Piggly Wiggly to buy personal items Jumpin' didn't carry, Kya stepped out of the grocery and nearly bumped right into Chase's parents—Sam and Patti Love. They knew who she was—everyone did.

She'd seen them in town occasionally through the years, mostly from a distance. Sam could be seen behind the counter in the Western Auto, dealing with customers, opening the cash register. Kya remembered how when she was a girl, he shooed her away from the window as though she might frighten away real customers. Patti Love didn't work full time at the store, allowing time for her to hurry along the street, handing out pamphlets for the Annual Quilting Contest or the Blue-Crab Queen Festival. Always dressed in a fine outfit with high-heel pumps, pocketbook, and hat, in matching colors demanded by the southern season. No matter the subject, she managed to mention Chase as being the best quarterback the town had ever seen.

Kya smiled shyly, looking right into Patti Love's eyes, hoping they would speak to her in some personal way and introduce themselves. Maybe acknowledge her as Chase's girl. But they halted abruptly, said nothing, and sidestepped around her—making a wider berth than necessary. Moved on.

The evening after bumping into them, Kya and Chase drifted in her boat under an oak so huge its knees jutted over the water, creating little grottoes for otters and ducks. Keeping her voice low, partly so she wouldn't disturb the mallards and partly in fear, Kya told Chase about seeing his parents and asked if she would meet them soon.

Chase sat silent, making her stomach lump up.

Finally he said, "'Course you will. Soon, I promise." But he didn't look at her when he said it.

"They know about me, right? About us?" she asked.

"A' course."

The boat must have drifted too close to the oak, because right then a great horned owl, plump and cushy as a down pillow, dropped from the tree on reaching wings, then stroked slow and easy across the lagoon, his breast feathers reflecting soft patterns on the water.

Chase reached out and took Kya's hand, wringing the doubt from her fingers.

For weeks, sunsets and moonrises followed Chase and Kya's easy movements through the marsh. But each time she resisted his advances, he stopped. Images of does or turkey hens alone with their demanding young, the males long gone to other females, weighed solid in her mind.

Lying around near naked in the boat was as far as it went, no matter what the townspeople said. Although Chase and Kya kept to themselves, the town was small and people saw them together in his boat or on the beaches. The shrimpers didn't miss much on the seas. There was talk. Tittle-tattle.

27.

Out Hog Mountain Road

1966

The shack stood silent against the early stir of blackbird wings, as an earnest winter fog formed along the ground, bunching up against the walls like large wisps of cotton. Using several weeks of mussel money, Kya had bought special groceries and fried slices of molasses ham, stirred redeye gravy, and served them with sour-cream biscuits and blackberry jam. Chase drank instant Maxwell House; she, hot Tetley tea. They'd been together nearly a year, though neither spoke of that. Chase said how lucky he was that his father owned the Western Auto: "This way we'll have a nice house when we get married. I'm gonna build you a two-story on the beach with a wraparound veranda. Or whatever kinda house you want, Kya."

Kya could barely breathe. He wanted her in his life. Not just a hint, but something like a proposal. She would belong to someone. Be part of a family. She sat straighter in her chair.

He continued. "I don't think we should live right in town. That'd be too much of a jump for you. But we could build a place on tha outskirts. Ya know, close to the marsh."

Lately, a few vague thoughts of marriage to Chase had formed in her mind, but she had not dared dwell on them. But here he was saying it out loud. Kya's breath was shallow, her mind disbelieving and sorting details all at the same time. *I can do this,* she thought. *If we live away from people it could work.*

Then, head low, she asked, "What about your parents? Have you told them?"

"Kya, ya gotta understand something 'bout my folks. They love me. If I say you're my choice, that'll be that. They'll just fall in love with ya when they get to know ya."

She chewed on her lips. Wanting to believe.

"I'll build a studio for all yo' stuff," he continued. "With big windows so ya can see the details of all those dad-burned feathers."

She didn't know if she felt about Chase the way a wife should, but in this moment her heart soared with something like love. No more digging mussels.

She reached out and touched the shell necklace under his throat.

"Oh, by the way," Chase said. "I have to drive over to Asheville in a few days to buy goods for the store. I was thinkin', why don't ya come with me?"

Eyes downcast, she'd said, "But that's a large town. There'd be lots of people. And I don't have the right clothes, or don't even know what the right clothes are, and . . ."

"Kya, Kya. Listen. You'd be with me. I know everything. We don't have to go anywhere fancy. You'd see a lot of North Carolina just driving over—the Piedmont, the Great Smoky Mountains, forchristsake. Then when we got there, we could just go to a drive-in for burgers. You can wear what you have on. You don't have to talk to one soul if you don't want to. I'll take care of everything. I've been lots of times. Even to Atlanta. Asheville's nothing. Look, if we're gonna get married, ya might as well start gettin' out in tha world a bit. Spread those long wings of yours."

She nodded. If nothing else, to see the mountains.

He continued. "It's a two-day job, so we'll have to stay overnight. In a casual place. You know, a small motel. It's okay, because we're adults."

"Oh," was all she said. Then whispered, "I see."

Kya had never driven up the road a piece, so, a few days later, as she and Chase rode west out of Barkley in his pickup, she stared out the window, holding on to the seat with both hands. The road wound through miles of saw grass and palmettos, leaving the sea in the rear window.

For more than an hour, the familiar reaches of grass and waterways slipped by the truck's window. Kya identified marsh wrens and egrets, comforted by the sameness, like she hadn't left home but brought it with her.

Then abruptly, at a line drawn across the earth, the marsh meadows ended, and dusty ground—hacked raw, fenced into squares, and furrowed into rows—spread before them. Fields of paraplegic snags stood in felled forests. Poles, strung with wires, trudged toward the horizon. Of course, she knew coastal marsh didn't cover the globe, but she'd never been beyond it. What had people done to the land? Every house, the same shoebox shape, squatted on sheared lawn. A flock of pink flamingos fed across a yard, but when Kya whirled in surprise, she saw they were plastic. The deer, cement. The only ducks flew painted on mailboxes.

"They're incredible, huh?" Chase said.

"What?"

"The houses. You've never seen anything like 'em, huh?"

"No, I haven't."

Hours later, out on the flatlands of the Piedmont, she saw the Appalachians sketched in gentle blue lines along the horizon. As they neared, peaks rose around them and forested mountains flowed softly into the distance as far as Kya could see.

Clouds lazed in the folded arms of the hills, then billowed up and drifted away. Some tendrils twisted into tight spirals and traced the warmer ravines, behaving like mist tracking the dank fens of the marsh. The same game of physics playing on a different field of biology.

Kya was of the low country, a land of horizons, where the sun set and the moon rose on time. But here, where the topography was a jumble, the sun balanced along the summits, setting behind a ridge one moment and then popping up again when Chase's truck ascended the next rise. In the mountains, she noticed, the time of sunset depended on where you stood on the hill.

She wondered where her grandpa's land was. Maybe her kin had kept pigs in a weather-grayed barn like the one she saw in a meadow, creek running by. A family that should have been hers once toiled, laughed, and cried in this landscape. Some would still be here, scattered through the county. Anonymous.

The road became a four-lane highway, and Kya held on tight as Chase's truck sped within feet of other fast-moving vehicles. He turned onto a curving roadway that rose magically into the air and led them toward the town. "A cloverleaf exit," he said proudly.

Enormous buildings, eight and ten stories high, stood against the outline of the mountains. Scores of cars scuttled like sand crabs, and there were so many people on the sidewalks, Kya pushed her face to the window, searching their faces, thinking surely Ma and Pa must be among them. One boy, tanned and dark-haired, running down the sidewalk, looked like Jodie, and she spun around to watch him. Her brother would be grown now, of course, but she tracked the boy until they turned a corner.

On the other side of town, Chase booked them into a motel out Hog Mountain Road, a single-story row of brown rooms, lit up by neon lights the shape of palm trees, of all things.

After Chase unlocked their door, she stepped into a room that seemed clean enough but reeked of Pine-Sol and was furnished in America cheap: fake-panel walls, sagging bed with a nickel vibrator machine, and a black-and-white TV secured to the table with an impossibly large chain and padlock. The bedspreads were lime green, the carpet orange shag. Kya's mind went back to all the places they had lain together—in crystal sand by tidal pools, in moonlit drifting boats. Here, the bed loomed as the centerpiece, but the room didn't look like love.

She stood knowingly near the door. "It's not great," he said, putting his duffel bag on the chair.

He walked toward her. "It's time, don't you agree, Kya? It's time."

Of course, it had been his plan. But she was ready. Her body had been longing for months and, after the talk of marriage, her mind gave in. She nodded.

He came toward her slowly and unbuttoned her blouse, then turned her gently around and unfastened her bra. Traced his fingers across her breasts. An excited heat flowed from her breasts to her thighs. As he pulled her down onto the bed in the glow of the red and green neon lights filtering through thin curtains, she closed her eyes. Before, during all those almost-times, when she had stopped him, his wandering fingers had taken on a magical touch, bringing parts of her to life, causing her body to arch toward him, to long and want. But now, with permission finally granted, an urgency gripped him and he seemed to bypass her needs and push his way. She cried out against a sharp tearing, thinking something was wrong.

"It's okay. It'll be better now," he said with great authority. But it didn't get much better, and soon he fell to her side, grinning.

As he passed into sleep, she watched the blinking lights of the *Vacancy* sign.

Several weeks later, after finishing a breakfast of fried eggs and hamgrits at Kya's shack, she and Chase sat at her kitchen table. She was wrapped snugly in a blanket after lovemaking, which had improved only slightly since their first attempt at the motel. Each time left her wanting, but she didn't have the faintest notion how to broach such a subject. And anyway, she didn't know how she was supposed to feel. Maybe this was normal.

Chase stood from the table and, lifting her chin with his fingers, kissed her, saying, "Well, I won't be out much in the next few days with Christmas comin' up and all. There's lots of events and stuff, and some relatives comin' in."

Kya looked up at him and said, "I was hoping maybe I could . . . you know, go to some of the parties and things. At least maybe Christmas dinner with your family."

Chase sat back down in his chair. "Kya, look, I've been wantin' to talk ta ya 'bout this. I wanta ask ya to the Elks Club dance and stuff like that, but I know how shy you are, how ya don't ever do stuff in town. I know you'd be miserable. You wouldn't know anybody, ya don't have the right clothes. Do ya even know how to dance? None a' those things are what you do. You understand that, right?"

Looking at the floor, she said, "Yes, and all that's true. But, well, I have to start fitting in with some of your life. Spread my wings, like you said. I guess I have to get the right clothes, meet some of your friends." She raised her head. "You could teach me to dance."

"Well sure, an' I will. But I think of you and me as what we have out here. I love our time here together, just you and me. To tell you the truth, I'm gittin' kinda tired a' those stupid dances. Been the same fer years. High school gym. Old folks, young folks all together. Same dumb music. I'm ready to move on. You know, when we're married, we won't do stuff like that anyway, so why drag ya into it now? Don't make any sense. Okay?"

She looked back at the floor, so he lifted her chin again and held her eyes with his own. Then, grinning big, he said, "And, man, as far as having Christmas dinner wif ma family. Ma ancient aunts come in from Florida. Never stop talkin'. I wouldn't wish that on anybody. 'Specially you. Believe me, you ain't missin' a thing."

She was silent.

"Really, Kya, I wantcha to be okay with this. What we have out here is the most special thing anybody could hope for. All that other stuff"—he swiped his hands through the air—"is just stupid."

He reached over and pulled her into his lap, and she rested her head on his shoulder.

"This is where it's at, Kya. Not that other stuff." And he kissed her, warm and tender. Then stood. "Okay. Gotta go."

Kya spent Christmas alone with the gulls, as she had every year since Ma left.

Two days after Christmas, Chase still hadn't come. Breaking her self-promise to never wait for anyone again, Kya paced the shore of the lagoon, her hair woven into a French braid, mouth painted with Ma's old lipstick.

The marsh beyond lay in its winter cloak of browns and grays. Miles of spent grasses, having dispersed their seeds, bowed their heads to the water in surrender. The wind whipped and tore, rattling the coarse stems in a noisy chorus. Kya yanked her hair down and wiped her lips with the back of her hand.

The morning of the fourth day, she sat alone in the kitchen pushing biscuits and eggs around her plate. "For all his talk of '*this being where it's at*,' where is he now?" she spat. In her mind, she saw Chase playing touch football with friends or dancing at parties. "Those stupid things he's getting tired of."

Finally the sound of his boat. She sprang from the table, banged the door shut, and ran from the shack to the lagoon, as the boat chugged into view. But it wasn't Chase's ski boat or Chase, but a young man with yellow-gold hair, cut shorter but still barely contained under a ski cap. It was the old fishing rig, and there, standing, even as the boat moved forward, was Tate, grown into a man. Face no longer boyish, but handsome, mature. His eyes formed a question, his lips a shy smile.

Her first thought was to run. But her mind screamed, *NO! This is my lagoon; I always run. Not this time.* Her next thought was to pick up a rock, and she hurled it at his face from twenty feet. He ducked quickly, the stone whizzing by his forehead.

"Shit, Kya! What the hell? Wait," he said as she picked up another rock and took aim. He put his hands over his face. "Kya, for God's sake, stop. Please. Can't we talk?"

The rock hit him hard on the shoulder.

"GET OUT OF MY LAGOON! YOU LOW-DOWN DIRTY CREEP! HOW'S THAT FOR TALK!" The screaming fishwife looked frantically for another rock.

"Kya, listen to me. I know you're with Chase now. I respect that. I just want to talk with you. Please, Kya."

"Why should I talk with you? I never want to see you again EVER!" She picked up a handful of smaller stones and slung them at his face.

He jerked to the side, bent forward, and grabbed the gunwale as his boat ran aground.

"I SAID, GET OUT OF HERE!" Still yelling but softer, she said, "Yes, I am with someone else now."

Tate steadied himself after the jolt of hitting the shore, and then sat on the bow seat of his boat. "Kya, please, there're things you should know about him." Tate had not planned on having a conversation about Chase. None of this surprise visit to see Kya was going as he'd imagined.

"What are you talking about? You have no right to talk to me about my private life." She had walked up to within five feet of him and spat her words.

Firmly he said, "I know I don't, but I'm doing it anyway."

At this, Kya turned to leave, but Tate talked louder at her back. "You don't live in town. You don't know that Chase goes out with other women. Just the other night I watched him drive away after a party with a blonde in his pickup. He's not good enough for you."

She whirled around. "Oh, really! YOU are the one who left me, who didn't come back when you promised, who never came back. You are the one who never wrote to explain why or even if you were alive or dead. You didn't have the nerve to break up with me. You were not man enough to face me. Just disappeared. CHICKEN SHIT ASSHOLE. You come floating in here after all these years . . . You're worse than he is. He might not be perfect, but you're worse by a long shot." She stopped abruptly, staring at him.

Palms open, he pleaded, "You're right about me, Kya. Everything you said is true. I was a chicken shit. And I had no right to bring up Chase. It's none of my business. And I'll never bother you again. I just need to apologize and explain things. I've been sorry for years, Kya, please."

She hung like a sail where the wind just went out. Tate was more than her first love: he shared her devotion to the marsh, had taught her to read, and was the only connection, however small, to her vanished family. He was a page of time, a clipping pasted in a scrapbook because it was all she had. Her heart pounded as the fury dissipated.

"Look at you—so beautiful. A woman. You doing okay? Still selling mussels?" He was astonished at how she had changed, her features more refined yet haunting, her cheekbones sharp, lips full.

"Yes. Yes."

"Here, I brought you something." From an envelope he handed her a tiny red cheek feather from a northern flicker. She thought of tossing it on the ground, but she'd never found this feather; why shouldn't she keep it? She tucked it in her pocket and didn't thank him.

Talking fast, he said, "Kya, leaving you was not only wrong, it was the worst thing I have done or ever will do in my life. I have regretted it for years and will always regret it. I think of you every day. For the rest of my life, I'll be sorry I left you. I truly thought that you wouldn't be able to leave the marsh and live in the other world, so I didn't see how we could stay together. But that was wrong, and it was bullshit that I didn't come back and talk to you about it. I knew how many times you'd been left before. I didn't want to know how badly I hurt you. I was not man enough. Just like you said." He finished and watched her.

Finally she said, "What do you want now, Tate?"

"If only you could, some way, forgive me." He breathed in and waited.

Kya looked at her toes. Why should the injured, the still bleeding, bear the onus of forgiveness? She didn't answer.

"I just had to tell you, Kya."

When still she said nothing, he continued. "I'm in graduate school, zoology. Protozoology mostly. You would love it."

She couldn't imagine it, and looked back over the lagoon to see if Chase was coming. Tate didn't miss this; he'd guessed right off she was out here waiting for Chase.

Just last week Tate had watched Chase, in his white dinner jacket, at the Christmas gala, dancing with different women. The dance, like most Barkley Cove events, had been held at the high school gymnasium. As "Wooly Bully" struggled from a too-small hi-fi set up under the basketball hoop, Chase whirled a brunette. When "Mr. Tambourine Man" began, he left the dance floor and the brunette, and shared pulls of Wild Turkey from his Tar Heels flask with other former jocks. Tate was close by chatting with two of his old high school teachers and heard Chase say, "Yeah, she's wild as a she-fox in a snare. Just what you'd expect from a marsh minx. Worth every bit a' the gas money."

Tate had to force himself to walk away.

A cold wind whipped up and rippled across the lagoon. Expecting Chase, Kya had run out in her jeans and light sweater. She folded her arms tightly around herself.

"You're freezing; let's go inside." Tate motioned toward the shack, where smoke puffed from the rusty stovepipe.

"Tate, I think you should leave now." She threw several quick glances at the channel. What if Chase arrived with Tate here?

"Kya, please, just for a few minutes. I really want to see your collections again."

As answer, she turned and ran to the shack, and Tate followed her. Inside the porch, he stopped short. Her collections had grown from a child's hobby to a natural history museum of the marsh. He lifted a scallop shell, labeled with a watercolor of the beach where it was found, plus insets showing the creature eating smaller creatures of the sea. For each specimen—hundreds, maybe thousands of them—it was the same. He had seen some of them before, as a boy, but now as a doctoral candidate in zoology, he saw them as a scientist.

He turned to her, still standing in the doorway. "Kya, these are wonderful, beautifully detailed. You could publish these. This could be a book—lots of books."

"No, no. They're just for me. They help me learn, is all."

"Kya, listen to me. You know better than anybody that the reference books for this area are almost nonexistent. With these notations, technical data, and splendid drawings, these are the books everyone's been waiting for." It was true. Ma's old guidebooks to the shells, plants, birds, and mammals of the area were the only ones printed, and they were pitifully inaccurate, with only simple black-and-white pictures and sketchy information on each entry.

"If I can take a few samples, I'll find out about a publisher, see what they say."

She stared, not knowing how to see this. Would she have to go somewhere, meet people? Tate didn't miss the questions in her eyes.

"You wouldn't have to leave home. You could mail your samples to a publisher. It would bring some money in. Probably not a huge amount, but maybe you wouldn't have to dig mussels the rest of your life."

Still, Kya didn't say anything. Once again Tate was nudging her to care for herself, not just offering to care for her. It seemed that all her life, he had been there. Then gone.

"Give it a try, Kya. What can it hurt?"

She finally agreed that he could take some samples, and he chose a selection of soft watercolors of shells and the great blue heron because of her detailed sketches of the bird in each season, and a delicate oil of the curved eyebrow feather.

Tate lifted the painting of the feather—a profusion of hundreds of the thinnest brushstrokes of rich colors culminating into a deep black so reflective it seemed sunlight was touching the canvas. The detail of a slight tear in the shaft was so distinctive that both Tate and Kya realized at the same second that this was a painting of the very first feather he'd gifted her in the forest. They looked up from the feather into each other's eyes. She turned away from him. Forcing herself not to feel. She would not be drawn back to someone she couldn't trust.

He stepped up to her and touched her shoulder. Tried gently to turn her around. "Kya, I'm so sorry about leaving you. Please, can't you forgive me?"

Finally, she turned and looked at him. "I don't know how to, Tate. I could never believe you again. Please, Tate, you have to go now."

"I know. Thank you for listening to me, for giving me this chance to apologize." He waited for a beat, but she said no more. At least he was leaving with something. The hope for a publisher was a reason to contact her again.

"Good-bye, Kya." She didn't answer. He stared at her, and she looked into his eyes but then turned away. He walked out the door toward his boat.

She waited until he was gone, then sat on the damp, cold sand of the lagoon waiting for Chase. Speaking out loud, she repeated the words she'd said to Tate. "Chase may not be perfect, but you're worse."

But as she stared deep into the dark waters, Tate's words about Chase—*"drive away after a party with a blonde in his pickup"*—wouldn't leave her mind.

. . .

Chase didn't come until a week after Christmas. Pulling into the lagoon, he said he could stay all night, ring in the New Year together. Arm in arm, they walked to the shack, where the same fog, it seemed, draped across the roof. After lovemaking, they cuddled in blankets around the stove. The dense air couldn't hold another molecule of moisture, so when the kettle boiled, heavy droplets swelled on the cool windowpanes.

Chase slipped the harmonica from his pocket and, pressing it along his lips, played the wistful tune "Molly Malone." "Now her ghost wheels her barrow through the streets broad and narrow, singing cockles and mussels, alive, alive-o."

It seemed to Kya that when Chase played these melancholy tunes was when he most had a soul.

28.

The Shrimper

1969

At beer time the Dog-Gone served up better gossip than the diner. The sheriff and Joe stepped inside the elongated, jam-packed beer hall and up to the bar, made from a single longleaf pine, which extended down the left side of the room, seemingly out of sight into the dim. Locals—all men, since women weren't allowed—bunched up to the bar or sat at scattered tables. The two barkeeps roasted hot dogs; fried shrimp, oysters, and hush puppies; stirred grits; poured beers and bourbon. The only light emitted from various flashing beer signs, giving off an amber glow, like campfires licking whiskered faces. The *clonks* and *clinks* of billiard balls sounded from the back quarter.

Ed and Joe eased into a midbar cluster of fishermen, and as soon as they ordered Millers and fried oysters, the questions began: Anything new? How come there's no fingerprints; that part true? Ya guys thoughta ol' man Hanson? He's crazy as a loon, be just like sump'm he'd do, climb the tower, push off whoever comes along. This 'un got ya bumfuzzled, ain't it?

Joe facing one way, Ed the other, they rode the buzz. Answering, listening, nodding. Then through the hubbub, the sheriff's ear caught the corner of an even voice, a balanced tone, and turned to face Hal Miller, shrimper crew for Tim O'Neal.

"Can I talk with ya a minute, Sheriff? Alone?"

Ed backed away from the bar. "Sure can, Hal, come with me." He led him to a small table next to the wall, and they sat. "Need a refill on that beer?"

"No, fine fer now. Thank ya, though."

"Something on your mind, Hal?"

"Yeah, sure is. Gotta git her out, too. Been drivin' me a bit ditty."

"Let's have it."

"Oh man." Hal shook his head. "I don't know. May be nothing, either that, or I shoulda told ya sooner. I been haunted by what I seen."

"Just tell me, Hal. Together, we'll sort out if it's important or not."

"Well, it's about the Chase Andrews thing. It was the very night he died, well, I was crewing for Tim, and we were comin' into the bay late, way past midnight, and me and Allen Hunt seen that woman, the one people call the Marsh Girl, motoring just outta the bay."

"Is that so? How long after midnight?"

"Must'a been 'bout one forty-five in the mornin'."

"Where was she motoring?"

"Well, that's the thing, Sheriff. She was headed right toward the fire tower. If she stayed her course, she woulda landed at that little bay out from the tower."

Ed breathed out. "Yeah, Hal. That's important info. Very important. Can you be sure it was her?"

"Well, Allen and I talked about it at the time and were pretty sure it was her. I mean, we both thought the same thing. Wondered what the hell she was doin' out that late, cruisin' along with no lights on. Lucky we seen her, might've run her over. Then we just forgot about it.

It was only later I put two and two together and realized it was the same night Chase died at the tower. Well, then I reckoned I better speak up."

"Did anybody else on the boat see her?"

"Well, I don't know 'bout that. Others were about, fer sure, we were headin' in. All hands up. But I never talked to the others 'bout it. Ya know, just no reason to at the time. And haven't asked 'em since."

"I understand. Hal, you did the right thing to tell me. It's your duty to speak up like this. Don't worry about anything. All you can do is tell me what you saw. I'll ask you and Allen in to make a statement. Can I buy you that beer now?"

"No, I think I'll just go on home. G'night."

"Good night. Thanks again." As soon as Hal stood, Ed waved for Joe, who had been glancing over every few seconds to read the sheriff's face. They gave Hal a minute to clear the room with good-byes, then stepped onto the street.

Ed told Joe what Hal had witnessed.

"Man," Joe said, "that just about does it. Don't you think?"

"I think the judge may issue a warrant on this. Not sure, and I'd like to be sure before I ask. With a warrant we can search her place for any trace of red fibers that match those found on Chase's clothes. We gotta find out her story for that night."

29.

Seaweed

1967

Through the winter, Chase came to Kya's shack often, usually spending one night each weekend. Even on cold, damp days, they glided through misty thickets, her collecting, him playing whimsical tunes on his harmonica. The notes floated with the fog, dissipating into the darker reaches of the lowland forests, and seemed somehow to be absorbed and memorized by the marsh because whenever Kya passed those channels again, she heard his music.

One morning in early March, Kya eased alone through the sea toward the village, the sky in a frumpy sweater of gray clouds. Chase's birthday was in two days, and she was headed to the Piggly to buy ingredients for a special supper—featuring her first caramel cake. Had pictured setting the candlelit cake in front of him at the table—an event that hadn't happened in the kitchen since Ma left. Several times recently he'd said he was saving money for their house. She reckoned she'd better learn to bake.

After securing her boat, as she walked along the dock toward the single file of shops, she saw Chase standing at the end talking with friends. His arms draped the shoulders of a slim, blond girl. Kya's mind strained to make sense of this, even as her legs kept moving on their own. She'd never approached him when he was with others or in town, but short of jumping into the sea, there was no way to avoid them.

Chase and his friends turned at once to look at her, and in the same instant, he dropped his arm from the girl. Kya was dressed in white cutoff denims, setting off her long legs. A black braid fell over each breast. The group stopped talking and stared. Knowing she couldn't run up to him burned her heart with the wrongness of things.

As she reached the end of the wharf, where they stood, he said, "Oh, Kya, hi."

Looking from him to them, she said, "Hi, Chase."

She heard him saying, "Kya, you remember Brian, and Tim, Pearl, Tina." He rattled off a few more names until his voice faded. Turning toward Kya, he said, "And this is Kya Clark."

Of course, she didn't remember them; she'd never been introduced to them. Only knew them as Tallskinnyblonde and the rest. She felt like seaweed dragged on a line but managed to smile and say hello. This was the opportunity for which she'd waited. Here she was standing among the friends she wanted to join. Her mind fought for words, something clever to say that might interest them. Finally, two of them greeted her coolly and turned abruptly away, the others following quickly like a school of minnows finning down the street.

"Well, so here we are," Chase said.

"I don't want to interrupt anything. I've just come for supplies, then back home."

"You're not interrupting. I just ran into them. I'll be out on Sunday, like I said."

Chase shifted his feet, fingered the shell necklace.

"I'll see you then," she said, but he'd already turned to catch the others. She hurried toward the market, stepping around a family of mallard ducks waddling down Main Street, their bright feet surprisingly orange against the dull pavement. In the Piggly Wiggly, pushing the vision of Chase and the girl from her head, she rounded the end of the bread aisle and saw the truant lady, Mrs. Culpepper, only four feet away. They stood there like a rabbit and a coyote caught together in a yard fence. Kya was now taller than the woman and much more educated, though neither would have thought of that. After all the running, she wanted to bolt, but stood her ground and returned Mrs. Culpepper's stare. The woman nodded slightly, then moved on.

Kya found the picnic items—cheese, French bread, and cake ingredients—costing all the money she'd managed to save for the occasion. But it seemed someone else's hand lifted the items and put them into the cart. All she could see was Chase's arm resting on the girl's shoulder. She bought a local newspaper because the headlines mentioned a marine laboratory that was to open up the coast nearby.

Once out of the store, head down, she scurried like a robber-ferret to the pier. Back at the shack, she sat down at the kitchen table to read the article about the new lab. Sure enough, a swanky scientific facility was being developed twenty miles south of Barkley Cove near Sea Oaks. Scientists would study the ecology of the marsh, which contributed to the survival of almost half of sea life in one way or another, and . . .

Kya turned the page to continue the story, and there loomed a large picture of Chase and a girl above an engagement announcement: *Andrews-Stone.* Bunches of words jumped out, then sobs, and finally ragged heaves. She stood, looking at the paper from a distance. Picked it up again to see—surely she had imagined it. There they were, their faces close together, smiling. The girl, Pearl Stone, beautiful, rich-looking, with a pearl necklace and lace blouse. The one his arm had been around. *Alwayswearspearls.*

Touching the wall, Kya made her way to the porch and fell on the bed, hands over her opened mouth. Then she heard a motor. Abruptly, she sat up, looked toward the lagoon, and saw Chase pulling his boat onto the shore.

Quick as a mouse escaping a lidless box, she slipped out the porch door before he saw her and ran into the woods, away from the lagoon. Squatting behind palmettos, she watched as he went into the shack, calling her. He would see the article spread open on the table. In a few minutes, he came out again and walked toward the beach, figuring he would find her there.

She didn't budge, even when he came back, still shouting her name. Not until he motored away did she emerge from the brambles. Moving sluggishly, she got food for the gulls and followed the sun to the beach. A strong ocean breeze pushed up the path, so that when she emerged on the beach, at least she had the wind to lean on. She called the gulls and flung large bits of French bread into the air. Then swore louder and meaner than the wind.

30.

The Rips

1967

From the beach, Kya ran to her rig and roared full throttle into the sea, headed straight for the rips. Holding her head back, she screamed, "You mean, SHIT . . . SUMBITCH!" Sloppy and confused waves jerked the bow sideways, pulling against the tiller. As always, the ocean seemed angrier than the marsh. Deeper, it had more to say.

Long ago, Kya'd learned how to read ordinary currents and riptides; how to ride them out or break away by cutting perpendicular to their course. But she'd never headed straight into the deeper currents, some of them stirred by the Gulf Stream, which gushes four billion cubic feet of water every second, more power than all the land rivers on Earth combined—all streaming just beyond North Carolina's outstretched arms. The surge produces cruel backcurrents, fisted eddies, and reverse circulations that swirl with coastal riptides, birthing one of the nastiest snake pits of the planet's seas. Kya had avoided these areas all her life, but not now. Today she aimed straight for their throats, anything to outrun the pain, the anger.

Roiling water pushed toward her, rising under the bow and yanking the boat starboard. It heaved heavily, then righted. She was pulled into a furious rip, which carried her a quarter faster. Turning out of it seemed too risky, so she fought to steer with the current, watching for sandbars, which formed ever-shifting barriers beneath the surface. One glancing touch could flip her.

Waves broke over her back, drenching her hair. Fast-moving, dark clouds streamed just above her head, blocking the sunlight and obscuring the signs of eddies and turbulence. Sucking the day's heat.

Still, fear eluded her, even as she longed to feel terrified, anything to dislodge the blade jammed against her heart.

Suddenly the dark tumbling waters of the current shifted, and the small rig spun starboard, rearing on its side. The force slammed her onto the bottom of the boat, seawater sloshing over her. Stunned, she sat in the water, bracing for another wave.

Of course, she was nowhere near the actual Gulf Stream. This was the training camp, the mere playing fields for the serious sea. But to her, she had ventured into the mean and meant to ride it out. Win something. Kill the pain.

Having lost all sense of symmetry and pattern, slate-colored waves broke from every angle. She dragged herself back into her seat and took the tiller but didn't know where to steer. Land slung as a distant line, surfacing only now and then between whitecaps. Just when she glimpsed solid earth, the boat spun or tilted and she lost sight of it. She'd been so sure about riding the current, but it had grown muscular, hauling her farther into the furious, darkening sea. The clouds bunched and settled low, blocking the sun. Wet through, she shivered as her energy drained, making it difficult to steer. She'd brought no foul-weather gear, no food, no water.

Finally the fear came. From a place deeper than the sea. Fear from knowing she would be alone again. Probably always. A life sentence.

Ugly gasping noises passed from her throat as the boat skewed and rolled broadside. Tipping dangerously with each wave.

By now six inches of foamy water covered the floor of the boat, burning her bare feet with its cold. How quickly the sea and clouds defeated the spring heat. Folding one arm over her chest, she tried to warm herself as she steered weakly with the other hand, not fighting the water, just moving with it.

At last, the waters calmed, and although the current swept her along to its own purpose, the ocean no longer thrashed and churned. Up ahead she saw a small, elongated sandbar, maybe a hundred feet long, glistening with sea and wet shells. Fighting the strong underflow, and just at the right second, Kya jerked the tiller and turned out of the current. She steered around to the leeward side of the bar and, in the stiller waters, beached as gently as a first kiss. She stepped onto the narrow slip and sank to the sand. Lay back and felt the solid land against her.

She knew it wasn't Chase she mourned, but a life defined by rejections. As the sky and clouds struggled overhead, she said out loud, "I have to do life alone. But I knew this. I've known a long time that people don't stay."

It hadn't been a coincidence that Chase slyly mentioned marriage as bait, immediately bedded her, then dropped her for someone else. She knew from her studies that males go from one female to the next, so why had she fallen for this man? His fancy ski boat was the same as the pumped-up neck and outsized antlers of a buck deer in rut: appendages to ward off other males and attract one female after another. Yet she had fallen for the same ruse as Ma: *leapfrogging sneaky fuckers.* What lies had Pa told her; to what expensive restaurants had he taken her before his money gave out and he brought her home to his real territory—a swamp shack? Perhaps love is best left as a fallow field.

Speaking out loud, she recited an Amanda Hamilton poem:

"I must let go now.
Let you go.
Love is too often
The answer for staying.
Too seldom the reason
For going.
I drop the line
And watch you drift away.

"All along
You thought
The fiery current
Of your lover's breast
Pulled you to the deep.
But it was my heart-tide
Releasing you
To float adrift
With seaweed."

The weak sun found space between the heavy-bottomed clouds and touched the sandbar. Kya looked around. The current, the grand sweep of the sea, and this sand had conspired as a delicate catch-net, because all around her lay the most astonishing collection of shells she'd ever seen. The angle of the bar and its gentle flow gathered the shells on the leeward side and laid them gently upon the sand without breaking them. She spotted several rare ones and many of her favorites, intact and pearly. Still glistening.

Moving among them, she chose the most precious and stashed them in a pile. She flipped the boat, drained the water, and lined the shells carefully along the bottom seam. Now she planned her trip back by standing tall and studying the waters. She read the sea and, having learned from the shells, would embark from the leeward side and head straight for land from here. Avoiding the strongest current altogether.

As she pushed off, she knew no one would ever see this sandbar again. The elements had created a brief and shifting smile of sand, angled just so. The next tide, the next current would design another sandbar, and another, but never this one. Not the one who caught her. The one who told her a thing or two.

Later, wandering her beach, she recited her favorite Amanda Hamilton poem.

"Fading moon, follow
My footsteps
Through light unbroken
By land shadows,
And share my senses
That feel the cool
Shoulders of silence.

"Only you know
How one side of a moment
Is stretched by loneliness
For miles
To the other edge,
And how much sky
Is in one breath

When time slides backward
From the sand."

If anyone understood loneliness, the moon would.

Drifting back to the predictable cycles of tadpoles and the ballet of fireflies, Kya burrowed deeper into the wordless wilderness. Nature seemed the only stone that would not slip midstream.

31.
A Book

1968

The rusted-out mailbox, mounted on a pole Pa cut, stood at the end of the road that had no name. Kya's only mail was bulk postings sent to all residents. She had no bills to pay, no girlfriends or old aunts to send silly-sweet notes. Except for that one letter from Ma years ago, her mail was a neutral thing, and sometimes she wouldn't empty the box for weeks.

But in her twenty-second year, more than a year after Chase and Pearl announced their engagement, she walked the sandy lane, blistering with heat, to the mailbox every day and looked inside. Finally one morning, she found a bulky manila envelope and slid the contents—an advance copy of *The Sea Shells of the Eastern Seaboard,* by Catherine Danielle Clark—into her hands. She breathed in, no one to show it to.

Sitting on her beach, she looked at every page. When Kya had written to the publisher after Tate's initial contact and submitted more drawings, they sent her a contract by return mail. Because all her paintings and text for each shell sample had been completed for years, her editor, Mr. Robert Foster, wrote to her that the book would be published in record time and that her second on birds would follow soon after. He included an advance payment of five thousand dollars. Pa would have tripped over his gimpy leg and spilled his poke.

Now in her hands, the final copy—every brushstroke, every carefully thought-out color, every word of the natural histories, printed in a book. There were also drawings of the creatures who live inside—how they eat, how they move, how they mate—because people forget about creatures who live in shells.

She touched the pages and remembered each shell and the story of finding it, where it lay on the beach, the season, the sunrise. A family album.

Over the coming months, up and down the coasts of North Carolina, South Carolina, Georgia, Virginia, Florida, and New England, gift shops and bookstores put her book in their windows or on display tables. The royalty checks would come in every six months, they said, and might be several thousand dollars each.

Sitting at the kitchen table, she drafted a letter of thanks to Tate, but as she read it over, her heart paused. A note did not seem enough. Because of his kindness, her love of the marsh could now be her life's work. Her life. Every feather, shell, or insect she collected could be shared with others, and no longer would she have to dig through mud for her supper. Might not have to eat grits every day.

Jumpin' had told her Tate was working as an ecologist at the new institute and laboratory near Sea Oaks, which had assigned him a spiffed-up research boat. At times, she'd seen him in the distance, but steered clear.

She added a postscript to the note: "If you're near my place sometime, stop by. I'd like to give you a copy of the book," and addressed it to him at the lab.

The next week she hired a fix-it man, Jerry, who put in running water, a water heater, and a full bathroom with a claw-foot tub in the back bedroom. He set a sink in a cabinet topped with tiles and installed a flush toilet. Electricity was brought in, and Jerry put in a range and new refrigerator. Kya insisted on keeping the old woodstove, firewood piled next to it, because it heated the shack, but mostly because it had baked a thousand biscuits from her mother's heart. What if Ma came back and her stove was gone? He made kitchen cabinets of heart pine, hung a new front door, a new screen on the porch, and made shelves for her specimens from floor to ceiling. She ordered a sofa, chairs, beds, mattresses, and rugs from Sears, Roebuck but kept the old kitchen table. And now she had a real closet to store a few mementos—a little scrap-closet of her fallen-away family.

As before, the shack stood unpainted on the outside, the weathered pine boards and tin roof rich in gray and rust colors, brushed by Spanish moss from the overhanging oak. Less rickety, but still woven into the weft of the marsh. Kya continued sleeping on the porch, except in the coldest of winter. But now she had a bed.

One morning, Jumpin' told Kya developers were coming to the area with big plans to drain the "murky swamp" and build hotels. Now and then, over the last year she'd seen large machines cutting entire stands of oaks in a week, then digging channels to dry the marsh. When finished, they moved on to new spots, leaving tracks of thirst and hardpan behind. Apparently, they had not read Aldo Leopold's book.

A poem by Amanda Hamilton said it clearly.

Child to child
Eye to eye
We grew as one,
Sharing souls.
Wing by wing,
Leaf by leaf
You left this world,
You died before the child.
My friend, the Wild.

Kya didn't know if her family owned the land or just squatted it, as had most marsh people for four centuries. Over the years, searching for clues of Ma's whereabouts, she'd read every scrap of paper in the shack and had never seen anything like a deed.

As soon as she got home from Jumpin's, she wrapped the old Bible in a cloth and took it to the Barkley Cove courthouse. The county clerk, a white-haired man with an enormous forehead and tiny shoulders, brought out a large leather volume of records, some maps, and a few aerial photographs, which he spread on the counter. Running her finger across the map, Kya pointed out her lagoon and outlined the rough boundaries of what she thought of as her land. The clerk checked the reference number and searched for the deed in an old wooden filing cabinet.

"Yep, here et is," he said. "It were surveyed proper and bought up in 1897 by a Mr. Napier Clark."

"That's my grandpa," Kya said. She thumbed through the thin pages of the Bible, and there, in the records of births and deaths, was one Napier Murphy Clark. Such a grand name. The same as her brother's. She told the clerk her pa was dead, which he probably was.

"It's ne'er been sold. So, yessiree bobtail, I reckon it b'longs to you.

But I'm afred to tell ya, there're some back taxes, Miz Clark, and to keep the land you gotta pay 'em. In fact, ma'am, the way the law reads, whoever comes along and pays off them back taxes owns the land even if they don't got no deed."

"How much?" Kya had not opened a bank account, and all the cash she owned after the improvements to her house, some three thousand dollars, was right in her knapsack. But they must be talking forty years of back taxes—thousands and thousands of dollars.

"Well, let's lookee here. It's listed as 'waste-land cateegory,' so the taxes fer most of them years was about five dollars. Let's see here, I gotta calc'late it." He stepped over to a fat and clunky adding machine, punched in numbers, and, after every entry, pulled back the crank handle, which made a churning sound as if it were actually summing up.

"Looks like it'll be 'bout eight hundr'd dollars total—put the land free and clear."

Kya walked out of the courthouse with a full deed in her name for three hundred ten acres of lush lagoons, sparkling marsh, oak forests, and a long private beach on the North Carolina coastline. "Wasteland *cateegory*. Murky swamp."

Pulling back into her lagoon at dusk, she had a talk with the heron. "It's all right. That spot's your'n!"

The next noon there was a note from Tate in her mailbox, which seemed strange and somehow formal since he'd only ever left messages for her on the feather stump. He thanked her for the invitation to stop by her place for a copy of her book and added that he'd be there that very afternoon.

Carrying one of the six copies of her new book the publishers had given her, she waited on the old reading-log. In about twenty minutes she heard the sound of Tate's old boat chugging up the channel and stood. As he eased into view from the undergrowth, they waved and smiled softly. Both guarded. The last time he'd pulled in here, she'd hurled rocks in his face.

After tying up, Tate stepped up to her. "Kya, your book is a wonder." He leaned slightly forward, as if to hug her, but the hardened rinds of her heart held her back.

Instead she handed him the book. "Here, Tate. This is for you."

"Thank you, Kya," he said as he opened it and paged through. He didn't mention that, of course, he'd already bought one at the Sea Oaks Bookshelf and marveled at every page. "Nothing like this has ever been published. I'm sure this is just a beginning for you."

She simply bowed her head and smiled slightly.

Then, turning to the title page, he said, "Oh, you haven't signed it. You have to inscribe it for me. Please."

She jerked her head up at him. Had not thought of that. What words could she possibly write to Tate?

He took a pen from his jeans pocket and handed it to her.

She took it and, after a few seconds, wrote:

To the Feather Boy

Thank you

From the Marsh Girl

Tate read the words, then turned away, staring far across the marsh because he couldn't hold her. Finally, he lifted her hand and squeezed it.

"Thank you, Kya."

"It was you, Tate," she said, and then thought, *It was always you.* One side of her heart longing, the other shielding.

He stood for a minute, and when she didn't say more, he turned to go. But as he got into his boat, he said, "Kya, when you see me out in the marsh, please don't hide in the grass like a spotted fawn. Just call out to me and we can do some exploring together. Okay?"

"All right."

"Thanks again for the book."

"Good-bye, Tate." She watched until he disappeared in the thicket and then said, "I could have at least invited him in for tea. That wouldn't hurt anything. I could be his friend." Then with rare pride she thought of her book. "I could be his colleague."

An hour after Tate left, Kya motored to Jumpin's wharf, another copy of her book tucked in her knapsack. As she approached, she saw him leaning against the wall of his weathered shop. He stood and waved to her, but she did not wave back. Knowing something was different, he waited silently as she tied up. She stepped up to him, lifted his hand, and put the book in his palm. At first he didn't understand, but she pointed to her name and said, "I'm okay now, Jumpin'. Thank you, and thank Mabel for all you did for me."

He stared at her. In another time and place, an old black man and a young white woman might have hugged. But not there, not then. She covered his hand with hers, turned, and motored away. It was the first time she'd seen him speechless. She kept on buying gas and supplies from him but never accepted a handout from them again. And each time she came to his wharf, she saw her book propped up in the tiny window for all to see. As a father would have shown it.

32.

Alibi

1969

Low dark clouds raced over a steel sea toward Barkley Cove. The wind hit first, rattling windows and hurling waves over the wharf. Boats, tied to the dock, bobbed up and down like toys, as men in yellow slickers tied this line or that, securing. Then sideways rain slammed the village, obscuring everything except the odd yellow form moving about in the grayness.

The wind whistled through the sheriff's window, and he raised his voice. "So, Joe, you had something to tell me?"

"Sure do. I found out where Miss Clark will claim she was the night Chase died."

"What? Did you finally catch up to her?"

"Ya kiddin'? She's slipperier'n a damn eel. Gets gone ever' time I get near. So I drove over to Jumpin's marina this morning to see if he knew when she'd be coming next. Like everybody else she hasta go there for gas, so I figured I'd catch her up sooner or later. You won't believe what I found out."

"Let's have it."

"I got two reliable sources say she was outta town that night."

"What? Who? She never goes out of town, and even if she did, who'd know about it?"

"Ya remember Tate Walker? Dr. Walker now. Works out at the new ecology lab."

"Yeah, I know him. His dad's a shrimper. Scupper Walker."

"Well, Tate says he knew Kya—he calls her Kya—quite well when they were younger."

"Oh?"

"Not like that. They were just kids. He taught her to read, 'parently."

"He tell you this himself?"

"Yep. He was there at Jumpin's. I was askin' Jumpin' if he knew where or how I could ask the Marsh Girl some questions. He said he didn't know from one minute to the next when he'd see her."

"Jumpin's always been good to her. Doubt if he'll tell us much."

"Well, I asked him if, by any chance, he knew what she was doin' the night Chase died. And he said that as a matter of fact he did, that she'd come to his place the second mornin' after Chase died, and that he was the very one who told her he was dead. He said she'd been in Greenville for two nights, including the night Chase died."

"Greenville?"

"That's what he said, and then Tate, who'd been standin' there all that time, he piped in and said, yeah, she'd been in Greenville, that he was the one who told her how to buy the bus ticket."

"Well, that is some news," Sheriff Jackson said. "And very convenient that they were both standing there with the same story. Why would she go over to Greenville?"

"Tate said that a publishing company—ya know, she's gone and written a book on shells and one of seabirds—well, they paid her expenses to go over there and meet 'em."

"Hard to imagine fancy publishing people wanting to meet her. I guess it'll be pretty easy to check out. What'd Tate say about teaching her to read?"

"I asked him how he knew her. He said he useta go out near her place to fish, and when he found out she couldn't read, he taught her."

"Um. That so?"

Joe said, "Anyway, this changes everything. She does have an alibi. A good one. I'd say being in Greenville's a pretty good alibi."

"Yeah. On the surface. You know what they say about good alibis. And we got that shrimper saying he saw her boating directly toward the fire tower the very night Chase fell off it."

"He could've been wrong. It was dark. No moon until after two A.M. Maybe she was in Greenville, and he saw somebody else out there in a boat looks like hers."

"Well, like I said, this supposed trip to Greenville should be easy to check out."

The storm abated into a whine and drizzle; still, instead of walking to the diner, the two lawmen sent a runner for a takeout of chicken 'n' dumplings, butter beans, summer squash casserole, cane syrup, and biscuits.

Right after lunch, a knock sounded on the sheriff's door. Miss Pansy Price opened it and stepped inside. Joe and Ed stood. Her turban hat glistened a rose color.

"Afternoon, Miss Pansy." Both nodded.

"Good afternoon, Ed. Joe. May I have a seat? I won't take long. I believe I have important information concerning the case."

"Yes, of course. Sit down, please." The two men sat as soon as Miss Pansy settled like a fair-sized hen into the chair, tucking feathers here and there, her pocketbook perching on her lap like a prized egg. The sheriff, continuing, couldn't resist. "And what case would that be, Miss Pansy?"

"Oh, for heaven's sake, Ed. You know what case. Who murdered Chase Andrews. That case."

"We don't know if he was murdered, Miss Pansy. All right? Now, what do you have for us?"

"As you know, I'm employed at Kress's." She never lowered her standing by referring to the entire name: Kress's Five and Dime. She waited for the sheriff to acknowledge her comment with a nod—even though they all knew she'd worked there since she sold toy soldiers to him as a boy—and then continued. "I believe the Marsh Girl is a suspect. Is that correct?"

"Who told you that?"

"Oh, lots of people are convinced, but Patti Love's the main source."

"I see."

"Well, from Kress's me and some other employees saw the Marsh Girl get on and off the bus on days that woulda put her out of town the night Chase died. I can testify to those dates and times."

"That so?" Joe and Ed exchanged glances. "What are the dates and times?"

Miss Pansy sat straighter in her chair. "She left on the 2:30 P.M. bus on October 28 and returned at 1:16 on the thirtieth."

"You said others saw her, too?"

"Yes. I can get a list if you like."

"That won't be necessary. We'll come over to the Five and Dime if we want statements. Thank you, Miss Pansy." The sheriff stood, so Miss Pansy and Ed did as well.

She moved toward the door. "Well, thank you for your time. As you said, you know where to find me."

They said good-byes.

Joe sat back down. "Well, there it is. Confirms what Tate and Jumpin' said. She was in Greenville that night, or leastwise, she got on a bus and went somewheres."

The sheriff blew out a long breath. "Appears so. But I reckon if somebody can bus over to Greenville by day, they can bus back here at night. Do their business. Bus back to Greenville. Nobody the wiser."

"I guess. Seems a bit of a stretch."

"Go get the bus schedules. We'll see if the times work out. If a return trip is possible in one night."

Before Joe stepped out, Ed continued. "Could be she wanted to be seen out there in broad daylight getting on and off of buses. When you think about it, she had to do something out of the ordinary for an alibi. To claim that she'd been alone in her shack the night Chase died, as she usually is, would be no alibi at all. Zip. So she planned up something that lots of people would see her do. Making a great alibi right in front of all those folks on Main Street. Brilliant."

"Well yeah, that's a good point. Anyhow, we don't have to play gumshoe anymore. We can set right here drinkin' coffee and let the ladies of this town waltz in and outta here with all the goods. I'll go get the bus schedules."

Joe returned fifteen minutes later.

"Well, you're right," he said. "See here, it would be possible to bus from Greenville to Barkley Cove and then back again all in one night. Easy, really."

"Yeah, plenty of time between the two buses to push somebody off the fire tower. I say we get a warrant."

33.

The Scar

1968

In the winter of 1968, Kya sat at her kitchen table one morning, sweeping orange and pink watercolors across paper, creating the plump form of a mushroom. She had finished her book on seabirds and now worked on a guide to mushrooms. Already had plans for another on butterflies and moths.

Black-eyed peas, red onions, and salt ham boiled in the old dented pot on the woodstove, which she still preferred to the new range. Especially in winter. The tin roof sang under a light rain. Then, suddenly the sounds of a truck laboring through sand came down her lane. Rumbling louder than the roof. Panic rising, she stepped to the window and saw a red pickup maneuvering the muddy ruts.

Kya's first thought was to run, but the truck was already pulling up to the porch. Hunched down below the windowsill, she watched a man in a gray-green military uniform step out. He just stood there, truck door ajar, looking through the woods, down the path toward the lagoon. Then, closing the door softly, he jogged through the rain to the porch door and knocked.

She cussed. He was probably lost, would ask directions and go on, but she didn't want to deal with him. She could hide here in the kitchen, hope he went away. But she heard him call. "Yo! Anybody home? Hello!"

Annoyed yet curious, she walked through the newly furnished sitting room to the porch. The stranger, tall with dark hair, stood on the front step holding the screen door open, five feet from her. His uniform seemed stiff enough to stand on its own, as if it were holding him together. The breast of his jacket was covered with colorful rectangular medals. But most eye-catching of all was a jagged red scar that cut his face in half from his left ear to the top of his lips. Kya gasped.

In an instant she returned to the Easter Sunday about six months before Ma left for good. Singing "Rock of Ages," she and Ma walked arm in arm through the sitting room to the kitchen and gathered up the brilliantly colored eggs they had painted the night before. The other kids were out fishing, so she and Ma had time to hide the eggs, then get the chicken and biscuits into the oven. The brothers and sisters were too old to hunt for treats, but they would run around searching, pretending not to find them, then holding each discovered treasure high in the air, laughing.

Ma and Kya were leaving the kitchen with their baskets of eggs and chocolate bunnies from the Five and Dime, just as Pa rounded the corner from the hall.

Yanking Kya's Easter bonnet from her head and waving it around, he screamed at Ma, "Whar ya git the money for these fancy thangs? Bonnets and shiny leather shoes? Them prissy eggs and chocolate bunnies? Say. Whar?"

"Come on, Jake, please hush. It's Easter; this is for the kids."

He shoved Ma backward. "Ya out whoring, that's what. That how you git the money? Tell me *now*." He grabbed Ma by the arms and shook her so hard her face seemed to rattle around her eyes, which stayed very still and wide open. Eggs tumbled from the basket and rolled in wobbly pastels across the floor.

"Pa, please, stop!" Kya cried out, then sobbed.

He lifted his hand and slapped Kya hard across the cheek. "Shut up, ya prissy-pot crybaby! Git that silly-looking dress and fancy shoes off ya. Them's whorin' clothes."

She ducked down, holding her face, chasing after Ma's hand-painted eggs.

"I'm talkin' to ya, woman! Whar ya gettin' yo' money?" He lifted the iron fire poker from the corner and moved toward Ma.

Kya screamed as loud as she could and grabbed at Pa's arm as he slammed the poker across Ma's chest. Blood popped out on the flowery sundress like red polka dots. Then a big body moved down the hall and Kya looked up to see Jodie tackle Pa from behind, sending them both sprawling across the floor. Her brother got between Ma and Pa and hollered for Kya and Ma to run, and they did. But before she turned, Kya saw Pa raise the poker and whack Jodie across the face, his jaw twisting grossly, blood spewing. The scene played out in her mind now in a flash. Her brother crumbling onto the floor, lying among purple-pink eggs and chocolate bunnies. She and Ma running through palmettos, hiding in brush. Her dress bloody, Ma kept saying it was fine, the eggs wouldn't break, and they could still cook the chicken. Kya didn't understand why they stayed hidden there—she was sure her brother was dying, needed their help, but she was too afraid to move. They waited for a long time and then snuck back, looking through the windows to make sure Pa was gone.

Jodie lay cold on the floor, blood pooled around him, and Kya cried that he was dead. But Ma roused him and moved him to the sofa, where she stitched up his face with her sewing needle. When all was quiet,

Kya snatched her bonnet from the floor and ran fast through the woods and threw it with all her might into the saw grass.

Now she looked into the eyes of the stranger standing on her porch and said, "Jodie."

He smiled, the scar going crooked, and replied, "Kya, I hoped you'd be here." They stared, each searching for the other in older eyes. Jodie couldn't know he had been with her all these years, that scores of times he had shown her the way through the marsh, taught her over and over about herons and fireflies. More than anyone else, she had wanted to see Jodie or Ma again. Her heart had erased the scar and all the pain in that package. No wonder her mind buried the scene; no wonder Ma had left. Hit by a poker across the chest. Kya saw those rubbed-out stains on the flowered sundress as blood again.

He wanted to hug her, fold her into his arms, but as he moved toward her, she hung her head low to the side in profound shyness and backed up. So he simply stepped onto the porch.

"Come in," she said, and led him into the small living room chockfull with her specimens.

"Oh," he said. "Yes, then. I saw your book, Kya. I didn't know for sure if it was you, but yes, now I can see it was. It's amazing." He walked around looking at her collections, also examining the room with its new furniture, glancing down the halls to the bedrooms. Not wanting to snoop, but taking it all in.

"Do you want coffee, tea?" She didn't know if he'd come for a visit or to stay. What did he want after all these years?

"Coffee would be great. Thank you."

In the kitchen, he recognized the old woodstove next to the new gas range and refrigerator. He ran his hand over the old kitchen table, which she had kept as it was. With all its peeling-paint history. She poured the coffee in mugs, and they sat.

"You're a soldier, then."

"Two tours in 'Nam. I'm staying in the army for a few more months. They've been good to me. Paid for my college degree—mechanical engineering, Georgia Tech. Least I can do is stay in a while."

Georgia wasn't all that far away—he could have visited sooner. But he was here now.

"You all left," she said. "Pa stayed a while after you, but then he went, too. I don't know where, don't know if he's alive or not."

"You've been here by yourself since then?"

"Yes."

"Kya, I shouldn't have left you with that monster. I've ached, felt terrible about it for years. I was a coward, a stupid coward. These damned medals don't mean a thing." He swiped at his chest. "I left you, a little girl, alone to survive in a swamp with a madman. I don't expect you to forgive me, ever."

"Jodie, it's okay. You were just a kid yourself. What could you do?"

"I could've come back when I was older. At first it was day-to-day survival on the back streets of Atlanta." He sneered. "I left here with seventy-five cents in my pocket. Stole it from the money Pa left in the kitchen; took it knowing it would leave you short. I scraped by on odd jobs till the army took me in. After training, it was straight to war. When I got home, so much time had passed, I figured you were long gone, run away yourself. That's the reason I didn't write; I think I signed up to go back as a kind of self-punishment. What I deserved for leaving you. Then after I graduated from Tech, a couple of months ago, I saw your book in a shop. Catherine Danielle Clark. My heart just broke and leapt for joy all at once. I had to find you—figured I'd start here and track you down."

"Well, here we are then." She smiled for the first time. His eyes were the same as they had been. Faces change with life's toll, but eyes remain a window to what was, and she could see him there. "Jodie, I'm so sorry you worried about leaving me. Not once did I blame you. We were the victims, not the guilty."

He smiled. "Thank you, Kya." Tears welled, and they both looked away.

She hesitated, then said, "This may be hard to believe, but for a while Pa was good to me. He drank less, taught me to fish, and we went out in the boat a lot, all over the marsh. But then, of course, he went back to drinking and left me to fend for myself."

Jodie nodded. "Yeah, I saw that side of him a few times, but he always went back to the bottle. He told me once it had something to do with the war. I've been to war myself and seen things that could drive a man to drink. But he shouldn't have taken it out on his wife, his own kids."

"What about Ma, the others?" she asked. "Did you ever hear from them, know where they went?"

"I don't know a thing about Murph, Mandy, or Missy. I wouldn't know them if I passed them in the street. By now I 'spose they've scattered with the wind. But Ma, well, Kya, that's another reason I wanted to find you. There is some news of her."

"Some news? What? Tell me." Chills flowed from Kya's arms to her fingertips.

"Kya, it's not good. I only found out last week. Ma died two years ago."

She bent at the waist, holding her face in her hands. Soft groans came from her throat. Jodie tried to hold her, but she moved away from him.

Jodie continued. "Ma had a sister, Rosemary, who tried to track us down through the Red Cross when Ma died, but they couldn't find us. Then a couple of months ago they found me through the army and put me in touch with Rosemary."

In hoarse tones Kya mumbled, "Ma was alive until two years ago. I've been waiting all these years for her to walk down the lane." She stood and held on to the sink. "Why didn't she come back? Why didn't somebody tell me where she was? And now it's too late."

Jodie went to her, and even though she tried to turn away, he put his arms around her. "I'm sorry, Kya. Come sit down. I'll tell you what Rosemary said."

He waited for her, then said, "Ma was ill from a major breakdown when she left us and went to New Orleans—that's where she grew up. She was mentally and physically ill. I remember New Orleans a little bit. I guess I was five when we left. All I remember is a nice house, big windows overlooking a garden. But once we moved here, Pa wouldn't let any of us talk about New Orleans, our grandparents, or any of it. So it was all wiped away."

Kya nodded. "I never knew."

Jodie continued. "Rosemary said their parents had been against Ma's marriage to Pa from the start, but Ma went off to North Carolina with her husband, not a penny to their names. Eventually Ma began writing to Rosemary and told her of her circumstances—living in a swamp shack with a drunk man who beat her and her children. Then one day, years later, Ma showed up. She had on those fake alligator heels that she cherished. Hadn't bathed or combed her hair in days.

"For months Ma was mute, didn't speak one word. She stayed in her old room in her parents' home, barely eating. Of course, they had doctors come out, but no one could help her. Ma's father contacted the sheriff in Barkley Cove to ask if Ma's children were all right, but his office said they didn't even try to keep track of the marsh people."

Kya sniffed now and then.

"Finally, almost a year later, Ma became hysterical and told Rosemary she remembered she had left her children. Rosemary helped her write a letter to Pa asking if she could come get us and bring us to live with her in New Orleans. He wrote back that if she returned or contacted any of us, he would beat us unrecognizable. She knew he was capable of such a thing."

The letter in the blue envelope. Ma had asked for her, for all of them. Ma had wanted to see her. But the outcome of the letter had been vastly different. The words had enraged Pa and sent him back to drinking, and then Kya had lost him as well. She didn't mention to Jodie that she still kept the letter's ashes in a little jar.

"Rosemary said Ma never made friends, never dined with the family or interacted with anybody. She allowed herself no life, no pleasure. After a while, she started talking more, and all she talked about was her children. Rosemary said Ma loved us all her life but was frozen in some horrible place of believing that we'd be harmed if she returned and abandoned if she didn't. She didn't leave us to have a fling; she'd been driven to madness and barely knew she'd left."

Kya asked, "How did she die?"

"She had leukemia. Rosemary said it was possibly treatable, but she refused all medication. She just became weaker and weaker, and slipped away two years ago. Rosemary said she died much as she had lived. In darkness, in silence."

Jodie and Kya sat still. Kya thought of the poem by Galway Kinnell that Ma had underlined in her book:

> I have to say I am relieved it is over:
> At the end I could feel only pity
> For that urge toward more life.
> . . . Goodbye.

Jodie stood. "Come with me, Kya, I want to show you something." He led her outside to his pickup and they climbed into the back.

Carefully, he removed a tarp and opened a large cardboard box, and one by one, pulled out and unwrapped oil paintings. He stood them up around the bed of the truck. One was of three young girls—Kya and her sisters—squatting by the lagoon, watching dragonflies. Another of Jodie and their brother holding up a string of fish.

"I brought them in case you were still here. Rosemary sent these to me. She said that for years, day and night, Ma painted us."

One painting showed all five children as if they were watching the artist. Kya stared into the eyes of her sisters and brothers, looking back at her.

In a whisper, she asked, "Who's who?"

"What?"

"There were never any photographs. I don't know them. Who's who?"

"Oh." He couldn't breathe, then finally said, "Well, this is Missy, the oldest. Then Murph. Mandy. Of course, this little cutie is me. And that's you."

He gave her time, then said, "Look at this one."

Before him was an astonishingly colorful oil of two children squatting in swirls of green grass and wild flowers. The girl was only a toddler, perhaps three years old, her straight black hair falling over her shoulders. The boy, a bit older, with golden curls, pointed to a monarch butterfly, its black-and-yellow wings spread across a daisy. His hand was on the girl's arm.

"I think that's Tate Walker," Jodie said. "And you."

"I think you're right. It looks like him. Why would Ma paint Tate?"

"He used to come around quite a bit, fish with me. He was always showing you insects and stuff."

"Why don't I remember that?"

"You were very young. One afternoon Tate boated into our lagoon, where Pa was pulling on his poke, really drunk. You were wading and Pa was supposed to be watching you. Suddenly, for no reason at all, Pa grabbed you by your arms and shook you so hard your head was thrown back. Then he dropped you in the mud and started laughing. Tate jumped out of the boat and ran up to you. He was only seven or eight years old, but he shouted at Pa. Of course, Pa smacked him and screamed at him to get off his land, never come back or he'd shoot him. By this time we'd all run down to see what was happening. Even with Pa ranting and raving, Tate picked you up and handed you to Ma. He made sure you were all right before he left. We still went fishing some after that, but he never came back to our place again."

Not until he led me home that first time I took the boat into the marsh, Kya thought. She looked at the painting—so pastel, so peaceful. Somehow Ma's mind had pulled beauty from lunacy. Anyone looking at these portraits would think they portrayed the happiest of families, living on a seashore, playing in sunshine.

Jodie and Kya sat on the rim of the truck bed, still looking quietly at the paintings.

He continued. "Ma was isolated and alone. Under those circumstances people behave differently."

Kya made a soft groan. "Please don't talk to me about isolation. No one has to tell me how it changes a person. I have lived it. I am isolation," Kya whispered with a slight edge. "I forgive Ma for leaving. But I don't understand why she didn't come back—why she abandoned me. You probably don't remember, but after she walked away, you told me that a she-fox will sometimes leave her kits if she's starving or under some other extreme stress. The kits die—as they probably would have anyway—but the vixen lives to breed again when conditions are better, when she can raise a new litter to maturity.

"I've read a lot about this since. In nature—out yonder where the crawdads sing—these ruthless-seeming behaviors actually increase the mother's number of young over her lifetime, and thus her genes for abandoning offspring in times of stress are passed on to the next generation. And on and on. It happens in humans, too. Some behaviors that seem harsh to us now ensured the survival of early man in whatever swamp he was in at the time. Without them, we wouldn't be here. We still store those instincts in our genes, and they express themselves when certain circumstances prevail. Some parts of us will always be what we were, what we had to be to survive—way back yonder.

"Maybe some primitive urge—some ancient genes, not appropriate anymore—drove Ma to leave us because of the stress, the horror and real danger of living with Pa. That doesn't make it right; she *should have chosen to stay.* But knowing that these tendencies are in our biological blueprints might help one forgive even a failed mother. That may explain her leaving, but I still don't see why she didn't come back. Why she didn't even write to me. She could've written letter after letter, year after year, until one finally got to me."

"I guess some things can't be explained, only forgiven or not. I don't know the answer. Maybe there isn't one. I'm sorry to bring you this bad news."

"I've had no family, no news of family for most of my life. Now within a few minutes I've found a brother and lost my mother."

"I'm so sorry, Kya."

"Don't be. Actually, I lost Ma years ago, and now you're back, Jodie. I can't tell you how much I wanted to see you again. This is one of the happiest and yet saddest days of my life." She touched his arm with her fingers, and he already knew her enough to know this was rare.

They walked back into the shack, and he looked around at the new things, the freshly painted walls, the handcrafted kitchen cabinets.

"How'd you manage, Kya? Before your book, how'd you get money, food?"

"Oh, that's a long boring story. Mostly I sold mussels, oysters, and smoked fish to Jumpin'."

Jodie threw his head back and laughed out loud. "Jumpin'! I haven't thought about him for years. Is he still around?"

Kya didn't laugh. "Jumpin' has been my best friend, for years my only friend. My only family unless you count herring gulls."

Jodie turned serious. "Didn't you have friends in school?"

"I only went to school one day in my life," she chuckled. "The kids laughed at me, so I never went back. Spent weeks outsmarting the truant officers. Which, after all the things you'd taught me, wasn't very hard."

He looked astonished. "How did you learn to read? To write your book?"

"Actually, it was Tate Walker who taught me to read."

"You ever see him anymore?"

"Now and then." She stood, faced the stove. "More coffee?"

Jodie felt the lonely life hanging in her kitchen. It was there in the tiny supply of onions in the vegetable basket, the single plate drying in the rack, the cornbread wrapped carefully in a tea towel, the way an old widow might do it.

"I've had plenty, thanks. But what about a ride around the marsh?" he asked.

"Of course. You won't believe it, I have a new motor but still use that same old boat."

The sun had broken up the clouds and shone bright and warm for a winter day. As she steered them through narrow channels and glassy estuaries, he exclaimed at a remembered snag, the same as it had been, and a beaver lodge still piled in the exact spot. They laughed when they came to the lagoon where Ma, Kya, and their sisters had grounded the boat in mud.

Back at the shack, she put together a picnic, which they ate on the beach with the gulls.

"I was so young when they all left," she said. "Tell me about the others." So he told her stories of their older brother, Murph, who carried her around on his shoulders through the woods.

"You used to laugh the whole time. He would jog and turn circles with you way up there. And one time you laughed so hard you wet your pants right on his neck."

"Oh no! I didn't." Kya leaned back, laughing.

"Yes, you did. He squealed some, but he kept on going, ran right into the lagoon until he was underwater, and you still riding his shoulders. We were all watching—Ma, Missy, Mandy, and me—and laughed till we cried. Ma had to sit right down on the ground, she was laughing so hard."

Her mind invented pictures to go with the stories. Family scraps and shreds Kya never thought she'd have.

Jodie continued. "It was Missy who started feeding the gulls."

"What? Really! I thought I started it on my own, after everybody left."

"No, she fed the gulls every day she could get away with it. She gave them all names. She called one Big Red, I remember that. You know, after that red spot on their bills."

"It's not the same bird, of course—I've gone through a few generations of Big Reds myself. But there, the one on the left, that's Big Red today." She tried to connect with the sister who had given her the gulls, but all she could see was the face in the painting. Which was more than she'd had before.

The red spot on a herring gull's bill, Kya knew, was more than decoration. Only when the chicks pecked at the spot with their bills would the parent release the captured food for them. If the red spot was obscured so that the chicks didn't tap it, the parent wouldn't feed them and they would die. Even in nature, parenthood is a thinner line than one might think.

They sat for a moment, then Kya said, "I just don't remember much about it at all."

"You're lucky, then. Just keep it that way."

They sat there like that, quietly. Not remembering.

She cooked a southern supper as Ma would have: black-eyed peas with red onions, fried ham, cornbread with cracklin', butter beans cooked in butter and milk. Blackberry cobbler with hard cream with some bourbon Jodie brought. As they ate, he told her he would like to stay a few days, if that was okay, and she said he was welcome as long as he liked.

"This is your land now, Kya. You earned it. I'm stationed at Fort Benning for a while yet, so I can't stay long. After that I'll probably get a job in Atlanta so we can stay in touch; I'd like to see you as often as I can get up here. Knowing you're okay is all I ever wanted in my life."

"I'd like that, Jodie. Please come whenever you can."

The next evening, as they sat on the beach, wave tips tickling their bare toes, Kya chatted in unusual fashion, and Tate seemed to be in every paragraph. There was the time he showed her the way home when she, as a little girl, was lost in the marsh. Or the first poem Tate read to her. She talked about the feather game and how he taught her to read, how he was a scientist at the lab now. He was her first love, but he had dropped her when he went to college, left her waiting on the lagoon shore. So it had ended.

"How long ago was that?" Jodie asked.

"About seven years, I guess. When he first went to Chapel Hill."

"Did you ever see him again?"

"He came back to apologize; said he still loved me. He was the one who suggested I publish reference books. It's nice to see him now and then in the marsh, but I'd never get involved again. He can't be trusted."

"Kya, that was seven years ago. He was just a boy, first time away from home, hundreds of pretty girls around. If he came back and apologized and says he loves you, maybe you should cut him a little slack."

"Most men go from one female to the next. The unworthy ones strut about, pulling you in with falsehoods. Which is probably why Ma fell for a man like Pa. Tate wasn't the only guy who left me. Chase Andrews even talked to me about marriage, but he married someone else. Didn't even tell me; I read it in the paper."

"I'm so sorry. I am, but, Kya, it's not just guys who are unfaithful. I've been duped, dropped, run over a few times myself. Let's face it, a lot of times love doesn't work out. Yet even when it fails, it connects you to others and, in the end, that is all you have, *the connections*. Look at us; you and I have each other now, and just think, if I have kids and you have kids, well, that's a whole new string of connections. And on it goes. Kya, if you love Tate, take a chance."

Kya thought of Ma's painting of Tate and herself as children, their heads close together, surrounded by pastel flowers and butterflies. Maybe a message from Ma after all.

On the third morning of Jodie's visit, they unpacked Ma's paintings—all but one, which Jodie kept—and hung some on the walls. The shack took on a different light, as though more windows had opened up. She stood back and stared at them—a miracle to have some of Ma's paintings back on the walls. Pulled from the fire.

Then Kya walked Jodie out to his pickup and gave him a bag lunch she'd made for his trip. They both looked through the trees, down the lane, everywhere except into each other's eyes.

Finally he said, "I better get going, but here's my address and phone number," as he held out a scrap of notepaper. She stopped breathing, and with her left hand held herself steady on the truck as she took the paper with her right. Such a simple thing: the address of a brother on a slip of paper. Such an astonishing thing: a family she could find. A number she could call and he would answer. She choked on her own throat as he pulled her to him, and finally, after a lifetime, she sagged against him and wept.

"I never thought I'd see you again. I thought you were gone forever."

"I'll always be here, I promise. Whenever I move, I'll send my new address. If you ever need me, you write or call, you hear?"

"I will. And come back for a visit whenever you can."

"Kya, go find Tate. He's a good man."

He waved from the truck window all the way down the lane, as she watched, crying and laughing all at once. And when he turned onto the track, she could see his red pickup through the holes of the forest where a white scarf had once trailed away, his long arm waving until he was gone.

34.

Search the Shack

1969

Well, again she's not here," Joe said, knocking on the frame of Kya's screen door. Ed stood on the brick-'n'-board steps, cupping his hands on the mesh to see inside. Enormous limbs of the oak, hung with long strands of Spanish moss, cast shadows on the weathered boards and pointy roof of the shack. Only gray patches of sky blinked through the late November morning.

"Of course she's not here. It doesn't matter; we have a search warrant. Just go on in, bet it isn't locked."

Joe opened the door, calling out, "Anybody home? Sheriff here." Inside, they stared at the shelves of her menagerie.

"Ed, lookit all this stuff. It keeps goin' in the next room yonder, and on down the hall. Looks like she's a bit off her rocker. Crazy as a three-eyed rat."

"Maybe, but apparently she's quite an expert on the marsh. You know she published those books. Let's get busy. Okay, here're the things to look for." The sheriff read out loud from a short list. "Articles of red-wool clothing that might match the red fibers found on Chase's jacket. A diary, calendar, or notes, something that might mention places and times of her whereabouts; the shell necklace; or stubs from those night buses. And let's not mess up her stuff. No reason to do that. We can look under, around everything; don't need to ruin any of this."

"Yeah, I hear ya. Almost like a shrine in here. Half a' me's impressed, the other half's got the heebie-jeebies."

"It's going to be tedious, that's for sure," the sheriff said as he carefully looked behind a row of bird nests. "I'll start back in her bedroom."

The men worked silently, pushing clothes around in drawers, poking in closet corners, shifting jars of snakeskins and sharks' teeth in search of evidence.

After ten minutes, Joe called, "Come look at this."

As Ed entered the porch, Joe said, "Did ya know that female birds only got one ovary?"

"What're ya talking about?"

"See. These drawings and notes show that female birds only got one ovary."

"Dang it, Joe. We're not here for a biology lesson. Get back to work."

"Wait a second. Look here. This is a male peacock feather, and the note says that over eons of time, the males' feathers got larger and larger to attract females, till the point the males can barely lift off the ground. Can't hardly fly anymore."

"Are you finished? We have a job to do."

"Well, it's very interesting."

Ed walked from the room. "Get to work, man."

Ten minutes later, Joe called out again. As Ed walked out of the small bedroom, toward the sitting room, he said, "Let me guess. You found a stuffed mouse with three eyes."

There was no reply, but when Ed walked into the room, Joe held up a red wool hat.

"Where'd you find that?"

"Right here, hangin' on this row of hooks with these coats, other hats, and stuff."

"In the open like that?"

"Right here like I said."

From his pocket, Ed pulled out the plastic bag containing the red fibers taken from Chase's denim jacket the night he died and held it against the red hat.

"They look exactly the same. Same color, same size and thickness," Joe said as both men studied the hat and sample.

"They do. Both of them have fuzzy beige wool mixed in with the red."

"Man, this could be it."

"We'll have to send the hat to the lab, of course. But if these fibers match, we'll bring her in for questioning. Bag and label the hat."

After four hours of searching, the men met in the kitchen.

Stretching his back, Ed said, "I reckon if there's anything else, we would've found it by now. We can always come back. Call it a day."

Maneuvering the ruts back to town, Joe said, "Seems like if she's guilty of this thing, she woulda hidden the red cap. Not just hung it in the open like that."

"She probably had no idea fibers would fall off the hat onto his jacket. Or that the lab could identify them. She just wouldn't know something like that."

"Well, she might not a' known that, but I bet she knows a bunch. Those male peacocks struttin' around, competin' so much for sex, they can't hardly fly. I ain't sure what it all means, but it adds up to something."

35.

The Compass

1969

One July afternoon in 1969, more than seven months after Jodie's visit, *The Eastern Seacoast Birds* by Catherine Danielle Clark—her second book, a volume of stark detail and beauty—appeared in her mailbox. She ran her fingers over the striking jacket—her painting of a herring gull. Smiling, she said, "Hey, Big Red, you made it to the cover."

Carrying the new book, Kya walked silently to the shady oak clearing near her shack, searching for mushrooms. The moist duff felt cool on her feet as she neared a cluster of intensely yellow toadstools. Midstride, she halted. There, sitting on the old feather stump, was a small milk carton, red and white, just like the one from so long ago. Unexpectedly, she laughed out loud.

Inside the carton, wrapped in tissue paper, was an old army-issue compass in a brass case, tarnished green-gray with age. She breathed in at the sight of it. She had never needed a compass because the directions seemed obvious to her. But on cloudy days, when the sun was elusive, the compass would guide her.

A folded note read: *Dearest Kya, This compass was my grandpa's from the First World War. He gave it to me when I was little, but I've never used it, and I thought maybe you would get the best out of it. Love, Tate. P.S. I'm glad you can read this note!*

Kya read the words *Dearest* and *Love* again. Tate. The golden-haired boy in the boat, guiding her home before a storm, gifting her feathers on a weathered stump, teaching her to read; the tender teenager steering her through her first cycle as a woman and arousing her first sexual desires as a female; the young scientist encouraging her to publish her books.

Despite gifting him the shell book, she had continued to hide in the undergrowth when she saw him in the marsh, rowing away unseen. The dishonest signals of fireflies, all she knew of love.

Even Jodie had said she should give Tate another chance. But every time she thought of him or saw him, her heart jumped from the old love to the pain of abandonment. She wished it would settle on one side or the other.

Several mornings later, she slipped through the estuaries in an early fog, the compass tucked in her knapsack, though she would not likely need it. She planned to search for rare wild flowers on a wooded tongue of sand that jutted into the sea, but part of her scanned the waterways for Tate's boat.

The fog turned stubborn and lingered, twisting its tendrils around tree snags and low-lying limbs. The air was still; even the birds were quiet as she eased forward through the channel. Nearby, a *clonk, clonk* sounded as a slow-moving oar tapped a gunwale, and then a boat emerged ghoul-like from the haze.

Colors, which had been muted by the dimness, formed into shapes as they moved into the light. Golden hair beneath a red cap. As if coming in from a dream, Tate stood in the stern of his old fishing boat poling through the channel. Kya cut her engine and rowed backward into a thicket to watch him pass. Always backward to watch him pass.

At sundown, calmer, heart back in place, Kya stood on the beach, and recited:

"Sunsets are never simple.
Twilight is refracted and reflected
But never true.
Eventide is a disguise
Covering tracks,
Covering lies.

"We don't care
That dusk deceives.
We see brilliant colors,
And never learn
The sun has dropped
Beneath the earth
By the time we see the burn.

"Sunsets are in disguise,
Covering truths, covering lies.

"A.H."

36.

To Trap a Fox

1969

Joe walked through the opened door of the sheriff's office. "Okay, got the report."

"Let's have a look."

Both men scanned quickly to the last page. Ed said, "That's it. A perfect match. Fibers from her hat were on Chase's jacket as he lay dead." The sheriff slapped the report across his wrist, then continued. "Let's review what we have here. Number one, the shrimper will testify that he saw Miss Clark boating toward the fire tower just before Chase fell to his death. His colleague will back him up. Two, Patti Love said Miss Clark made the shell necklace for Chase, and it disappeared the night he died. Three, fibers from her hat were on his jacket. Four, motive: the woman wronged. And an alibi we can refute. That should do it."

"A better motive might help," Joe said. "Being jilted doesn't seem like enough."

"It's not like we're finished with the investigation, but we have enough to bring her in for questioning. Probably enough to charge her. We'll see how it goes once we get her here."

"Well, that's the problem, isn't it? How? She's outrun everybody for years. Truant officers, census takers, *you name it,* she's outwit 'em all. Includin' us. We go out there chasin' her through swamp grass, we'll make fools of ourselves."

"I'm not afraid of that. Just because nobody else could catch her doesn't mean we can't. But that wouldn't be the smartest way of doing it. I say we set a trap."

"Oh yeah. Well," the deputy said, "I know a thing or two 'bout trappin'. And when you go to trap a fox, it's usually the trap that gets foxed. It's not like we have surprise on our side. We been out there knockin' on her door enough to scare off a brown bear. What about the hounds? That'd be a sure thing."

The sheriff was silent a few seconds. "I don't know. Maybe I'm getting old and soft at the grand ol' age of fifty-one. But running down a woman with hounds for questioning doesn't seem right. It's fine for escaped convicts, people already convicted of some crime. But, like everybody else, she's innocent until proven guilty, and I can't see setting hounds on a female suspect. Maybe as a last resort, but not yet."

"Okay. What kinda trap?"

"That's what we gotta figure out."

On December 15, as Ed and Joe discussed options of how to bring Kya in, someone knocked on the door. The large form of a man loomed behind the frosted glass.

"Come on in," the sheriff called.

As the man stepped inside, Ed said, "Well, hello, Rodney. What can we do for you?"

Rodney Horn, a retired mechanic, spent most of his days fishing with his pal Denny Smith. The villagers knew him as quiet and settled, always in bib overalls. Never missed church, but wore his overalls there as well, with a nice fresh shirt ironed and starched stiff as a plank by his wife, Elsie.

Rodney took off his felt hat and held it in front of his belly. Ed offered him a chair, but Rodney shook his head. "This won't take long," he said. "Just something might be rel'vant to the Chase Andrews thing."

"What ya got?" Joe asked.

"Well, it was a while back, now. Me and Denny were out fishin' on August 30, this year, and we seen something out at Cypress Cove. Think it might be of interest to ya."

"Go ahead," the sheriff said. "But please sit down, Rodney. We'd all feel more comfortable if you sat."

Rodney took the chair offered and, for the next five minutes, told them his story. After he left, Ed and Joe looked at each other.

Joe said, "Well, now we've got motive."

"Let's get her in here."

37.

Gray Sharks

1969

Just days before Christmas and earlier in the morning than usual, Kya motored slowly and quietly toward Jumpin's. Ever since the sheriff or his deputy had been sneaking out to her place, trying to catch her at home—failed efforts she'd observed from the palmettos—she'd bought her gas and supplies before first light, when only fishermen were about. Now, low clouds scudded just above a sloshing sea, and to the east, a squall—twisted tightly like a whip—threatened from the horizon. She'd have to finish at Jumpin's quickly and get home before it hit. From a quarter of a mile out, she saw his wharf billowed in with fog. She slowed even more and looked around for other boats in the soggy quiet.

Finally, at about forty yards out, she could see Jumpin's form in the old chair leaning against the wall. She waved. He did not. He did not stand. He shook his head slightly, just a whisper. She let go of the throttle.

She waved again. Jumpin' stared at her, but did not move.

Jerking the stick, she turned abruptly back toward the sea. But coming in from the fog was a large boat, the sheriff at the helm. Another couple of boats, flanking. And just behind them, the squall.

Gunning her engine, she threaded the needle between the oncoming rigs, her boat banging whitecaps as she raced for the open sea. She wanted to cut back toward the marsh, but the sheriff was too close; he'd catch her before she got there.

The sea no longer swelled in symmetrical waves but tossed in confusion. The water grew meaner as the edge of the storm engulfed her. In seconds it released a torrent. She was soaked through, long strands of hair stringing across her face. She turned into the wind to keep from capsizing, but the sea pushed over the bow.

Knowing their boats were faster, she hunched forward into the ragged wind. Maybe she could lose them in this soup or dive into the sea and make a swim for it. Her mind raced through the details of jumping in, which seemed her best chance. This close to shore, there'd be a backwash or rip, which would zip her along underwater, much faster than they'd think she could swim. Popping up to breathe now and then, she could get to land and sneak out on a brushy shore.

Behind her their motors raced louder than the storm. Getting closer. How could she simply stop? She'd never given up. She had to jump now. But suddenly, like gray sharks they massed around her, pulling close. One of the boats whipped in front of her, and she rammed its side. Thrown back against the outboard, her neck jerked. The sheriff reached out and grabbed her gunwale, all of them wallowing in the churning wakes. Two men swung into her boat as the deputy said, "Miss Catherine Clark, you're under arrest for the murder of Mr. Chase Andrews. Ya have the right to remain silent . . ."

She didn't hear the rest of it. No one hears the rest of it.

38.

Sunday Justice

1970

Kya's eyes blinked shut against sharp light that poured from overhead lamps and windows as tall as the ceiling. For two months she'd lived in dimness, and now, opening her eyes again, caught a soft edge of the marsh outside. Rounded oaks sheltering shrub-sized ferns and winter holly. She tried to hold the vital green a second longer but was led by firm hands toward a long table and chairs where her attorney, Tom Milton, sat. Her wrists were cuffed in front, forcing her hands into an awkward prayer pose. Dressed in black slacks and a plain white blouse, with a single braid falling between her shoulder blades, she didn't turn her head to look at the spectators. Still, she felt the heat and rustle of people knotted into the courtroom for her murder trial. Could sense people's shoulders and heads waggling to catch a glimpse of her. To see her in handcuffs. A smell of sweat, old smoke, and cheap perfume increased her nausea. Coughing noises ceased but the hubbub rose as she neared her seat—all distant sounds to her, because mostly she heard the sickness of her own jagged breathing. She stared at the floorboards—highly polished heart pine—while the cuffs were removed, and then sat heavy into the chair. It was 9:30 A.M. on February 25, 1970.

Tom leaned close to her and whispered that everything would be all right. She said nothing but searched his eyes for sincerity, anything to hang on. Not that she believed him, but for the first time ever, she had to put herself in the charge of another. Rather tall for seventy-one years, he wore his thick white hair and frumpy linen suits with the accidental if clichéd grace of a country statesman. He moved gently and spoke quietly behind a pleasant smile that lived on his face.

Judge Sims had appointed a young attorney for Miss Clark, since she had taken no action to do so herself, but when Tom Milton heard of this, he came out of retirement and requested to represent her pro bono. Like everyone else, he had heard stories about the Marsh Girl, and over the years had seen her occasionally, either drifting sleekly through waterways as part of the current or scurrying from the grocery like a coon from a rubbish bin.

When he first visited Kya in jail two months ago, he'd been led into a small dark room, where she sat at a table. She had not looked up at him. Tom had introduced himself, saying he would represent her, but she didn't speak or raise her eyes. He had an overpowering urge to reach out and pat her hand, but something—maybe her upright posture or the way she stared, vacant-eyed—shielded her from touch. Moving his head at different angles—trying to capture her eyes—he explained the court procedures, what she should expect, and then asked her some questions. But she never answered, never moved, and never looked at him. As they led her from the room, she turned her head and glimpsed through a small window where she could see the sky. Seabirds shrieked over the town harbor, and Kya seemed to be watching their songs.

On his next visit Tom reached into a brown paper bag and slid a glossy coffee-table book toward her. Titled *The Rarest Shells of the World,* it opened to life-sized oil paintings of shells from the most distant shores on Earth. Her mouth partly open, she turned slowly through the pages, nodding at particular specimens. He gave her time. Then, once again he spoke to her, and this time she looked into his eyes. With easy patience, he explained the court procedures and even drew a picture of the courtroom, showing the jury box, the judge's bench, where the attorneys and she would sit. Then he added stick figures of the bailiff, the judge, and the recorder and explained their roles.

As on the first meeting, he tried to explain the evidence against her and to ask about her whereabouts on the night Chase died, but she pulled back into her shell at any mention of details. Later, when he stood to leave, she slid the book back across the table, but he said, "No, I brought it for you. It's yours."

She bit her lips and blinked.

And now in the courtroom for the first time, he tried to distract her from the bustle behind them by pointing out the features of the courtroom in the drawing. But diversion was useless. By 9:45 A.M. the gallery overflowed with villagers filling every pew and buzzed with high-pitched comments about the evidence, the death penalty. A small balcony at the rear seated twenty more, and though not marked, everybody understood colored people were restricted to the balcony. Today, it was filled mostly with whites, with only a few blacks, this being a white case through and through. Sectioned off near the front sat a few journalists from the *Atlanta Constitution* and the *Raleigh Herald.* People who couldn't find seats bunched along the back wall and along the sides by the tall windows. Fidgeting, muttering, gossiping. The Marsh Girl put up for murder; it didn't get any better than this. Sunday Justice, the courthouse cat—his back black, his face white with a black mask around green eyes—stretched out in a puddle of sunlight in one of the deep windowsills. A courthouse fixture for years, he cleared the basement of rats and the courtroom of mice, earning his place.

Because Barkley Cove was the first village settled in this torn and marshy stretch of the North Carolina coast, the Crown had declared it the county seat and built the original courthouse in 1754. Later, even though other towns such as Sea Oaks became more populated and developed, Barkley Cove remained the official hub for county government.

Lightning struck the original courthouse in 1912, burning much of the wooden structure to ashes. Rebuilt the next year on the same square at the end of Main Street, it was a brick two-story with twelve-foot windows trimmed in granite. By the 1960s, wild grasses and palmettos, and even a few cattails, had moved in from the marsh and taken over the once-groomed grounds. A lily-choked lagoon flooded in spring and, over the years, had eaten part of the sidewalk.

In contrast, the courtroom itself, designed to replicate the original, was imposing. The elevated judge's bench, made of dark mahogany with a colorful inlay of the state's seal, stood under multiple flags, including the Confederate. The half wall of the jury box, also of mahogany, was trimmed in red cedar, and the windows that lined one side of the room framed the sea.

As the officials entered the courtroom, Tom pointed to the stick figures in his drawing and explained who they were. "That's the bailiff, Hank Jones," he said as a lanky man of sixty with a hairline that receded past his ears, making his head almost exactly half bald and half not, walked to the front of the room. He wore a gray uniform and a wide belt, hung with a radio, a flashlight, an impressive set of keys, and a holstered Colt six-shooter.

Mr. Jones called out to the crowd. "Sorry, folks, but y'all know the fire marshal's rules. If ya don't have a seat, ya gotta leave."

"That's Miss Henrietta Jones, the bailiff's daughter, the court recorder," Tom explained as a young woman, as tall and thin as her father, walked in quietly and sat at a desk near the judge's bench. Already seated, the prosecuting attorney, Mr. Eric Chastain, unpacked note pads from his briefcase. Eric, a broad-chested, redheaded man of nearly six feet, dressed in blue suits and wide bright ties purchased at Sears, Roebuck in Asheville.

Bailiff Jones called, "All rise. This court is in session. The Honorable Judge Harold Sims presiding." Sudden silence fell. The chamber door opened and Judge Sims entered and nodded for everyone to sit, and asked both the prosecuting and defense attorneys to approach the bench. A large-boned man with a round face and bold white sideburns, he lived in Sea Oaks but had officiated over Barkley Cove cases for nine years. He was generally considered to be a no-nonsense, levelheaded, and fair arbitrator. His voice boomed across the room.

"Mr. Milton, your motion to relocate this trial to another county on the grounds that Miss Clark cannot get a fair trial due to prejudices against her in this community is denied. I accept that she has lived in unusual circumstances and been subjected to some prejudice, but I see no evidence that she has endured more prejudices than many people on trial in small towns all across this nation. And some large towns, for that matter. We will proceed here and now." Nods of approval eased through the room as the attorneys returned to their seats.

He continued. "Catherine Danielle Clark of Barkley County, North

Carolina, you are charged with murder in the first degree of Chase Lawrence Andrews, formerly of Barkley Cove. First-degree murder is defined as a premeditated act and, in such cases, the state is allowed to seek the death penalty. The prosecutor has announced that they will do so if you are found guilty." The room murmured.

Tom seemed to have inched slightly closer to Kya, and she didn't deny herself that comfort.

"We will begin the jury selection." Judge Sims turned toward the first two rows filled with potential jurors. As he read off a list of rules and conditions, Sunday Justice jumped down from the windowsill with a thud and, in one fluid motion, leapt onto the judge's bench. Absent-mindedly, Judge Sims stroked the cat's head as he continued.

"In capital cases, the State of North Carolina allows a juror to be excused if he or she does not believe in the death penalty. Please raise your hand if you will not or cannot impose the death sentence if a guilty verdict is delivered." No hands were raised.

"Death penalty" was all Kya heard.

The judge continued. "Another legitimate reason to be excused from the jury is if you have now or had in the past such a close relationship with either Miss Clark or Mr. Andrews that you cannot be objective in this case. Please let me know now if you feel this is true."

From the middle of the second row, Mrs. Sally Culpepper lifted her hand and stated her name. Her gray hair was pulled back severely in a tiny knot, and her hat, suit, and shoes bore the same dull brown.

"All right, Sally, tell me what's on your mind," the judge said.

"As you know, I was the truant officer for Barkley County for nearly twenty-five years. Miss Clark was one of my cases, and so I had some dealings with her, or tried to."

Kya couldn't see Mrs. Culpepper or anyone in the main gallery unless she turned around, which of course she'd never do. But she remembered clearly the last time Mrs. Culpepper sat in the car while the man in the fedora tried to chase her down. Kya had been as easy on the old man as she could, taking off noisily through brambles to give him a clue, then circling back and hiding in some bushes next to the car. But Fedora ran in the opposite direction toward the beach.

Crouching there, Kya shook a holly branch against the car door, and Mrs. Culpepper looked out the window directly into her eyes. She thought at the time that the truant lady smiled slightly. In any case, she made no attempt to give her away when Fedora returned, cussing up a streak, then driving down the road for good.

Now, Mrs. Culpepper said to the judge, "Well, since I had dealings with her, I don't know if that means I should be excused."

Judge Sims said, "Thank you, Sally. Some of you may have dealt with Miss Clark in the shops or in official ways, as in Mrs. Culpepper's case, the truant officer. The point is: can you listen to the testimony given here and decide whether she's guilty or innocent based on the evidence, not on past experience or feelings?"

"Yessir, I'm sure I can do that. Your Honor."

"Thank you, Sally, you can stay."

By 11:30 seven women and five men sat in the jury box. From there Kya could see them and stole glances at their faces. Most of them she recognized from the village, though she knew few of the names. Mrs. Culpepper sat squarely in the middle and gave slight comfort to Kya. But next to her sat Teresa White, blond wife of the Methodist preacher, who years ago had rushed from the shoe shop to whisk her daughter away from Kya as she stood on the curb after having lunch in the diner with Pa—that one and only time. Mrs. White, who had told her daughter that Kya was dirty, now sat on the jury.

Judge Sims called for a lunch recess until 1:00 P.M. The diner would bring over tuna fish, chicken salad, and ham sandwiches for the jurors, who would eat in the deliberation room. To be fair to the town's two eating establishments, the Dog-Gone Beer Hall would deliver hot dogs, chili, and shrimp po'boys on alternative days. They always brought something for the cat, too. Sunday Justice preferred the po'boys.

39.

Chase by Chance

1969

A fog was lifting from an August morning in 1969 as Kya motored to a remote peninsula the locals called Cypress Cove, where she had once seen rare toadstools. August was late for mushrooms, but Cypress Cove was cool and moist, so perhaps she could find the rare species again. More than a month had passed since Tate had left the compass for her on the feather stump, and though she'd seen him in the marsh, she hadn't ventured close enough to thank him for the gift. Neither had she used the compass, though it was tucked safely in one of the many pockets of her knapsack.

Moss-draped trees hugged the bank, and their low-hanging limbs formed a cave close to the shore through which she glided, searching the thickets for small orange mushrooms on slender stalks. And finally she saw them, bold and brilliant, clinging to the sides of an old stump, and, after beaching her boat, sat cross-legged in the cove, drawing them.

Suddenly she heard footsteps on the duff and then a voice: "Well, look who's here. My Marsh Girl." Whirling around, standing at the same time, she stood face-to-face with Chase.

"Hello, Kya," he said. She looked around. How had he gotten here? She'd heard no boat. He read her question. "I was fishing, saw ya pass, so landed over yonder on the other side."

"Please just go," she said, stuffing her pencils and pad in the knapsack.

But he put his hand on her arm. "C'mon, Kya. I'm sorry about how things turned out." He leaned in, wisps of breakfast bourbon on his breath.

"Don't touch me!"

"Hey, I said I'm sorry. Ya knew we couldn't get married. Ya never coulda lived near town. But I always cared about ya; I stayed by ya."

"Stayed by me! What does that mean? Leave me alone." Kya tucked the knapsack under her arm and walked toward the boat, but he grabbed her arm, holding hard.

"Kya, there'll never be anybody else like ya, never. And I know ya love me." She ripped her arm from his hands.

"You're wrong! I'm not sure I ever loved you. But you talked to *me* about marriage, remember? You talked about building a house for you and me. Instead I found out about *your* engagement *to somebody else* in the newspaper. Why'd you do that? Why, Chase!"

"C'mon, Kya. It was impossible. Ya must've known it wouldn't work. What's wrong with how things were? Let's go back to what we had." He reached for her shoulders and pulled her toward him.

"Let go of me!" She twisted, tried to yank away, but he gripped her with both hands, hurting her arms. He put his mouth on hers and kissed her. She threw her arms up, knocking his hands away. She pulled her head back, hissing, "Don't you dare."

"There's my lynx. Wilder than ever." Grabbing her shoulders, he clipped the back of her knees with one of his legs and pushed her to the ground. Her head bounced hard on the dirt. "I know ya want me," he said, leering.

"No, stop!" she screamed. Kneeling, he jammed his knee in her stomach, knocking the breath from her, as he unzipped his jeans and pulled them down.

She reared up, pushing him with both hands. Suddenly he slugged her face with his right fist. A sick popping sound rang out inside her head. Her neck snapped back, and her body was thrown backward onto the ground. Just like Pa hitting Ma. Her mind blanked for seconds against a pounding pain; then she twisted and turned, trying to squirm out from under him, but he was too strong. Holding both her arms over her head with one hand, he unzipped her shorts and ripped down her panties as she kicked at him. She screamed, but there was no one to hear. Kicking at the ground, she struggled to free herself, but he grabbed her waist and flipped her over onto her stomach. Shoved her throbbing face into the dirt, then reached under her belly and pulled her pelvis up to him as he knelt behind.

"I'm not lettin' ya go this time. Like it or not, you're mine."

Finding strength from somewhere primal, she pushed against the ground with her knees and arms and reared up, at the same time swinging her elbow back across his jaw. As his head swung to the side, she struck him wildly with her fists until he lost his balance and sprawled backward onto the dirt. Then, taking aim, she kicked him in his groin, square and solid.

He bent double and rolled on his side, holding his testicles and writhing. For good measure, she kicked him in the back, knowing exactly where his kidneys lay. Several times. Hard.

Pulling up her shorts, she grabbed the knapsack and ran to her boat. Snapping the starter rope, she looked back as he rose to his hands and knees, moaning. She cussed until the motor cranked. Expecting him to chase after her any second, she turned the tiller sharply and accelerated away from the bank just as he stood. Her hands shaking, she zipped up her pants and held her body tight with one arm. Wild-eyed, she looked out to sea and saw another fishing rig nearby, two men staring at her.

40.

Cypress Cove

1970

After lunch, Judge Sims asked the prosecutor, "Eric, are you ready to call your first witness?"

"We are, Your Honor." In former murder cases, Eric usually called the coroner first because his testimony introduced material evidence such as the murder weapon, time and place of death, and crime scene photographs, all of which made sharp impressions on the jurors. But in this case, there was no murder weapon, no fingerprints or footprints, so Eric intended to begin with motive.

"Your Honor, the People call Mr. Rodney Horn."

Everyone in court watched Rodney Horn step onto the witness stand and swear to tell the truth. Kya recognized his face even though she'd seen it for only a few seconds. She turned away. A retired mechanic, he was one of them, spending most of his days fishin', huntin', or playin' poker at the Swamp Guinea. Could hold his likker like a rain barrel. Today, as ever, he wore his denim bib overalls with a clean plaid shirt, starched so stiff the collar stood at attention. He held his fishing cap in his left hand as he was sworn in with the right, then sat down in the witness box, hat on his knee.

Eric stepped casually to the witness stand. "Good morning, Rodney."

"Mornin', Eric."

"Now, Rodney, I believe you were fishing with a friend near Cypress Cove on the morning of August 30, 1969? Is that correct?"

"That's 'xactly right. Me and Denny were out there fishin'. Been there since dawn."

"For the record, that would be Denny Smith?"

"Yeah, me 'n' Denny."

"All right. I would like you to tell the court what you saw that morning."

"Well, like I said, we been there since dawn, and it was near 'leven I reckon, and hadn't had a nibble for some time, so we was 'bout to pull our lines and head out, when we heard a commotion in the trees over on the point. In the woods."

"What kind of commotion?"

"Well, there was voices, kinda muffled at first, then louder. A man and a woman. But we couldn't see 'em, just heard them like they was fussin'."

"Then what happened?"

"Well, the woman started hollerin', so we motored over to get a better look. See if she was in trouble."

"And what did you see?"

"Well, by the time we got closer, we seen the woman was standin' next to the man and was kicking him right in the . . ." Rodney looked at the judge.

Judge Sims said, "Where did she kick him? You can say it."

"She kicked him right in the balls and he slumped over on his side, moanin' and groanin'. Then she kicked him again and again in his back. Mad as a mule chewin' bumblebees."

"Did you recognize the woman? Is she in the courtroom today?"

"Yeah, we knew 'er all right. It's that 'un there, the defendant. The one folks call the Marsh Girl."

Judge Sims leaned toward the witness. "Mr. Horn, the defendant's name is Miss Clark. Do not refer to her by any other name."

"A'right, then. It was Miss Clark we seen."

Eric continued. "Did you recognize the man she was kicking?"

"Well, we couldn't see him then 'cause he was writhin' and wigglin' around on the ground. But a few minutes later he stood up and it was Chase Andrews, the quarterback a few years back."

"And then what happened?"

"She came stumblin' out toward her boat, and well, she was part-way undressed. Her shorts 'round her ankles and her knickers 'round her knees. She was tryin' to pull up her shorts and run at the same time. The whole time shoutin' at him. She went to her boat, jumped in, and zoomed away, still pullin' at her pants. When she passed us by, she looked at us right in the eyes. That's how I know 'xactly who it was."

"You said she was shouting at him the entire time she was running toward her boat. Did you hear exactly what she said?"

"Yeah, we could hear her plain as day by then 'cause we were pretty close."

"Please tell the court what you heard her shout."

"She was screamin', 'Leave me alone, you bastard! You bother me again, I'll kill ya!'"

A loud murmur shot through the courtroom and didn't stop. Judge Sims banged his gavel. "That's it. That'll do it."

Eric said to his witness, "That will be all, thank you, Rodney. No further questions. Your witness."

Tom brushed past Eric and stepped to the witness stand.

"Now, Rodney, you testified that at first, when you heard those muffled but loud voices, you couldn't see what was going on between Miss Clark and Mr. Andrews. Is that correct?"

"That's right. We couldn't see 'em till we moved up some."

"And you said the woman, who you later identified as Miss Clark, was hollering as if she was in trouble. Correct?"

"Yeah."

"You didn't see any kissing or any sexual behavior between two consenting adults. You heard a woman shouting like she was being attacked, as if she was in trouble. Isn't that correct?"

"Yeah."

"So, isn't it possible that when Miss Clark kicked Mr. Andrews she was defending herself—a woman alone in the woods—against a very strong, athletic man? A former quarterback, who had attacked her?"

"Yeah, I reckon that's possible."

"No further questions."

"Redirect?"

"Yes, Your Honor," Eric said, standing at the prosecution table.

"So, Rodney, no matter whether certain behavior was consensual or not between the two of them, is it accurate to say that the defendant, Miss Clark, was extremely mad at the deceased, Chase Andrews?"

"Yeah, plenty mad."

"Mad enough to scream that if he bothered her again, she would kill him. Isn't that correct?"

"Yeah, that's how it was."

"No further questions, Your Honor."

41.

A Small Herd

1969

Kya's hands fumbled at the tiller as she looked back to see if Chase was following in his boat from Cypress Cove. She motored fast to her lagoon and limp-ran to the shack on swelling knees. In the kitchen, she dropped to the floor, crying, touching her swollen eye and spitting grit from her mouth. Then listened for sounds of him coming.

She had seen the shell necklace. He still wore it. How could that be?

"You're mine," he'd said. He'd be mad as hell that she kicked him and he'd come for her. He might come today. Or wait for night.

She couldn't tell anybody. Jumpin' would insist they call in the sheriff, but the law would never believe the Marsh Girl over Chase Andrews. She wasn't sure what the two fishermen had seen, but they'd never defend her. They'd say she had it coming because, before Chase left her, she'd been seen smooching with him for years, behaving unladylike. *Actin' the ho,* they'd say.

Outside, the wind howled from the sea and she worried that she'd never hear his motor coming, so, moving slowly from the pain, she packed biscuits, cheese, and nuts in her knapsack and, head low against a manic gale, hurried through cord grass along channels toward the reading cabin. The walk took forty-five minutes, and at every sound her sore and stiff body flinched and her head jerked to the side, scanning the undergrowth. Finally, the old log structure, up to its knees in tall grasses and clinging to the creek bank, whispered into view. Here the wind was calmer. The soft meadow quiet. She'd never told Chase about her hideout, but he might have known about it. She wasn't sure.

The packrat smell was gone. After the ecology lab hired Tate, he and Scupper fixed up the old cabin so he could stay overnight on some of his expeditions. They had shored up the walls, straightened the roof, and brought in basic furniture—a small quilt-covered bed, a cookstove, a table and chair. Pots and pans hung from the rafters. Then, out-of-place and plastic covered, a microscope sat on a folding table. In the corner, an old metal trunk stored tins of baked beans, sardines. Nothing to bring the bears in.

But inside, she felt trapped, unable to see if Chase was coming, so she sat on the edge of the creek, searching the grassy water land with her right eye. The left was swollen shut.

Downstream a herd of five female deer ignored her and wandered along the water's edge nibbling leaves. If only she could join in, belong to them. Kya knew it wasn't so much that the herd would be incomplete without one of its deer, but that each deer would be incomplete without her herd. One lifted her head, dark eyes searching north into the trees, stomping her right front foot, then the left. The others looked up, then whistled in alarm. Instantly, Kya's good eye probed the forest for signs of Chase or some other predator. But all was quiet. Perhaps the breeze had startled them. They stopped stomping but slowly moved away into the tall grass, leaving Kya alone and uneasy.

She scanned the meadow again for intruders, but the listening and searching sucked all her energy, so she went back into the cabin. Dug sweaty cheese from her bag. Then slumped on the floor and ate mindlessly, touching her bruised cheek. Her face, arms, and legs were cut and smeared with bloody grit. Knees scratched and throbbing. She sobbed, fighting shame, suddenly spitting the cheese out in a chunky, wet spray.

She'd brought this on herself. Consorting unchaperoned. A natural wanting had led her unmarried to a cheap motel, but still unsatisfied. Sex under flashing neon lights, marked only by blood smudged across the sheets like animal tracks.

Chase had probably bragged about their doings to everyone. No wonder people shunned her—she was unfit, disgusting.

As the half moon appeared between fast-moving clouds, she searched through the small window for manlike forms, hunched and sneaking. Finally she crawled into Tate's bed and slept under his quilt. Waking often, listening for footsteps, then pulling the soft fabric closely around her face.

More crumbling cheese for breakfast. Her face darkened to green-purple now, eye swollen like a boiled egg, neck stove-up. Parts of her upper lip twisted grotesquely. Like Ma, monstrous, afraid to go home. In sudden clarity Kya saw what Ma had endured and why she left. "Ma, Ma," she whispered. "I see. Finally I understand why you had to leave and never come back. I'm sorry I didn't know, that I couldn't help you." Kya dropped her head and sobbed. Then jerked her head up and said, "I will never live like that—a life wondering when and where the next fist will fall."

She hiked home that afternoon, but even though she was hungry and needed supplies, she didn't go to Jumpin's. Chase might see her there. Besides, she didn't want anyone, especially Jumpin', to see her battered face.

After a simple meal of hard bread and smoked fish, she sat on the edge of her porch bed, staring through the screen. Just at that moment she noticed a female praying mantis stalking along a branch near her face. The insect was plucking moths with her articulated forelegs, then chewing them up, their wings still flapping in her mouth. A male mantis, head high and proud as a pony, paraded along to court her. She appeared interested, her antennae flailing about like wands. His embrace might have been tight or tender, Kya couldn't tell, but while he probed about with his copulatory organ to fertilize her eggs, the female turned back her long, elegant neck and bit off his head. He was so busy humping, he didn't notice. His neck stump waved about as he continued his business, and she nibbled on his thorax, and then his wings. Finally, his last foreleg protruded from her mouth as his headless, heartless lower body copulated in perfect rhyme.

Female fireflies draw in strange males with dishonest signals and eat them; mantis females devour their own mates. Female insects, Kya thought, know how to deal with their lovers.

After a few days, she boated into the marsh, exploring areas Chase wouldn't know, but was jumpy and alert, making it difficult to paint. Her eye was still puffed around a thin slit, and the bruise had leached its nauseated colors across half her face. Much of her body throbbed with pain. At the chirp of a chipmunk she whirled around, listened keenly to the caws of crows—a language before words were, when communication was simple and clear—and wherever she went, mapped an escape route in her mind.

42.

A Cell

1970

Murky shafts of light streamed through the tiny window of Kya's cell. She stared at dust motes, dancing silently in one direction as though following some dreamy leader. When they hit the shadows, they vanished. Without the sun they were nothing.

She pulled the wooden crate, her only table, under the window, which was seven feet above the floor. Dressed in a gray jumpsuit with *COUNTY INMATE* printed on the back, she stood on the crate and stared at the sea, just visible beyond the thick glass and bars. Whitecaps slapped and spat, and pelicans, heads turning for fish, flew low over the waves. If she stretched her neck far to the right she could see the dense crown of the marsh's edge. Yesterday she had seen an eagle dive and twist toward a fish.

The county jail consisted of six twelve-by-twelve cells in a cement-block, one-story building behind the sheriff's office at the edge of town. The cells were in a row down the length of the building—only on one side, so inmates couldn't see one another. Three of the walls were damp cement blocks; the fourth was made of bars including the locked door.

Each cell had a wooden bed with a bumpy cotton mattress, a feather pillow, sheets, one gray wool blanket, a sink, and a wooden-crate table, plus a toilet. Over the sink was not a mirror but a picture of Jesus, framed there by the Ladies' Baptist Auxiliary. The only allowance made for her, the first female inmate—other than overnighters—in years, was a gray plastic curtain that could be pulled around the sink and toilet.

For two months before the trial, she'd been held in this cell without bail because of her failed attempt to escape the sheriff in her boat. Kya wondered who started using the word *cell* instead of *cage*. There must have been a moment in time when humanity demanded this shift. Self-scratched red webbing streaked her arms. For untracked minutes, sitting on her bed, she studied strands of her hair, plucking them like feathers. As the gulls do.

Standing on the crate, craning her neck toward the marsh, she recalled an Amanda Hamilton poem:

Broken Gull of Brandon Beach

Winged soul, you danced the skies,
And startled dawn with shrilling cries.
You followed sails and braved the sea,
Then caught the wind back to me.

You broke your wing; it dragged the land
And etched your mark upon the sand.
When feathers break, you cannot fly,
But who decides the time to die?

. . .

You disappeared, I know not where.
But your wing-marks still linger there.
A broken heart cannot fly,
But who decides the time to die?

Even though the inmates couldn't see one another, the only other occupants—two men at the far end of the row—spent much of each day and evening jabbering. Both were doing thirty days for starting a fight, which ended in broken bar mirrors and a few bones, over who could spit the farthest at the Dog-Gone Beer Hall. Mostly they lay on their beds, calling to each other from their adjoining cells, sounding like drum squatters. Much of the banter was gossip they'd heard about Kya's case from their visitors. Especially her odds of getting the death penalty, which had not been issued in the county for twenty years, and never to a woman.

Kya heard every word. Being dead didn't bother her; they couldn't scare her with threats of ending this shadow life. But the process of being killed by another's hand, planned out and set to schedule, was so unthinkable it stopped her breath.

Sleep avoided her, slinking around the edges, then darting away. Her mind would plunge along deep walls of sudden slumber—an instant of bliss—then her body would shudder her awake.

She stepped down from the crate and sat on the bed, knees tucked under her chin. They'd brought her here after court, so it might be six by now. Only one hour passed. Or maybe not even that.

43.

A Microscope

1969

In early September, more than a week after Chase attacked her, she walked down her beach. The wind ripped at a letter in her hand, so she held it against her breasts. Her editor had invited her to meet him in Greenville, writing that he understood she didn't come to town often, but he wanted to meet her, and the publisher would pay her expenses.

The day stood clear and hot, so she motored into the marsh. At the end of a narrow estuary, she rounded a grassy bend and saw Tate squatting on a wide sandbar, dipping up water samples in little vials. His cruiser–cum–research vessel was tied to a log and drifted across the channel, blocking it. She heaved on the tiller. Some of the swelling and bruising on her face had diminished, but ugly green and purple splotches still circled her eye. She panicked. She could not let Tate see her battered face and tried to turn her boat around quickly.

But he looked up and waved. "Pull in, Kya. I've got a new microscope to show you."

This had the same effect as the truant officer calling to her about chicken pie. She slowed but didn't answer.

"Come on. You won't believe this magnification. You can see the pseudopods on the amoebas."

She'd never seen an amoeba, certainly not its body parts. And seeing Tate again brought a peace, a calmness. Deciding that she could keep her bruised face turned away from him, she beached her boat and walked through the shallow water toward his. She wore cutoff jeans and a white T-shirt, her hair free. Standing at the top of the stern ladder, he held out his hand and she took it, looking away from him.

The cruiser's soft beige blended into the marsh, and Kya had never seen anything as fine as the teak deck and brass helm. "Come on down," he said, stepping below into the cabin. She scanned the captain's desk, the small kitchen outfitted better than her own, and the living area that had been converted into an onboard laboratory with multiple microscopes and racks of vials. Other instruments hummed and blinked.

Tate fiddled with the largest microscope and adjusted the slide.

"Here, just a minute." He touched a drop of marsh water onto the slide, covered it with another, and focused the eyepiece. He stood. "Have a look."

Kya leaned over gently, as if to kiss a baby. The microscope's light reflected in her dark pupils, and she drew in a breath as a Mardi Gras of costumed players pirouetted and careened into view. Unimaginable headdresses adorned astonishing bodies so eager for more life, they frolicked as though caught in a circus tent, not a single bead of water.

She put her hand on her heart. "I had no idea there were so many and so beautiful," she said, still looking.

He identified some odd species, then stepped back, watching her. *She feels the pulse of life,* he thought, *because there are no layers between her and her planet.*

He showed her more slides.

She whispered, "It's like never having seen the stars, then suddenly seeing them."

"Would you like some coffee?" he asked softly.

She raised her head. "No, no, thank you." Then she backed away from the microscope, moving toward the galley. Awkwardly, keeping her brown-green eye turned away.

Tate was accustomed to Kya being guarded, but her behavior seemed more distant and stranger than ever. Continuously keeping her head turned at an angle.

"Come on, Kya. Just have a cup of coffee." He'd already moved into the kitchenette and poured water into a machine that dripped out a strong brew. She stood by the ladder to the deck above, and he handed her a mug, motioning for her to go up. He invited her to sit on the cushioned bench, but she stood at the stern. Catlike, she knew the exit. The brilliant white sandbar curved away from them under sheltering oaks.

"Kya . . ." He started to ask a question, but when she faced him, he saw the fading bruise on her cheek.

"What happened to your face?" He walked toward her, reaching to touch her cheek. She turned away.

"Nothing. I ran into a door in the middle of the night." He knew that wasn't true by the way she flung her hand to her face. Someone had hit her. Had it been Chase? Was she still seeing him even though he was married? Tate worked his jaw. Kya moved to put her mug down, as if she were going.

He forced calm. "Have you started a new book?"

"I'm almost finished with the one on mushrooms. My editor's coming to Greenville sometime at the end of October and wants me to meet him there. But I'm not sure."

"You should go. It'd be good to meet him. There's a bus from

Barkley every day, one at night, too. It doesn't take long. An hour and twenty minutes maybe, something like that."

"I don't know where to buy a ticket."

"The driver'll know everything. Just show up at the bus stop on Main; he'll tell you what you need to do. I think Jumpin' has the schedule tacked up in his store." He almost mentioned that he had ridden the bus many times from Chapel Hill, but thought it better not to remind her of those days, of her waiting on a July beach.

They were quiet for a while, sipping their coffee, listening to a pair of hawks whistling along the walls of a tall cloud.

He hesitated to offer more coffee, knowing she would leave if he did. So he asked about her mushroom book, explained the protozoans he studied. Any bait to keep her.

The afternoon light softened and a cool wind picked up. Putting the mug down again, she said, "I have to go."

"I was thinking of opening some wine. Would you like some?"

"No, thanks."

"Wait a second before you go," Tate said as he went below to the galley and returned with a bag of leftover bread and biscuits. "Please give my regards to the gulls."

"Thanks." She climbed down the ladder.

As she walked toward her boat, he called out, "Kya, it's gotten cooler, don't you want a jacket or something?"

"No. I'm fine."

"Here, at least take my cap," and he tossed a red ski cap toward her. She caught it and slung it back to him. He threw it again, farther, and she jogged across the sandbar, leaned low and scooped it up. Laughing, she jumped into her boat, cranked the motor, and, as she boated near him, pitched the hat back into his boat. He grinned and she giggled. Then they stopped laughing and simply looked at each other as they lobbed the cap back and forth until she motored around the bend. She sat down hard on the stern seat and put her hand over her mouth. "No," she said out loud. "I cannot fall for him again. I will not get hurt all over again."

Tate stayed at the stern. Clenching his fists at the image of someone hitting her.

She hugged the coastline just beyond the surf, heading south. On this route she would pass her beach before reaching the channel that led through the marsh to her shack. Usually she didn't stop at her beach, but motored through the maze of waterways to her lagoon, and then walked to the shore.

But as she passed by, the gulls spotted her and swarmed the boat. Big Red landed on the bow, bobbing his head. She laughed. "Okay then, you win." Breaking through the surf, she beached her boat behind tall sea oats and stood at the shoreline tossing the crumbs Tate had given her.

As the sun spread gold and pink across the water, she sat on the sand while the gulls settled around her. Suddenly she heard a motor and saw Chase's ski boat racing toward her channel. He could not see her boat behind the sea oats, but she was in plain sight on the open sand. Instantly she lay flat, turning her head to the side, so she could watch him. He stood at the helm, hair blowing back, face in an ugly scowl. But he didn't look in her direction as he turned into the channel toward her shack.

When he was out of sight, she sat up. If she hadn't beached here with the gulls, he would have caught her at home. She'd learned over and over from Pa: these men had to have the last punch. Kya had left Chase sprawled on the dirt. The two old fishermen had probably seen her flatten him. As Pa would have it, Kya had to be taught a lesson.

As soon as he discovered she wasn't at the shack, he'd walk here to her beach. She ran to her boat, throttled up, and headed back toward Tate. But she didn't want to tell Tate what Chase had done to her; shame overwhelmed reason. She slowed down and drifted on swells as the sun disappeared. She had to hide and wait for Chase to leave. If she didn't see him go, she wouldn't know when it was safe to motor home.

She turned into the channel, panicked that he could roar in her direction at any second. Her motor just above idle, so she could hear his boat, she eased into a backwater thicket of overhanging trees and brush. She reversed deeper into the undergrowth, pushing limbs aside until layers of leaves and the falling night hid her.

Breathing hard, she listened. Finally she heard his engine screaming across the soft evening air. She ducked lower as he approached, suddenly worried that the tip of her boat was visible. The sound came very close, and in seconds his boat zoomed by. She sat there for nearly thirty minutes until it was truly dark, then cruised home by starlight.

She took her bedding to the beach and sat with the gulls. They paid her no mind, preening outstretched wings before settling down on the sand like feathered stones. As they chortled softly and tucked their heads for the night, she lay as close to them as she could get. But even among their soft cooing and ruffling, Kya couldn't sleep. Mostly she tossed from one side to the other, sitting up each time the wind mimicked footfalls.

Dawn surf roared on a slapping wind that stung her cheeks. She sat up among the birds, who wandered nearby, stretching and kick-scratching. Big Red—eyes wide, neck cocked—seemed to have found something most interesting in his underwing, an act that would normally have made Kya laugh. But the birds brought her no cheer.

She walked to the water's edge. Chase would not let this go. Being isolated was one thing; living in fear, quite another.

She imagined taking one step after the other into the churning sea, sinking into the stillness beneath the waves, strands of her hair suspending like black watercolor into the pale blue sea, her long fingers and arms drifting up toward the backlit blaze of the surface. Dreams of escape—even through death—always lift toward the light. The dangling, shiny prize of peace just out of grasp until finally her body descends to the bottom and settles in murky quiet. Safe.

Who decides the time to die?

44.

Cell Mate

1970

Kya stood in the middle of her cell. Here she was in jail. If those she'd loved, including Jodie and Tate, hadn't left her, she wouldn't be here. Leaning on someone leaves you on the ground.

Before being arrested, she'd caught glimpses of a path back to Tate: an opening of her heart. Love lingering closer to the surface. But when he'd come to visit her in jail on several occasions, she had refused to see him. She wasn't sure why jail had closed her heart even tighter. Why she hadn't embraced the comfort he could give her in this place. It seemed that now, Kya being more vulnerable than ever, was reason to trust others even less. Standing in the most fragile place of her life, she turned to the only net she knew—herself.

Being thrown behind bars with no bail made clear how alone she was. The sheriff's offer of a phone call starkly reminded her: there was no one to call. The only phone number she knew in the world was Jodie's, and how could she call her brother and say she was in jail accused of murder? After all those years, how could she bother him with her troubles? And maybe shame played a part.

They had abandoned her to survive and defend herself. So here she was, by herself.

Once more she lifted the wondrous shell book Tom Milton had given her, by far her most treasured volume. Some biology texts were stacked on the floor, which the guard said Tate had brought, but she couldn't hold the words in place. Sentences wandered off in several directions, circling back to the beginning. Shell pictures were easier.

Footsteps clanked on the cheap tile floor and Jacob, a small black man who served as guard, appeared in front of her door. He held a large brown-paper package. "Sorry to bother ya, Miz Clark, but ya got a viz'tor. Ya gotta come with me."

"Who is it?"

"It's yo' lawya, Mr. Milton." Metal-to-metal *clanks* sounded, as Jacob unlocked her door and handed her the package. "An' this here's from Jumpin'." She laid the parcel on the bed and followed Jacob down the hall and into a room—even smaller than her cell. Tom Milton rose from his chair as she entered. Kya nodded at him and then looked out the window, where an enormous cumulus cloud with peach-colored cheeks puffed itself up.

"Good evening, Kya."

"Mr. Milton."

"Kya, please call me Tom. And what's wrong with your arm? Have you hurt yourself?"

She jerked her hand, covering the webs she'd scratched on her arms. "Just mosquito bites, I think."

"I'll talk to the sheriff; you shouldn't have mosquitoes in your—room."

Head down, she said, "Please, no, it's okay. I'm not worried about insects."

"All right, of course, I won't do anything you don't want. Kya, I came to talk about your options."

"What options?"

"I'll explain. It's hard to know at this point how the jury is leaning. The prosecution has a good case. It's not solid by any means, but considering how people in this town are prejudiced, you have to be prepared that it won't be easy for us to win. But there's the option of a plea bargain. Do you know what I'm referring to?"

"Not exactly."

"You have pleaded not guilty to first-degree murder. If we lose, you lose big: life in prison or, as you know, they are seeking the death penalty. Your option is to plead guilty to a lesser charge, say, manslaughter. If you were willing to say, yes, you did go to the tower that night, you did meet Chase there, you had a disagreement, and in a horrible accident he stepped backward through the grate, the trial might end immediately, you wouldn't have to go through any more of this drama, and we could negotiate with the prosecution over a sentence. Since you've never been charged with anything before, they'd probably sentence you to ten years, and you could be out in, say, six years. I know that sounds bad, but it's better than spending life in prison or the other."

"No, I won't say anything that implies guilt. I will not go to prison."

"Kya, I understand, but please take some time to think about it. You don't want to live your entire life in jail, nor do you want—the other."

Kya looked out the window again. "I don't need to think about it. I won't stay in jail."

"Well, we don't have to decide now. We have some time. Let's see how it goes. Before I leave, is there anything you want to discuss with me?"

"Please get me out of here. One way or—the other."

"I'll do my best to get you out, Kya. But don't give up. And please help me. Like I've mentioned before, you need to be engaged, look at the jurors now and then . . ."

But Kya had turned to leave.

Jacob led her back to the cell, where she picked up the package from Jumpin'—unwrapped by the warden and taped up haphazardly again. She opened it, saving and folding the paper. Inside was a basket with some tiny vials of paint, a brush, paper, and a paper bag of Mabel's corn muffins. The basket was lined with a nest of pine straw, some oak leaves, a few shells, and long strands of cattails. Kya sniffed deeply. Pinched her lips. Jumpin'. Mabel.

The sun had set; no dust motes to follow.

Later Jacob cleared away her supper tray. "I declare, Miz Clark, ya didn't eat much a'tall. Them poke chops and greens as good as dey git." She smiled lightly at him, then listened as his steps clomped to the end of the hall. She waited to hear the thick metal door shut with heavy finality.

Then something moved on the hall floor, just outside the bars. Her eyes swung there. Sunday Justice sat on his haunches staring at her dark eyes with his green ones.

Her heart raced. Locked up alone all these weeks, and now this creature could step wizardlike between the bars. Be with her. Sunday Justice broke the stare and looked down the hall, toward the inmates' talk. Kya was terrified that he would leave her and walk to them. But he looked back at her, blinked in obligatory boredom, and squeezed easily between the bars. Inside.

Kya breathed out. Whispered, "Please stay."

Taking his time, he sniffed his way around the cell, researching the damp cement walls, the exposed pipes, and the sink, all the while compelled to ignore her. A small crack in the wall was the most interesting to him. She knew because he flicked his thoughts on his tail. He ended his tour next to the small bed. Then, just like that, he jumped onto her lap and circled, his large white paws finding soft purchase on her thighs. Kya sat frozen, her arms slightly raised, so as not to interfere with his maneuvering. Finally, he settled as though he had nested here every night of his life. He looked at her. Gently she touched his head, then scratched his neck. A loud purr erupted like a current. She closed her eyes at such easy acceptance. A deep pause in a lifetime of longing.

Afraid to move, she sat stiff until her leg cramped, then shifted slightly to stretch her muscles. Sunday Justice, without opening his eyes, slid off her lap and curled up next to her side. She lay down fully clothed, and they both nestled in. She watched him sleep, then followed. Not falling toward a jolt, but a drifting, finally, into an empty calm.

Once during the night, she opened her eyes and watched him sleeping on his back, forepaws stretched one way, hind paws the other. But when she awoke at dawn, he was gone. A moan struggled against the strength of her throat.

Later, Jacob stood outside her cell, holding the breakfast tray with one hand, unlocking the door with the other. "Gotcha yo' oatmeal, Miz Clark."

She took the tray, saying, "Jacob, the black and white cat that sleeps in the courtroom. He was here last night."

"Oh, sorry as can be. That's Sundee Justice. Sometimes he slips in wif me and I don't see 'im 'cause of carryin' the suppa trays. I end up closin' 'im in with y'all." Kind enough not to say *locking*.

"It's fine. I liked having him here. Please, will you let him in whenever you see him after supper? Or anytime."

He looked at her with soft eyes. "'Course I can. I'll do that, Miz Clark; I sho' will. Can see he'd be mighty good comp'ny."

"Thank you, Jacob."

That evening, Jacob returned. "Here's yo' food now, Miz Clark. Fried chicken, mashed taters wif gravy from the diner. Hope ya can eat sump'm tonight, now."

Kya stood, looking around his feet. She took the tray. "Thank you, Jacob. Have you seen the cat?"

"Nome. Not a'tall. But I'll keep an eye out."

Kya nodded. She sat on the bed, the only place to sit, and stared at the plate. Here in jail was better food than she had seen all her life. She poked around the chicken, pushed the butter beans. Having found food, her stomach was lost.

Then, the sound of the lock turning, the heavy metal door swinging.

At the end of the hall she heard Jacob say, "Thar ya go, then, Mista Sundee Justice."

Without breathing, Kya stared at the floor outside her cell and within a few seconds Sunday Justice stepped into view. His markings were surprisingly stark and soft at the same time. No hesitation this time, he stepped into her cell and walked up to her. She put the plate on the floor and he ate the chicken—pulled the drumstick right onto the floor—then lapped up the gravy. Skipped the butter beans. She smiled through it all, then wiped the floor clean with tissue.

He jumped on her bed, and a sweet sleep wrapped them together.

Jacob stood outside her door the next day. "Miz Clark, ya got anotha viz'ter."

"Who is it?"

"It's Mr. Tate again. He's done come sev'ral times now, Miz Clark, either brings sump'm or asks to see ya. Won't ya see him today, Miz Clark? It's Saderdee, no court, nothin' to do in here the livelong day."

"All right, Jacob."

Jacob led her to the same dingy room where she had met Tom Milton. As she stepped through the door, Tate rose from his chair and walked quickly toward her. He smiled lightly, but his eyes revealed the sadness from seeing her here.

"Kya, you look good. I've been so worried. Thank you for seeing me. Sit down." They sat opposite each other while Jacob stood in the corner reading a newspaper with considerate concentration.

"Hello, Tate. Thanks for the books you brought." She acted calm, but her heart pulled into pieces.

"What else can I do for you?"

"Maybe you could feed the gulls if you're out my way."

He smiled. "Yes, I've been feeding them. Every other day or so." He made it sound easygoing but had driven or boated to her place every dawn and dusk to feed them.

"Thank you."

"I was in court, Kya, sitting right behind you. You never turned around, so I didn't know if you knew that. But I'll be there every day."

She looked out of the window.

"Tom Milton's very good, Kya. Probably the best lawyer in this part of the state. He'll get you out of here. Just hang on."

When again she didn't speak, he continued. "And as soon as you're out of here, we'll get back to exploring lagoons like in the old days."

"Tate, please, you have to forget me."

"I have never and will never forget you, Kya."

"You know I'm different. I don't fit with other people. I cannot be part of your world. Please, can't you understand, I'm afraid to be close with anybody ever again. I can't."

"I don't blame you, Kya, but . . ."

"Tate, listen to me. For years I longed to be with people. I really believed that someone would stay with me, that I would actually have friends and a family. Be part of a group. But no one stayed. Not you or one member of my family. Now I've finally learned how to deal with that and how to protect myself. But I can't talk about this now. I appreciate your coming to see me in here, I do. And maybe someday we can be friends, but I can't think about what comes next. Not in here."

"Okay. I understand. Really, I do."

After a short silence, he continued. "The great horns are already calling."

She nodded, almost smiled.

"Oh, and yesterday when I was at your place, you won't believe it, but a male Cooper's hawk landed right on your front steps."

Finally a smile as she thought of the Coop. One of her many private memories. "Yes, I believe it."

Ten minutes later, Jacob said their time was up and Tate had to leave. Kya thanked him again for coming.

"I'll keep feeding the gulls, Kya. And I'll bring you some books."

She shook her head and followed Jacob.

45.

Red Cap

1970

On Monday morning, after Tate's visit, when Kya was led into the courtroom by the bailiff, she kept her eyes away from the spectators, as she had before, and looked deep into the shadowy trees outside. But she heard a familiar sound, maybe a soft cough, and turned her head. There in the first row of seats, sitting with Tate, were Jumpin' and Mabel, who wore her church bonnet decked out with silk roses. Folks had made a stir when they walked in with Tate and sat downstairs in the "white area." But when the bailiff reported this to Judge Sims, still in his chambers, the judge told him to announce that anybody of any color or creed could sit anywhere they wanted in his courtroom, and if somebody didn't like it, they were free to leave. In fact, he'd make sure they did.

On seeing Jumpin' and Mabel, Kya felt a smidge of strength, and her back straightened slightly.

The next witness for the prosecution, Dr. Steward Cone, the coroner, had graying hair cut very short and wore glasses that sat too far down his nose, a habit that forced him to tilt his head back to see through the lenses. As he answered Eric's questions, Kya's mind wandered to the gulls. These long months in jail, she had pined for them, yet all along, Tate had been feeding them. They had not been abandoned. She thought of Big Red, how he always walked across her toes when she threw crumbs to them.

The coroner tossed his head back to adjust his glasses, the gesture bringing Kya back to the courtroom.

"So to recap, you've testified that Chase Andrews died between midnight and two o'clock on the night of October 29 or the morning of the thirtieth, 1969. The cause of death was extensive injuries to the brain and spinal cord due to a fall through an open grate of the fire tower, sixty-three feet to the ground. As he fell, he hit the back of his head on a support beam, a fact confirmed by blood and hair samples taken from the beam. Is all that correct according to your expert opinion?"

"Yes."

"Now, Dr. Cone, why would an intelligent and fit young man like Chase Andrews step through an open grate and fall to his death? To rule out one possibility, was there alcohol or any other substance in his blood that could have impaired his judgment?"

"No, there was not."

"Evidence presented previously demonstrates that Chase Andrews hit the back of his head on that support beam, not his forehead." Eric stood in front of the jury and took a large step. "But when I step forward, my head ends up slightly ahead of my body. Were I to step into a hole here in front of me, the momentum and the weight of my head would pitch me forward. Correct? Chase Andrews would have hit his forehead on the beam, not the back of his skull, if he was stepping forward. So isn't it true, Dr. Cone, that the evidence suggests that Chase was going backward when he fell?"

"Yes, the evidence would support that conclusion."

"So we can also conclude that if Chase Andrews was standing with his back to the opened grate and was pushed by someone, he would have fallen backward, not forward?" Before Tom could object, Eric said very quickly, "I'm not asking you to state that this is conclusive evidence that Chase was pushed backward to his death. I am simply making it clear that if someone pushed Chase backward through the hole, the wounds to his head from the beam would have coincided with those actually found. Is that correct?"

"Yes."

"All right. Dr. Cone, when you examined Chase Andrews in the clinic, the morning of October 30, was he wearing a shell necklace?"

"No."

To suppress the rising nausea, Kya focused on Sunday Justice grooming himself on a windowsill. Pretzeled into an impossible position, one leg straight in the air, he licked the inside tip of his tail. His own bath seemed to absorb and entertain him entirely.

A few minutes later, the prosecutor was asking, "Is it correct that Chase Andrews wore a denim jacket the night he died?"

"Yes, that is correct."

"And according to your official report, Dr. Cone, did you not find red wool fibers on his jacket? Fibers that were not from any piece of clothing he was wearing?"

"Yes."

Eric held up a clear plastic bag containing bits of red wool. "Are these the red fibers that were found on Chase Andrews's jacket?"

"Yes."

Eric lifted a larger bag from his desk. "And isn't it true that the red wool fibers found on Chase's jacket matched those on this red cap?" He handed it to the witness.

"Yes. These are my labeled samples, and the fibers from the cap and jacket matched exactly."

"Where was this cap found?"

"The sheriff found the cap in Miss Clark's residence." This was not generally known, and murmurs rippled through the crowd.

"Was there any evidence that she had ever worn the cap?"

"Yes. Strands of Miss Clark's hair were found in the cap."

Watching Sunday Justice in court got Kya thinking about how her family had never had a pet. Not one dog or cat. The only thing close was the female skunk—a silky, slinky, and sassy creature—who lived under the shack. Ma called her Chanel.

After a few near misses, they'd all gotten to know one another, and Chanel became very polite, only flashing her armament when the kids got too rowdy. She'd come and go, sometimes within feet of whoever was coming up or down the brick 'n' boards.

Every spring she'd escort her little kits on forays into the oak woods and along the slipstreams. Them scurrying behind, running into and over one another in black-and-white confusions.

Pa, of course, was always threatening to get rid of her, but Jodie, showing maturity far beyond his father's, deadpanned, "Another one'll just move in, and I always reckoned it's better the skunk ya know than the skunk ya don't know." She smiled now, thinking of Jodie. Then caught herself.

"So, Dr. Cone, on the night Chase Andrews died, the night he fell backward through an open grate—a posture consistent with being pushed by someone—fibers on his jacket came from a red cap found at Miss Clark's residence. And there were strands of Miss Clark's hair in the cap."

"Yes."

"Thank you, Dr. Cone. I have no further questions."

Tom Milton looked briefly at Kya, who watched the sky. The room leaned physically toward the prosecution as though the floor tipped, and it didn't help that Kya sat rigid and detached—carved from ice. He flicked his white hair from his forehead and approached the coroner for the cross-examination.

"Good morning, Dr. Cone."

"Good morning."

"Dr. Cone, you testified that the wound on the back of Chase Andrews's head was consistent with him going backward through the open hole. Isn't it true that if he stepped backward on his own and fell through the hole by accident, the results of hitting the back of his head would have been exactly the same?"

"Yes."

"Were there any bruises on his chest or arms that would coincide with him being pushed or shoved?"

"No. There was, of course, heavy bruising over his entire body from the fall. Mostly on the back of his body and legs. There were none that could be identified specifically as developing from a push or shove."

"In fact, isn't it true that there is no evidence whatsoever that Chase Andrews was pushed into the hole?"

"That is true. There's no evidence that I'm aware of that Chase Andrews was pushed."

"So, Dr. Cone, there is no evidence from your professional examination of Chase Andrews's body that proves this was a murder and not an accident?"

"No."

Tom took his time, letting this answer sink into the jury, then continued. "Now, let's talk about those red wool fibers found on Chase's jacket. Is there any way to determine how long the fibers had been on the jacket?"

"No. We can say where they came from, but not when."

"In other words, those fibers could have been on that jacket for a year, even four years?"

"That's correct."

"Even if the jacket had been washed?"

"Yes."

"So there's no evidence that those fibers became attached to that jacket the night Chase died?"

"No."

"There has been testimony that the defendant knew Chase Andrews for four years prior to his death. So you're saying that anytime during those four years, when they met wearing those items of clothing, it's possible the fibers were transferred from the cap to the jacket."

"From what I have seen, yes."

"So the red fibers do not prove that Miss Clark was with Chase Andrews the night he died. Was there any evidence at all that Miss Clark was in close proximity to Chase Andrews that night? For example, her skin fragments on his body, under his fingernails, or her fingerprints on the buttons or snaps of his jacket? Strands of her hair on his clothes or body?"

"No."

"So, in fact, since the red fibers could have been on his jacket for as long as four years, there's no evidence whatsoever that Miss Catherine Clark was near Chase Andrews the night of his death?"

"From my examination that is correct."

"Thank you. No more questions."

Judge Sims declared an early lunch recess.

Tom touched Kya's elbow gently and whispered that it had been a good cross-examination. She nodded slightly as people stood and stretched. Almost all stayed long enough to watch Kya being handcuffed and led from the room.

As Jacob's steps echoed down the hall after leaving her in her cell, Kya sat hard on her bed. When she was first incarcerated, they hadn't allowed her to bring her knapsack into the cell but let her take some of its contents with her in a brown paper bag. She reached into the bag then and pulled out the scrap of paper with Jodie's phone number and address. Since being there, she'd looked at it almost every day and thought of phoning her brother, asking him to come be with her. She knew he would, and Jacob had said she could use the phone to call him. But she had not. How would she say the words: *Please come; I'm in jail, charged with murder.*

Carefully, she put the paper back into the bag and lifted out the World War I compass Tate had given her. She let the needle swing north and watched it settle true. She held it against her heart. Where else would one need a compass more than in this place?

Then she whispered Emily Dickinson's words:

> The sweeping up the heart,
> And putting Love away
> We shall not want to use again
> Until Eternity.

46.

King of the World

1969

The September sea and sky glistened pale blue from a soft sun as Kya churned in her little boat toward Jumpin's to get the bus schedule. The thought of busing with strange people to a strange town unnerved her, but she wanted to meet her editor, Robert Foster. For more than two years, they had exchanged short notes—and even some long letters—mostly discussing editorial adjustments for the prose and art in her books, but the correspondence, written so often in biological phrases blended with poetic descriptions, had become a bond welded in its own language. She wanted to meet this person on the other end of the mail line, who knew how ordinary light is shattered by microscopic prisms in the feathers of hummingbirds, creating the iridescence of its golden-red throat. And how to say it in words as startling as the colors.

As she stepped onto the wharf, Jumpin' greeted her and asked if she needed gas.

"No thanks, not this time. I need to write down the bus schedule. You have a copy, right?"

"Sho' do. Tacked up right on the wall, left a' the doah. Hep yurself."

After she stepped from the shop with the schedule, he asked, "Ya goin' on a trip somewheres, Miss Kya?"

"I might. My editor invited me to Greenville to meet him. Not sure yet."

"Well then, thata' be mighty fine. It's a fur piece over there, but a trip a' do ya good."

As Kya turned to get back into her boat, Jumpin' leaned in and looked at her more closely. "Miss Kya, what's done happened to yo' eye, yo' face? Look like you been beat up, Miss Kya." Quickly she turned her face away. The bruise from Chase's slug, almost a month old, was faded to a faint yellowish stain, which Kya thought no one would notice.

"No, I just walked into a door in—"

"Don't ya go tellin' me a story now, Miss Kya. I didn't jus' fall off the turnip truck. Who done hit ya like that?"

She stood silent.

"Was it Mr. Chase done this to ya? Ya know ya can tell me. In fact, we gwine stand right here tills ya tell me."

"Yes, it was Chase." Kya could barely believe the words came from her mouth. She never thought she had anyone to tell such things. She turned away again, fighting tears.

Jumpin's entire face frowned. He didn't speak for several seconds. And then, "What else he done?"

"Nothing, I swear. He tried, Jumpin', but I fought him off."

"That man gotta be horsewhupped, then run outta this town."

"Jumpin', please. You can't tell anybody. You know you can't tell the sheriff or anybody. They'd drag me into the sheriff's office and make me describe what happened to a bunch of men. I can't live through that." Kya dropped her face in her hands.

"Well, sump'm gotta be done. He cain't go an' do a thing like that, and then just go on boatin' 'round in that fancy boat a' his. King of the World."

"Jumpin', you know how it is. They'll take his side. They'll say I'm just stirring up trouble. Trying to get money out of his parents or something. Think what would happen if one of the girls from Colored Town accused Chase Andrews of assault and attempted rape. They'd do nothing. Zero." Kya's voice became more and more shrill. "It would end in big trouble for that girl. Write-ups in the newspaper. People accusing her of whoring. Well, it'd be the same for me, and you know it. Please promise me you won't tell anybody." She ended in a sob.

"Ya right, Miss Kya. I know ya right. Ya don't gotta worry 'bout me doin' anythang to make this thang worse. But how d'ya know he ain't comin' after ya again? And ya a'ways on yo' lonesome out there?"

"I've always protected myself before; I just slipped up this time because I didn't hear him coming. I'll stay safe, Jumpin'. If I decide to go to Greenville, when I come back, maybe I could live out at my reading cabin awhile. I don't think Chase knows about it."

"A'right, then. But I wantcha to come in here more of'en, I wantcha to come by and let me know how things're goin'. Ya know ya can always come out and stay with Mabel and me, ya know that."

"Thank you, Jumpin'. I know."

"When ya goin' over to Greenville?"

"I'm not sure. The editor's letter mentioned late October. I haven't made arrangements, haven't even accepted the invitation." She knew now she couldn't go unless the bruise had disappeared completely.

"Well, ya let me know when ya gwine over thar and when ya get back. Ya hear? I gotta know if ya outer town. 'Cause, if'n I don't see ya fer more'n a day or so, I'm goin' out to yo' place maself. Bring along a posse if need be."

"I will. Thank you, Jumpin'."

47.

The Expert

1970

Prosecutor Eric Chastain had been questioning the sheriff about the two boys who discovered Chase Andrews's body at the base of the fire tower on October 30, the doctor's examination, and the initial investigation.

Eric continued. "Sheriff, please tell us what led you to believe that Chase Andrews had not fallen from the tower by accident. What made you think a crime had been committed?"

"Well, one of the first things I noticed was there weren't any footprints around Chase's body, not even his own. Except those made by the boys who found him, so I figured somebody had destroyed them to cover up a crime."

"Isn't it also true, Sheriff, that there were no fingerprints and no vehicle tracks at the scene?"

"Yeah, that's correct. The lab reports stated there were no fresh fingerprints on the tower. Not even on the grate, which somebody had to open. My deputy and I searched for vehicle tracks, and there weren't any of those either. All this indicated that someone had purposely destroyed evidence."

"So when the lab reports proved that red wool fibers from Miss Clark's hat were found on Chase's clothing that night, you . . ."

"Objection, Your Honor," Tom said. "Leading the witness. And besides, testimony has already established that the red fibers could have been transferred from Miss Clark's clothing to those of Mr. Andrews prior to the night of October 29 to 30."

"Sustained," the judge boomed.

"No more questions. Your witness." Eric had known the sheriff's testimony would be somewhat weak for the prosecution—what can you do with no murder weapon and no finger-, foot-, or truck prints—but there was still enough meat and gravy to convince the jury someone had murdered Chase, and considering the red fibers, that someone could've been Miss Clark.

Tom Milton walked to the witness box. "Sheriff, did you or anybody else ask an expert to look for footprints or for evidence that footprints were wiped out?"

"That wasn't necessary. I am the expert. Footprint examination is part of my official training. I didn't need another expert."

"I see. So was there evidence that footprints had been wiped off the ground? I mean, for example, were there marks from a brush or branch to cover tracks? Or was there mud moved on top of other mud? Any evidence, any photographs of such an act?"

"No. I'm here to testify as an expert that there were no footprints under the tower except ours and the boys'. So somebody had to have wiped them out."

"Okay. But, Sheriff, it's a physical characteristic of the marsh that as the tides come in and out, the groundwater—even far beyond the tide—goes up and down, making areas dry for a while, then a few hours later the water rises again. In many places, as the water rises it soaks the area, wiping out any marks in the mud, such as footprints. Clean slate. Isn't that true?"

"Well, yeah, it can be like that. But there's no evidence that something like that occurred."

"I have here the tide table for the night of October 29 and the morning of October 30, and see, Sheriff Jackson, it shows that low tide was around midnight. So, at the time Chase arrived at the tower and walked to the steps, he would have made tracks in the wet mud. Then when the tide came in and the groundwater rose, his tracks were wiped out. That's the reason you and the boys made deep tracks, and the same reason that Chase's prints were gone. Do you agree that this is possible?"

Kya nodded slightly—her first reaction to testimony since the trial began. Many times she'd seen marsh waters swallow yesterday's story: deer prints by a creek or bobcat tracks near a dead fawn, vanished.

The sheriff answered, "Well, I've never seen it wipe out anything so complete as that, so I don't know."

"But, Sheriff, as you said, you're the expert, trained in footprint examination. And now you say you don't know if this common occurrence happened that night or not."

"Well, it wouldn't be that hard to prove one way or the other, would it? Just go out there at low tide, make some tracks, and see if they are wiped out when the tide comes in."

"Yes, it wouldn't be that hard to determine one way or the other, so why wasn't it done? Here we are in court, and you have no proof whatsoever that a person wiped away footprints to cover a crime. It's more likely that Chase Andrews did leave prints under the tower and that they were washed away by the rising groundwater. And if some friends had been with him to climb the tower for fun, their footprints would have been washed away as well. Under these very likely circumstances, there is no suggestion whatsoever of a crime. Isn't that correct, Sheriff?"

Ed's eyes darted left, right, left, right, as if the answer were on the walls. People shifted on the benches.

"Sheriff?" Tom repeated.

"In my professional opinion, it seems unlikely that a normal cycle of rising groundwater would completely wash away footprints to the extent that they disappeared in this case. However, since there was no sign of a cover-up, the absence of footprints does not, by itself, prove there was a crime. But—"

"Thank you." Tom turned toward the jury and repeated the sheriff's words. "The absence of footprints does not prove there was a crime. Now, moving on, Sheriff, what about the grate that was left open on the floor of the fire tower? Did you examine it for Miss Clark's fingerprints?"

"Yes, of course we did."

"And did you find Miss Clark's fingerprints on the grate or anywhere on the tower?"

"No. No, but we didn't find any other fingerprints either, so . . ."

The judge leaned over. "Only answer the questions, Ed."

"What about hair? Miss Clark has long black hair—if she had climbed all the way to the top and was busy on the platform, opening a grate and such, I would expect there to be strands of her hair. Did you find any?"

"No." The sheriff's brow glistened.

"The coroner testified that, after examining Chase's body, there was no evidence that Miss Clark was in close proximity to him that night. Oh, there were those fibers, but they could have been four years old.

And now, you're telling us that there is no evidence whatsoever that Miss Clark was even on the fire tower that night. Is that a correct statement?"

"Yes."

"So we have no evidence that proves Miss Clark was on the fire tower the night Chase Andrews fell to his death. Correct?"

"That's what I said."

"So that's a yes."

"Yeah, that's a yes."

"Sheriff, isn't it true that those grates on top of the tower were left open quite frequently by kids playing up there?"

"Yeah, they were left open sometimes. But like I said earlier, it was usually the one you had to open to climb on top, not the other ones."

"But isn't it true that the grate by the stairs and occasionally the others were left open so often and considered so dangerous that your office submitted a written request to the U.S. Forest Service to remedy the situation?" Tom held a document out to the sheriff. "Is this the official request to the Forest Service on July 18 of last year?" The sheriff looked at the page.

"Yeah. That's it."

"Who exactly wrote this request?"

"I did it myself."

"So only three months before Chase Andrews fell to his death through an open grate on the fire tower, you submitted a written request to the Forest Service asking them to close the tower or secure the grates so that no one would be hurt. Is that correct?"

"Yeah."

"Sheriff, would you please read to the court the last sentence of this document that you wrote to the Forest Service? Just the last sentence, here." He handed the document to the sheriff, pointing at the last line.

The sheriff read out loud to the court, "'I must repeat, these grates are very dangerous and if action is not taken, a serious injury or even death will occur.'"

"I have no further questions."

48.

A Trip

1969

On October 28, 1969, Kya eased up to Jumpin's dock to tell him goodbye, as promised, then motored to the town wharf, where fishermen and shrimpers as always stopped their work to watch her. Ignoring them, she tied up and carried a faded cardboard suitcase—pulled from the back of Ma's old closet—onto Main Street. She had no purse, but toted her knapsack packed with books, some ham and biscuits, and a small amount of cash, after burying most of her royalty money in a tin can near the lagoon. For once, she looked quite normal, dressed in a brown Sears, Roebuck skirt, white blouse, and flats. Shopkeepers busied about, tending customers, sweeping the sidewalk, every one of them staring at her.

She stood on the corner under the *Bus Stop* sign and waited until the Trailways bus, its air brakes hissing, pulled up, blocking the ocean. Nobody got off or on as Kya stepped forward and bought a ticket to Greenville from the driver. When she asked about the return dates and times, he handed her a printed schedule and then stowed her suitcase. She held tightly to her knapsack and boarded. And before she had time to think much about it, the bus, which seemed as long as the town, drove out of Barkley Cove.

Two days later, at 1:16 in the afternoon, Kya stepped off the Trailways from Greenville. Now even more villagers were about, staring and whispering as she tossed her long hair over her shoulder and took her suitcase from the driver. She crossed the street to the wharf, stepped into her boat, and motored straight home. She wanted to stop by and tell Jumpin' that she was back, as she had promised to do, but other boats were lined up waiting for gas at his wharf, so she figured she'd come back the next day. Besides, this way she'd get back to the gulls faster.

So, the next morning, October 31, as she pulled up to Jumpin's wharf, she called to him, and he stepped out from the small store.

"Hey, Jumpin', I'm just letting you know I'm home. Got back yesterday." He said nothing as he walked toward her.

As soon as she stepped onto his wharf, he said, "Miss Kya. I . . ."

She cocked her head. "What is it? What's wrong?"

He stood looking at her. "Kya, have ya heard the news 'bout Mr. Chase?"

"No. What news?"

He shook his head. "Chase Andrews is dead. Died in tha middle of the night while ya were over'n Greenval."

"What?" Both Kya and Jumpin' looked deep into the other's eyes.

"They found 'im yestadee mornin' at the bottom of the ol' far towa with a . . . well, they say his neck broke an' his skull smashed right in. They reckon he fell right off from the top."

Kya's lips remained parted.

Jumpin' went on. "Whole town's buzzed up. Some folks're puttin' it down as a accident, but the word is, the sheriff itn't so sure. Chase's mama's all riled up, says there was foul play. It's a sho'-nuff mess."

Kya asked, "Why do they think foul play was . . . ?"

"One a' them grates on the towa flo' was left wide open, and he fell plumb through, and they reckoned that was suspicious. Some people're sayin' them grates are left open all the time with kids always messin' 'round up there, and Mr. Chase coulda fell through by accident. But some folks cryin' murder."

Kya was silent, so Jumpin' continued. "One reason was, when Mr. Chase was found, he wan't wearin' that shell necklace he wore ever' day fer years, and his wife says he was wearin' it that very night when he lef' the house, 'fore he went to his folks for dinah. A'ways wore it, she said."

Her mouth went dry at the mention of the necklace.

"Then, those two young'uns that found Chase, well, they heard the sheriff say thar weren't no footprints at the scene. Nary a one. Like somebody done rubbed out evidence. Them boys been yappin' all over town 'bout it."

Jumpin' told her when the funeral would be but knew Kya wouldn't go. What a spectacle that would be for the sewing bees and Bible study groups. For sure, the speculation and gossip would include Kya. *Thank tha Lawd she'd been in Greenval at the time 'a his death, or they'd'a put this on 'er,* Jumpin' thought.

Kya nodded at Jumpin' and churned home. She stood on the mud bank of the lagoon, whispering one of Amanda Hamilton's verses:

"Never underrate
the heart,
Capable of deeds
The mind cannot conceive.
The heart dictates as well as feels.
How else can you explain
The path I have taken,
That you have taken
The long way through this pass?"

49.

Disguises

1970

Stating his name as Mr. Larry Price—a man with curly white hair, cut short, and dressed in a blue suit that shone cheaply—and that he drove the Trailways bus on varying routes in this area of North Carolina, the next witness was sworn in. As Eric questioned him, Mr. Price confirmed that it was possible to bus from Greenville to Barkley Cove and back again on the same night. He also stated that he was driving the bus from Greenville bound for Barkley Cove the night Chase died, and none of the passengers looked like Miss Clark.

Eric said, "Now, Mr. Price, you told the sheriff during his investigation that there was a skinny passenger on that bus who could've been a tall woman disguised as a man. Is that correct? Please describe this passenger."

"Yeah, that's right. A young white man. Reckon he was 'bout five ten, and his pants just hung on him like sheets on a fence post. He wore a big bulky cap, blue. Kept his head down, didn't look at anybody."

"And now that you've seen Miss Clark, do you believe it's possible that the skinny man on the bus was Miss Clark in disguise? Could her long hair have been hidden in that bulky cap?"

"Yeah, I do."

Eric asked the judge to request that Kya stand up, and she did so with Tom Milton by her side.

"You can sit back down, Miss Clark," Eric said, and then to the witness, "Would you say that the young man on the bus was the same height and stature as Miss Clark?"

"I'd say 'bout exactly the same," Mr. Price said.

"So all things considered, would you say that it's likely that the skinny man on the 11:50 P.M. bus traveling from Greenville to Barkley Cove on the night of October 29 of last year was in fact the defendant Miss Clark?"

"Yeah, I'd say that's very possible."

"Thank you, Mr. Price. No further questions. Your witness."

Tom stood in front of the witness stand and, after five minutes of questioning Mr. Price, he summed up. "What you've told us is this: one, there was no woman who looked like the defendant on the bus from Greenville to Barkley Cove on the night of October 29, 1969; two, there was a tall, thin man on the bus, but at the time, even though you saw his face very close, you didn't think of him as a woman in disguise; three, this idea of disguise only came to you when the sheriff suggested it."

Tom continued before the witness could respond. "Mr. Price, tell us how you're sure the thin man was on the 11:50 P.M. bus of October 29? Did you take notes, write it down? Maybe it was the night before or the night after. Are you one hundred percent sure it was October 29?"

"Well, I see what you gettin' at. And, when the sheriff was jogging my memory, it seemed like that man was on that bus, but now, I reckon I can't be one hundred percent sure."

"Also, Mr. Price, wasn't the bus very late that night? In fact, it was twenty-five minutes late and didn't arrive in Barkley Cove until 1:40 in the morning. Is that correct?"

"Yeah." Mr. Price looked at Eric. "I'm just trying to help out here, do the right thing."

Tom reassured him. "You've been a great help, Mr. Price. Thank you very much. No further questions."

Eric called his next witness, the driver for the 2:30 A.M. bus from Barkley Cove to Greenville on the morning of October 30, a Mr. John King. He testified that the defendant, Miss Clark, was not on the bus, but there was an older lady, ". . . tall like Miss Clark, who had gray hair, short with curls, like a permanent wave."

"Looking at the defendant, Mr. King, is it possible that if Miss Clark had disguised herself as an older lady, she would have looked similar to the woman on the bus?"

"Well, it's hard to picture it. Maybe."

"So it's possible?"

"Yes, I guess."

On cross, Tom said, "We cannot accept the word *guess* in a murder trial. Did you see the defendant, Miss Clark, on the 2:30 A.M. bus from Barkley Cove to Greenville in the early morning of October 30, 1969?"

"No, I did not."

"And was there another bus from Barkley Cove to Greenville that night?"

"No."

50.

The Journal

1970

When Kya was led into the courtroom the next day, she glanced toward Tate, Jumpin', and Mabel and held her breath at seeing a full uniform, a slight smile across a scarred face. Jodie. She nodded slightly, wondering how he'd learned of her trial. Probably the Atlanta paper. She tucked her head in shame.

Eric stood. "Your Honor, if it please the court, the People call Mrs. Sam Andrews." The room breathed out as Patti Love, the grieving mother, made her way to the witness stand. Watching the woman she'd once hoped would be her mother-in-law, Kya now realized the absurdity of that notion. Even in this sullen setting, Patti Love, dressed in the finest black silks, seemed preoccupied with her own appearance and importance. She sat straight with her glossy purse perched on her lap, dark hair swept into the perfect bun under a hat, tipped just so, with dramatic black netting obscuring her eyes. Never would she have taken a barefoot marsh dweller as a daughter-in-law.

"Mrs. Andrews, I know this is difficult for you, so I'll be as brief as possible. Is it true that your son, Chase Andrews, wore a rawhide necklace hung with a shell?"

"Yes, that's true."

"And when, how often, did he wear that necklace?"

"All the time. He never took it off. For four years I never saw him without that necklace."

Eric handed a leather journal to Mrs. Andrews. "Can you identify this book for the court?"

Kya stared at the floor, working her lips, enraged at this invasion of her privacy as the prosecutor held her journal for all the court to see. She'd made it for Chase very soon after they met. Most of her life, she'd been denied the joy of giving gifts, a deprivation few understand. After working for days and nights on the journal, she'd wrapped it in brown paper and decorated it with striking green ferns and white feathers from snow geese. She'd held it out as Chase stepped from his boat onto the lagoon shore.

"What's this?"

"Just something from me," she had said, and smiled.

A painted story of their times together. The first, an ink sketch of them sitting against the driftwood, Chase playing the harmonica. The Latin names of the sea oats and scattered shells were printed in Kya's hand. A swirl of watercolors revealed his boat drifting in moonlight. The next was an abstract image of curious porpoises circling the boat, with the words of "Michael Row the Boat Ashore" drifting in the clouds. Another of her swirling among silver gulls on a silver beach.

Chase had turned the pages in wonder. Ran his fingers lightly over some of the drawings, laughed at some, but mostly was silent, nodding.

"I've never had anything like this." Leaning over to embrace her, he had said, "Thank you, Kya." They sat on the sand awhile, wrapped in blankets, talking, holding hands.

Kya remembered how her heart had pounded at the joy of giving, never imagining anyone else would see the journal. Certainly not as evidence at her murder trial.

She didn't look at Patti Love when she answered Eric's question. "It's a collection of paintings that Miss Clark made for Chase. She gave it to him as a present." Patti Love remembered finding the journal under a stack of albums while cleaning his room. Apparently hidden from her. She'd sat on Chase's bed and opened the thick cover. There, in detailed ink, her son lying against driftwood with that girl. The Marsh Girl. Her Chase with trash. She could barely breathe. *What if people find out?* First cold, then sweaty, her body reeled.

"Mrs. Andrews, would you please explain what you see in this picture painted by the defendant, Miss Clark."

"That's a painting of Chase and Miss Clark on the top of the fire tower." A murmur moved through the room.

"What else is going on?"

"There—between their hands, she is giving him the shell necklace."

And he never took it off again, Patti Love thought. *I believed that he told me everything. I thought I'd bonded with my son more than other mothers; that's what I told myself. But I knew nothing.*

"So, because he told you and because of this journal, you knew your son was seeing Miss Clark, and you knew she gave him the necklace?"

"Yes."

"When Chase came to your house for dinner on the night of October 29, was he wearing the necklace?"

"Yes, he didn't leave our house until after eleven, and he was wearing the necklace."

"Then when you went into the clinic the next day to identify Chase, did he have the necklace on?"

"No, he did not."

"Do you know of any reason why any of his friends or anyone else, besides Miss Clark, would want to take the necklace off Chase?"

"No."

"Objection, Your Honor," Tom called quickly from his seat. "Hearsay. Calls for speculation. She can't speak to the reasoning of other people."

"Sustained. Jurors, you must disregard the last question and answer." Then, lowering his head ganderlike at the prosecutor, the judge said, "Watch your step, Eric. For crying out loud! You know better than that."

Eric, unfazed, continued. "All right, we know from her own drawings that the defendant, Miss Clark, climbed the fire tower with Chase at least once; we know she gave the shell necklace to him. After that, he wore it continuously until the night he died. At which time it disappeared. Is all that correct?"

"Yes."

"Thank you. No further questions. Your witness."

"No questions," Tom said.

51.

Waning Moon

1970

The language of the court was, of course, not as poetic as the language of the marsh. Yet Kya saw similarities in their natures. The judge, obviously the alpha male, was secure in his position, so his posture was imposing, but relaxed and unthreatened as the territorial boar. Tom Milton, too, exuded confidence and rank with easy movements and stance. A powerful buck, acknowledged as such. The prosecutor, on the other hand, relied on wide, bright ties and broad-shouldered suit jackets to enhance his status. He threw his weight by flinging his arms or raising his voice. A lesser male needs to shout to be noticed. The bailiff represented the lowest-ranking male and depended on his belt hung with glistening pistol, clanging wad of keys, and clunky radio to bolster his position. *Dominance hierarchies enhance stability in natural populations, and some less natural,* Kya thought.

The prosecutor, wearing a scarlet tie, stepped boldly to the front and called his next witness, Hal Miller, a rake-thin twenty-eight-year-old with moppy brown hair.

"Mr. Miller, please tell us where you were and what you saw the night of October 29 to 30, 1969, at about 1:45 A.M."

"Me and Allen Hunt were crewing for Tim O'Neal on his shrimp boat, and we were headed back to Barkley Cove Harbor late, and we seen her, Miz Clark, in her boat, about a mile out, east of the bay, headed north-northwest."

"And where would that course take her?"

"Right smack to that cove near the fire tower."

Judge Sims banged his gavel at the outburst, which rumbled for a full minute.

"Could she not have been going somewhere else?"

"Well, I reckon, but there's nothing up that way but miles of swamped-out woods. No other destination I know of 'cept the fire tower."

Ladies' funeral fans pumped against the warming, unsettled room. Sunday Justice, sleeping on the windowsill, flowed to the floor and walked to Kya. For the first time in the courtroom, he rubbed against her leg, then jumped onto her lap and settled. Eric stopped talking and looked at the judge, perhaps considering an objection for such an open display of partiality, but there seemed no legal precedent.

"How can you be sure it was Miss Clark?"

"Oh, we all know her boat. She's been boatin' around on her own fer years."

"Were there lights on her boat?"

"No, no lights. Might've run her over if we hadn't seen her."

"But isn't it illegal to operate a boat after dark without lights?"

"Yeah, she was s'posed to have lights. But she didn't."

"So on the night that Chase Andrews died at the fire tower, Miss Clark was boating in exactly that direction, just minutes before the time of his death. Is that correct?"

"Yeah, that's what we seen."

Eric sat down.

Tom walked toward the witness. "Good morning, Mr. Miller."

"Good mornin'."

"Mr. Miller, how long have you been serving as a crew member on Tim O'Neal's shrimp boat?"

"Going on three years now."

"And tell me, please, what time did the moon rise the night of October 29 to the 30?"

"It was waning, and didn't rise till after we docked in Barkley. Sometime after two A.M. I reckon."

"I see. So when you saw the small boat motoring near Barkley Cove that night, there was no moon. It must have been very dark."

"Yeah. It was dark. There was some starlight but, yeah, pretty dark."

"Would you please tell the court what Miss Clark was wearing as she motored past you in her boat that night."

"Well, we weren't near close enough to see what she was wearing."

"Oh? You weren't near enough to see her clothes." Tom looked at the jury as he said this. "Well, how far away were you?"

"I reckon we was a good sixty yards away at least."

"Sixty yards." Tom looked at the jury again. "That's quite a distance to identify a small boat in the dark. Tell me, Mr. Miller, what characteristics, what features of this person in this boat made you so sure it was Miss Clark?"

"Well, like I said, 'bout everybody in this town knows her boat, how it looks from close and far. We know the shape of the boat and the figure she cuts sittin' in the stern, tall, thin like that. A very particular shape."

"A particular shape. So anybody with this same shape, any person who was tall and thin in this type of boat would have looked like Miss Clark. Correct?"

"I guess somebody else coulda looked like her, but we get to know boats and their owners real good, you know, being out there all the time."

"But, Mr. Miller, may I remind you, this is a murder trial. It cannot get more serious than this, and in these cases we have to be certain. We can't go by shapes or forms that are seen from sixty yards away in the dark. So, please can you tell the court you are certain the person you saw on the night of October 29 to October 30, 1969, was Miss Clark?"

"Well, no, I can't be completely sure. Never said I could be completely sure it was her. But I'm pretty—"

"That will be all, Mr. Miller. Thank you."

Judge Sims asked, "Redirect, Eric?"

From his seat, Eric asked, "Hal, you testified that you've been seeing and recognizing Miss Clark in her boat for at least three years. Tell me, have you ever thought you saw Miss Clark in her boat from a distance and then once you got closer, you discovered that it wasn't Miss Clark after all? Has that ever happened?"

"No, not once."

"Not once in three years?"

"Not once in three years."

"Your Honor, the State rests."

52.

Three Mountains Motel

1970

Judge Sims entered the courtroom and nodded at the defense table. "Mr. Milton, are you ready to call your first witness for the defense?"

"I am, Your Honor."

"Proceed."

After the witness was sworn and seated, Tom said, "Please state your name and what you do in Barkley Cove." Kya raised her head enough to see the short, elderly woman with the purplish-white hair and tight perm who years ago asked her why she always came alone to the grocery. Perhaps she was shorter and her curls tighter, but she looked remarkably the same. Mrs. Singletary had seemed nosey and bossy, but she had given Kya the net Christmas stocking with the blue whistle inside the winter after Ma left. It was all the Christmas Kya had.

"I'm Sarah Singletary, and I clerk at the Piggly Wiggly market in Barkley Cove."

"Sarah, is it correct that from your cash register within the Piggly Wiggly, you can see the Trailways bus stop?"

"Yes, I can see it clearly."

"On October 28 of last year, did you see the defendant, Miss Catherine Clark, waiting at the bus stop at 2:30 P.M.?"

"Yes, I saw Miss Clark standing there." At this, Sarah glanced at Kya and remembered the little girl coming barefoot into the market for so many years. No one would ever know, but before Kya could count, Sarah had given the child extra change—money she had to take from her own purse to balance the register. Of course, Kya was dealing with small sums to start with, so Sarah contributed only nickels and dimes, but it must have helped.

"How long did she wait? And did you actually see her step onto the 2:30 P.M. bus?"

"She waited about ten minutes, I think. We all saw her buy her ticket from the driver, give him her suitcase, and step onto the bus. It drove away, and she was most definitely inside."

"And I believe you also saw her return two days later on October 30 on the 1:16 P.M. bus. Is that correct?"

"Yes, two days later, a little after 1:15 in the afternoon, I looked up as the bus stopped, and there was Miss Clark stepping off it. I pointed her out to the other checkout ladies."

"Then what did she do?"

"She walked to the wharf, got in her boat, and headed south."

"Thank you, Sarah. That will be all."

Judge Sims asked, "Any questions, Eric?"

"No, Your Honor, I have no questions. In fact, I see from the witness list that the defense intends to call several townspeople to testify that Miss Clark got on and off the Trailways bus on the dates and times

Mrs. Singletary has stated. The prosecution does not refute this testimony. Indeed, it is consistent with our case that Miss Clark traveled on those buses at those times and, if it please the court, it is not necessary to hear from other witnesses on this matter."

"All right. Mrs. Singletary, you can step down. What about you, Mr. Milton? If the prosecution accepts the fact that Miss Clark got on the 2:30 bus on October 28, 1969, and returned at about 1:16 on October 30, 1969, do you need to call other witnesses to this effect?"

"No, Your Honor." His face appeared calm, but Tom swore inside. Kya's alibi of being out of town at the time of Chase's death was one of the strongest points for the defense. But Eric had successfully diluted the alibi simply by accepting it, even stating that he didn't need to hear testimony that Kya traveled to and from Greenville during the day. It didn't matter to the prosecution's case because they claimed Kya had returned to Barkley at night and committed the murder. Tom had foreseen the risk but thought it crucial that the jury hear testimony, to visualize Kya leaving town in daylight and not returning until after the incident. Now, they'd think her alibi wasn't important enough even to be confirmed.

"Noted. Please proceed with your next witness."

Bald and fubsy, his coat buttoned tight against a round belly, Mr. Lang Furlough testified that he owned and operated the Three Mountains Motel in Greenville and that Miss Clark had stayed at the motel from October 28 until October 30, 1969.

Kya detested listening to this oily-haired man, who she never thought she'd see again, and here he was talking about her as though she weren't present. He explained how he had shown her to her motel room but failed to mention he had lingered too long. Kept thinking of reasons to stay in her room until she opened the door, hinting for him to leave. When Tom asked how he could be sure of Miss Clark's comings and goings from the motel, he chuckled and said she was the kind of woman men notice. He added how strange she was, not knowing how to use the telephone, walking from the bus station with a cardboard suitcase, and bringing her own bagged dinner.

"Mr. Furlough, on the next night, that being October 29, 1969, the night Chase Andrews died, you worked at the reception desk all night. Is that correct?"

"Yes."

"After Miss Clark returned to her room at ten P.M. after dinner with her editor, did you see her leave again? At any time during the night of October 29 or the early-morning hours of October 30, did you see her leave or return to her room?"

"No. I was there all night and I never saw her leave her room. Like I said, her room was directly across from the reception counter, so I would have seen her leave."

"Thank you, Mr. Furlough, that's all. Your witness."

After several minutes of cross-examination, Eric continued. "Okay, Mr. Furlough, so far we have you leaving the reception area altogether to walk to your apartment twice, use the restroom, and return; the pizza boy bringing pizza; you paying him, et cetera; four guests checking in, two checking out; and in between all that, you completed your receipts account. Now I'd submit, Mr. Furlough, that during all that commotion, there were plenty of times that Miss Clark could have quietly walked out of her room, quickly crossed the street, and you would never have seen her. Isn't that entirely possible?"

"Well, I guess it's possible. But I never saw a thing. I didn't see her leave her room that night—is what I'm saying."

"I understand that, Mr. Furlough. And what I'm saying is that it's very possible that Miss Clark left her room, walked to the bus station, bused to Barkley Cove, murdered Chase Andrews, and returned to her room, and you never saw her because you were very busy doing your job. No more questions."

After the lunch recess, just as everyone was settled and the judge had taken his seat, Scupper stepped inside the courtroom. Tate turned to see his father, still in his overalls and yellow marine boots, walking down the aisle. Scupper had not attended the trial because of his work, he'd said, but mostly because his son's long attachment to Miss Clark confounded him. It seemed Tate had never had feelings for any other girl, and even as a grown, professional man, he still loved this strange, mysterious woman. A woman now accused of murder.

Then, that noon, standing on his boat, nets pooled around his boots, Scupper breathed out heavily. His face blazed with shame as he realized that he—like some of the ignorant villagers—had been prejudiced against Kya because she had grown up in the marsh. He remembered Tate proudly showing him Kya's first book on shells and how Scupper himself was taken aback by her scientific and artistic prowess. He had bought himself a copy of each of her books but hadn't mentioned that to Tate. What bullshit.

He was so proud of his son, how he had always known what he wanted and how to achieve it. Well, Kya had done the same against much bigger odds.

How could he not be there for Tate? Nothing mattered except supporting his son. He dropped the net at his feet, left the boat wallowing against the pier, and walked directly to the courthouse.

When he reached the first row, Jodie, Jumpin', and Mabel stood to allow him to squeeze by and sit next to Tate. Father and son nodded at each other, and tears swelled in Tate's eyes.

Tom Milton waited for Scupper to sit, the silence in the room complete, then said, "Your Honor, the defense calls Robert Foster." Dressed in a tweed jacket, tie, and khaki pants, Mr. Foster was trim, of medium height, and had a neat beard and kind eyes. Tom asked his name and occupation.

"My name is Robert Foster, and I'm a senior editor for Harrison Morris Publishing Company in Boston, Massachusetts." Kya, hand to her forehead, stared at the floor. Her editor was the only person she knew who didn't think of her as the Marsh Girl, who had respected her, even seemed awed at her knowledge and talent. Now he was in court seeing her at the defendant's table, charged with murder.

"Are you the editor for Miss Catherine Clark's books?"

"Yes, I am. She is a very talented naturalist, artist, and writer. One of our favorite authors."

"Can you confirm that you traveled to Greenville, North Carolina, on October 28, 1969, and that you had meetings with Miss Clark on both the twenty-ninth and the thirtieth?"

"That is correct. I was attending a small conference there, and knew I would have some extra time while in town but wouldn't have enough time to travel to her place, so I invited Miss Clark to Greenville so we could meet."

"Can you tell us the exact time that you drove her back to her motel on the night of October 29, last year?"

"After our meetings, we dined at the hotel and then I drove Kya back to her motel at 9:55 P.M."

Kya recalled standing on the threshold of the dining room, filled with candlelit tables under soft chandeliers. Tall wineglasses on white tablecloths. Stylishly dressed diners conversed in quiet voices, while she wore the plain skirt and blouse. She and Robert dined on almond-crusted North Carolina trout, wild rice, creamed spinach, and yeast rolls. Kya felt comfortable as he kept the conversation going with easy grace, sticking to subjects about nature familiar to her.

Remembering it now, she was astonished how she had carried it off. But in fact, the restaurant, with all its glitter, wasn't nearly as grand as her favorite picnic. When she was fifteen, Tate had boated to her shack one dawn, and, after he'd wrapped a blanket around her shoulders, they cruised inland through a maze of waterways to a forest she'd never seen. They hiked a mile to the edge of a waterlogged meadow where fresh grass sprouted through mud, and there he laid the blanket under ferns as large as umbrellas.

"Now we wait," he'd said, as he poured hot tea from a thermos and offered her "coon balls," a baked mixture of biscuit dough, hot sausage, and sharp cheddar cheese he had cooked for the occasion. Even now in this cold courtroom setting, she remembered the warmth of his shoulders touching hers under the blanket, as they nibbled and sipped the breakfast picnic.

They didn't have to wait long. Moments later, a ruckus as loud as cannons sounded from the north. "Here they come," Tate had said.

A thin, black cloud appeared on the horizon and, as it moved toward them, it soared skyward. The shrieking rose in intensity and volume as the cloud rapidly filled the sky until not one spot of blue remained. Hundreds of thousands of snow geese, flapping, honking, and gliding, covered the world. Swirling masses wheeled and banked for landing. Perhaps a half million white wings flared in unison, as pink-orange feet dangled down, and a blizzard of birds came in to land. A true whiteout as everything on Earth, near and far, disappeared. One at a time, then ten at a time, then hundreds of geese landed only yards from where Kya and Tate had sat under the ferns. The sky emptied as the wet meadow filled until it was covered in downy snow.

No fancy dining room could compare to that, and the coon balls offered more spice and flare than almond-crusted trout.

"You saw Miss Clark go into her room?"

"Of course. I opened her door and saw her safely inside before I drove away."

"Did you see Miss Clark the next day?"

"We had arranged to meet for breakfast, so I picked her up at 7:30 A.M. We ate at the Stack 'Em High pancake place. I took her back to her motel at 9:00. And that was the last I saw of her until today." He glanced at Kya, but she looked down at the table.

"Thank you, Mr. Foster. I have no further questions."

Eric stood and asked, "Mr. Foster, I was wondering why you stayed at the Piedmont Hotel, which is the best hotel in the area, while your publishing company only paid for Miss Clark—such a talented author, one of the favorites, as you put it—to stay in a very basic motel, the Three Mountains?"

"Well, of course, we offered, even recommended that Miss Clark stay at the Piedmont, but she insisted on staying at the motel."

"Is that so? Did she know the motel's name? Did she specifically request to stay at the Three Mountains?"

"Yes, she wrote a note saying she preferred to stay at the Three Mountains."

"Did she say why?"

"No, I don't know why."

"Well, I have an idea. Here's a tourist map of Greenville." Eric waved the map around as he approached the witness stand. "You can see here, Mr. Foster, that the Piedmont Hotel—the four-star hotel that you offered to Miss Clark—is located in the downtown area. The Three Mountains Motel, on the other hand, is on Highway 258, near the Trailways bus station. In fact, if you study the map as I have, you will see that the Three Mountains is the closest motel to the bus station . . ."

"Objection, Your Honor," Tom called out. "Mr. Foster is not an authority on the layout of Greenville."

"No, but the map is. I see where you're going, Eric, and I'll allow it. Proceed."

"Mr. Foster, if someone were planning a quick trip to the bus station in the middle of the night, it is logical that they would choose the Three Mountains over the Piedmont. Especially if they planned to walk. All I need from you is the confirmation that Miss Clark asked specifically to stay at the Three Mountains and not the Piedmont."

"As I said, she requested the Three Mountains."

"I have nothing more."

"Redirect?" Judge Sims asked.

"Yes, Your Honor. Mr. Foster, how many years have you worked with Miss Clark?"

"Three years."

"And even though you didn't meet her until the visit in Greenville last October, would you say that you've gotten to know Miss Clark quite well through correspondence over those years? If so, how would you describe her?"

"Yes, I have. She is a shy, gentle person, I believe. She prefers to be alone in the wilderness; it took some time for me to convince her to come to Greenville. Certainly she would avoid a crowd of people."

"A crowd of people like one would encounter at a large hotel such as the Piedmont?"

"Yes."

"In fact, wouldn't you say, Mr. Foster, that it is not surprising that Miss Clark—who likes to keep to herself—would choose a small, rather remote motel over a large bustling hotel right in town? That this choice would fit her character?"

"Yes, I would say that."

"Also, doesn't it make sense if Miss Clark, who is not familiar with public transport and knew she had to walk from the bus station to her hotel and back again, carrying a suitcase, that she would select a hotel or motel closest to the station?"

"Yes."

"Thank you. That will be all."

When Robert Foster left the witness stand, he sat with Tate, Scupper, Jodie, Jumpin', and Mabel, behind Kya.

That afternoon, Tom called the sheriff back as his next witness.

Kya knew from Tom's list of witnesses that there weren't many more to be called, and the thought sickened her. The closing arguments came next, then the verdict. As long as a stream of witnesses supported her, she could hope for acquittal or at least a delay of conviction. If the court proceedings trailed on forever, a judgment would never be handed down. She tried to lead her mind into fields-of-snow-geese distractions as she had since the trial began, but instead she saw only images of jail, bars, clammy cement walls. Mental inserts now and then of an electric chair. Lots of straps.

Suddenly, she felt she couldn't breathe, couldn't sit here any longer, her head too heavy to hold up. She sagged slightly, and Tom turned from the sheriff to Kya as her head dropped onto her hands. He rushed to her.

"Your Honor, I request a short recess. Miss Clark needs a break."

"Granted. Court dismissed for a fifteen-minute recess."

Tom helped her stand and whisked her out the side door and into the small conference room, where she sank into a chair. Sitting next to her, he said, "What is it? Kya, what's wrong?"

She buried her head in her hands. "How can you ask that? Isn't it obvious? How does anyone live through this? I feel too sick, too tired to sit there. Do I have to? Can't the trial continue without me?" All she was capable of, all she wanted, was to return to her cell and curl up with Sunday Justice.

"No, I'm afraid not. In a capital case, such as this, the law requires your presence."

"What if I can't? What if I refuse? All they can do is throw me in jail."

"Kya, it's the law. You have to attend, and anyway, it's better for you to be present. It's easier for a jury to convict an absent defendant. But, Kya, it won't be for much longer."

"That doesn't make me feel any better, don't you see? What comes next is worse than this."

"We don't know that. Don't forget, we can appeal if this doesn't go our way."

Kya didn't answer. Thoughts of an appeal sickened her more, the same forced march through different courtrooms, farther from the marsh. Probably large towns. Some gull-less sky. Tom stepped out of the room and returned with a glass of sweet iced tea and a package of salted peanuts. She sipped at the tea; refused the nuts. A few minutes later, the bailiff knocked on the door and led them back into court. Kya's mind faded in and out of reality, catching only snippets of the testimony.

"Sheriff Jackson," Tom said, "the prosecution is claiming that Miss Clark snuck out of her motel late at night and walked from the Three

Mountains Motel to the bus station—a trip of at least twenty minutes. That she then took the 11:50 P.M. night bus from Greenville to Barkley Cove, but the bus was late, so she couldn't have arrived in Barkley until 1:40 A.M. They claim that from the Barkley bus stop, she walked to the town wharf—three or four minutes—then she boated to the cove near the water tower—at least twenty minutes—walked to the tower, another eight minutes; climbed it in pitch dark, say, four to five minutes at least; opened the grate, a few seconds; waited for Chase—no time estimate—and then all of this in reverse.

"Those actions would have taken one hour seven minutes minimum, and that does not count time supposedly waiting for Chase. But the bus back to Greenville, which she had to catch, departed only fifty minutes after she arrived. Therefore, it is a simple fact: there was not enough time for her to commit this alleged crime. Isn't that correct, Sheriff?"

"It would've been tight, that's true. But she could've jogged from her boat to the tower and back, she could've cut a minute here and there."

"A minute here and there won't do it. She would have needed twenty extra minutes. At least. How could she have saved twenty minutes?"

"Well, maybe she didn't go in her boat at all; maybe she walked or ran from the bus stop on Main, down the sandy track to the tower. That would be much quicker than going by sea." From his seat at the prosecution table, Eric Chastain glared at the sheriff. He had convinced the jury there was enough time for Kya to commit the crime and return to the bus. They didn't need much convincing. In addition, they had a superior witness, the shrimper, who testified that he had seen Miss Clark headed to the tower by boat.

"Do you have any evidence whatsoever that Miss Clark went by land to the tower, Sheriff?"

"No. But going by land is a good theory."

"Theory!" Tom turned to the jury. "The time for *theories* was before you arrested Miss Clark, before you held her in jail for two months. The fact is you cannot prove that she went by land, and there was not enough time for her to go by sea. No more questions."

Eric faced the sheriff for the cross. "Sheriff, isn't it true that the waters near Barkley Cove are subjected to strong currents, riptides, and undertows that can influence the speed of a boat?"

"Yeah, that's true. Everybody lives here knows that."

"Someone who knew how to take advantage of such a current could boat very quickly to the tower from the harbor. In such a case, it would be very feasible to cut twenty minutes off the round trip. Isn't that correct?" Eric was annoyed that he had to suggest yet another theory, but all he needed was some plausible concept the jurors could latch on to and pull them in.

"Yeah, that's correct."

"Thank you." As soon as Eric turned from the witness stand, Tom stood for the redirect.

"Sheriff, yes or no, do you have any evidence that a current, riptide, or strong wind occurred on the night of October 29 to the 30 that could have decreased the time for someone to boat from the Barkley Cove Harbor to the fire tower, or any evidence that Miss Clark went to the tower by land?"

"No, but I'm sure there—"

"Sheriff, it doesn't make any difference what you're sure of or not. Do you have any evidence that a strong riptide was flowing the night of October 29, 1969?"

"No, I don't."

53.

Missing Link

1970

The next morning, Tom had only one more witness. His last card.

He called Tim O'Neal, who had operated his own shrimping boat in the waters off Barkley Cove for thirty-eight years. Tim, nearing sixty-five, tall yet stout, had thick brown hair with only whispers of gray, yet a full beard, nearly white. Folks knew him to be quiet and serious, honest and gracious, always opening doors for ladies. The perfect last witness.

"Tim, is it correct that on the night of October 29 to the 30 of last year, you were skippering your boat into Barkley Cove Harbor at approximately 1:45 to 2:00 A.M.?"

"Yes."

"Two of your crew members, Mr. Hal Miller, who testified here, and Mr. Allen Hunt, who signed an affidavit, both claim they saw Miss Clark motoring north past the harbor in her boat at approximately the times mentioned. Are you aware of their declarations?"

"Yes."

"Did you see the same boat, at that time and place, that both Mr. Miller and Mr. Hunt saw?"

"Yes, I did."

"And do you agree with their statements that it was Miss Clark in her boat that you saw motoring north?"

"No. I do not."

"Why not?"

"It was dark. There was no moon until later. And that boat was too far away to recognize with any certainty. I know everybody 'round here with that kinda boat, and I've seen Miss Clark in hers plenty a' times, and known right away it was her. But that night, it was too dark to recognize that boat or who was in it."

"Thank you, Tim. No more questions."

Eric walked up close to the witness stand. "Tim, even if you could not identify that boat, or who exactly was in it, do you agree that a rig about the same size and shape as Miss Clark's boat was headed toward the Barkley Cove Fire Tower at approximately 1:45 A.M. the night Chase Andrews died at the fire tower around that time?"

"Yes, I can say the boat was a similar shape and size as Miss Clark's."

"Thank you very much."

On redirect, Tom rose and spoke from where he stood. "Tim, to confirm, you testified that you have recognized Miss Clark in her boat many times, but on that evening, you saw nothing at all to identify that boat or boater to be Miss Clark in her rig. Correct?"

"Correct."

"And can you tell us, are there very many boats the same size and shape as Miss Clark's boat operating in this area?"

"Oh yes, hers is one of the most common types of boat around. There's lots of boats just like hers operating here."

"So the boater you saw that night could have been any number of other persons in a similar boat?"

"Absolutely."

"Thank you. Your Honor, the defense rests."

Judge Sims said, "We'll recess for twenty minutes. Court dismissed."

For his closing, Eric wore a tie with wide gold and burgundy stripes. The gallery was quietly expectant as he approached the jury and stood at the railing, passing his eyes deliberately from one to the next.

"Ladies and gentlemen of the jury, you are members of a community, of a proud and unique town. Last year you lost one of your own sons. A young man, a shining star of your neighborhood, looking forward to a long life with his beautiful . . ."

Kya barely heard him as he repeated his account of how she murdered Chase Andrews. She sat, elbows on the table, her head in her hands, catching only fragments of his discourse.

". . . Two well-known men in this community saw Miss Clark and Chase in the woods . . . heard her saying the words *I will kill you!* . . . a red wool cap that left fibers on his denim jacket . . . Who else would want to remove that necklace . . . you know these currents and winds can drastically increase the speed . . .

"We know from her lifestyle that she is very capable of boating at night, of climbing the tower in the dark. It all fits together like clockwork. Every single move she made that night is clear. You can and must find that the defendant is guilty of first-degree murder. Thank you for doing your duty."

. . .

Judge Sims nodded at Tom, who approached the jury box.

"Ladies and gentlemen of the jury, I grew up in Barkley Cove, and when I was a younger man I heard the tall tales about the Marsh Girl. Yes, let's just get this out in the open. We called her the Marsh Girl. Many still call her that. Some people whispered that she was part wolf or the missing link between ape and man. That her eyes glowed in the dark. Yet in reality, she was only an abandoned child, a little girl surviving on her own in a swamp, hungry and cold, but we didn't help her. Except for one of her only friends, Jumpin', not one of our churches or community groups offered her food or clothes. Instead we labeled and rejected her because we thought she was different. But, ladies and gentlemen, did we exclude Miss Clark because she was different, or was she different because we excluded her? If we had taken her in as one of our own—I think that is what she would be today. If we had fed, clothed, and loved her, invited her into our churches and homes, we wouldn't be prejudiced against her. And I believe she would not be sitting here today accused of a crime.

"The job of judging this shy, rejected young woman has fallen on your shoulders, but you must base that judgment on the facts presented in this case, in this courtroom, not on rumors or feelings from the past twenty-four years.

"What are the true and solid facts?" Just as with the prosecution, Kya's mind caught only snippets. ". . . the prosecution has not even proved that this incident was indeed a murder and not simply a tragic accident. No murder weapon, no wounds from being pushed, no witnesses, no fingerprints . . .

"One of the most important and proven facts is that Miss Clark has a sound alibi. We know she was in Greenville the night Chase died . . .

no evidence that she dressed as a man, bused to Barkley . . . In fact, the prosecution has failed to prove that she was in Barkley Cove that night at all, failed to prove that she went to the tower. I say again: there is not one single piece of evidence that proves Miss Clark was on the fire tower, in Barkley Cove, or killed Chase Andrews.

". . . and the skipper, Mr. O'Neal, who has operated his own shrimp boat for thirty-eight years, testified that it was too dark to identify that boat.

". . . fibers on his jacket, which could have been there for four years . . . These are uncontested facts . . .

"Not one of the witnesses for the prosecution was sure of what they saw, not one. Yet in her defense, every witness is one hundred percent certain . . ."

Tom stood for a moment in front of the jury. "I know most of you very well, and I know you can set aside any former prejudices against Miss Clark. Even though she only went to school one day in her life—because the other children harassed her—she educated herself and became a well-known naturalist and author. We called her the Marsh Girl; now scientific institutions recognize her as the Marsh Expert.

"I believe you can put all of the rumors and tall tales aside. I believe you will come to a judgment based on the facts you heard in this court room, not the false rumors you have heard for years.

"It is time, at last, for us to be fair to the Marsh Girl."

54.

Vice Versa

1970

Motioning toward mismatched chairs in a small conference room, Tom offered seats to Tate, Jodie, Scupper, and Robert Foster. They sat around the rectangular table, stained with coffee-mug circles. The walls were two tones of flaking plaster: lime green around the top, dark green around the bottom. An odor of dankness—as much from the walls as from the marsh—permeated.

"You can wait in here," Tom said, closing the door behind him. "There's a coffee machine down the hall across from the assessor's, but it's not fit for a three-eyed mule. The diner has okay coffee. Let's see, it's a little after eleven. We'll make a plan for lunch later."

Tate walked to the window, which was crisscrossed with a mesh of white bars, as if other verdict-waiters had tried escape. He asked Tom, "Where'd they take Kya? To her cell? Does she have to wait in there alone?"

"Yes, she's in her cell. I'm going to see her now."

"How long do you think the jury will take?" Robert asked.

"It's impossible to say. When you think it'll be quick, they take days, and vice versa. Most of them have probably already decided—and not in Kya's favor. If a few jurors have doubts and try to convince the others that guilt has not been proven definitively, we have a chance."

They nodded silently, weighed down by the word *definitively,* as though guilt had been proven, just not absolutely.

"Okay," Tom continued. "I'm going to see Kya and then get to work. I have to prepare the appeals request and even a motion for a mistrial due to prejudice. Please keep in mind, if she's convicted, this is not the end of the road. Not by any means. I'll be in and out, and I'll certainly let you know if there's any news."

"Thanks," Tate said, then added, "Please tell Kya we're here, and will sit with her if she wants." This, though she had refused to see anyone but Tom for the last few days and almost no one for two months.

"Sure. I'll tell her." Tom left.

Jumpin' and Mabel had to wait for the verdict outside among the palmettos and saw grass of the square, along with the few other blacks. Just as they spread colorful quilts on the ground and unpacked biscuits and sausage from paper bags, a rain shower sent them grabbing things and running for cover under the overhang of the Sing Oil. Mr. Lane shouted that they had to wait outside—a fact they'd known for a hundred years—and not to get in the way of any customers. Some whites crowded in the diner or the Dog-Gone for coffee, and others clustered in the street beneath bright umbrellas. Kids splashed in sudden puddles and ate Cracker Jacks, expecting a parade.

Tutored by millions of minutes alone, Kya thought she knew lonely. A life of staring at the old kitchen table, into empty bedrooms, across endless stretches of sea and grass. No one to share the joy of a found feather or a finished watercolor. Reciting poetry to gulls.

But after Jacob closed her cell with the clank of bars, disappeared down the hall, and locked the heavy door with a final thud, a cold silence settled. Waiting for the verdict of her own murder trial brought a loneliness of a different order. The question of whether she lived or died did not surface on her mind, but sank beneath the greater fear of years alone without her marsh. No gulls, no sea in a starless place.

The annoying cellmates down the hall had been released. She almost missed their constant nattering—a human presence no matter how lowly. Now she alone inhabited this long cement tunnel of locks and bars.

She knew the scale of the prejudices against her and that an early verdict would mean there had been little deliberation, which would mean conviction. Lockjaw came to mind—the twisting, tortured life of being doomed.

Kya thought of moving the crate under the window and searching for raptors over the marsh. Instead she just sat there. In the silence.

Two hours later, at one in the afternoon, Tom opened the door into the room where Tate, Jodie, Scupper, and Robert Foster waited. "Well, there's some news."

"What?" Tate jerked his head up. "Not a verdict already?"

"No, no. Not a verdict. But I think it's good news. The jurors have asked to see the court record of the bus drivers' testimonies. This means, at least, they're thinking things through—not simply jumping to a verdict. The bus drivers are key, of course, and both said they were certain Kya was not on their respective buses and weren't certain about the disguises either. Sometimes seeing testimony in black and white makes it more definitive to the jurors. We'll see, but it's a glimmer of hope."

"We'll take a glimmer," Jodie said.

"Look, it's past lunchtime. Why don't y'all go over to the diner? I promise, I'll get you if anything happens."

"I don't think so," Tate said. "They'll all be talking about how guilty she is over there."

"I understand. I'll send my clerk for some burgers. How's that?"

"Fine, thanks," Scupper said, and pulled some dollars from his wallet.

At 2:15, Tom returned to tell them the jurors had asked to see the coroner's testimony. "I'm not sure if this is favorable or not."

"Shit!" Tate swore. "How does anybody live through this?"

"Try to relax; this may take days. I'll keep you posted."

Unsmiling and drawn, Tom opened the door again at four o'clock. "Well, gentlemen, the jurors have a verdict. The judge has ordered everyone back to the courtroom."

Tate stood. "What does it mean? Happening so fast like this."

"Come on, Tate." Jodie touched his arm. "Let's go."

In the hallway, they joined the stream of townspeople jostling shoulder to shoulder from outside. Dank air, smelling of cigarette smoke, rain-wet hair, and damp clothes, flowed with them.

The courtroom filled in less than ten minutes. Many couldn't get a seat and bunched in the hall or on the front steps. At 4:30 the bailiff led Kya toward her seat. For the first time, he supported her by her elbow, and indeed, it appeared she might drop if he did not. Her eyes never moved from the floor. Tate watched every twitch in her face. His breath labored against nausea.

Miss Jones, the recorder, entered and took her seat. Then, like a funeral choir, solemn and cheerless, the jurors filed into their box. Mrs. Culpepper glanced at Kya. The others kept their eyes ahead. Tom tried to read their faces. There was not one cough or shuffle from the gallery.

"All rise."

Judge Sims's door opened, and he sat at his bench. "Please be seated. Mr. Foreman, is it correct that the jury has reached a verdict?"

Mr. Tomlinson, a quiet man who owned the Buster Brown Shoe Shop, stood in the first row. "We have, Your Honor."

Judge Sims looked at Kya. "Would the defendant please rise for the reading of the verdict." Tom touched Kya's arm, then guided her up. Tate placed his hand on the railing as close to Kya as he could get. Jumpin' lifted Mabel's hand and held it.

No one in the room had ever experienced this collective heart pounding, this shared lack of breath. Eyes shifted, hands sweated. The shrimper crew, Hal Miller, knotted his mind, fighting to confirm that it truly was Miss Clark's boat he had seen that night. Suppose he'd been wrong. Most stared, not at the back of Kya's head, but at the floor, the walls. It seemed that the village—not Kya—awaited judgment, and few felt the salacious joy they had expected at this juncture.

The foreman, Mr. Tomlinson, handed a small piece of paper to the bailiff, who passed it to the judge. He unfolded it and read it with a vacant face. The bailiff then took it from Judge Sims and handed it to Miss Jones, the recorder.

"Would somebody read it to us," Tate spat.

Miss Jones stood and faced Kya, unfolded the paper, and read: "We the jury find Miss Catherine Danielle Clark not guilty as charged in the first-degree murder of Mr. Chase Andrews." Kya buckled and sat. Tom followed.

Tate blinked. Jodie sucked in air. Mabel sobbed. The gallery sat motionless. Surely they had misunderstood. "Did she say not guilty?" A stream of whispers quickly rose in pitch and volume to angry questions. Mr. Lane called out, "This ain't right."

The judge hammered his gavel. "Silence! Miss Clark, the jury has found you not guilty as charged. You are free to go, and I apologize on behalf of this State that you served two months in jail. Jury, we thank you for your time and for serving this community. Court dismissed."

A small covey gathered around Chase's parents. Patti Love wept. Sarah Singletary scowled like everybody else but discovered that she was greatly relieved. Miss Pansy hoped no one saw her jaw relax. A lone tear trailed down Mrs. Culpepper's cheek, and then a shadow smile for the little swamp truant escaping again.

A group of men in overalls stood near the back. "Them jurors have some explainin' to do."

"Cain't Eric declare a mistrial? Do the whole thing over?"

"No. Remember? Cain't be tried for murder twice. She's free. Got away with the whole thing."

"It's the sheriff who messed it up for Eric. Couldn't keep his story straight, kep' makin' it up as he went. Theory this, theory that."

"Been struttin' 'round like he's on *Gunsmoke*."

But this small band of disgruntlement fell apart quickly, some wandering out the door, talking about work to catch up on; how the rain had cooled things down.

Jodie and Tate had rushed through the wooden gate to the defense table. Scupper, Jumpin', Mabel, and Robert followed and encircled Kya. They did not touch her, but stood close as she sat there unmoving.

Jodie said, "Kya, you can go home. Do you want me to drive you?"

"Yes, please."

Kya stood and thanked Robert for coming all the way from Boston. He smiled. "You just forget about this nonsense and continue your amazing work." She touched Jumpin's hand, and Mabel hugged her into her cushy bosom. Then Kya turned to Tate. "Thank you for the things you brought me." She turned to Tom and lost words. He simply enfolded her in his arms. Then she looked at Scupper. She'd never been introduced to him, but knew from his eyes who he was. She nodded a soft thank-you, and to her surprise, he put his hand on her shoulder and squeezed gently.

Then, following the bailiff, she walked with Jodie toward the back door of the courtroom and, as she passed the windowsill, reached out and touched Sunday Justice's tail. He ignored her, and she admired his perfected pretense of not needing good-bye.

When the door opened she felt the breath of the sea on her face.

55.

Grass Flowers

1970

As Jodie's truck bumped off the pavement onto the sandy marsh road, he talked gently to Kya, saying she'd be fine; it would just take some time. She scanned cattails and egrets, pines and ponds flashing past. Craned her neck to watch two beavers paddling. Like a migrating tern who has flown ten thousand miles to her natal shore, her mind pounded with the longing and expectation of home; she barely heard Jodie's prattle. Wished he would be quiet and listen to the wilderness within him. Then he might see.

Her breath caught as Jodie turned the last bend of the winding lane, and the old shack came into view, waiting there beneath the oaks. The Spanish moss tossed gently in the breeze above the rusted roof, and the heron balanced on one leg in the shadows of the lagoon. As soon as Jodie stopped the truck, Kya jumped out and ran into the shack, touching the bed, the table, the stove. Knowing what she would want, he'd left a bag of crumbs on the counter, and, finding new energy, she ran to the beach with it, tears streaming her cheeks as the gulls flew toward her from up and down the shore. Big Red landed and tramped around her, his head bobbing.

Kneeling on the beach, surrounded by a bird frenzy, she trembled. "I never asked people for anything. Maybe now they'll leave me alone."

Jodie took her few belongings into the house and made tea in the old pot. He sat at the table and waited. Finally, he heard the porch door open, and as she stepped into the kitchen, she said, "Oh, you're still here." Of course, he was still there—his truck was in plain view outside.

"Please sit down a minute, would you?" he said. "I'd like to talk."

She didn't sit. "I'm fine, Jodie. Really."

"So, does that mean you want me to go? Kya, you've been alone in that cell for two months, thinking a whole town was against you. You've hardly let anyone visit you. I understand all that, I do, but I don't think I should drive away and leave you alone. I want to stay with you a few days. Would that be okay?"

"I've lived alone almost all my life, not two months! And I didn't *think*, I *knew* a whole town was against me."

"Kya, don't let this horrible thing drive you further from people. It's been a soul-crushing ordeal, but this seems to be a chance to start over. The verdict is maybe their way of saying they will accept you."

"Most people don't have to be acquitted of murder to be accepted."

"I know, and you have every reason in the world to hate people. I don't blame you, but . . ."

"That's what nobody understands about me." She raised her voice, "I never hated people. *They* hated *me. They* laughed at *me. They* left *me. They* harassed *me. They* attacked *me.* Well, it's true; I learned to live without them. Without you. Without Ma! Or anybody!"

He tried to hold her, but she jerked away.

"Jodie, maybe I'm just tired right now. In fact, I'm exhausted.

Please, I need to get over all this—the trial, jail, *the thought of being executed*—by myself, because *by myself* is all I've ever known. I don't know how to be consoled. I'm too tired to even have this conversation. I . . ." Her voice trailed off.

She didn't wait for an answer but walked from the shack and into the oak forest. Knowing it was futile, he didn't go after her. He would wait. The day before, he'd supplied the shack with groceries—just in case of acquittal—and now set about chopping vegetables for her favorite: homemade chicken pie. But as the sun set he couldn't stand keeping her from her shack another minute, so he left the hot, bubbling pie on the stovetop and walked out the door. She had circled to the beach, and when she heard his truck driving slowly down the lane, she ran home.

Whiffs of golden pastry filled the shack to the ceiling, but Kya still wasn't hungry. In the kitchen she took out her paints and planned her next book on marsh grasses. People rarely noticed grasses except to mow, trample, or poison them. She swept her brush madly across the canvas in a color more black than green. Dark images emerged, maybe dying meadows under storm cells. It was hard to tell.

She dropped her head and sobbed. "Why am I angry now? Why now? Why was I so mean to Jodie?" Limp, she slid to the floor like a rag doll. Curling into a ball, still crying, she wished she could snuggle with the only one who'd ever accepted her as she was. But the cat was back at the jail.

Just before dark, Kya walked back to the beach where the gulls were preening and settling in for the night. As she waded into the surf, shards of shells and chips of crabs brushed her toes as they tumbled back to the sea. She reached down and picked up two pelican feathers just like the one Tate had put in the *P* section of the dictionary he had given her for Christmas years ago.

She whispered a verse by Amanda Hamilton:

"You came again,
Blinding my eyes
Like the shimmer of sun upon the sea.
Just as I feel free
The moon casts your face upon the sill.
Each time I forget you
Your eyes haunt my heart and it falls still.
And so farewell
Until the next time you come,
Until at last I do not see you."

The next morning before dawn, Kya sat up in her porch bed and breathed the rich scents of the marsh into her heart. As faint light filtered into the kitchen, she cooked herself some grits, scrambled eggs, and biscuits, as light and fluffy as Ma's. She ate every bite. Then, as the sun rose, she rushed to her boat and chugged across the lagoon, dipping her fingers into the clear, deep water.

Churning through the channel, she spoke to the turtles and egrets and lifted her arms high above her head. Home. "I'll collect all day, anything I want," she said. Deeper in her mind was the thought that she might see Tate. Maybe he'd be working nearby and she'd come across him. She could invite him back to the shack to share the chicken pie Jodie had baked.

Less than a mile away, Tate waded through shallow water, dipping samples in tiny vials. A wake of gentle ripples fanned out from each step, from each dip. He planned to stay near Kya's place. Maybe she'd boat out into the marsh, and they'd meet. If not, he'd go to her shack that evening. He hadn't decided exactly what he'd say to her, but kissing some sense into her came to mind.

In the distance an angry engine roared, higher-pitched and much louder than a motorboat—defeating the soft sounds of the marsh. He tracked the noise as it moved in his direction, and suddenly one of those new airboats, which he hadn't seen, raced into view. It glided and gloated above the water, above even the grasses, sending behind a fantail of spray. Emitting the noise of ten sirens.

Crushing shrubs and grasses, the boat broke its own trail across the marsh and then sped across the estuary. Herons and egrets squawking. Three men stood at its helm, and seeing Tate, they turned in his direction. As they neared, he recognized Sheriff Jackson, his deputy, and another man.

The flashy boat sat back on its haunches as it slowed and eased near. The sheriff shouted something to Tate, but even cupping his ears with his hands and leaning toward them, he couldn't hear above the din. They maneuvered even closer until the boat wallowed next to Tate, sloshing water up his thighs. The sheriff leaned down, hollering.

Nearby, Kya had also heard the strange boat and, as she boated toward it, she saw it approaching Tate. She backed into a thicket and watched him take in the sheriff's words, then stand very still, head lowered, shoulders sagging in surrender. Even from this distance she read despair in his posture. The sheriff shouted again, and Tate finally reached up and let the deputy pull him into the boat. The other man hopped into the water and climbed into Tate's cruiser. Chin lowered, eyes downcast, Tate stood between the two uniformed men as they turned around and sped back through the marsh toward Barkley Cove, followed by the other man driving Tate's boat.

Kya stared until both boats disappeared behind a point of eelgrass.

Why had they apprehended Tate? Was it something to do with Chase's death? Had they arrested him?

Agony ripped her. Finally, after a lifetime, she admitted it was the chance of seeing Tate, the hope of rounding a creek bend and watching him through reeds, that had pulled her into the marsh every day of her life since she was seven. She knew his favorite lagoons and paths through difficult quagmires; always following him at a safe distance. Sneaking about, stealing love. Never sharing it. You can't get hurt when you love someone from the other side of an estuary. All the years she rejected him, she survived because he was somewhere in the marsh, waiting. But now perhaps he would no longer be there.

She stared at the fading noise of the strange boat. Jumpin' knew everything—he'd know why the sheriff had taken Tate in and what she could do about it.

She pull-cranked her engine and sped through the marsh.

56.

The Night Heron

1970

The Barkley Cove graveyard trailed off under tunnels of dark oaks. Spanish moss hung in long curtains, creating cavelike sanctuaries for old tombstones—the remains of a family here, a loner there, in no order at all. Fingers of gnarled roots had torn and twisted gravestones into hunched and nameless forms. Markers of death all weathered into nubbins by elements of life. In the distance, the sea and sky sang too bright for this serious ground.

Yesterday the cemetery moved with villagers, like constant ants, including all the fishermen and shopkeepers, who had come to bury Scupper. People clustered in awkward silence as Tate moved among familiar townspeople and unfamiliar relatives. Ever since the sheriff found him in the marsh to tell him his father had died, Tate simply stepped and acted as guided—a hand behind his back, a nudge to his side. He remembered none of it and walked back to the cemetery today to say good-bye.

During all those months, pining for Kya, then trying to visit her in jail, he'd spent almost no time with Scupper. Guilt and regret needed clawing away. Had he not been so obsessed with his own heart, perhaps he would have noticed his father's was failing. Before her arrest, Kya had shown signs of coming back—gifting him a copy of her first book, coming onto his boat to look through the microscope, laughing at the hat toss—but once the trial began she had pulled away more than ever. Jail could do that to a person, he thought.

Even now, walking toward the new grave, carrying a brown plastic case, he found himself thinking more of Kya than of his dad and swore at that. He approached the fresh-scarred mound under the oaks, the wide sea beyond. The grave lay next to his mother's; his sister's on the far side, all enclosed in a small wall of rough stones and mortar embedded with shells. Enough space left for him. It didn't feel as if his dad were here at all. "I should've had you cremated like Sam McGee," Tate said, almost smiling. Then, looking over the ocean, he hoped Scupper had a boat wherever he was. A red boat.

He set the plastic case—a battery-operated record player—on the ground next to the grave and put a 78 on the turntable. The needle arm wobbled, then dropped, and Miliza Korjus's silvery voice lifted over the trees. He sat between his mother's grave and the flower-covered mound. Oddly, the sweet, freshly turned earth smelled more like a beginning than an end.

Talking out loud, head low, he asked his dad to forgive him for spending so much time away, and he knew Scupper did. Tate remembered his dad's definition of a man: one who can cry freely, feel poetry and opera in his heart, and do whatever it takes to defend a woman. Scupper would have understood tracking love through mud. Tate sat there quite awhile, one hand on his mother, the other on his father.

Finally, he touched the grave one last time, walked back to his truck, and drove to his boat at the town wharf. He would go back to work, immerse himself in squirming life-forms. Several fishermen walked to him on the dock, and he stood awkwardly, accepting condolences just as awkward.

Head low, determined to leave before anyone else approached, he stepped onto the aft deck of his cabin cruiser. But before he sat behind the wheel, he saw a pale brown feather resting on the seat cushion. He knew right away it was the soft breast feather of a female night heron, a long-legged secretive creature who lives deep in the marsh, alone. Yet here it was too near the sea.

He looked around. No, she wouldn't be here, not this close to town. He turned the key, churned south through the sea, and finally the marsh.

Going too fast in the channels, he brushed past low branches that slapped at the boat. The agitated wake sloshed against the bank as he pulled into her lagoon and tied his boat next to hers. Smoke rose from the shack's chimney, billowing and free.

"Kya," he yelled. "Kya!"

She opened the porch door and stepped under the oak. She was dressed in a long, white skirt and pale blue sweater—the colors of wings—hair falling about her shoulders.

He waited for her to walk to him, then took her shoulders and held her against his chest. Then pushed back.

"I love you, Kya, you know that. You've known it for a long time."

"You left me like all the others," she said.

"I will never leave you again."

"I know," she said.

"Kya, do you love me? You've never spoken those words to me."

"I've always loved you. Even as a child—in a time I don't remember—I already loved you." She dipped her head.

"Look at me," he said gently. She hesitated, face downcast. "Kya, I need to know that the running and hiding are over. That you can love without being afraid."

She lifted her face and looked into his eyes, then led him through the woods to the oak grove, the place of the feathers.

57.

The Firefly

They slept the first night on the beach, and he moved into the shack with her the next day. Packing and unpacking within a single tide. As sand creatures do.

As they walked along the tide line in late afternoon, he took her hand and looked at her. "Will you marry me, Kya?"

"We are married. Like the geese," she said.

"Okay. I can live with that."

Each morning they rose at dawn and, while Tate percolated coffee, Kya fried corn fritters in Ma's old iron skillet—blackened and dented—or stirred grits and eggs as sunrise eased over the lagoon. The heron posing one-legged in the mist. They cruised estuaries, waded waterways, and slipped through narrow streams, collecting feathers and amoebas. In the evenings, they drifted in her old boat until sunset, then swam naked in moonlight or loved in beds of cool ferns.

Archbald Lab offered Kya a job, but she turned it down and continued writing her books. She and Tate hired the fix-it man again, and he built a lab and studio—of raw wood, hand-hewn posts, and tin roof—for her behind the shack. Tate gave her a microscope and installed worktables, shelves, and closets for her specimens. Trays of instruments and supplies. Then they refurbished the shack, adding a new bedroom and bath, a larger sitting room. She insisted on keeping the kitchen as it was and the exterior unpainted, so that the dwelling, more of a cabin now, remained weathered and real.

From a phone in Sea Oaks she called Jodie and invited him and his wife, Libby, for a visit. The four of them explored the marsh and fished some. When Jodie pulled in a large bream, Kya squealed, "Lookee there. You got one big as Alabamee!" They fried up fish and hush puppies big as "goose aigs."

Kya never went to Barkley Cove again in her life, and for the most part, she and Tate spent their time in the marsh alone. The villagers saw her only as a distant shape gliding through fog, and over the years the mysteries of her story became legend, told over and over with buttermilk pancakes and hot pork sausages at the diner. The theories and gossip over how Chase Andrews died never stopped.

As time passed, most everyone agreed the sheriff never should've arrested her. After all, there was no hard evidence against her, no real proof of a crime. It had been truly cruel to treat a shy, natural creature that way. Now and then a new sheriff—Jackson was never elected again—would open the folder, make some inquiries about other suspects, but not much came of it. Over the years the case, too, eased into legend. And though Kya was never completely healed from the scorn and suspicion surrounding her, a soft contentment, a near-happiness settled into her.

Kya lay on the soft duff near the lagoon one afternoon, waiting for Tate to return from a collecting trip. She breathed deep, knowing he would always come back, that for the first time in her life she would not be abandoned. She heard the deep purr of his cruiser, chugging up the channel; could feel the quiet rumble through the ground. She sat up as his boat pushed through the thickets and waved to him at the helm. He waved back but didn't smile. She stood.

He tied to the small wharf he had built and walked up to her on the shore.

"Kya, I'm so sorry. I have bad news. Jumpin' died last night in his sleep."

An ache pushed against her heart. All those who left her had chosen to do so. This was different. This was not rejection; this was like the Cooper's hawk returning to the sky. Tears rolled down her cheeks, and Tate held her.

Tate and almost everyone in town went to Jumpin's funeral. Kya did not. But after the services, she walked to Jumpin' and Mabel's house, with some blackberry jam long overdue.

Kya paused at the fence. Friends and family stood in the dirt yard, swept clean as a whistle. Some talked, some laughed at old Jumpin' stories, and some cried. As she opened the gate everyone looked at her, then stepped aside to make a path. Standing on the porch, Mabel rushed to Kya. They hugged, rocking back and forth, crying.

"Lawd, he loved ya like his own dawder," Mabel said.

"I know," Kya said, "and he was my pa."

Later, Kya walked to her beach and said farewell to Jumpin' in her own words, in her own way, alone.

And as she wandered the beach remembering Jumpin', thoughts of her mother pushed into her mind. As though Kya were once again the little girl of six, she saw Ma walking down the sandy lane in her old gator shoes, maneuvering the deep ruts. But in this version, Ma stopped at the end of the trail and looked back, waving her hand high in farewell. She smiled at Kya, turned onto the road, and disappeared into the forest. And this time, finally, it was okay.

With no tears or censure, Kya whispered, "Good-bye, Ma." She thought of the others briefly—Pa, her brother and sisters. But she didn't have enough of that bygone family to bid farewell.

That regret faded too when Jodie and Libby began bringing their two children—Murph and Mindy—to visit Kya and Tate several times a year. Once again the shack swelled with family around the old cookstove, serving up Ma's corn fritters, scrambled eggs, and sliced tomatoes. But this time there was laughter and love.

Barkley Cove changed over the years. A man from Raleigh built a fancy marina where Jumpin's shack had leaned for more than a hundred years. With bright blue awnings over each slip, yachts could pull in. Boaters from up and down the coastline moseyed up to Barkley Cove and paid $3.50 for an espresso.

Little sidewalk cafés with smart-colored umbrellas and art galleries with seascapes sprouted on Main. A lady from New York opened a gift shop that sold everything the villagers didn't need but every tourist had to have. Almost every shop had a special table displaying the books by *Catherine Danielle Clark ~ Local Author ~ Award-Winning Biologist*. Grits were listed on the menus as polenta in mushroom sauce and cost $6.00. And one day, some women from Ohio walked into the Dog-Gone Beer Hall, never imagining they were the first females to pass through the door, and ordered spicy shrimp in paper boats, and beer, now on draft. Adults of either sex or any color can walk through the door now, but the window, which was cut out of the wall so that women could order from the sidewalk, is still there.

Tate continued his job at the lab, and Kya published seven more award-winning books. And though she was granted many accolades—including an honorary doctorate from the University of North Carolina at Chapel Hill—she never once accepted the invitations to speak at universities and museums.

Tate and Kya hoped for a family, but a child never came. The disappointment wove them closer together, and they were seldom separated for more than a few hours of any day.

Sometimes Kya walked alone to the beach, and as the sunset streaked the sky, she felt the waves pounding her heart. She'd reach down and touch the sand, then stretch her arms toward the clouds. Feeling the *connections*. Not the connections Ma and Mabel had spoken of—Kya never had her troop of close friends, nor the connections Jodie described, for she never had her own family. She knew the years of isolation had altered her behavior until she was different from others, but it wasn't her fault she'd been alone. Most of what she knew, she'd learned from the wild. Nature had nurtured, tutored, and protected her when no one else would. If consequences resulted from her behaving differently, then they too were functions of life's fundamental core.

Tate's devotion eventually convinced her that human love is more than the bizarre mating competitions of the marsh creatures, but life also taught her that ancient genes for survival still persist in some undesirable forms among the twists and turns of man's genetic code.

For Kya, it was enough to be part of this natural sequence as sure as the tides. She was bonded to her planet and its life in a way few people are. Rooted solid in this earth. Born of this mother.

. . .

At sixty-four Kya's long black hair had turned as white as the sand. One evening she did not return from a collecting trip, so Tate puttered around in the marsh, searching. As dusk eased in, he came around a bend and saw her drifting in her boat in a lagoon surrounded by sycamores touching the sky. She had slumped backward, her head lying against the old knapsack. He called her name softly, and, when she didn't move, he shouted, then screamed. Pulling his boat next to hers, he stumbled awkwardly into the stern of her boat. Reaching out his long arms, he took her shoulders and gently shook her. Her head slumped farther to the side. Her eyes not seeing.

"Kya, Kya, no. No!" he screamed.

Still young, so beautiful, her heart had quietly stopped. She had lived long enough to see the bald eagles make a comeback; for Kya that was long enough. Folding her in his arms, he rocked back and forth, weeping. He wrapped her in a blanket and towed her back to her lagoon in the old boat through the maze of creeks and estuaries, passing the herons and deer for the last time.

> And I'll hide the maid in a cypress tree,
> When the footstep of death is near.

He got special permission for her to be buried on her land under an oak overlooking the sea, and the whole town came out for the funeral. Kya would not have believed the long lines of slow-moving mourners. Of course, Jodie and his family came and all of Tate's cousins. Some curiosity-seekers attended, but most people came out of respect for how she had survived years alone in the wild. Some remembered the little girl, dressed in an oversized, shabby coat, boating to the wharf, walking barefoot to the grocery to buy grits. Others came to her graveside because her books had taught them how the marsh links the land to the sea, both needing the other.

By now, Tate understood that her nickname was not cruel. Only few become legend, so he chose as the epitaph for her tombstone:

CATHERINE DANIELLE CLARK
"KYA"
THE MARSH GIRL
1945–2009

The evening of her funeral, when everyone was finally gone, Tate stepped into her homemade lab. Her carefully labeled samples, more than fifty years' worth, was the longest-running, most complete collection of its kind. She had requested that it be donated to Archbald Lab, and someday he would do so, but parting with it now was unthinkable.

Walking into the shack—as she always called it—Tate felt the walls exhaling her breath, the floors whispering her steps so clear he called out her name. Then he stood against the wall, weeping. He lifted the old knapsack and held it to his chest.

The officials at the courthouse had asked Tate to look for her will and birth certificate. In the old back bedroom, which had once been her parents', he rummaged through the closet and found boxes of her life stuffed in the bottom, almost hidden, under some blankets. He pulled them onto the floor and sat beside them.

Ever so carefully he opened the old cigar box, the one where all the collecting began. The box still smelled of sweet tobacco and little girl. Among a few birds' feathers, insects' wings, and seeds was the small jar with the ashes from her ma's letter, and a bottle of Revlon fingernail polish, Barely Pink. The bits and bones of a life. The stones of her stream.

Tucked in the bottom was the deed for the property, which Kya had put in a conservation easement, protecting it from development. At least this fragment of the marsh would always be wild. But there was no will or personal papers, which did not surprise him; she would not have thought of such things. Tate planned to live out his days at her place, knowing she had wanted that and that Jodie would not object.

Late in the day, the sun dipping behind the lagoon, he stirred corn mush for the gulls and mindlessly glanced at the kitchen floor. He cocked his head as he noticed for the first time that the linoleum had not been installed under the woodpile or the old stove. Kya had kept firewood stacked high, even in summer, but now it was low, and he saw the edge of a cutout in the floorboard. He moved the remaining logs aside and saw a trapdoor in the plywood. Kneeling down, he slowly opened it to find an enclosed compartment between the joists, which held, among other things, an old cardboard box covered in dust. He pulled it out and found inside scores of manila envelopes and a smaller box. All the envelopes were marked with the initials *A.H.*, and from them he pulled out pages and pages of poetry by Amanda Hamilton, the local poet who had published simple verses in regional magazines. Tate had thought Hamilton's poems rather weak, but Kya had always saved the published clippings, and here were envelopes full of them. Some of the written pages were completed poems, but most of them were unfinished, with lines crossed out and some words rewritten in the margin in the poet's handwriting—*Kya's handwriting.*

Amanda Hamilton *was Kya*. Kya was the poet.

Tate's face grimaced in disbelief. Through the years she must have put the poems in the rusty mailbox, submitting them to local publications. Safe behind a nom de plume. Perhaps a reaching-out, a way to express her feelings to someone other than gulls. Somewhere for her words to go.

He glanced through some of the poems, most about nature or love. One was folded neatly in its own envelope. He pulled it out and read:

The Firefly

Luring him was as easy
As flashing valentines.
But like a lady firefly
They hid a secret call to die.

A final touch,
Unfinished;
The last step, a trap.
Down, down he falls,
His eyes still holding mine
Until they see another world.

I saw them change.
First a question,
Then an answer,
Finally an end.

And love itself passing
To whatever it was before it began. A.H.

Still kneeling on the floor, he read it again. He held the paper next to his heart, throbbing inside his chest. He looked out the window, making certain no one was coming down the lane—not that they would, why would they? But to be sure. Then he opened the small box, knowing what he would find. There, laid out carefully on cotton, was the shell necklace Chase had worn until the night he died.

Tate sat at the kitchen table for a long while, taking it in, imagining her riding on night buses, catching a riptide, planning around the moon. Softly calling to Chase in the darkness. Pushing him backward. Then, squatting in mud at the bottom, lifting his head, heavy with death, to retrieve the necklace. Covering her footprints; leaving no trace.

Breaking kindling into bits, Tate built a fire in the old woodstove and, envelope by envelope, burned the poems. Maybe he didn't need to burn them all, maybe he should have destroyed just the one, but he wasn't thinking clearly. The old, yellowed papers made a great *whoosh* a foot high, then smoldered. He took the shell off the rawhide, dropped the rawhide in the fire, and put the boards back in the floor.

Then, in near dusk, he walked to the beach and stood on a sharp bed of white and cracked mollusks and crab pieces. For a second he stared at Chase's shell in his open palm and then dropped it on the sand. Looking the same as all the others, it vanished. The tide was coming in, and a wave flowed over his feet, taking with it hundreds of seashells back into the sea. Kya had been of this land and of this water; now they would take her back. Keep her secrets deep.

And then the gulls came. Seeing him there, they spiraled above his head. Calling. Calling.

As night fell, Tate walked back toward the shack. But when he reached the lagoon, he stopped under the deep canopy and watched hundreds of fireflies beckoning far into the dark reaches of the marsh. Way out yonder, where the crawdads sing.

Acknowledgments

To my twin brother, Bobby Dykes, my deepest thanks for a lifetime of unimaginable encouragement and support. Thank you to my sister, Helen Cooper, for always being there for me, and to my brother Lee Dykes, for believing in me. I am so grateful to my forever friends and family for their unwavering support, encouragement, and laughter: Amanda Walker Hall, Margaret Walker Weatherly, Barbara Clark Copeland, Joanne and Tim Cady, Mona Kim Brown, Bob Ivey and Jill Bowman, Mary Dykes, Doug Kim Brown, Ken Eastwell, Jesse Chastain, Steve O'Neil, Andy Vann, Napier Murphy, Linda Denton (and for the horse and ski trails), Sabine Dahlmann, and Greg and Alicia Johnson.

For reading and commenting on the manuscript, I thank: Joanne and Tim Cady (multiple readings!), Jill Bowman, Bob Ivey, Carolyn Testa, Dick Burgheim, Helen Cooper, Peter Matson, Mary Dykes, Alexandra Fuller, Mark Owens, Dick Houston, Janet Gause, Jennifer Durbin, John O'Connor, and Leslie Anne Keller.

To my agent, Russell Galen, thank you for loving and understanding Kya and fireflies, and for your enthusiastic determination to get this story told.

Thank you, G. P. Putnam's Sons, for publishing my words. I am so grateful to my editor, Tara Singh Carlson, for all your encouragement, beautiful editing, and vision for my novel. Also at Putnam, my thanks to Helen Richard for helping at every turn.

Special thanks to Hannah Cady for your cheerful assistance with some of the more mundane and gritty jobs—like the bonfires—of writing a novel.

CRY OF THE KALAHARI

Paperback coming in 2022

The incredible memoir by the author of *Where the Crawdads Sing*, Delia Owens and fellow nature conservationist Mark Owens is out now. Charting their time researching wildlife in the Kalahari Desert, *Cry of the Kalahari* is a gripping account of how they survived the dangers of living in one of the last and largest pristine areas on Earth and will be reissued with full colour photographs for the first time since its original publication in 1984.